DEVIL OF A FIX

Also by Marcus Palliser

Matthew's Prize

DEVIL OF A FIX

Marcus Palliser

WILLIAM HEINEMANN : LONDON

First published in the United Kingdom in 2000 by
William Heinemann

1 3 5 7 9 10 8 6 4 2

William Heinemann
The Random House Group Limited
20 Vauxhall Bridge Road, London, SW1V 2SA

Random House Australia (Pty) Limited
20 Alfred Street, Milsons Point, Sydney, New South Wales 2061, Australia

Random House New Zealand Limited
18 Poland Road, Glenfield
Auckland 10, New Zealand

Random House South Africa (Pty) Limited
Endulini, 5a Jubilee Road, Parktown 2193, South Africa

A CIP catalogue record for this book is available from the British Library

Papers used by Random House are natural, recyclable products made from wood
grown in sustainable forests. The manufacturing processes conform to the
environmental regulations of the country of origin

Typeset by SX Composing DTP, Rayleigh, Essex
Printed and bound in the United Kingdom by
Creative Print and Design (Wales), Ebbw Vale

ISBN 0 434 00763 3

To David, the future

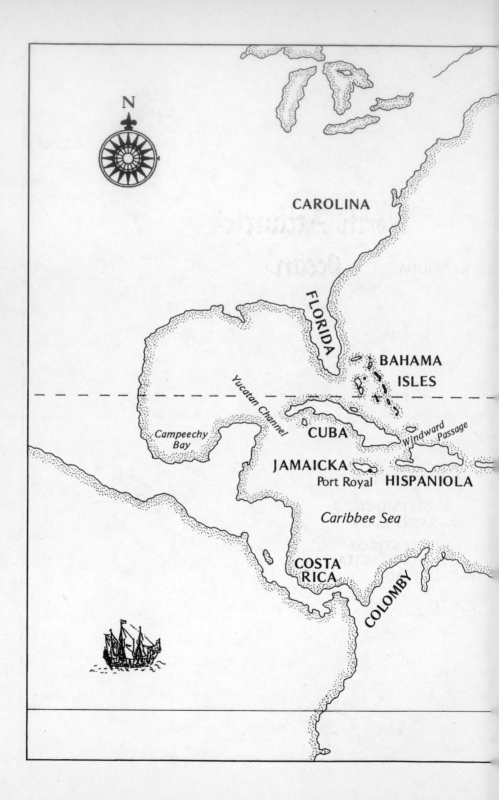

N

CAROLINA

FLORIDA

BAHAMA
ISLES

Yucatan Channel

Campeechy
Bay

CUBA

Windward Passage

JAMAICKA
Port Royal

HISPANIOLA

Caribbee Sea

COSTA
RICA

COLOMBY

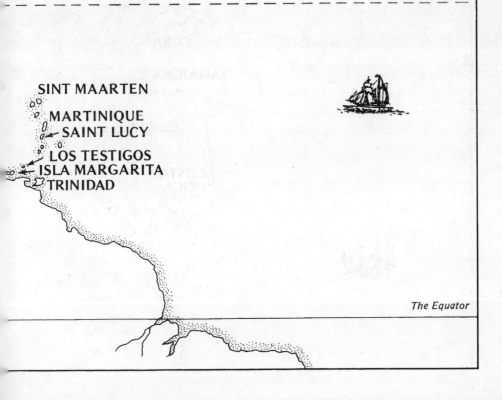

AZORES

North Attantick
Ocean

BERMUDA

Tropick of Cancer

SINT MAARTEN
MARTINIQUE
SAINT LUCY
LOS TESTIGOS
ISLA MARGARITA
TRINIDAD

The Equator

1

VILLAINY AFOOT

Port Royal, Kingstown Bay, Spring 1702

It was dusk and the inn's lamps glowed yellow in the heated Tropick air as I padded up the alleyway, come to make a trade, to sell a plain cargo honestly obtained. Here in Jamaicka the merchants gathered, lobsters in their caves, clustered together in Sally Cox's Tavern. A handsome bargaining meant auspicious prospects, and if only I could put gold in my seamen's pockets, their loyalty would be undivided and my captaincy assured.

Pausing, I glanced back down the sloping, crooked street towards the water's edge a few hundred paces off, trying to pick out my bark, the graceful *Cornelius*. But amongst the lattice of rigs and yards and sprits of the many anchored vessels, their tracery still faintly mirrored in the darkening glassy surface, she was one amongst too many. Her swooping sheerline and three tall masts were lost in a forest of spars, for in Kingstown Roads lay a hundred vessels or more engaged in all the English and Dutch business of the Caribbee Sea.

I pursed my lips. The dark hours favoured all the base and wretched traffick of Port Royal, the painted ladies and sharp-eyed gamblers, the merchants and slave-buyers and molasses dealers, the ruffians, the sot-wenches, the crimps, and the taphousemen. And each night, what was meat and drink to these thieves landed succulently on to their waiting plates: the seamen ordinary and the Navy's impressed men alike, the renegades and buccaneers, the ships' officers and the lawful traders, their pockets full of money and heads full of drink. What sort of plain dealing was to be found here? Had I brought the *Cornelius* after all to the right place?

In the vaporous heat of the Tropick night, I mopped my brow with a linen cloth, girded up my belt and checked my weapons, a brace of charged pistols and a cutlass. With a sudden burst of noise and laughter, a brawl of ruffians and their women spilled from the tavern, jostling a fellow attempting to pass inside, playfully making as if to wrest from under his arm the long paper roll he carried. Angrily pushing them away, he turned instead for a nearby doorway and began to pin up posters. The brawlers soon drifted off laughing. Putting aside all misgivings, I took my chance and strode directly into Sally Cox's alehouse.

The sweat and noise were enveloping, the air gaggingly hot and heady, like the inside of a small-beer cask left in the sun. I shouldered my way through the press of men and women drinkers until I came to a hatch where ale was sold. A mug was filled and I passed a coin across in return. Noticing a group of sombre-faced men at a table, I made my way over. Unhatted and unwigged though these fellows were, nevertheless their cotton and silk shirts, watch-chains and felt weskits betrayed them as prosperous traders. They sucked their clays, sending up a fug, and smacked at their ale-mugs, nodding when I indicated my wish to join them. As I took up a place on the bench, a hand was laid heavily on my arm.

'Ship's captain?' a voice said, and I saw a deep-lined, pinched face, bristled and pock-scarred, with its single eye fixed on me. In the matching socket where its pair should be was a blank of skin marked by a two-inch red weal crossed with the crude stitchmarks of a sailmaker's whalebone needle.

'Aye, sir. I am a master who wishes to announce himself and his bark.'

2

He thrust his face close. 'To trade?'

'Indeed. My ship's name is –'

'What cargo? From Africka? Blackamoors – good and strong 'uns? Maybe a piece of fresh black veal-calf, tender and youthful, as Smiley likes 'em.' He cackled to his friends. 'Bring Smiley Bankes tender flesh and he'll suck it like sweet sugar-cane. Give him a dark maiden-girl for his worn old bone, master, and his friendship's yours.'

Bankes' companion merchants grinned in concert, presenting an array of crooked gapes. One was red-faced with mirth at what he took for Smiley's wit, gasping and hacking and banging the table until the tears sprang from his eyes, of which he still had two, one more than he owned front teeth.

'Sirs,' I began with a forced smile, as leery of these fellows as a seaman in a cole-mine, 'my bark's no slaver. And far from touching at the Africk coast, we hauled here from Carolina.'

'From Carolina, eh?' said Bankes, sitting back. 'What commerce did you make there?'

He had betrayed an interest of sorts, so I pressed onwards. 'I must tell you we made a good bargain with the native tribes of that country, and I have no doubt you shall find our trade rewarding.'

I reached into my jacket pocket for Abigail's manifest. Mister Jeffreys' daughter had enscribed it with all her usual care and faith, working under a candle-lamp at the table in the *Cornelius*'s Great Cabin, now and then glancing up to smile my way. Merchant Seth Jeffreys himself had begged to accompany me ashore, but though his knowledge of commerce might be wide I reckoned him untrustworthy in bargaining and he remained aboard, sulking.

'Allow me to describe what we offer,' I said, and read off the list. 'A hundred dozen skins for tanning, the finest of deer and fox and suchlike, just the variety to fetch fine prices in Amsterdam for hats and mitts and coats. Also forty hundredweight of horn for tool-making, and two hundred quarters of hoof for boiling into glues. We hold a quantity of handsome American timber such as pine-wood and log-wood in lengths for planking and studding, amounting to twelve tuns.'

I glanced up, only to be met by silent stares. Even to me, such merchandise began to sound out of place.

'As you are aware,' I said, clearing my throat, 'demand for timber and tools is much enhanced by the Navy's station here.'

The merchants gave no sign, encouraging or otherwise, so I read on.

'Well now, in small stows and caskets, we offer a variety of scarce herbs and potions for ailments such as the fevers and the pox. Balms to ease the condition of bursted belly, a medicine for contradicting black gum, and many other valuable Physicks unknown to English apotheckaries.' I laid the list on the table. 'If you study this manifest, sirs, we may quickly agree a price, for like your goodselves I have no time to waste on idle talk.'

I took up my ale and swallowed half of it, confident at least of having laid out our wares in a direct and merchanting a manner. Wiping my mouth, I set down the mug and looked expectantly at my commercial counterparts, from one to the other and back again. Their faces were as blank as statues of stone. Their lips were drawn – set tight, rather. It began to enter my mind that they were not such canny merchants after all, for they seemed slow.

Smiley Bankes' one eye flickered, and the lid twitched and trembled as if he were struggling within himself. His shoulders began to heave. At last, his mouth opened, the awful gape reappeared and a harsh, rasping noise like a mule bewailing its burden emanated from the cavern. The head went back, the horrible eye screwed itself shut, and he roared and roared. His mates joined in, guffawing, casting aside their clays, banging their chests, spitting yellow juice on the straw-strewn floor, thumping the table-top and drumming their feet. The laughter all but silenced the whole tavern.

'What the Devil's the matter?' I said, casting around in annoyance.

4

Their mirth abated but the company retained their flushed faces and smirks. Bankes put a paw up and knuckled his weeping eye, then turned his peculiar gaze on me.

'Master, what you bring to trade' – he jabbed a bent finger at the Bill of Lading on the table – 'is an assortment of goods valued by us less than straw. If the Good Lord grants you a next time,' he went on, 'load your bark with salt-cod or with whale oil, so we can fill our bellies and light our lamps. Better still, bring strong black men without no red-spot or pox on them. Or silver and gold and jewels taken from the Dagoes, or muskets and powder lifted off the Frenchies.'

'Sir, my offer represents a trade in necessary plain goods, fairly obtained,' I protested. 'A bounty of materials for colonists and Naval authorities alike.'

'Not at Port Royal,' said Bankes. 'This is the last place on God's globe to make a trade of such stuff. We want flesh and muscle and gold and arms. You'll get no price for this.'

Suddenly their game unfolded in front of me. Merchants commonly drive down a price by demeaning what was on offer, and it was fair play in commerce, as the weasel-faced sometime-merchant Mister Jeffreys liked to say. Sitting back in my chair, I levelled my gaze with Bankes' lopsided countenance.

'Let me invite you to name the value you would put on these goods,' I said, and made ready to bargain lower than I had intended.

'I make no offer,' he said, 'and shall not bargain.'

'Indeed?' I said, unsmiling, and turned to his companions. 'Let us see who else is prepared to strike a deal. Sirs?'

Every man seated round the table folded his arms, or shook his head, or lifted his mug to drink. No one made an offer.

'In that case,' I said, with a shrug, 'this table misses the chance. I shall be obliged to make my way to other merchants.'

'Save yourself the voyage, master. These fellows here are all the merchants you shall find in Port Royal.'

There was unmistakable threat in Bankes' tone. At once, my

skin felt hot. The shirt under my confining jacket had crept into the folds of my armpits, clinging damply. No doubt of it, this was a thieves' den and best done with altogether.

'If that is so, sir,' I said, half rising, 'I bid you a goodnight till the pleasure of our meeting another day.'

Smiley Bankes laid his hand across my arm with a grip like an octopus. 'You strike me as no merchant, sir,' he said, 'more the master of a bad bargain. This stuff you bring is little more than heathen waste – vile poisons and turd-ridden skins and stinking horn. It insults the Guild of Merchants of Port Royal.'

'Very well,' I retorted, making as if to go. 'You leave me no choice but to approach the port authorities who direct refitting and supply in the Navy's yards.'

'O, you shan't be approaching them, my friend, for no one goes aside of us, not in Port Royal.' Smiley's hold on my arm relaxed. He picked up the manifest and held it between finger and thumb. 'We control all the trade, our little guild here.'

With that, he tore Abigail's list in two from top to bottom. His single eye held me as he crumpled the pieces and let them fall to the filthy floor. Dumbly, I watched them flutter downward. He had gone too far.

'Why, dammit, sir,' I said, standing away. 'Take your common insults and blasted grins and go to the Devil.'

'Blast me not, master, nor send me to Hades.'

Smiley Bankes was strangely still when he spoke. It was then I noticed the pistol in his hand, pointing at my belly. His body remained motionless and the loathsome gaze steady as his crooked thumb prised back the lock. The throng around us moved away. The hubbub of the tavern hushed to nothing.

I spread my hands wide. 'I came to treat with fair and honest men.'

'The way I sees it, young captain,' said Smiley, 'a fellow who insults the Merchant Bankes, and gives threat to the livelihood of straight-dealing traders, has the same number of chances to depart here alive as I have eyes to see with. Take his weapons.'

Smiley's head jerked and on the instant powerful arms pinned my wrists. In seconds, a couple of fellows had stripped me of my pistols and cutlass and searched every pocket and fold of my dress. Pitched out on the table were a few paltry items, amongst them some coins and my seaman's knife.

'Nothing more?' said Bankes mockingly. He fingered the weapons, assessing their value, then scooped up the coins and my knife and pocketed them. 'Master, you must be the only unarmed soul in Kingstown Bay, and all of Sally Cox's Tavern knows it. You shall have to be fleet of foot.'

He had as good as set the mob upon me.

Dry mouthed, I took my chance without delay. The drinkers parted, smirking and nudging each other as I crossed towards the door. Once outside, I found the street deserted, at least as far as the pools of light from the tavern windows showed. Silently I thanked the stars for a chance to escape, reckoning it best to live to trade another day. Hardly had I taken a step towards the alleyway than a rough voice croaked close by, at once whining and full of menace.

'Over here, jack-tar.'

A hand reached out and grabbed my weskit, pulling me off balance and into a doorway. Thinking myself attacked, I brought up my fist to strike but just then a reek of cheap powder mingling with sweat reached my nostrils.

'Save your ardour for my bed, won't you,' the woman spat. Her eyes rolled slug-like from the depths of an over-painted face and her breath stank.

'I've no desire for your second-hand pleasures,' I answered, lowering my raised hand, and turned to go. My eye caught the flash of white posters pinned to the door behind the raddled harlot. Startled, I shoved her aside, and none too courteously. The sheets were askew, one partly obscuring another, but the freshest one on top held me. Blaring from it in bold lettering stood out a ship's name. In crude print, letters two inches high, the script proclaimed:

'Somethin' there catch your fancy better than me, queer boy?' sneered the whore, ducking back into the tavern.

I stared stupidly at the poster. It condemned both me and my young Navigator, Adam Pyne, to be hunted like animals. In black and white, the poster advertised us as fair game for any opportunist bounty hunter – pirates, privateers and the Navy alike, on the high seas or in harbour. For two hundred golden guineas, any spy or the least of common sailors might deliver us, any private bark or the greatest of warships might launch themselves without warning in attack against the *Cornelius*. Two hundred guineas for the ship, ten for Adam, thirty for me – the sums tolled in my head like an execution bell.

I ripped the poster from the door and ran off down the alleyway. After fifty paces I paused, panting, to look back down the lane. Nothing moved. A clamour of coarse shouts drifted down to me from the tavern's glowing doorway, but no one followed.

How close I had come to announcing in that tavern for all to hear my own and my vessel's name! Thank the Lord that Smiley Bankes had cut me off. I darted anxious glances about the alley, fearing bounty seekers, believing guilt to be inked on my features as bold as the print on the poster. Pacing on, I kept repeating over and again, but we are innocent, dammit, innocent.

As the first shock of spying the poster subsided, it was replaced by outrage. How could we be so falsely accused? My men of the *Cornelius* were the very fellows who had fought to save her from the traitorous ship-stealers amongst her crew. Far from taking the privateer for our own ends, we had agreed, on the death of her captain, to try for honest trade, to repay the bark's Amsterdam owners and redeem ourselves of any illegality. And after this night, when my trading bid had led only to ridicule and loss, it was not just frightening but galling in the extreme to find myself charged with such crimes.

And what of Adam – poor Adam Pyne, former midshipman in His Majesty's Navy? He had likewise resisted a mutiny aboard his own vessel, yet in the heat of battle, and through no fault of his own, had ended up willy nilly on our privateer. He had since proved himself a most trustworthy Navigator, yet the Navy did not want him back for his skills and loyal service. No, they wanted only his neck, stretched and broken from the gibbet, to serve as an example to others. Blast and dam' them, I cursed out loud. As long as I am captain, they shall not catch us.

The alleyway of ramshackle dwellings crowded close and I watched for footpads at every hidden corner. To either side, glints of yellow light shone through gaps in the loose-boarded huts, and I imagined muttered plottings lit by hissing whale-oil lamps and fuelled by sugar-rum. The town to which I had brought the *Cornelius* only that morning was no more than a nest of rough buildings in the crook of the sand spit called the Palisadoes fringing the seaward side of Kingstown Bay. It was a dismal place of perhaps four or five hundred houses in all, their dereliction plain even in the gloom. Port Royal had burned itself to cinders not five years before, but the purge was short-lived and the town had been rebuilt, stinks and drains and crevices and all, to satisfy the greed and convenience of men. For this natural anchorage was the securest in the Caribbee Sea and, with the island in English hands and the King's Navy vigilant in patrolling its shores, it was a true port of refuge. Whatever else Port Royal boasted, for vessels to jostle so for swinging room in its roads, at least the trade ought to have been worth the while. The trade! How wrong I had been – or rather how mistaken Seth Jeffreys in his estimations. Whatever Abigail said, her father's designs would never again sway my mind.

Now, the Navy had set its net and, all unwitting, I had brought us into the seat of its power and justice. I had delivered the entire company of the *Cornelius* – not just the seamen, but Abigail and Adam too – into the very heart of danger. And what of me? With every step, I felt as if I approached closer to the scaffold.

The alleyway ended and the open strand stretched ahead. Drawn up in ranks on the beach were a dozen boats, a small portion of the many wherries, cutters and gigs that ran about ferrying officers and traders and masters and mates and super-cargoes on their ships' business. Standing by their boats, oars raised, the watchmen followed my passing with wary looks until out of the darkness appeared my own cutter. Two figures waited by it, the Dutch boy Gaspar Rittel and his sea-daddy Eli Savary, my second mate of steerboard watch, better than sixty but still as nimble aloft as a lad.

'Quickly, Gaspar – my calf-boots,' I said, raising one foot.

When the boy knelt and pulled off my shore-going footwear, my bare feet touched the warm cloying sand, soft and treacherous. At the strandline was a rime of blackened scum like the weed growing at a bark's waterline, while the air reeked of tar and oil and pump-waste discharged from the anchored fleets.

'This place stinks like a jack-tar's briches dipped in the piss-dale,' said Eli, chewing noisily on a cheek-sized baccy plug and scowling around as if the very beach would rise up and throttle him.

10

'You're right there, second mate,' I said, 'even though I was assured Port Royal offered the best of prospects. And by none other than the Merchant Jeffreys.'

At the name, Savary ceased chewing and gobbed pointedly into the water. Gaspar handed my boots with care over the cutter's stem and I boarded.

'Back to the *Cornelius*, sir?' he said.

'Quiet!' I said, whirling round. 'Don't use the ship's name.'

Eli was already pushing the cutter out. 'What's happened, captain? What about the trade?'

'There'll be no trade for us here, old fellow,' I told him. 'Take up your sweeps and pull as fast as you can.'

They waded a few paces in the shallows to shove off the boat, then leapt in after me. As their blades dipped in the black water and the strand receded, I threw anxious looks astern, but our little cutter, crossing the dark surface of the roads, was quite alone.

'There's not to be any distribution for the seamen, then?' asked Eli, without breaking his rhythm.

'Not after this night,' I told him.

Then Savary said, 'I just want you to know, captain, I shall do my best for you with steerboard watch.' He spat emphatically over the gunnels. 'The voting, I mean.'

Such is the lot of a privateering master, I thought grimly. The seamen may show their hand for you one day and cast you out the next. And what might they think of the bounty sums if they got to hear? Worth delivering their captain and his Navigator to the Admiralty's hangman?

'I'll vote for you, sir,' piped up the Dutch boy brightly, 'whatever they may say.'

I caught his arm so hard he let out a yelp. He had to stop rowing and the boat spun, coming to a swirling halt.

'What do they say, Gaspar?' I demanded.

Eli shipped his oar and leaned forward, cutting in over the boy's stammering confusion.

11

'Captain, them jack-tars of ours does nothing but moan about the stinks from the furs and horns and stuffs in the hold. Why trade in animal skins, they say? What are we privateers for unless we get rich in silver dollars?'

'How short their memories are. Who was it voted me captain to take the bark into trade?' I muttered, and let go of Gaspar's wrist. 'Let's stroke on, fellows.'

'I'm right behind you, captain,' said Savary, pulling away as if nothing had happened. 'You shan't hear me carping.'

'Nor me neither, sir,' said Gaspar, fumbling with his oar, eager to expatiate his mistake.

The cutter moved steadily, the silence broken only by the rhythmical splash of the oars as we progressed through the packed anchorage. All around loomed the dim outlines of moored barks with rigs of every shape and design. There were schooners and sloops, ketches and flyers and full ship-rigged barks, of burthen great and small alike, rafted up together, their yards boxed and their sails in tight harbour stows. There were vessels in all states of trim and readiness for sea, from worm-eaten, split-planked old hulks to well-caulked, deck-scrubbed beauties with gilded work at their stern galleries and painted figureheads at the bows.

Most magnificent of all were the Navy barks – cruzers, three-deckers, schooners and ketches, all rafted up in ranks right across the bay. All at once it seemed to me as if they were blocking our path to the sea.

At last, recognising her graceful sternlights lit from inside the Great Cabin and ablaze with a welcoming glow, we closed the *Cornelius*. She was double-moored alongside an armed merchantman, an awkwardness made necessary by the sheer number of vessels berthed in the roads. Our companion was a powerful twenty gunner, a hundred tuns burthen bigger and thirty foot longer than us, and something of an unequal match. On the decorated stern was painted her name, the *Willingminde of Dartmouth*. Lord, I wondered, had there been a chance yet for her to send a party ashore who might see the bill-poster's handiwork elsewhere in town and mark our ship's name?

The night was damp and foreboding and the air still as a fog, the familiar eerie quiet that threatens a squall. For that alone, I was bent on clearing away to sea at once. Yet it was not the augury of a storm in the dangerously crowded anchorage that drove me, nor even the abysmal failure of my attempt at trade.

Still bunched in my hand was the reward poster, crumpled into a fist-sized ball. Tossing it away with all my strength, I watched it bob whitely on the scummy surface before disappearing astern, and wished only that I could as easily dismiss its sentence of death.

2

A SQUALL OF TROUBLES

'Sailing-master!' I bellowed, swinging bodily over the *Cornelius*'s rail.

To my astonishment, not fifteen feet away at the larboard side, a bare-fisted fight was under way between half a dozen of my crew and a like number of unknown men. And Youssef the Barbar was in the thick of it. My shout ended the encounter and the intruders, seizing their chance of escape, vaulted the rail with many guffaws and jeers and went aboard the *Willingminde*.

The Barbar came over, his narrow, bony brown features wearing a shame-faced look.

'What is your explanation for this, sailing-master?' I demanded.

'Captain Mattoo, Youssef try to stop fight – but they are cheats. Owe money from cards.'

'You know the rules against gaming,' I snapped. 'I'll deal with that later. I want the anchor up smartly and the ship under way.'

'We put to sea? No trading?'

'The night's gone thick as ink,' I said. 'We'll need a tow in this still air, so send down the Great Launch with as many rowing men as you can muster.'

He peered into the darkness as if to see for himself but

14

dammit, there was little need to question it. He soon caught my look and went off to obey.

The weather-deck came alive as the jack-tars sprang into a bustle of action, swarming aloft and running to the belays, the sound of their working chanties ringing out lusty as ever. But there came too an unfamiliar low groaning sound and I crossed to the larboard rail to look down. Heavy hempen cables, knotted into bunches, hung between our topsides and the *Willingminde*'s to prevent the channels and the chainplates touching, with canvases slung over to save the timbers from damage. A surge entering the roads from outside the harbour made the two barks creak and strain, shifting against each other and chafing away the rope protectors.

With each oily swell passing, the *Willingminde* heeled, her great bulk graunching against us. She was proving an uncomfortable berthing partner for the *Cornelius*, as I had feared from the moment she towed in earlier that evening just as the boat was readying to take me ashore and I had reluctantly consented to let her lie alongside. Her officers had been curt to the point of rudeness and her captain, an overdressed man of stiff bearing and pompous demeanour, had insolently fixed his gaze on Abigail's figure as she bent above the open holds checking items on her list. Catching my annoyance, he had bowed, grudgingly and self-importantly, and turned away.

I scanned the merchantman's decks, thinking to call across and demand that the captain at once lay his vessel back on her anchor and let the *Cornelius* slip free. But he was nowhere to be seen and this was no time to go aboard and seek him out. The sea was building quickly.

Alarmed, I left the waist and mounted the quarter-deck. There, by the wheel, stood Abigail. Under the riding-lamp's flickering glow she appeared almost afloat in her white cotton dress and neat linen bonnet, such a light-footed and delicate girl. She was reading a manifest, with a satchel of ship's papers held close to her bosom. Seeing me, she smiled.

15

'Matthew, how did our trade go?'

It did not seem the right time to worry her with the uncomfortable truth.

'We're leaving at all speed,' I said, taking her in my arms and pulling her close. The satchel came between us, so instead I gave her hand a comforting squeeze. 'There's bad weather on the way.'

Around us the ship's company were readying the bark for sea. Men ran hither and thither across the waist shouting directions and the anchor windlass clanked its pawls as a party laboured at the levers.

Abigail frowned. 'You know there's been an argument? Some of our seamen took your books and instruments. They sold them to the *Willingminde* for pots of rum.'

'My Navigation books?' I gasped. 'And the sighting instruments? Why did you not stop them?'

'They forced themselves into the Great Cabin.' She bit her lip. 'If only we could have paid them, even a little, it might not have happened.'

'Lord, those books and tools are irreplaceable,' I muttered.

She pointed at my belt. 'Matthew, you've lost your pistols too. What happened in Port Royal? Have you sold our cargo? Why are we leaving?'

All at once the story came blurting out. 'We're wanted, Adam and me. The Navy's after us. They've declared the ship renegade and there's a reward. We must stay not a minute longer.'

'What about the stolen things?'

'I shall get them back,' I said, but just then the ship shifted awkwardly as a large swell passed beneath her keel. The *Willingminde*'s heaving topsides grated horribly against ours, and Abigail's eyes widened in fear.

'The quarter's going to be dangerous,' I said. Brooking no argument, I swept her off to the hatchway, sending her down the companion to the sanctuary of the Great Cabin, then went swiftly to the break and called up my sailing-master.

'Youssef, make sure we're cast off alongside and no snags. Is the launch out with the tow?'

'Aye aye, captain,' he said.

'Good. Ready to brace up on larboard for when we come free – and lively about it.'

He disappeared into the darkness, rousing the watchmen to action. Glancing over the side, I saw a sickening swell heaving on the black waters below. Dammit, there was going to be no chance to get aboard the merchantman and salvage my instruments. The ship herself must come first.

With so many vessels tightly anchored either side, getting under way in the pitch of night was a nerve-wracking prospect. A rising swell was bad enough, but if the wind and rain came down hard then the difficulty would worsen by an order of magnitude. I had never seen such numbers of ships at close anchor, even in my boyhood days at Whitby. Then I had thrilled at the whalers, Baltick traders, Dutch flyers and Tyne colliers jammed by the dozen into the roads or moored fore-and-aft in the narrow tide-wracked Esk. Here in the stagnant Tropick waters of Kingstown Bay, swinging to their moorings in far greater numbers, were merchant-adventurers, warships, slavers, sugar-ships, molasses carriers, tobacco haulers, packet boats and island traders of all kinds. Yet now all this magnificent variety was no sailor boy's heart-stirring sight. To a sea-captain, it was little short of a threatening trap.

The *Willingminde* had made no move to get under way so, as our anchor cable came home, we had pulled ahead until her beak was level with our midships. Her bows heaved to the incoming seas and her great head bucked like a horse. At every surge, she bore against the *Cornelius*'s stern parts with such force I wondered what must give.

Even after clearing the anchored fleets, there was a narrow passage to steer through to gain the open sea. All at once I remembered that since coming back aboard there had been no sign of my Navigator. Just after dawn, with his pilot books spread out on the quarter-deck, Adam Pyne had brought us safely into Kingstown Roads, darting glances from the charts to the Jamaicka coastline and back, sighting carefully along the cross-staff for bearings on Plumb Point and the Palisadoes. Between us and the land behind had lain shoals and spits, reefs and low sandy cays, and the safe channel was hard enough to find in the day, let alone at night. Now I needed Adam on the quarter-deck, and quickly.

Checking around, I searched the men milling about in the waist. The second mate of larboard watch, the Frieslander Jackob Tosher, was passing across the weather-deck.

'Ya, captain, Mister Pyne was here not long back,' he said in answer to my question. He cast about uncertainly. 'But where he is now I do not know.'

'Very well, second mate, back to your station. And send me Gannes.'

'Gannes to the wheel!' he called, and went off.

Soon, a strong-built seaman lumbered up to the binnacle. Without a word, he hefted the spokes, centred the wheel and peered down intently at the compass card just visible in the light thrown by a miniature oil-lamp above it. Henrik Gannes was the steadiest steersman a captain could wish for.

There came a rattle of gear overhead as the gaskets were freed and the topsails fell from the yards. It seemed to my impatient eye as if the sailors going aloft clambered up the ratlines with cannon balls chained to their feet. When the sails fell loose, they did so reluctantly, hanging limp, held back by the very weight of the air. There was no breeze, only the ominously building swell. On deck, the second mates sent men to the belays to brace up ready to sheet in, but for me the jack-tars moved as though walking in treacle. The anchor cable ratcheted home with agonising slowness, fathom by dragging fathom. The whole ship seemed tethered by invisible hawsers. In the seamen's natural way, they were hastening slowly, as I knew full well. Yet it was all happening too tardily.

18

'Hurry, fellows,' I silently urged.

The first gust took us by ambush. From the enveloping thick stillness of the night it came unseen, tearing down upon our ship, a blow straight from God. The loosened topsails flogged like untamed beasts, all but throwing men clean off the yards. Blasting in from dead south, the wind pressed us hard against the *Willingminde*. Both barks sheered round, heeling, grinding their sides together as if bent on ripping out the chainplates. When the wind abated momentarily, the merchantman tore free and sagged off astern, but at the next gust she gave a mighty heave forward. Her thirty foot bowsprit lunged across the *Cornelius*'s quarter-deck. Henrik Gannes and I ducked for our lives. With a tearing crash, the sprit's end tore into the mizen shrouds only feet away. Its jib-boom and fore-topgallant mast-stay lodged in our rigging, binding the vessels together like prisoners at the courthouse.

There were men at her beak, crouched by the anchor windlass.

'Let her cable run out!' I called across. 'Lay back clear!'

They looked confusedly at each other.

'It's jammed!' came the cry.

Another gust punched into the rigging, whistling through the shrouds. The merchantman's bowsprit leapt forward again. This time, her stem struck the rail and split it, cracking open the deckboards. The huge weight rose up and crashed back down, sending splinters flying.

Then, as suddenly as it had come, the wind died to nothing. The *Willingminde*, like an attacker seeking respite, retreated, ripping and tearing at our broken timbers as she went. Yet she withdrew only half the length of her bowsprit, leaving us locked in harness still.

Heart in mouth, I went to the break of the poop and called, 'Sheet in topsails on larboard tack. She'll heel on the next gust and come free.'

The sailing-master repeated the order and a dozen tars ran to sweat the topsail sheets home. A gust bore in and the *Cornelius* swayed over. The mizenmast gave a tortured groan from deep below, taking a strain it was never meant to bear. Raggedly, with a gruesome rending sound, the bark tore herself clear of the invading bowsprit. Two of the three larboard mizen shrouds parted above the chainplates and a mess of rigging – ratlines, blocks, deadeyes, shrouds, bracelines, sheets, haulyards – was ripped out in a clattering mayhem and sent flying. Again, Henrik went down flat on the deck-boards as I threw myself under the far rail, hands over my head. Pieces of broken wood struck me on the back and hempen lines whipped my shoulders, snapping away into the night. At last, the *Willingminde* fell clear and the *Cornelius* slowly hauled ahead.

Breathing hard, I got to my feet and ran over to help Henrik, who was dazed but unhurt, back to the wheel. Then I called out to the sailing-master, 'Bring the launch in, Youssef. And where the Hell is Mister Pyne?'

He jerked his head towards the rail.

My heart somersaulted. 'Has he gone overboard?'

'No – in launch. Captain said all hands to tow out.'

'Dammit, where's the launch now?'

'Not sure – towing line parted.'

'What? Then have every man keep his eyes skinned.' I needed no reminding that there were at least twelve men in that launch.

Youssef disappeared into the waist just as another gust of wind hit. The rigging sang, the sails flogged and filled. The *Cornelius* gathered way, leaving the *Willingminde*'s bowsprit further behind, a sorry mess of tangled dead-eyes, ratlines, shrouds and blocks hanging from it. With an anxious glance astern, I muttered under my breath, Keep moving, *Cornelius*, just keep going and the wind'll take us into clear water.

To my consternation, just then I heard Youssef cry, 'Let go sheets fore and main!'

What in blazes was he doing? Had he not seen? In seconds, she would fall back on the *Willingminde*.

'Keep her going ahead!' I bellowed above the howling noise of the squall.

20

The Barbar whirled round with a wild look. 'Captain, we sail over anchor.'

'Stand on – that's an order!' I shouted.

The *Cornelius* sailed on. Seconds later, she reached the end of her anchor cable. It came taut with a brutal snatch that sent men crashing to the boards. Where it ran out through the hawse-hole and bore on the fairlead, the cable groaned and the deck timbers creaked. The ship, all three hundred tuns of her, was trapped on her own anchor, twisting round against the hawser as she tried to sail herself off.

'Spy the launch!' came a lookout's cry. 'Great Launch to steerboard!'

Pandemonium broke out, with jack-tars running to free sheets, to let fly bracelines, to shoot heaving lines or to run out cable, as their instincts dictated, while the sailing-master and mates cursed at them to wait for orders. Above the din and rattle, no one heard my command. Fighting to keep calm, I strode down the steps and roughly took hold of Youssef's arm.

'Cut the cable, sailing-master,' I shouted in his ear. The noise of the straining rig was terrible.

'What about Great Launch?' he yelled back.

The dim shape of the launch, a few yards off the steerboard side, rose and fell on the high swells now surging into the roads. The exhausted men in the boat were clinging to the broken stumps of their oars, shoulders drooping, their strength sapped. One of them, I now knew, was my Navigator. Astern, the *Willingminde*'s bulk charged forward once more as windblasts struck her topsides with renewed force. She was bound to strike us again, and much harder. Caught on our anchor, we were hooked like a tunny fish awaiting its death blow.

Youssef stared, then turned to me in alarm.

'The ship comes first,' I said baldly. 'Give the order – go forward and cut the cable.'

All around the weather-deck, sailors stood holding coiled lines

21

at the ready, waiting for the order to pull in the launch.

'Cut cable,' muttered Youssef, his eyes flicking from me to the Great Launch and back.

Then he broke away and yelled the order at the top of his voice. Seconds later, seamen with axes were hacking at the four-strand hempen cable, thick as a man's thigh. Blow after blow was struck until, at the final crash of the blade, the shipboard part of the cable flew backwards with a force that knocked one man flat. The outboard part disappeared through the hawse-hole in a cloud of dust, taking with it the whole tun weight of our second main bower and the Lord knew how many fathoms of precious cable.

All at once, the bulging canvas above at last allowed to do its work, we sheered off and in seconds the *Willingminde* was lost to sight. As the *Cornelius* gathered speed, the Great Launch disappeared too. Henrik strained at the wheel against the forces on the rudder blade. White-topped rollers rushed at the bows, striking with a booming sound and sending up walls of spray. Suddenly she was going much too fast.

Not fifty fathoms off, broad on the steerboard bow, loomed the fudged outline of an anchored vessel, a huge, towering two-decker. We bore down, close-hauled and making such a lee board as to smash into her with force enough to split our frames and stove in the topsides. It had happened so quickly there was no room to bring up, no distance left between the vessels. Collision seemed the only outcome.

'Put the helm down, Henrik,' I said, dry-mouthed.

The wheel span. With all my might, I shouted into the waist, 'Wear ship!'

Startled faces turned my way as the ship began to bear off. Aloft, the sails bellied to breaking point and rainwater streamed from the hempen sheets coming taut as iron bars. Youssef stood in the waist, gripping the rail, transfixed, making no move to obey.

'Wear ship, dammit!' I bellowed.

A great commotion ensued. At once, the sailing-master called orders and jack-tars shouted their ayes in response, instantly leaping for the belays or scrambling up the ratlines. The ship veered off. The canvas flogged, blocks rattled and she began to come upright, her yards arcing across the night sky. The men already aloft were caught by surprise and had to grapple for the jack-stays, holding on for their lives. The big two-decker appeared dead ahead, so close that I picked out on her decks a row of blank-faced, rigid figures. Everyone waited, sensing the motion through the deck-boards.

The *Cornelius*'s stern yawed and a tremor told me the rudder had bitten. The sails snapped full of wind. Her head shied away and she turned, swinging dizzily through ninety or a hundred degrees. The side of the bark we had seemed bent on ramming swept past, scooped away as if by a great hand, our bowsprit missing her timbered side by less than the length of a long-pike. An instant later we shot past her lighted stern windows, glimpsing anxious faces peering out through the mullions. Then in the blackness she was gone.

'Helm amidships,' I ordered Henrik, then called out, 'Sailing-master, bring her on a reach.'

Youssef issued a rapid series of commands and, with topsails and jibsails stretching under the buffeting wind, the *Cornelius* rushed onwards into the darkness. Excited shouts came up from the weather-deck. The seamen were all looking off to larboard, pointing and squinting through swirling curtains of rain.

'Launch there,' the Barbar called, pointing.

'Helm up,' I ordered. 'Back the main-topsail. Free jibsails.'

The jibsails shook as the sheets were let fly and the *Cornelius* lost way. The mainyard swung round and the topsail went aback. Men shuffled against the rail, peering into the gloom, ropes and heaving lines at the ready. A cry went up, the lines were shot across and in no time the Great Launch was hauled in alongside, bucking like an unbroken colt. A tun or more of boat lifted and fell, crashing time and again into the topsides and

23

chainplates, but one by one the sailors hauled themselves up a knotted boarding rope. As the last man struggled aboard, the bark gave a lurch. He lost his grip and fell back into the launch, flailing for a handhold, on the point of being tossed out. In a flash, Youssef was over the side and down the rope. He grabbed the fellow and with an effort of will heaved him safe aboard. The bedraggled figure lay inert on the boards, half dead with fatigue, until he was lifted up and borne off to the foc'sle for the surgeon's ministrations. When Youssef reported to the break, his news was bad. It was Adam Pyne.

'Very well, it can't be helped,' I said shortly. 'Get under way again, sailing-master – closehauled, larboard tack. Tow the launch for now.'

Second mate Eli Savary quickly bent on a fifty fathom line and let the Great Launch tail astern. Rain streaming down my face, I stood near Henrik at the wheel, examining the compass as it lurched crazily in its gimbals, the card spinning in its bath of oil. With my Navigator incapacitated, it fell to me to pilot the ship. By now we had fallen too far west of the roads ever to beat back for the main channel. Beyond that, I had altogether lost my bearings. Worse, having earlier delegated the pilotage into Adam's hands, I had paid only brief attention to the charts. All I knew was that a second escape route lay close to the curve of Kingstown Bay's shoaling, reef-strewn western shore. Much narrower than the main channel, it was a hazardous passage between the heads of two low lying cays. For a few minutes, the bark lurched blindly onwards, heading south as I tried to reckon the best course to have any hope of finding the pass. Then there came a cry from right forward at the beak.

'Four fathom and falling!'

It was the leadsman. Even through the driving wind and rain, every man jack aboard heard it. Forty seamen on the weather-deck or aloft, their faces white ovals in the gloom, turned to watch me on the quarter-deck. We were running into shoal water.

Snatching up the spy-glass, I raked back and forth, scanning the night for a clue. I caught a gleam of illumination to the southeast. The riding-lamp of another anchored bark? No, the lights of a town – the stinking pit of Port Royal. It was enough to give me a clue, a line of bearing to work from. Perched like a limpet on the very eastern point of the long spit of land called the Palisadoes, the den of thievery that had all but undone me now told me which way to steer.

'Henrik, come steerboard eight points and head due west by the compass,' I said at once.

Then, loud and clear, I ordered Youssef to ease her round to run off downwind. Again came the welter of gear going over aloft and the grunts of many seamen labouring at the belays.

At the end of the spit lurked the two cays guarding the entrance to the second channel. Beyond them to the west lay shallow water and coral reefs, while to the north there were only more rocks. Behind us stood the roads and the hundred moored vessels, no doubt half of them trying to get under way to clear the squall. There was no going back, no anchoring, and only one way out. Standing at the weather rail, I searched the night seascape again and again, looking for the elusive cays.

'Three fathom and a half!' cried the leadsman.

Suddenly I saw, only a few boat lengths distant, disturbances on the surface and a pale patch of water. Surf swirling around the cays? I could not be sure. I wiped the rain from the tube's end-glass and looked again. Two froths of white foam appeared in the distance and as quickly vanished again. A pair of low cays for certain, but were they the Gun Rock and Drunkenman Cay, barely a cable's width between them, lying like way-markers on opposite sides of the exit passage? Or might they be Maiden's Reef and Rackam Cay, laid out in a line north and south and leading to nowhere but destruction on the western reef? I looked at the compass, then back into the waist where the seamen waited with bated breath. Then I bet on the Drunkenman.

'Hold your course, steersman,' I called out loud enough for all the seamen to hear.

'Only three fathom found!' sang the leadsman.

Lord, this was all too tight. Raising my voice again, I cried, 'Prepare to come on a reach, sailing-master.'

Youssef repeated the order and all forty men moved to their stations, ready and waiting. Broken waters foamed past our larboard side barely a ship's length away.

'Ready, Henrik?' I said in a low voice. He nodded. I counted ten seconds, then called, 'Put the helm up hard – now!'

The wheel spun and the compass card whirled. With a clatter of gear and a rattle of blocks overhead, the *Cornelius* swung her beak through a quarter of a full circle. Tars ran to the lines and chantied home the sheets. She heeled and came on to a beam reach. Our speed increased.

'Steady amidships and keep her dead south,' I told Henrik. His massive arms worked again to centre the wheel and I craned over to watch the swinging card settle. The needle pointed to the south cardinal mark.

'Steer small,' I urged.

A minute passed, every seaman aboard straining to see as the ship shouldered onwards, oblivious and unheeding. Catching the faint splash of a swell breaking on the shoals off to either side, I flicked my gaze from the compass card to the waters ahead, black and unbroken. This had to be the channel or I was sending us to disaster.

Suddenly, I sensed the *Cornelius* lift to a higher and longer swell, the motion of a ship in deep water.

'Ten fathom!' came the leadsman's cry, and half a minute later, 'Bottom found at twenty fathom!'

We were clear.

The rain streamed down my cheeks, cool and soothing, as I stood immobile, gripping the rail, relief flooding over me. Gradually, I became aware of a ragged hubbub rising from the waist. All the jack-tars were looking my way, and every last man

26

cheering. It took me half a second to find my voice.

'All right, lads,' I said, 'and well done. Sailing-master, bring her hard up to weather. We'll stand away closehauled on larboard.'

They sprang to the work, sweating home the bracelines, hardening the sheets until they were taut, thrumming bars, a thousand square feet of topsails set and drawing hard. We gained a league off the coast before I slowed ship to hoist the launch aboard. The gale blew harder and, as the squall passed over, ended up in the west. The rain increased, filling the air with cool, liquid drops that hissed on the surging wave-tops. In the Caribbee Sea a westerly is lusty yet short-lived and sure enough in two hours the wind tailed off and broke into odd, boxing gusts from all points. Then it filled from just south of east, built to a fair breeze and settled. We eased sheets and swung on to a broad reach, running clear of the land to the north and into the open sea. The rain ceased and stars peeped from behind the scurrying clouds until the whole canopy of the night sky came aglow with pinpricks of glitter. As the warm tradewind resumed its natural order, our sodden clothes dried and our spirits lifted. A merry chanty carried down from aloft where the tars were busy shaking out the main and forecourses for best speed and a ready helm.

I called the Barbar to the quarter. A moment later, he stepped up, stripped naked to the waist during the struggle to save the ship, his body glistening wetly in the glow of the binnacle lamp.

'Your report, sailing-master,' I said briskly.

'Carpenter Sedgewick found mizen step loose. Quarter-deck a little bit broken.' He gestured aft, where the shattered deckboards and lifted planks were plain to see. '*Cornelius* need shelter – find a place to repair.'

'Still carry nothing on the mizen, then,' I said. 'And how's Adam Pyne?'

'Nothing bad, bruises only.'

'Thank the Lord. That was a brave act of yours, Youssef.' His eyes were averted, looking vacantly over my shoulder. The tension between us was palpable. 'Have you anything more to report?'

He shrugged. 'One bower anchor and fifty fathom of cable gone.' There was a short, expectant silence before he added, 'Cutting cable good thing. Captain find passage out. Save ship.'

Still he refused to meet my eye. Dammit, back there he had as good as doubted my judgement. What would happen once he learned of the bounty on my head? The boil had to be lanced.

'Listen, Barbar,' I said, my voice low and urgent, 'as long as I remain captain, never question an order again.'

The ship staggered into a trough and we were flung together, our faces so close I heard his breathing even above the gush and swirl of the bark's progress.

'Aye, captain,' was all he said.

His calm eyes remained without expression. I pushed him away and for some seconds neither of us spoke. In the weak glow of the compass light, his countenance was as blank and unreadable as a North Sea sky.

'Tell me, Youssef,' I said at last, in the most deliberate tones, 'will the vote go against me?'

After a thoughtful pause, he quietly replied, 'Mattoo can stay as captain if no trading. Go for prizes. Back to old ways.'

The ship plunged on. A loud crack rang out above and the after mizen shroud on the steerboard side flew loose. Even without canvas on the mizenmast, she was overpressed and straining.

'We're running too fast.' My tone was curt. 'Shorten aloft, sailing-master. At once.'

'Aye aye, captain,' he said, and loped off to see it done.

3

HIDDEN FLAW

'Seamen say, ship on run, captain wanted. So why not go for prizes?'

We lay in Flawless Cove, anchored under the hot sun, and as Youssef spoke I shot a glance at my Navigator. Young Pyne was still shaken from his accident in the launch, but that was the slightest of his troubles. With the *Cornelius* declared a renegade – liable to reported on sight by any bark, private or Navy, if not attacked outright – my concern was for all the ship's complement, from Abigail to the lowest sea-boy. Yet of all of them, it was only Adam and myself who were wanted alive or dead.

We could have sailed no further without repairs, so I had brought us to this hidey-hole thirty leagues along the Jamaickan shore. We were skulking in a lagoon that was as much a trap as a haven, and my most urgent desire was to get away again in the shortest time. In the meantime, I trusted the Navy would have little cause to visit Flawless Cove.

As we sat on the blistering quarter-deck sheltering under the awning, the officers' disconsolate faces were ranged before me – Youssef the Barbar, the second mates Eli Savary and Jakob Tosher, and Navigator Adam Pyne. A little apart stood Abigail, concerned, listening closely. No one spoke for a full half minute while we watched the carpenter's crew busy at work with their mallets and adzes. Overhead, blocks creaked as a party took a line from the mizen truck to the chainplate and hauled the mast straight while a fellow aloft with a plumbline called instructions to his mates below. From deep within the hull resonated the rhythmic thuds of hammer blows as the step was laboriously worked tight and true.

'The *Cornelius* may be accused, sailing-master,' growled old Eli, chewing determinedly on a baccy plug, 'but Captain Matthew wants to keep her in honest trade and prove we never stole her. And by Saint Mary's blood, that's what we'll do.'

In truth, rather than being a ship-stealer, I had led the fight to prevent the *Cornelius* falling into the hands of mutineers, and it was they who had killed the English officer. Adam, a midshipman loyal then to the Navy, had risked his life to save the *Success* when it too was taken in mutiny. Far from deserting, he had been blown clean off her decks in the battle, and only come aboard our privateer to save his life. Yet the poster branded us murderers. Was there a way to prove our innocence? For sure, not in the Admiralty Courts of Jamaicka or the Bahama Isles, even if we were fortunate enough to appear there alive. These were no true seats of English justice but rather a source of fear that spread throughout the Antilles. The Naval judges, it was said amongst sailors, would as lightly flog a man to death as eat a breakfast.

Jakob Tosher puffed at a delicately curved clay pipe, sending contemplative clouds into the air.

'Ya, the captain's right,' he said in a melancholy tone. 'Either we bring her back to Amsterdam with a profit for the owners or every man jack of us is a ship-stealer.' He pointed at Youssef with his stem. 'So we must remain legal, and free.'

'Free but poor,' said the sailing-master, fixing me with his Barbary look, gaunt-featured and hook-nosed. 'Men say, dollar a week not enough. As well go aboard slaver, or into King's Navy.'

Every captain knows his sailing-master's word is law below

30

decks. For the jack-tars who spend their lives running aloft at a moment's notice, slopping out the bilges or emptying the piss-dales, caulking seams and bloodying their knuckles scraping barnacles off the bottom – for these hardy fellows who eat and sleep in the foc'sle far from the grace and comfort of the Great Cabin, the sailing-master's word counts above the captain's.

'They'll get their chance to vote,' I said levelly, 'as soon as the repairs are done and we're safely at sea. I'm depending on you officers to put the choices to them fair and square.'

I cast around the company, wondering if anyone might rather offer up their wanted master and his pilot in hopes of keeping the ship for themselves. My eye fell once more on the Barbar, who gazed out across the lagoon where the waters ruffled in the tradewind breeze. At twenty three he had only a year the better of me, but his service aboard the *Cornelius* stretched back far longer than mine. His resentment at my rise to the captaincy was plain.

The brooding silence was prolonged, so I changed tack.

'Now fellows, the stripe of white paint along her gunports makes a good enough disguise,' I told them, 'but I want a new name too.'

Everyone breathed more easily, shifting and stretching their tensed limbs. Adam was first to speak.

'Second mate Tosher's come up with an idea, sir,' he said brightly.

Jakob withdrew the clay from his lips and sent aromatic clouds wafting upwards to the awning.

'The *Saskia*, captain,' he offered with a doleful grin. 'The girl I left behind in Harlingen.'

I gave Abigail a smile. 'The woman's name suits our graceful bark, so the *Saskia* it shall be.' I stood up. 'As agreed, then, soon as we're fit we set course for the Colomby coast and Cartagena, to seek a peaceful trade there. Once the cargo's sold, we shall clear the holds and start afresh.' As if it hardly mattered a jot, I added lightly, 'Unless the vote changes everything.'

31

Eli looked sad. 'In the squall, we split a keg or two of that savages' medicine. It's set up a vile nose in the pump-well, quite enough to make me a queasy sailor.'

'Horns and furskins make big stinks,' grimaced Youssef. 'We trade quick, by Allah, or get rid.'

'Miss Abigail is seeing to all cargo matters,' I said firmly. 'Sailing-master, see that all the men not engaged in repair work are kept busy. Set up a gunnery drill after eight bells of the noontime watch. Dismissed.'

Moments later, Abigail and I dropped down the companion-way and entered the Great Cabin. Her father, the merchant Seth Jeffreys, rose with a false smile that utterly failed to disguise his habitually shifty demeanour. To my eye he cut a ridiculous figure when he wore, as now, his tricorn atop a short wig, with a weskit over his shirt and a long-coat on too. He must be off his head to be garbed in full rig in such heat. Then I realised the landlubber merchant, taking no account of our shipboard troubles, had readied himself to go ashore, scenting the prospect of profitable merchanting.

'Matthew – Captain Loftus – are we to go to the next trading port at once?' he said, taking a little mincing step forward, his small eyes alight with fervour. 'As soon as these mast mounts or whatever they are have been fixed. Is that the idea? With the ship disguised, can the trading at Port Royal not be resurrected?'

'We're certainly not going back to any Jamaickan port, sir,' I said testily. 'Have you forgotten we are wanted?'

'Well, I insist upon going ashore in future. As I told you, it is necessary to speak the proper language of commerce in order to make the best of such poor trade as we have aboard.'

'Not poor, but honest trade,' I corrected, glaring.

'Ah, so like your misguided father and his nonsense against the Africkan commerce.' Now the merchant wore a small regretful smile, as if someone had tipped his arm and spilled small beer on a clean shirt. 'You are forever clinging to unattainable dreams. Why, back in Whitby you progressed around the town with your head in the air and your book under your arm, quite as if you were no more in life than a little apprenticed cole-boy.'

'And you,' I said, jabbing a finger at his narrow bird-like chest, 'cheated and beggared good men with your lendings at ten and twelve per cent. We're not going to an English port and I'm certainly not taking any advice from you. I've decided we shall put to sea for Cartagena, and the officers agree.'

Open-mouthed, he spun towards his daughter. 'Abigail, I thought you said –'

'That's enough, sir,' I snapped, and bade him exit from the Great Cabin.

When he had sidled out, not without protestations, Abigail and I sat alone together at last. The sun streamed in through the mullioned sternlights, throwing her sweet face now into illumination, now into shadow as the *Cornelius* swung gently at anchor. It must be so hard for her, I thought, to resist her father's incessant carping.

'Matthew, I have been thinking,' she began, 'if you and Adam are accused, we must have money and gold to put up for your defence.'

'There's no defence in the colonial courts, my dearest,' I told her.

'Well, a pardon may be bought, so father says. I worry that we shall not get enough for the wares in Cartagena.'

I squeezed her hand. 'The medicines are prized by apotheckaries of the Spanish Navy and the timbers are greatly needed by the shipyard there. I understand the port bulges with vessels bound back for Europe, where skins and horns command fine prices. We shall make a good trade. It's the only way to return the ship to Amsterdam and clear ourselves of all the charges. And pay the seamen.'

'Can we truly make enough by commerce? They came aboard for prizes and gold, did they not?'

'Aye, but since then they voted for trading fair and square. All agreed, trade's better than plunder – it keeps a man whole, with his limbs intact. Our cargo's worth between two and three thousand dollars, yet it cost less than a hundred. Surely that's profit enough.'

Abigail looked thoughtful. 'It's worth nothing if no one will buy it.' She brightened. 'Why could we not sell the ship? She's more valuable than the cargo. She'd fetch two thousand pounds, father estimates. Enough to pay off the men and buy land with a house, for growing tobacco or cane.'

'If we sold her, then we would truly be ship stealers,' I sighed.

She took up both my hands in hers. 'Would it not be safer ashore somewhere, my love? If we had a plantation, the Navy would never find you.'

'I'm not going to hide, I'm going to fight to prove my innocence.'

She was downcast. 'Perhaps I shall never again have a proper house. With well-made furnishings, and a maid too. And look at my hands – rough from handling flax and canvas, tugging at bales of furs. I haven't even a silken dress left.'

I squeezed her waist and planted a consoling kiss on her lips. She wriggled her body snugly against mine. Of course it was tempting to think of taking some easy prize, turning the *Cornelius* into a plundering privateer and paying the jack-tars handsomely in gold coin. In the lawless Caribbee Sea, we would likely get away with such crimes. Yet a single act of piracy would leave me without defence, living forever as a wanted man, each minute of every day fearing denunciation, followed by condemnation and the rope around my neck. I could not live – would never live – like a cur.

'We could seek a French galleon or Spanish treasure ship, you know,' Abigail was saying. 'Surely that would not be wrong, for they are the enemies of the King. And father says, if we catch a fish, it might as well be the biggest we can find.'

I stopped kissing her. Her head was full of Mister Jeffreys' notions about prizes and profits. All at once it seemed a long time since she had been the demure girl of our Whitby days, tripping up and down the steep streets in her leather-heeled shoes and best Sabbath Day bonnet.

'Abigail,' I said, 'seizing ships when there's no war is outright piracy, no matter whether a Catholick country is sworn against a Protestant King. It would make the charges against us undefendable. And I'm sure a woman ought not to be thinking of such a thing.'

'I've heard of women pirates,' she challenged me, 'with diamonds in their ears.'

'Aye,' I said, kissing her again, 'and hanged on the gibbet by the Admiralty Courts at the Bahama Isles or in Port Royal.'

'You always see the black side,' she murmured. 'Father says we might come upon a plunder-ship working off the Colomby coast to join her convoy, and if we took her –'

'"Father this and Father that"! I've heard enough from him!' I pushed her away, the heat of my passion turned in a flash to anger. 'The *Cornelius* – dammit, the *Saskia* – is going to make her peaceful trade or she can go on without me.' My temper was rising and I banged a fist hard down on the table 'As long I am commander I shall fight to be free with our heads held high. And to keep all aboard safe and whole against attack from prize seekers.'

She sat back, shocked at my vehemence. Of a sudden, she rose and went to sit on the window-seat, arms folded.

'I'm half minded,' I continued intemperately, 'to lock you in the sleeping cabin along with your father, to plot your fortunes together.'

'Why must you be so stubborn!' she said. Slowly, tears welled up and trickled down her cheeks, turning her face blotchy and red. Still annoyed, I fell to wondering why a woman takes on such a look when she grows distressed.

'I wanted your trading to succeed,' she sniffled, 'but you won't admit it's failed.'

'We've hardly allowed it a chance,' I protested.

She sat up, wiping away the tears and recomposing herself.

Some locks of her thick hair had come loose under the linen bonnet, and her eyes were large with sadness. Her forlorn look, the hurt on her face, and the way she sadly smoothed down the faded dress all combined to take me quite aback. I wanted to go to her, cover her with kisses, beg forgiveness, prostrate myself and ask what she would have me do to make amends.

Just as I thought to embark on this, to kiss and comfort my girl, put my arms around her waist and draw her body to mine, speaking words of contrition and love and tenderness, the little world we had created was split asunder.

'Sail ahoy!' cried the lookouts from far aloft. 'A sail entering the cove!'

I ran from the Great Cabin and bounded up the steps, fearing the worst. The entire ship's company was likewise assembling on deck, men bursting from the foc'sle, some already craning over the rail, others scrambling into the ratlines.

'English ensign, captain,' said Youssef grimly, handing me the tube.

Though the vessel's hull was hidden by high ground around the entrance, we saw her three topgallant masts plain enough as she glided in towards the anchorage.

'Drill as we have practised,' I ordered, my heart thudding. 'Kedge and tow her round.'

I hoped we were ready enough to defend ourselves. Youssef shouted commands and twelve men scrambled into the Great Launch, pulling away at the sweeps. Eight more ran up on the quarter and hauled at the kedge anchor's cable, bringing aboard the dripping rope and taking it to the deck capstan. As the coils wound on, the stern began its slow swing to bring us broadside on to meet the newcomer.

'To the guns,' I called. 'Charge up with doubled roundshot.'

In an anchorage, and at such close quarters, chainshotting the rigging to disable the newcomer from sailing was pointless. If we hit her at all, we had to hit hard – and hit first.

As Tosher and Eli sprang away, what any landsman might

think a scene of chaos ensued as men ran hither and thither, dropping their mallets and brushes, making off the tackles at the mizen, shouting and gesticulating. Yet in a flash, shot-garlands were racked out behind the pieces, and ramrods, sponges, wads and horns placed by each one. The decks rumbled as each crew heaved on the tackles and ran their heavy gun out through the open ports. In under three minutes, we transformed ourselves from a scene resembling a shipyard works into a fully-armed vessel of war, with our larboard broadside charged with two round balls each and double primed. Peaceful repairs had been abandoned and gunnery begun.

The newcomer passed swiftly through the narrow entrance passage. Thank the angels, she was no Navy bark. Instead, she revealed herself to be a two-decker of twelve guns, an armed merchantman capable of putting up a fight but no outright man o'war. Her ports were open and the guns run out, but until she was brought round they could not range either side's six guns our way. The *Cornelius*, on the other hand, had all but kedged herself beam on and in another half minute would be able to loose off an eight-gun broadside.

I called the signalsman over. 'Hoist an English ensign and make the signal of friendship.'

As she nosed into the lagoon, my spy-glass showed her watches busy aloft with the canvas and at the catheads unstowing the bower for letting go. A launch was in the water with a tow off her beak and a smaller cutter stroked out ahead sounding the depths. Yet though the guns were run out, few men stood behind them and I could make out no immediate preparedness to fire. Far from bracing herself for a frenzy of gunnery she appeared quite unready, yet they must have seen our masts from outside the entrance. My hopes rose that her intentions were peaceful and this would not end in battle. If she did not know us and was not a prize seeker, there was no need for a fight.

With a roar at my shoulder and a blast of white smoke, the

37

signal piece discharged. I scanned the merchantman for a reply, or any clue to her provenance. The *Cornelius* – the *Saskia* now – shifted uneasily in her chains, held beam on against the tradewind. I went to the break and put my hands on the rail. Again all the seamen's faces were fixed on me, from the gale-hardened salty dogs to the youngest sea-boy. This time they waited for their captain to put it to them in a show of hands, the long-time privateers' way, whether we should give fight or make flight. This was not the open sea, so flight was out of the question. And everyone could see we had the better of the twelve gunner in a straight fight.

A voice hissed insistently into my ear. It was the Barbar. 'They smell a prize, Captain Mattoo. Say we fight. They vote for you.'

A pool of expectancy enveloped the whole ship. Every last jack-tar, gunner and powder-boy was gathered on the weather-deck and crowded by the guns. They stared up, ready for their captain to propose the action that would bring them the coins of gold and silver they craved. Poised by the foc'sle were the ship's surgeon and old Carpenter Sedgewick, doubtless already reckoning up their idlers' share. Even the lookouts gazed intently down from their perches in the tops.

There was no doubt the stranger was off her guard. If our aim was good first time, she had no defence against a sudden broadside. With luck, she might strike her colours without reply. What a fine prize she would make! There would be a handsome distribution to settle the men's grievances, and gold to buy more arms and powder. Far from the *Cornelius* being caught in the trap of Flawless Cove, this plump fruit had fallen into our lap. With one word of command, I could transform my captaincy from one of failed trading into a gilt-edged triumph of prize-taking. At a stroke, I could alter our fate forever and set us on a course of plunder and mayhem, gorging on spoils, enriching ourselves at the expense of those weaker or more unready to fight. Yet with that single order to fire the guns, I would throw away forever any chance of acquittal or pardon or reprieve.

As the silence extended and my palms grew damp on the smooth wood, I was full of uneasy misgivings, not so much for the future but this very minute. There was a look about this newcomer that was not as it should be. Something was badly amiss.

At the sound of a step behind, I half turned to catch sight of the Merchant Jeffreys emerging from the companionway, the tricorn in place, his nose twitching at the whiff of a plunder. But my gaze carried beyond this absurd figure, past the taff-rail and across the lagoon. Behind the spit near the entrance, there was a movement.

'Lookouts, dam' you!' I cried, pointing. 'Sails ahoy!'

All eyes followed my extended arm. At the heads of the only passage into the cove there had appeared two more sets of masts, their soaring height signifying ships of great size. A brace of vessels was following the twelve gunner into Flawless Cove, one of them clearly a far mightier bark than ours. Though as yet we could not see their hulls, the leader's trucks stood even higher than either of its companions', and it was plain the three barks represented a force that outweighed our firepower by a multiple. Belatedly, the errant lookouts began shouting, calling out the number of masts they spied, the spread of canvas on display, the state of the sails. They were behind events by a long shot.

'Stand at your positions,' I commanded, and amidst the nervous shuffling as everyone rearranged themselves before the guns, some taking up linstocks, others fingering their muskets, I snatched a look at our flagstaff. The friendly signal still fluttered there boldly, thank the Lord.

The massive three-master barged into the cove under tow, crowding the little sanctuary. She was a heavyweight two-decked vessel of thirty guns, a full-rigged fighting ship with a broadside capable of smashing clean through our four-inch timbers. Even the most shortsighted of sail-stitchers could see her guns were all run out, the rails busy with men, the whole ship astir in the expectation of a fight. No wonder the first bark had shown such insouciance.

Astern of this fearsome warship, following like a tame gundog, came a third vessel, smaller but nevertheless of about twenty guns, enough on her own to outmatch the *Saskia*. Her foreparts looked oddly arranged, with the bowsprit askew and drooping, the forestays hanging slackly. My heart missed a beat. By the Lord's own blood, she was the *Willingminde*.

Not more than two cables distant, the water rustled at the thirty gunner's great stem as she fetched grandly across the bay with sails bunted up and towing launches on station. She let go her bower with a mighty splash, lay back to set the flukes, then ran out more cable. Far from letting her tail into the tradewind, the launches swung her stern round and ranged the broadside directly upon us, fifteen menacing black mouths gaping our way.

There settled on her a stillness of the same intensity as on our own bark. Dozens of pairs of eyes must have been trained on us, but the only sounds in the lagoon were the swish of the Tropick breeze stirring the coco palm fronds and the sighing surf on the encircling shore.

Then her signal gun fired once, shattering the fragile calm. It was a command, not a request, for us to show that we would give no fight. I looked at my officers. Adam's face was pale. The Barbar turned his mouth down at the corners and shrugged. Eli gobbed a cheekful of brown liquid on the boards.

'It's as well for us, captain,' said the old salt, 'that you had eyes for what was coming.'

The lugubrious Jakob, glum as ever, said, 'If we avoid being blown to pieces, that would be, I think, a cause for celebration.'

Mister Jeffreys' tricorn bobbed back down into the hatchway. Did he know that a well-ranged six-pound shot could penetrate even the stoutest timbers of the stern quarters as if they were mere falls of sacking cloth?

'Haul up the flag of truce,' I said quietly.

Now the thirty gunner's red and white English standard was downhauled and replaced by the strangest four-yard colour. On a brilliant red ground, picked out in gold and white, was a terrifying defacement, a death's head bold against the field, supported by crossed cutlasses under. It signalled no quarter. But above the skull's forbidding motif was another emblem, a pair of hands clasped in friendship. This was no common pirate's flag, but a contradiction. It professed force and fear and death, yet equally it declared an offer of alliance. What the Devil was she about?

In the *Saskia*'s waist, forty figures stood immobile, some hunched by the guns, others standing tall with rammers in their hands, each man staring fixedly at the great flagship, puzzling out her meaning.

Fervently hoping our flag of friendship, hauled to the cross-trees and now fluttering and snapping in the hot Caribbee trade-wind, had been seen and noted, I brought up the spy-glass. On the big ship's quarter-deck, her officers were gathered together, consulting. One figure stood out taller than the rest, magnificently attired in white hose, golden briches, silken shirt and feather-trimmed hat – the master or captain, or even a gentleman-landsman by the look of it. A launch went briefly alongside, hoisted a blue trucial flag and pushed off. As the boat closed, her bows displayed the name of the mother ship. Picked out in fancy gold lettering, it declared her to be the *Prometheus*.

'She's offering to meet halfway for a parley,' I said, lowering the tube.

I scanned the faces of my officers one by one. Every man of us knew that – parley or no parley – the moment these fearsome ships had entered the lagoon, the *Saskia*'s fate was settled.

4

OUTGUNNED

'Gentlemen, should we not drink to your stroke of good fortune?'

The speaker was the magnificently attired figure I had spied not long before on the *Prometheus*'s quarter-deck when she hove into Flawless Cove. As he spoke, he held me with his eye. Longing for escape from the stuffy confines of this grand Great Cabin, broad and high though it was, I returned his scrutiny like for like.

The Merchant Jeffreys, a pair of half-lenses balanced on the sharp bone of his nose, was perched on a chair reading a long, unrolled parchment. At my officers' behest, I had taken him with me to oversee the arrangements. Against his apparent ease, I stood straight-backed by the table, refusing to be seated.

Opposite Jeffreys sprawled the most handsome figure of Sir Thomas Filligrew, noted and feared privateer, commodore of a flota comprising not only his thirty-gun *Prometheus* but the *Hannah Rebacka* of twelve and the twenty-gun *Willingminde*. His ships had defeated us without firing a shot and now the *Cornelius* – keeping her new disguise as the *Saskia* – was being forced to agree to run with his flota. The man looked impossibly pleased with himself for having added a fine and well-armed flyer to his assembly at the cost of no bloodshed, nor any depletion of his arms, nor any damage to his barks.

'Captain Sprang, the brandy if you will,' said Filligrew, his gaze unwavering while Willem Sprang, a Dutchman introduced as a captain presently between commands, took himself obediently to a pane-fronted cabinet. He brought out glasses and a decanter, and set them on the elegant oaken table-top.

'Are you done yet, Mister Jeffreys?' boomed the commodore in rich, bass tones. He kept smiling at me all the while, and I guessed him to be as slippery as a pollock in a pool.

The merchant looked up, allowing a little smile to continue its play across his face, and simpered, 'A few details to consider, Sir Thomas. Just for the sake of clarity, you understand.'

Filligrew studied him for a second, then his eyes flicked back to me.

'Loftus, you're a damm'd good seafaring man, a captain with handsome prospects. The way you got your bark clear of Kingstown Bay shows that indisputably.'

The *Willingminde*'s captain, spying me on the quarter-deck as he hove into Flawless Cove not half glass earlier, had of course recognised the *Cornelius* from the unhappy double anchoring episode in Port Royal. Not only that, but the vessel we had nearly rammed while getting under way in the squall turned out to be the *Prometheus* herself, anchored not far off. So, despite our attempts at disguise, it was all in vain and Commodore Filligrew knew exactly who we were the moment his barks had entered the cove.

'Not such fine prospects,' I said quietly. 'I intend to step down on my return to the *Saskia*.'

The mere notion of facing the stares of my men if I returned reduced yet clinging to the captaincy was impossible to bear. And setting apart my own self-interest in avoiding ignominy, remaining in command would needlessly add to my crew's jeopardy. I had decided never to allow that.

Sir Thomas took up the brandy and charged four glasses, pushing one across the table towards me, which I ignored. He nodded in turn at Mister Jeffreys and Captain Sprang, at which the gentlemen threw back the shots.

'A first-rate palate-soother,' declared the commodore, lifting his glass towards the tall, mullioned sternlights and examining the colour of the red-brown liquid. He assumed a brisker tone. 'Resoluteness is laudable, Loftus, but stubborn pride a sign of one lacking conviction in himself.'

'I want no lesson in conduct, sir, if you will.'

'Precisely so, for I see your character,' said Filligrew. Leaving the observation hanging in the air between us, he held out his glass for Sprang to recharge.

I broke the silence. 'It is a question of authority. I was voted captain to keep the vessel legal, seek profitable trade and eventually bring her back to Amsterdam. You have as good as destroyed my chance of doing that.'

Mister Jeffreys, hand fussily over his mouth, gave a polite cough and uncrossed his legs.

'Commodore Sir Thomas, we shall be honoured to run under your flag,' he said. 'Your renown has gone before you all along the coast of Carolina amongst the settlers. I well remember how your letters from the Governour of the Bahama Isles and commissions from the King himself allowed us to bring into Jamestown a hundred and fifty Negroes for planting work – in two trading barks, right under the Dagoes' noses. You uphold the expansion of trade and the settlement of the New World, bringing glory and wealth to His Majesty the King.'

He bent from the waist, an awkward manoeuvre when seated close at a table, and smiled ingratiatingly. The commodore contemplated him without expression.

'That is what the King's Navy is for, my good merchant,' he said. 'Protection of the new colonies, the expansion of trade, safety on the high seas, upholding of the law. A humble privateer such as myself is obligated to aid the nation when the Sovereign calls him to a duty.' He leaned back lazily, made the tips of his fingers into a pitched roof, and studied me once more. 'Is that not the Navy's purpose, Loftus?'

The man's self-importance irritated me. 'Aye, it is,' I said, 'along with escorting slave ships on their foul errands, bombarding undefended settlements and blowing traders out of the water if they disobey a signal to haul over and give up their vessel. Just like privateers. That is so, too, is it not, sir?'

'A brave riposte! There speaks an independent mind,' he said, smiling broadly, before drinking from the goblet and swallowing noisily.

The commodore leaned across the table and absently fingered a copy of the poster that had brought pursuit and death onto my head and Adam's. Its top was scrunched as though the paper had been torn from its pinnings, and now it lay there in full view, mocking every least ambition or dread that I harboured. A hateful, scornful thing, it seemed to know my weakness – that I feared not so much death as the means of dying, the rope's rough chafing at the jawline, its iron grip on the windpipe, then the tongue blocking the back of the throat and each breath becoming more tortured than the last, the arms twisting against the wrist lashings, the legs writhing absurdly, the crowd below laughing, a rising roar and din in my ears, then – at last – oblivion.

My likely companion choking on the scaffold alongside me would be young Adam, his life smothered almost before it had properly begun. I could not confront this prospect with anything but a pounding heart and muscle-loosening fear deep in my belly. Yet the commodore seemed wholly unmindful of the turmoil that poster caused within me. Perhaps he was used to dealing with condemned men.

'As I take it you could never ally yourself with the King's own cause,' he said smoothly, 'let me recapitulate what advantages there are in joining mine. First, you retain authority as master aboard your own vessel, with the rank of junior alongside my senior captains. Next, the *Cornelius* – I'm so sorry, the *Saskia* – is eligible for a division of one sixth share of any prize she might take. Further, she gets twelve and one half per cent of anything agreed under a parley, the distribution amongst officers and men to be decided by her captain.'

I said nothing, only shaking my head. Jeffreys nodded and smiled encouragingly at the commodore, his eagerness undisguised. Sir Thomas, ignoring him, sipped from his goblet and continued to address me.

'Why did you choose Flawless Cove for a refuge?'

I took a long breath, relieved at the chance to speak about an ordinary matter of sailing, and said, 'It was the only place we could reach with our damaged mast. The nearest safe haven.'

'My reason too for coming here – an unlucky choice, as you would see it, but the *Willingminde* wants immediate repairs. You know this coast, I assume? Not many could find this cove unless they had piloted here before.'

Exasperated at this assumption, I said curtly, 'No sir, I directed my bark here by the Navigation.'

'The celestial Navigation? Are you a taught Navigator?'

'Aye, and we brought ourselves right to the cove despite, I might add, a severe depletion of my charts and instruments.'

Filligrew cocked his head. 'They were lost in that squall?'

'Spirited away by greed. Stolen and sold off by seamen ignorant of their value.'

'Ah, the savagery of the common seaman!'

'They're aboard your bark, the *Willingminde*, and I formally demand their return.' I was thinking that if by regaining possession of my instruments, I might slip away with Abigail and work my way aboard ships as Navigator, eventually reaching home and seeking pardon.

'What have you lost?'

'My pilot books, many sea-charts, nearly all my sight tables and almanacks. Two ordinary cross-staffs, a Davis back-staff with good brass fitments, and an excellent quadrant.'

His eyebrows lifted. Then he rose and crossed the cabin, which was half as wide again as my own aboard the *Saskia*. Throwing open a walnut roll-top stand, he drew out a bundle of sea-charts and pilots and spread them flat. Even from where I stood, it was at once clear they were excellent drawings, new and pristine.

'Did you study at Trinity House?' he asked. 'With charts such as these?'

'No, but I was taught the calculations and methods by a Navigator once of the King's Navy. I practised with many fine instruments, though none as good as the quadrant stolen from my cabin – a reflecting quadrant with a mirror-glass and green shades.'

Filligrew seemed impressed. 'Ah, the best, an instrument of great accuracy, and of new design. Loftus, I beg you, have regard for this.'

He ceremoniously slid open a three-foot wide drawer beneath the chart table. There was revealed a cache of valuable instruments such as I had never before laid eyes upon, except in sweated dreams.

Each piece nestled in its own shaped compartment made to fit and lined with green felt, like a card table. The glint of polished brass, of shiny steel and of flashing lenses met my widening eyes. Here were not the unwieldy, wooden tools of the common sea-captain for capturing the sun's meridian altitude, nor even my sorely missed mirror-glass quadrant for shooting the angle on Venus or Altair or Aldebaran at dusk. Here were instruments of invention and production far exceeding the intellect and craft of the men who had fashioned mine. Here too were tubes beyond mere spy-glasses, and I knew them from drawings in books to be the new telescopes. One was two foot in length, others eighteen inches, and amongst them was even a model in miniature, perhaps a prentice's work-piece, yet equally exquisite.

Clocks, telescopes, parallel rules, dividers – it was a treasure of magnificence. My own pieces were by comparison nothing but crude outmoded tools as clumsy as axes. I craned over, the better to see, tingling at the prospect of laying hand upon these bejewelled works.

'Do you admire my display?' boomed the commodore.

I straightened, realising my guard had dropped.

'Good instruments are so vital,' he said. 'I want my barks

Navigated as proficiently as we fight them. Sit down, Loftus, and drink.'

Still wary, I took the offered chair and grasped the glass. When I swallowed heartily, the brandy's fire was soothing.

Sir Thomas fixed his attention on me. 'You're well grounded in Natural Philosophy, I take it? A little of the Mathematicks, perhaps? How I yearn to converse with a fellow enquirer and discoverer! You are familiar with Napier's Tables?'

'The logarithms?' I said, remembering my lessons long ago. 'O aye, Napier's work cuts the Navigator's task of calculation by half.'

'And too few damm'd captains properly learn the methods. We're lifelong seamen, they cry, and we reckon from the log and the leadline. But I say, they must learn to learn. And does it not astonish you that only now does the Navy Board begin to require a Navigator, conversant with the calculations, to sail aboard their largest vessels?'

I allowed a brief smile, relaxing a degree. 'Aye, and even then he must purchase his own instruments as if he were nothing but a journeyman.'

Filligrew laughed and generously refilled my glass. 'Such irony. The tardiest institution in adopting the Navigation is the very one most in need. Drink, Loftus, to the King's Navy, and to the poor benighted pilots who man the poops of their frigates and as often as not send them upon the stony shore.'

I took another draught, finding the drink had softened my mood.

'If you value the Navigation, commodore,' I said, 'I presume you are conversant with the new theory of tabulating the positions of stars against the motions of the Moon? In hopes of solving the Longitude.'

'The Lunar Distance Method?' he boomed, cheeks flushing. 'I find myself impressed, Loftus, with your breadth. Not many, even amongst Navigators, have heard of such things. It's true, there's important work issuing from Greenwich.'

'The Royal Observatory?'

'Aye, Loftus. I'm well-met with John Flamsteed, the Astronomer Royal. Known him twenty years, and he's as dry a stick as ever. And mistaken over the Lunar Distance Method, of course.'

'Mistaken, sir?' I said, trying to cover my astonishment at being in the company of one acquainted with so exalted a figure as the Astronomer Royal himself. 'Surely the Method he propounds is the best hope of finding a Longitude?'

'Ah, true, true, captain. By the book, to measure the distance of the Moon from the known position of a star, or even in the day from the sun herself, is a sweet way to consult God's clock to find the time and thus a Longitude. Finding the Longitude! Good God, Loftus, think what it means. The first nation to master the mystery can send its barks around the oceans at will, and gain control of all the carrying trade of the entire world. What prizes await.'

'Aye, and the Longitude –'

'Imagine too, Loftus, the advantages in war.' Filligrew leaned across the table, eyes agleam. 'A nation might send her barks against another Navy in the certainty of arriving intact at the desired destination. Warships might approach the enemy's fast-nesses in the confidence of knowing where the offshore rocks and shoals lay. Squadrons might remain at sea for months without touching the shore for a fix, never exposing themselves to enemy batteries, forever able to outwit coastal patrols. Knowledge of the Longitude wins the war at sea once and for all.'

'Aye, indeed, but –'

'The rewards, Loftus! Think of the riches for the first man to discover the Longitude. From Batavia to the Cape of Storms, from the Spice Isles to the Caribbee, from the New World to the Narrow Seas, from the Baltick to the Levant, think of the advantages to ocean trade.'

'And the seamen, Sir Thomas,' I got in at last. 'Think too of the lives to be saved, the barks no longer needlessly wrecked. I was taught that the prime importance of the Navigation was to save men from drowning.'

'Ah, I do admire the principle you display.' He smiled sadly. 'Nonetheless, Flamsteed is mistaken. Not about the Method itself, mark you, but in his approach. His tables do not achieve the aim intended. Take his best work so far, *The Catalogue Of One Hundred Stars*. Even for the most recently published edition – 1688, I believe – there have been no observations for more than a handful of latitudes. And the volumes are replete with errors. Mindful of these shortcomings he refuses to publish further tables, saying they cause more mishaps than they prevent.'

'You seem to admit defeat, sir,' I said, taking a gulp of brandy. 'Surely the Longitude is not forever lost to us?'

Filligrew chuckled richly. 'We are in a fix, Loftus, because we are without a fix. Yet in the end, our Longitude shall be found. And by astronomers, too, even if not by Flamsteed. Consider the revolution in instrument-making. See!' With a triumphant flourish, he lifted from its compartment the miniature, quarter-sized telescope I had thought a practice piece. 'This mechanism of advanced opticks,' he said, eyes glinting, 'resolves the satellites of Jupiter and thus in future may allow a Navigator to time those moonlets' eclipses. From that and an almanack – yet unpublished or even devised – he shall one day be able to calculate his Longitude.'

Though I had read of a telescope to view Jupiter's tiny moons, that instrument had been fourteen foot in length, and fixed atop a hill at Greenwich, where even on *terra firma* the slightest tilt of its base or tremor of its tube rendered the sighting faulty. What, then, might this mere prentice's toy accomplish? How could such a model-piece be held steady at sea on a rolling bark?

'A reflecting telescope,' declared Filligrew, placing it on the table-top with loving reverence. 'A copy of one made by a genius, almost thirty years ago. It resolves not only the craters of our own large Moon, but even the Ring of Saturn. It sharpens the heavens more distinctly than any refractor on Earth, however well-made, of whatever length. It uses mirrors instead of lenses, and is a gift from God to the mariner.'

The beautiful artifice stood on three small brass legs supporting a cylinder of six inches' length. Its shape, its detail and its coherence unmistakably bespoke its perfection.

'I had this copy made against the opposition of my Fellows,' said Sir Thomas, 'but with the express permission of he who made its original.'

'How does it work?' I asked.

'Inside are many small, jewel-like mirrors, polished to a dazzle, smoother than any lens. They reduce the distortion of light – the spherickal and chromatick aberrations – near to nothing. By doubling and redoubling the image back on itself, the power to magnify is many times that of a refractor. It was designed by a giant amongst pygmies, a Natural Philosopher of light and opticks, and an uncommon experimenter with whose alchemickal works I am intimate. A gentleman called Isaac Newton.'

'I once read of his works,' I said, marvelling at the fine-tooled eyepiece. 'And who was the craftsman who built it?'

'The same, the very same!'

I looked up, open mouthed.

'Remarkable, is it not, Loftus, that one man should possess not only the wit to design such a work, but the skill to fashion it? And those Philosophickal fools –' he beat his fist into his palm '– disbelieved and ignored its worth for years. I speak of the Fellows of the Royal Society, sir, of which I am one myself, and who suppressed this instrument, blind to its significance.'

'You are a Fellow of the Royal Society of London?'

'Indeed,' he chuckled, 'though I hardly expected my election to entail life-long tribulations with other Natural Philosophers.' Rising, Filligrew took up the telescope with great care. 'Come on deck, Loftus. See what it can do.'

In thrall, I followed him out of the Great Cabin and up to the quarter-deck, where we took turns with the instrument.

51

Balancing it atop the compass binnacle, I squinted into the eye-piece and, quite to my amazement, found a new world. In the circle of view, a green patch turned out to be the single frond of a coco palm more than a mile off on the far side of the bay. It so defeated the plain refracting tube of a sea-captain's spy-glass, like my own, that I shook my head in awe.

'This invention,' said Filligrew when I at last relinquished it, 'allows the Lunar Distance Method to triumph. As soon as Flamsteed's works are all done, Loftus, we shall know our Longitude at sea!'

His face was suffused with fervour. What a remarkable fellow, I thought, with such enthusiasm for knowledge and the Navigation.

He adopted a solemn tone. 'Take note, young sir. My captains may be notable seamen, but fellows of Natural Philosophy they are not. I need a man who shares my faith and my fascination. Someone who can steer my barks better than any Navy squadron or Frenchy flotilla or lumbering convoy of Spanish treasure-ships. A man like you, Loftus, could direct us further and faster than any fleet before, bringing us to our destined ports with a precision no others dream of, crossing the open seas to come upon our landfall without fail.' Sir Thomas drew me closer. 'And I have a secret, something the great Flamsteed himself would dearly wish to have in his own hands.' He wore a look of unadulterated smugness. 'The secret of the Longitude. But I have it now, Loftus – now!'

My mouth fell open, and I said stupidly, 'What is it – the secret?'

He laughed and shook a finger at me. 'You shall have to agree to run as captain with the flota first, my good fellow. And before you decide,' he said, leaning conspiratorially near, 'I urge you to reflect on your prospects as a wanted man. If you join me and Navigate the flota, in a twelvemonth you may learn about my discovery. Then I shall bring you in triumph to London and negotiate your pardon.'

52

'Negotiate?' I said. 'You do not mean a bought pardon, I trust?'

'O aye, money is a deft persuader.'

'Sir, I am innocent,' I said hotly, 'and refuse to buy a false pardon.'

'You would rather the scaffold, then?'

A vision of the Port Royal poster floated before me once again. Filligrew caught my look of consternation and seemed amused.

'I gather you would not,' he said. 'If you cannot bear to be bought a pardon, then you must seek a relief from all charges, a declaration of innocence.'

'Then an acquittal is what I seek, sir, for myself and Pyne.'

'Call it how you will, you must appear before a court to get it. Would you risk that, knowing the wilful caprice of the Admiralty Courts? On the other hand, a pardon may be granted by an individual with authority – a judge, say, or an admiral, open to persuasion. A paid-for pardon is also a clear and unmistakable document, recognised everywhere.'

His reasoning was undeniably sound. I was thinking hard, and Filligrew could see it.

'I can win you that pardon, Loftus,' he said quickly. 'Just reckon on the value of my secret – solving the Longitude. Indeed, if you work with me, the nation's gratitude might extend even beyond pardon or acquittal. Lands, privilege – perhaps a gentleman's rank, or better.'

All this talk of pardons and prizes made my head spin. I began to consider the ruse of going along with Sir Thomas just so far, keeping the *Saskia* as honest as possible yet still paying off the men in silver dollars and rum. Could I not benefit too from his Navigation techniques and even learn the secret he spoke of? After all, it might have been far worse – if our barks had engaged in a needless and bloody fight or if Filligrew's flota had instead been a Navy squadron. Most of all, I thought of escaping the rope, and of young Adam's life. Even so, there was a mighty stumbling block.

'Sir Thomas,' I said, measuring my words, 'I shall not remain captain whatever you or I might wish. The *Saskia*'s men are going to vote me out.'

'What? Vote? No, no, no.' He suddenly gripped me by the elbow. 'Good Lord, man, this flota runs by its commodore's rule, along with my captains. Each decision is arrived at solely by me and my officers.'

'Not by any vote of the private seamen?'

'By command of the captains, Loftus, the more politick way.' He placed an arm around my shoulder. 'You burden yourself with too many difficulties by allowing your seamen a vote. You should silence their demands with gold.'

'It was the practice of our respected former captain,' I protested, 'to hold a vote on the bark's destiny.'

'That was in the past. You must look to now. And then there's your trading, Loftus. This is the Caribbee Sea. There's too much gold and rum, too many spoils for Dutch and English seamen to be satisfied with hauling salt-cod or animal skins. Leave that to the natives.'

I thought of Abigail craving a modicum of comfort, and how a little gold might make our love more secure. Youssef and the jack-tars would respond warmly to a generous distribution of prize money. And I thought, too, of finding the price of a couple of pardons. The more I pondered, the more I had to admit the advantages. As old Eli said, there were always two ways to caulk a deck seam and three to pay the Devil. Perhaps I could after all go along with Filligrew, just until I got what I desired.

The commodore must have guessed at my calculating, for he beamed. 'Go back to the *Saskia*, assemble your men, tell them what generous terms you have secured. My dear fellow, let it never be said that two Navigators could pass in the night like unlit ships on the ocean, or fail to be mutual in their Art.'

With that, he replaced the precious telescope in its box and, taking my arm, propelled me towards the companionway and down to the Great Cabin, where we found Mister Jeffreys and

Captain Sprang still poring over the unrolled parchment. Filligrew bustled about until he had collected a pile of books – tables, pilots, methods and calculations – and a handsome selection of instruments.

He gestured at the lapidary collection. 'Yours, Loftus. What do you say?'

The treasures were undoubtedly seductive. Suddenly, I found myself saying, 'Aye, very well. It's agreed.'

The merchant looked up. 'What is agreed?'

'It concerns you no longer, Mister Jeffreys,' I said shortly. Reaching past him, I took up the quill and signed boldly across the bottom of the document over whose irrelevant details he had been so fussily vacillating. His face was a picture of incredulity.

'An admirable show of leadership,' Filligrew chuckled. 'And so the flota is herewith enlarged by one bark. Now, Merchant Jeffreys, my commercial affairs are proving more intricate and multifarious by the day – contractual arrangements, commissions, orders of submission, prize divisions, bargaining of captured goods, trading agreements and the like. I require a gentleman of integrity and high aptitude to oversee them.'

Seth Jeffreys blushed. 'Why, of course, sir, I have much experience of commerce and bargaining, indeed, but –'

Filligrew clicked his fingers and Captain Sprang jumped up, holding out a quill. The commodore leant forward and tapped the parchment.

'Just your signature as witness, then.'

The merchant's glance darted from the quill to Sir Thomas's face, then up at mine. Nervously, he fingered the agreement.

'Sign, Mister Jeffreys,' I cut in, 'or I'll exchange your comfortable stern for a foc'sle berth below decks with the common seamen.'

He blenched and took the quill, dipping it and scratching the point across the vellum. Captain Sprang dusted powder on the ink, melted a drop of wax on the bottom corner and pressed down a seal.

I turned to Sir Thomas. 'May I propose Miss Abigail Jeffreys as trusted scribe and assistant to the merchant? She has an excellent commercial mind.'

Filligrew smiled broadly. 'Assuredly, Loftus. Women are commonly assiduous in such tasks. It is all agreed then? Very well, at eight bells of the morning watch, all captains are to assemble here for orders.'

He began hefting the trophies into my arms. There were too many to carry on my own.

'Mister Jeffreys, be so kind,' I said, indicating the items remaining on the table, 'as to bring those boxes and volumes.'

With that, we left the *Prometheus*'s Great Cabin, passing into the low passageway that led forward into the waist. Brought up short by the sound of a ghastly hacking cough, I spied in a sleeping cabin to the side, through the half open door, a miserable sight. A shrunken old man sat disconsolately on a bunk, muttering and croaking. On seeing me, he rose, fluttering like a bat, and shuffled to the opening, his mouth working.

'Sir, O sir!' cried this pathetic figure, extending a clawed hand. 'Shall you go to England? I beg of you to help me. O, help me with the Longitude, aid my cause, my *magnum opus* –'

'Be silent, you old fool!' barked Sir Thomas, only a step behind. He thrust the fellow back in and slammed the door shut. Smoothing his shirtfront, he said, with an apologetic smile, 'Deranged – beyond the help of sane men.'

As we left, from behind the cell door issued a whimpering, lachrymose wail, sounding like nothing so much as a recitation of numbers, over and over.

The weather-deck was busy with seamen and officers preparing the launch for our return to the *Saskia*. I sent the merchant scrambling daintily down the boarding rope, then handed my booty of treasures safe into his waiting grasp and descended after.

'God be with you,' cried the commodore, waving as the launch was stroked away.

And on these equable terms, I left the *Prometheus*, bent on imparting the good news that I had secured a future for the entire company of the *Saskia*, her captain and Navigator included.

Only the merchant seemed discontent. He sat in the stern-sheets clutching the burden of my instruments, his rat's face pinched into a scowl.

5

WATCHES OF THE NIGHT

As dusk fell that night, I yawned and stretched in the Great Cabin, listening to the sounds of the ship's repair work dwindle to silence and the murmurs of the off-watch men resting after their sustained effort of repair. I had sent a party ashore to kill two small pigs and a supper was under way at the galley furnace, yet I had no appetite nor desire to break from my work. Instead, alone under the clear light of a whale-oil lamp, I pored over Filligrew's astonishing gifts.

The door opened and Abigail put her head round.

'Matthew?' she began.

With a smile, I pushed aside the Navigation works.

Coming to my table, she said, 'I'm so pleased you intend to stay in your command. The men have such regard for your seamanship.'

'And what do you think of the agreement?' I patted the seat for her to sit beside me. We had had no chance to be alone since I had put my plans to the officers. 'My arrangements to pay the men? The new percentages? We shall hear no more griping about pay and prize money, not now the seamen on the *Saskia* get two tenths.'

She gave me a squeeze and said, 'You're too generous. My father says few privateers allocate to the foc'sle more than one tenth.'

I smiled. 'It was you who insisted we paid the seamen as much as we could. That's what I've done, and it'll make them toe the line – no more stealing and fighting, that's for sure. And if the *Saskia*'s got to run with Sir Thomas, then I'm bent on keeping her as far clear of illegality as possible and I shall need their undying support to do it. It isn't going to be easy under a man like Filligrew, but it's worth it if we get our pardons.'

'O yes!' she said, eyes shining. Then she hesitated. 'But Matthew, my father suggests you might have kept more back for the ship – for the officers, for us.'

My smile faded. I heartily wished she would not cite Mister Jeffreys' opinions so dutifully. After all, I had managed to retain the captaincy, despite Filligrew scoffing at my principles.

'Dearest, the agreement's the main thing,' I said, convinced she would see sense in the end, 'because I can still run the ship my way.'

'Father believes the commodore might have offered more, well, more *generous* terms.'

I laughed lightly. 'What, faced with the might of three armed vessels, we should have held out for another two per cent or five per cent? Is that your father's opinion? Abigail, you should not always listen to him.'

'Of course not!' she said hotly. 'But perhaps you were too much preoccupied with the Navigation. If only you had let him parley –'

'Your father's eye for commercial matters may be acute,' I cut in, 'but he's a landsman and when it comes to a ship's fortunes, his opinions are of no more consequence than a rat's droppings in the bilges.'

'Matthew, there's no call to be coarse. He has tried to speak with the sailing-master and the second mates, and I thought –'

'I am astonished! Your father agreed to the enterprise, there on the *Prometheus*. When we returned here, he consented to the terms I put to the officers. Everyone's behind me now, all the officers and the men.' She said nothing, and I kissed the top of her head. 'You must be tired. Will you go to your cabin now, and shall I come to you later?'

Looking a touch downcast, she nodded and withdrew, and I turned back to my studies. When the doorlatch clicked shut behind her, I threw down the books and pounded a fist into my palm. Curse the blasted merchant! Running with the flota was going to be difficult enough without Seth Jeffreys interposing himself between me and his daughter. The sooner I sent him aboard the *Prometheus* to organise the flota's affairs and see it about its business according to whatever commissions Filligrew obtained, the better for us all. In time I would persuade the commodore to be rid of Jeffreys altogether, perhaps ashore to the slave market in Sint Maarten where he could enjoy bargaining lower prices for the Negroes, or at a plantation exhorting poor indentured fellows to work for less than nothing on pain of punishment. Whatever happened, the slippery merchant was not to divert me. I resolved again to wash him and his venal ways from my mind. Now I had settled the future of the ship – and my own – on the most honourable terms possible, there were far more rewarding concerns to occupy my time.

The volumes and instruments laid out before me were exquisite. The almanacks represented the very latest issue from the Astronomer Royal at Greenwich and the most advanced calculating tables from Geneva, all produced to a quality of design that improved on any I had seen. There were sea-charts from the Royal Navy's own chart-makers, and harbour pilot books of encompassing detail and freshness. My eye ranged over the instruments too, for although there was not amongst them such a remarkable creation as the Newton telescope, yet there was a quadrant equal to the one lost to my ignorant crew's greed for a few silver coins.

Alone, I worked late into the night watches, quite absorbed and heedless of movements in the ship all around, for I had left all the work in the charge of the Barbar the better to concentrate on my Navigation. The sounds of carousing began to filter through, yet

I cared nothing for joining my fellows at the sugar-rum. At intervals, the anchor cable groaned, its sound travelling along the wooden walls as far as the Great Cabin, but I barely heard it. Perhaps a launch bumped alongside once or twice, but I put it out of my mind. My head whirled in the realms of arithmeticks and departures and angles and the magic of the logarithmick columns. Then, tiring of the arithmeticks, I perused volume after volume of Filligrew's pilot books covering harbours and lagoons and coves on coral islands throughout the Antilles, Greater and Lesser, and all along the shores of the Colomby Coast and the Rich Coast on the Spanish Main. Half imagining myself there, I sailed deep inside the reefs of the Darien Isthmus, and cruised along the palm-fringed shores of Costa Reeka. In my mind's eye, I dodged round the Yucatan and into Campeechy Bay until it seemed as though I could direct my bark anywhere in the Caribbee Sea. With effort and discipline, what a captain I would become!

And then there was the Longitude, the prize above all prizes of gold or booty. If Filligrew truly would let me into his secret, and I proved that the new methods worked at sea, then what magnificent rewards might follow.

All these dreams dissolved the instant the door flew back with a crash. Several figures burst into the cabin all at once, and there was jostling behind in the narrow passageway. Leaping half out of my seat, I sent volumes and instrument cases cascading to the cabin sole. By instinct, I had laid a hand on my cutlass before my head cleared enough to recognise the intruder. Or visitor, I thought, relaxing my guard, for the personage who strode forward from the throng was Sir Thomas himself.

'Why, commodore,' I said, recovering from my discomposure, 'this is a surprise. I welcome you aboard, but perhaps you might have signalled me –'

I trailed off when behind him followed half a dozen armed men, cutlasses drawn, one or two with pistols at the ready. To my confusion, Youssef was amongst them, armed likewise and hawk-faced.

'I would hardly forewarn you, Loftus,' said Sir Thomas, 'that your vessel was to be boarded and taken.'

My chest pounded. 'What the Devil are you talking about?'

I at once became aware of many heavy treads on deck, shouts and orders ringing out across the weather-deck, and the movement of a large number of men. Without thinking, I once more lifted my cutlass.

Filligrew raised an arm. 'There is little point resisting. The vessel is in my hands, Loftus. From now forward, she shall go under Captain Percy Gamble, formerly of the *Willingminde*. He is on the quarter-deck taking charge here, while Captain Willem Sprang is to command the twenty gunner. The sailing-master, this Barbar Youssef, shall keep his post along with the bulk of your seamen, though the ones who resisted are being taken off and replaced by prize crew. You are henceforth confined in your quarters.'

Shaken to the core, I felt as though all my powers were slipping away. 'But – what about our agreement?'

'There is a new agreement,' said Filligrew, 'which I am sure shall be for the better.'

'For the better!' I exploded. 'For whom?'

'Better for the flota. Paying your men two-tenths does not suit me. It disrupts and undermines the other ships.'

'It was my decision as captain. You said you would not interfere with that.'

'On the contrary, it's my decision as commodore. Nor can I permit you to pay any seaman's wage, as you propose. The rule is that the flota goes by prize distribution alone. I cannot allow a captain the degree of independence you now appear to claim. Nor your insistence on continuing to attempt to trade in goods of little value. Nor the preposterous suggestion that my flota may not attack the barks of France and Spain.'

'How did you hear all this?' I said, rapping the table angrily. Someone had broken the confidence of my officers' briefing.

'What matters is the truth of it,' the commodore said. 'I have learnt you are a misguided man. What might hold good in the English Channel or the Narrow Seas has no place here. Neither the law of England nor that of France, nor of Spain, stretches this far. As perennial enemies of the Sovereign, they lay open their vessels to attack on the high seas.'

'We are at peace,' I protested.

'What peace is there when they make war on our innocent seamen and ships? My flota shall continue to strike at the barks of those warmongering nations, whether you like it or not. Frankly Loftus, I believed you were converted from such unworkable notions. Yet the minute you set foot back aboard here, you relapsed. I trust you did not think you might dangle me along on the end of a string?' He shook his head in disbelief. 'Three dollars for a sea-boy! Twenty per cent of prize distribution to end up below decks! Trading in skins!'

My every word had been betrayed. While I sat below in the Great Cabin, there had been machinations and treachery above my head. Then I noticed the merchant Jeffreys skulking like a jackal behind the commodore.

'You should learn to listen to your betters,' he trilled from this safety. 'Once Sir Thomas heard your unwise notions about trading and payments –'

'And he heard it from you? How? When?' I demanded angrily.

The merchant's voice grew more confident. 'You were a little too – ah, occupied, Matthew, to notice the launch taking me off.'

'Back to the *Prometheus*? I should have put you in chains.'

'The commodore soon saw how you would stand in the way of things,' said the merchant, still cravenly keeping cover. 'Our noble and gracious commodore.' He turned and beamed at Sir Thomas, giving a little half bow from the waist.

Filligrew constructed a shallow smile. 'Jeffreys, what an ingratiating and servile character you are. A greasier eel might not be found this side of the Baltick Sea.'

The merchant's smile remained fixed but a shade of misgiving crept over his features.

'You've done your good works for this night, Merchant, so there's no need to crow. If he had half a chance, who could blame Loftus for seeing you boiled in a tar-barrel, dipped in hot-wax and trennelled to the stem for a figurehead?'

The weakening smile on the merchant's face froze into a rictus.

The commodore turned to me. 'Loftus, however it was done, you must nevertheless accept what has happened. In time, you may recognise the merits of it. Seamanship and Navigation are your undoubted strengths, but as for captaincy – well, you are young, not tempered yet. You have much to learn.'

Filligrew nodded at Youssef. The Barbar came over and removed the useless cutlass from my hand.

'Not end of world, my friend,' he said. 'You lose now, you win another day.'

I glowered back. 'This is pure treachery, Barbar.'

'No treachery, by Allah. Commodore can win more prize money than Mattoo. More chance for sailors to live well.'

'More money for you, you mean. And that counts higher than any loyalty – to me, or to the ship.'

'Loyalty, treachery. Only words. Seamen live on pleasures. Fill bellies with rum and pig, make happy time with girls.'

I had underestimated the degree to which Youssef saw the world in such visceral terms. Racking my memory for the worst of his countrymen's curses that could be laid upon an Arab, I said, 'Youssef, I spit on the soles of your feet.'

He pursed his lips. 'By Allah, that is bad thing.' Then he brightened. 'But you see – all fine, men very pleased.'

There was the rustle of a dress at the doorway behind Filligrew's men.

'Let me speak to him,' said Abigail, pushing through.

'Mister Barbar, dismissed to your duties,' said the commodore. Youssef left without another word and Filligrew's men parted to allow my girl passage. She came and stood beside me, hands clasped, eyes cast down.

'Abigail?' I said, reaching for her, but she refused to look up.

'You guessed what your father was doing? You tried to tell me, didn't you?'

She gave the slightest nod, and my spirits fell away in tatters.

Filligrew ordered his men to remove all weapons and arms from my Great Cabin. Then he approached the table.

'I read men, Loftus, that is my true art. You are a fine seaman and Navigator, but you stagger under a load of pointless morals and quandaries.' All benignity was gone from his tone, and he spoke without a flicker of the fellow feeling we had so recently enjoyed. 'My captains are grasping, bloody fellows – great prize-takers, jolly deceivers and beggars of the truth. Like your dam' Barbar there. These are the men who make commanders of private ships.' He cast an eye over the opened volumes strewn across my table. 'You were well seduced by my treasures, were you not? And as a consequence, in my coming over to put things back on an even keel, there has been not a trickle of blood spilt on your deck-boards.' He smoothed the loose cotton shirt under his braided coat. 'I shall let the instruments remain here, for nonetheless I still require your talents as Navigator. You shall direct our course for the entire flota.'

I gaped. The man had robbed me of command and humiliated me. Probably my chance of pardon was gone too. How could he expect me to guide his flota to raid settlements and chasing down prizes?

'Not for all the gold in Colomby,' I retorted.

'Think on it. Your reward for this service shall be two and one half per cent of all flota prizes, excepting those taken by the *Saskia* herself, in which case you shall receive four per cent. Less than one third the division a captain warrants, but generous enough in the circumstance. What do you say?'

'Never,' I muttered.

'Ah, you're thinking that you will not aid the man who took your bark from you,' said Sir Thomas, 'and that you can no longer hold up your head before your once loyal fellows. But you were bound to lose her, Loftus, trading in furs and horns and such poor stuff. Your crew was on the point of uprising, though I daresay you deny even that.'

I opened my mouth to deny it, then thought better.

'Yet now you may Navigate with the finest of instruments and a first-rate chance of enriching yourself. A single Spaniard bark we took last year realised a sum of better than twenty thousand dollars. Calculate four per cent of that.' Filligrew bent over the table and grasped my arm. 'Why, man, you can still hold up your head. You're a high-blooded young fellow, but a few years will chamfer the edges off you.' He started for the door, then turned. 'The last fellow to cross me was roped to the catheads for three days while we beat to weather. Consider that too, then give me an answer.'

'There's nothing to think about,' I said levelly. 'I shall never Navigate your flota.'

'Have it your way,' he shrugged. 'Stew in your quarters until you see sense. You are allowed on deck only at Captain Gamble's word. The flota is making ready to sail this night, in two hours. The *Saskia* is one of my party and fully under her commodore's command. Understood?'

'I understand perfectly,' I said, 'but the men of the *Cornelius* – the *Saskia*, dammit – may not. No sooner do they hear about the new divisions than you take them away again. Remember, they are accustomed to voting. They won't have a captain imposed on them. Every man aboard here has his vote, down to the lowest ship's boy. Go against that, and you're inviting trouble.'

Filligrew took several paces back towards me. 'Still you fail to understand. If we fight and take a prize, they get far more gold than ever you could pay by trading.' He shook his head in mock despair, as if he had just lost an inconsequential hand at cards. 'And this voting notion! I've no time for such niceties. Men respond to a call to action, to the promise of rewards. Voting corrupts purpose. It saps a nation's spirit, let alone a bark's. Above all, at sea there is no place for such levelling notions. Common seamen, Loftus, always run with the money.'

We were worlds apart. Filligrew took my resentful silence as the end of the argument, and departed with his guards. Their booted feet clumped heavily on the treads and I caught a muffled gasp as of someone stifling their mirth. Then they were gone.

Abigail and I were left alone in the Great Cabin. Sick to my belly, I slumped into the chair. It was as if I had been thrown down the pump-well of a ship to wallow in the bilges. Wordlessly, she turned and stood by the sternlights, her back to me, gazing out at the dark Tropick landscape beyond. After a prolonged pause, she broke the silence.

'It's for the better in the long run, Matthew.'

I started to protest. 'But what about –'

'O, I know all about those principles of yours,' she said sadly, coming back to sit beside me. 'They're too high minded for the Antilles and the Caribbee. Sooner or later, we'd have lost the ship anyway, been taken for a prize by force of arms. We'd never have kept her well armed and stored up with shot and powder, never have kept good seamen and gunners aboard. With your trading, we'd have become poorer and poorer until we fell into captivity and were murdered. Think of the habits of those Spanish, and of the natives.' She shuddered. 'A European woman feels unprotected, vulnerable.'

I grasped her hands. 'My dearest, I had no idea how you felt.'

'It's not only fear of what can happen aboard a ship,' she said quietly, 'but of the future. We lost our place in Whitby society, father and I, our house, all our possessions. This ship was a chance to lift ourselves. You were ready to throw it all away.'

I was exasperated. 'Dammit, that's unjust. I signed up to the flota. Did your father forget to tell you? It was for you. I was thinking of you, of our future together.' I wound an arm round her waist and squeezed. 'For us to be together, safe aboard a ship. Look at me, Abigail.'

When she did, my confidence evaporated. She could see right through me, as if looking down into the clear depths of a lagoon. Her eyes penetrated to the bottom where she saw no bright future, no silvery prosperity. Not only had my plan to play along with Filligrew failed miserably but, worse, it was plain she saw I had been seduced by the quadrants and the books, the promises and blandishments. My eye ranged over the instruments carelessly scattered across the table, the treasures which had absorbed me while my bark was stolen away to satisfy the venal desires of Jeffreys and the Barbar – traitors, both of them. And these instruments are traitors too, I thought, nothing but golden, bejewelled traitors.

Abigail's arms encircled me, hugging tightly. We stayed like that a long time, in the silence of the Great Cabin, in privacy but without intimacy. Somehow, an unbridgeable distance had opened between us.

Filligrew was as good as his word, and made ready to leave the cove within half a watch. When Abigail retired, I refused to join her and sat uncomforted in the Great Cabin listening to the bustle of my bark getting under way.

The *Saskia* hauled up her bower anchor and set her topsails. With shouts and the splash of oars, the launch towed her towards the entrance. She eased between the heads of the channel, lifted her bows to the sea and unfurled her courses to the tradewind. Then the swells heaved beneath the bark's keel and the flota pressed onwards into the darkness, gathering speed. Yet in all this I had given no order, spoken to no officer, been consulted by not a single soul. Staring out through the sternlights trying to pick out from the gloom of night the receding shores that bounded Flawless Cove, it came home to me that my command was gone.

Those first hours passed as if I were in the grip of something akin to fever. My mind was thronged with confusing images as I listened to the quarter-deck exchanges above my head. A new voice, clipped and authoritative – Captain Gamble's, I supposed, to whom Filligrew had handed the captaincy – called out the compass course. The steersman – Henrik Gannes, of course –

68

acknowledged and Youssef repeated the sailing orders loud and clear. Eli and Jakob sang out to the watchmen, while sailors' chanties came drifting down from far aloft at the topgallant yards. They were sailing my ship without me.

The *Saskia* settled into her sea routine. The quiet murmur of seamen's chatter mingled with the rustle and slop of water against her planks, the creak of the deck knees and mast steps, the hull timbers working, the snick of greased rudder chains responding to the wheel. Soon there was a great deal of activity on deck and from within the lower holds came thuds and scrapes and shouts. I listened hard for many minutes on end, until it came to me. Blast them, I said aloud, and dam' them to Hell.

In a flash, I was out of the Great Cabin and along the passage. The only guard stood at the top of the companionway, for I was taken as a compliant enough captive. Too damm'd compliant, I cursed, mounting the steps in a rush and shoving the unsuspecting fellow aside. Gaining the quarter, breathing hard, I instantly saw their game. Both main hatch covers, fore and midships, were thrown back like gaping mouths. Parties of a dozen men a-piece were bringing our precious cargo to the hatchways bale after bale, box following bundle. They chain-handed them up on deck where more jack-tars caught the goods and cast them over the rail. As the parcels flew through the air and splashed into the black waters, laughter and ribald shrieks rang out. Astern, dozens and dozens of bales and packages bobbed and wallowed in our wake, some half-sunk, others stubbornly, futilely, remaining afloat.

Youssef the Barbar oversaw the deck operation. He worked with a will as did the seamen, my erstwhile crew, the same men who had once voted me captain and acclaimed my seamanship. It seemed to count for nothing now.

Nearby on the quarter stood Abigail. Next to her was the officer I had seen aboard the *Willingminde* when we were anchored alongside in Port Royal. With his straight-backed stance, the Naval-looking attire and elaborate sword at his belt, he was unmistakable. Round-faced and smooth skinned, short of

69

stature, he was barely older than me and already thick at the waist, like a fattened hog.

Now this Captain Percy Gamble turned and appraised me. He and Abigail had the air of those between whom there has been an intimacy of conversation, broken by my unexpected presence. I advanced quickly and seized her arm.

'What are you doing?' I demanded. 'There's no need – it's still valuable stuff.'

Shocked, she seemed unable to reply. Gamble butted in.

'Valuable? This animal waste?' he said mockingly. 'I should have thought , Loftus, you had learned the lesson from that most estimable merchant, Smiley Bankes. Now there's a sharp one-eyed jack to bargain with. Not that I am greatly informed, of course, on matters of trade.'

He uttered the last word as if it had been 'dung' or 'piss'.

'Go to the Devil, Gamble,' I said, glaring.

He smirked. 'By all accounts, the demon dealer of Sally Cox's made a prick of you. And in front of all those charming souls, too.'

I stepped forward with my fist up, but he shrank back and agitatedly signalled for his guards.

'Take this troublemaker in hand,' he commanded.

In another half second, a pair of seamen, fellows unknown to me, were wrestling me to the deck-boards. Though I landed a blow or two, I paid for my resistance threefold over. Despite Abigail's cries of anguish, the cracking onslaught continued. They delivered punch after punch until I quit the battle and put my hands up to save my head.

'Don't throw it all away, Abigail!' I cried.

Percy Gamble's clipped tones rang out. 'Teach the awkward cove a lesson,' he said, 'before you take him below.'

A blow from what might have been a belay pin laid me down. Through a nauseous mix of anger and pain, I heard Abigail calling my name. Somewhere inside my skull stars exploded, and my resistance was stilled.

6

DEMON NUMBERS

A single great drum of war beat regular and slow, dinning into my head with rhythmic stabs of pain. Inside my skull-case, a chorus of voices chanted incessantly, accompanied by the jangling of a thousand blades and pikes as if an army marched across a hilltop on their way to battle.

Opening my eyes, I found myself flat on my back in darkness. The moment I tried to rise, that terrible clattering army struck up once more and I fell back defeated. Still the drummer beat his pommel and the skin boomed, and it said *treach-er-ee, treach-er-ee, treach-er-ee*. After a while, a pale glow swam before me until the beams of a deckhead grew distinct and at last I remembered about ships, and being aboard them. What vessel this might be, I could not tell, but she lurched and yawed, rolling along with a hiss and rush of water inches away outside the wooden walls. We were at sea and going fast.

There came a rustle of movement. Someone glided close.

'Abigail –' I began, cracking my painful eyelids wider, but hers was not the face before me. Instead there were the lines and pocks of an old fellow wearing a look of concern, a potful of worry.

'Eli, is it you?' I croaked. 'Some water, if you will.'

'No-ooooo-ooo,' wheezed the ancient, and coughed moistly. 'Not your Eli, I am not he. It is Noah Spatchears, condemned to

71

his cell *in perpetuum*. And bound to tend his fellow prisoner, for no one else is here.'

'A sip of water then, for the Lord's sake,' I muttered, and gingerly raised myself off the hard shelf bunk. When I put my legs over the side, they clanked as I planted them on the deck-boards. There were shackles round my ankles, connected by a two-foot length of heavy chain links. What, was I imprisoned? For the love of mercy, was it not enough to lose my command without being deprived of liberty too? Then I remembered Abigail on the quarter-deck as the cargo was jettisoned. She had stared at me almost in contempt. My anger dissolved, replaced by oak-hard determination. This downward rush in my fortunes had to end. I resolved that as soon as my body revived, I would turn my mind to escape, and restoration.

The fellow called Noah attended me with a pewter mug.

'Drink!' he said, in a high-pitched screech. It rang against my bruised temples like an unoiled sawblade being worked through green wood. Gratefully, I sluiced the liquid into my throat.

'Drink,' wailed the old man, 'for it lubricates the brains of men and frees the discourses of their mind. Quench away, for water is the liquid of life.'

'This is small beer,' I said, but nevertheless supped it grate-fully. As I revived, I listened to the boom and rumble of rudder chains coming from somewhere deep in the afterparts and realised that it was a great ship were we aboard, much more massive than the *Saskia*. Gradually it dawned on me it must be Filligrew's flagship, the *Prometheus*. Then I remembered the madman – locked in a cell in the warren of rooms near the Great Cabin – who had accosted me as we left with the instruments.

'Small beer for a large world,' came the old man's voice, 'and for an even greater Universe, extending beyond the reach of sight but not beyond believing, for with diligence and resilience and providence we shall number and mark and divine our progress towards –'

'Sir, peace a-while, for pity's sake,' I said, putting up my hand.

Noah Spatchears backed away as if I had made to strike him. He puckered his lips, folding them back into his toothless mouth, and smacked them rapidly up and down. His eyes watered, the chin trembled and his neck wobbled. I thought the man was breaking down, until he opened his mouth and let out a barking cough that spattered mucus around the cabin, some gobbets of which fell across me. His shoulders shook and he gave in to a fit of such wheezing and drawing that I thought he must die on the spot.

'Ooo-oooooooh,' he gurgled, champing his lips and swallowing like a pelican. After sucking several more rattling breaths into his chest, he let out another cry. 'Help here! Assault, assault! O, salvation from this agent! The tables are turned, give up the tables. No, you cannot wrest them from me. I have burnt them – they are gone!'

This alarming outburst had a markedly poor effect on me. The drum struck up inside my skull with renewed vigour and my eyeballs throbbed in time. A minute more of this and my own mind would become unbalanced.

'Calm yourself,' I begged, but he shrilled on, screaming all the louder.

Clambering heavily in my chains into the sanctuary of the upper bunk, troubled and beset by the ranting, I lay down with my hands over my ears. In this disturbed solitude, I could not help but dwell on my condition.

I must have slipped into a half slumber, for I next remember lying awake in the cell listening to the creak and protest of the ship's beams as she heaved her way along a boisterous sea. It was night still, and the *Prometheus* ran before a grand swell in half a gale which sent her surging forward, yawing broadly, then lifting her stern to the next wave. In the quiet between the passing rollers came the strains of a low-sung song.

It was Noah Spatchears. He chanted as if to a prayer-string, his voice rising and falling in time with the waves. At first, I set my ears against the chant and dipped between sleep and wakefulness, but by degrees the sounds distinguished themselves into words. Or rather numbers. The song was nothing more than a stream of threes and sixes and twos and noughts – all the single numbers, in lots of four and five at a time. Once or twice, he uttered something like 'next column', or he would intone 'full integer'. After an hour or more of this, I rose up and sipped half-heartedly at my mug of beer, debating whether smothering him to death with his own palliasse could in any way be counted a kindness.

The chanting ceased. Next, there came a voice right by my ear.

'Sir, I beg pardon for the noise,' it whispered, 'but I can hardly keep my mind in this place.' A fine drizzle of spittle landed on my face as he spoke.

'So it seems,' I said, pushing him away. 'Must you chant these random numbers for hour after hour?'

'Not random! It is the only way I can remember. You must hear my case.'

'I care nothing for your case, sir. I want only peace.'

His tone hardened at once. 'I am a spy for His Majesty the King, and command you to aid the cause.'

The madness again, I thought. 'I have no wish to act as a spy, not even in the cause of King William.'

The ghostly oval of his face was close. 'Not he, O no! The King of the Catholicks is for whom I act.'

'I follow no religious cause,' I said wearily.

'My King might be the Pretender, but my cause is the Longitude.'

The Longitude? The very mention of it seared into my consciousness. Filligrew's words rang in my head: the rewards and riches, the winning of trade, the end of sea wars, my own elusive pardon – and all for finding the Longitude.

I put a hand on his thin arm. 'What do you have to say about the Longitude?'

'It is a Catholick cause, *nota bene*.' His voice was breathy and conspiratorial. 'The Pope spends his treasure towards its

74

solution. The faithful Kings likewise fund the endeavour. Once it was Charles and James in England but now the torch is borne aloft by King Louis and young James in France – the Catholick Kings, defenders and pretenders alike. The just and lordly patrons of Papish men everywhere.'

I sighed in despair. 'It's the Navigation I'm interested in, not your religious ideas.'

'UnGodliness rules, but most of all in trade and commerce,' said the madman, ignoring me. 'Why, consider insurance – a machination straight from the Devil. It is for Protestants. For bankers.' His voice rose. 'Usury is for puritans, ventures are for dissenters!'

'I see why Filligrew keeps you confined,' I said in disgust, sickened by the gale of putrid breath and spittle. He could not keep a grip on his thoughts for more than half a sentence without setting up a rant of the purest nonsensickality.

He coughed for a full minute until his lungs had settled. Then he issued a drawn out sigh, a sound resembling a cable groaning at the hawse-hole. Issuing from deep in his gullet, it rose in pitch while I listened in helpless fascination. His features slackened as though the life had been sucked from him, then refilled like the wind ballooning into sails. In an instant, his demeanour changed from lamentation to consuming rage.

'Spy, spy, spy, spy!' he screamed, pointing a finger and backing away as far as the narrow cabin allowed. 'The coffee houses are full of heathen beliefs and nonconformism! The Longitude is the only Godly truth! My quest is for Our Saviour, the Lord Jesus Christ!'

'Get in your bunk and stay quiet,' I said harshly, 'or I shall silence you without qualm.'

He did not speak further, but wheezed and groaned the night long. Every minute or two, from his broken, consumptive chest, he brought up gobbets and expelled them with surprising vigour. We passed that night close together in the crowded cell, but worlds apart in our minds.

In the morning, when light came, I spied Commodore Filligrew passing into the passageway. Lurching off the bunk, I shuffled, clanking, to the doorway.

'Sir Thomas, we must speak together,' I called. 'Where are we going? Let me see Abigail!'

The man with whom I had sat in the Great Cabin and conversed over the mysteries of Natural Philosophy and Alchemy and instruments and Methods, the gentleman who was a Fellow of the Royal Society and acquainted with the Astronomer Royal himself, swept past without so much as a word or a glance, preoccupied, his stride not faltering nor his demeanour changing in any regard. He looked past me and headed up the steps quite as though I did not live and breathe half a yard distant. It was as clear as the watch-bell I was no longer worthy of his least attention.

Despairing, I sank to the deck-boards and hung my head. Noah Spatchears lifted me back to the bunk, an effort which sent him into a spasm of chestiness. When the coughing ceased, he called out for food and drink, and rattled our little door and stamped his feet until a seaman came up and left us hard bread and a bowl of cold pottage. The old lunatick guzzled gleefully on his share, while I chewed without relish on a single mouthful and pushed the rest away.

When Spatchears was done eating, his noise began.

'Sir,' he said, 'I beg pardon for last night, as –'

'I wish you would keep it to yourself,' I said unkindly. 'Your madness all but unhinges me.'

'I am not mad, sir,' he said in hurt tones, 'merely ill. Rendered liable to a derangement brought on by fear of the night, and which is peculiar to the hours of darkness.'

I studied him. He was an ancient fellow, tiny of stature, wren-like, the skin hanging off his bones like loose sacking. True enough, in daylight his countenance was serene and tranquil, utterly changed from the scream and rant of a few hours before.

'The illness,' he said, eyes peering intently from the dry folds

76

of his parchment face, 'mixes up the compartments of my mind with a mash of memories and dreams so that I do not know myself what is right. Chanting numbers through the dark hours is my only handhold on sanity. Yet in the day, as I trust you hear, I am quite *compos mentis*, as whole in mind and active in thought as any man and better than many.' He fingered the grubby cuffs of his shirt and eyed me nervously. 'I observe much, even though I can no longer study the heavens.'

'You study the heavens?'

'Until the night fears prevented me.' He glanced from side to side, then spoke low. 'But sir, we must fly from here. I have seen where the keys are kept, and where the commodore stows his weapons, and when the guards –'

'Pass me that broth, Mister Spatchears,' I said, cutting off his rant. 'Escape's out of the question. We're imprisoned aboard a mighty flagship, surrounded by officers and men, shackled by our feet. It would be more use if you knew our destination, or at what port we might be let off ashore.' I spooned down the grey liquid. 'As we sail west, I take it to be Campeechy, perhaps? Or the Silver Coast?'

'West? How do you know that? There is no window here.'

I observed him closely for a full second, and concluded he truly was not mocking me.

'By the bark's motion, of course. We're rolling and yawing in a downwind way, so we can't be close-hauled or reaching. And we are going fast – recklessly, I'd say.'

He thought for a few seconds. 'You cannot conclude our heading is west. The wind or weather might be blowing us to the east, or south, or north.'

This time I laughed out loud. 'No sir! The tradewind blows only from northeast or southeast. If we're running before it, we're heading west.'

'It seems revealed to you, but not to me,' he said, staring at the remains of his pottage. 'After a life labouring at the stars and planets, I know astronomickal directions of all kinds, and nothing about barks or the winds. Yet you can tell all this *prima facie* – from below decks without sight of the sun or the land?'

'It's natural to a sailor,' I said. 'And if you, sir, have laboured with the stars, it cannot have been as Navigator on ships.'

'Most certainly not,' he said, as if someone had suggested he were a common beggar. 'For nigh on three decades, I was salaried at the Greenwich Observatory.'

This made me sit up. 'At Greenwich? As what?'

'I worked under the Astronomer Royal, on a method for improving the Navigation. You are addressing,' he said, stretching himself up, 'Chief Assistant Observator Noah Spatchears.'

'Did you work, by any chance,' I asked, suspicion rising, 'on the Lunar Distance Method?'

'You know of it? O lucky day, that I should fall upon so sympathetic a gentleman!'

'Now I see why Filligrew has you here. There are connections.'

'Perhaps, but connections of an uneasy nature.'

'Observator Spatchears, in the night, you talked about the Longitude. Was that just the illness?'

He looked hurt again. 'Do not remind me of the night.'

'Aye, but can you speak about it sensibly?'

'I have no one to tell, and no one to trust but you, sir.' He took a breath, but it caught in his throat. He coughed to clear it, then swallowed something sloppy and glutinous. 'It is the absolute truth, sir,' he said at last, 'that I have in more than a quarter century's observations collected sightings enough to bring forward in great measure the Lunar Distance Method. It is a great and important work, an advance for finding the Longitude.'

So this must be the secret Filligrew had talked about. Yet Spatchears' night madness made me sceptickal.

'No single astronomer, however capable,' I said, 'could have completed all those Moon sightings and calculated the predictions. There are millions to be done to make the Lunar Distance Method work. And observations can only be done at night-time, which is the occasion of your illness.'

'Indeed,' he said in a defiant tone, 'but I laboured at the Observatory with twenty waged assistants and scribblers and prentices and clerks under me. These results are not of my own endeavours alone, but of many men's.'

'Even if that's so, still the resulting Method is of great complexity, and far too difficult for use at sea.'

'No longer! For I have designed new calculations – integers, logarithmick methods and all the advances of Mathematicks to refine the Navigator's sightings and angles into the necessary numbers. The *modus operandi* is quite practickal in use, for my systems simplify the sums needed to compute a Longitude such that the least of arithmetickers may do it, even mariners.'

I could not stifle a snort of laughter. 'Shooting the Moon from the deck of a bark? Have you tried it yourself, sir?'

'At sea? No, indeed. But I have worked it on terra firma.'

'So your instruments are on land, set up firmly and kept steady, perhaps with tripod legs?'

'Indeed so, on the hill above Greenwich overlooking the great river.'

'And you have never raised the cross-staff on deck, in a seaway, at night, with the bark lifting and dipping?'

'I am no mariner, sir!' he spluttered.

'That's clear, Observator Spatchears. The cross-staff is six-foot long and very hard to aim at any given star. With the sea's motion, the bar jumps and dives, the star leaps away, your hand slips on the transom slide, and time and again you miss getting the angles.'

'O indeed, I understand the difficulty,' conceded old Noah, 'but when you do get an angle, then have you only to observe the Moon's limb.'

'Within a very brief time, is that not so?'

'Indeed, you must set a minute-glass and hasten.'

'Hasten about a lurching deck at night, trying not to fumble with the cross-staff,' I pointed out. 'Now, if the Moon is obliging and reveals herself between racing clouds just the instant of a fly's wingbeat, you might be able to freeze the sphere and read the sight. You have to be quick to capture the angle, for if the minute-glass has run its seconds through, then the Moon has moved too far and you must begin again.'

Noah Spatchears tried to interrupt but I raised my hand.

'Any Navigator, sir, is bound to point out,' I went on, 'that though your Method may be logical, its practickal use at sea is another matter entirely.'

Spatchears leaned forward. 'No, sir. The task is made easy by my tables. The Navigator has Napier's help too, and not more than forty five or fifty separate sums to calculate. Then, *ceteris paribus*, he need only find the columnar for his day and date, reckon the hour of night in local time, enter the arithmeticks to select his estimated latitude and –'

'Exactly!' I cried, shaking my head. 'Far too difficult.'

'But you have not seen the works. My new tables reduce the matter by an order of magnitude.'

'Perhaps, but as I understand it, for most latitudes, the necessary observations are barely begun. How many are contained in your tables?'

He smiled shyly. 'I have completed all the necessary observations for many dozens of the important lines of latitude, including most of those for the Narrow Seas, the greater part of the Middle Sea and almost all for the northern Tropick latitudes.'

I sat up quickly.

'Truly? Then that is a most astonishing advance,' I said. 'But how do your tables compare with those few already published by Astronomer Royal Flamsteed?'

Instantly, his voice rose to a wail. 'John Flamsteed! Dam' his eyes! Dam' his soul!'

I reached over and gripped his arm. 'Hush, sir. Why do you dam' Flamsteed?'

'O, the obstinacy! He refuses to publish my works. He

maintains that only the complete works may be printed – for all latitudes and positions, for all the Moon's variances, and for all the observable stars too. But that is the task of many, many years more. Meanwhile, he rails against the tables already published, saying their errors are too many, and their incompleteness a cause of mishap. So he delays, because he controls all Naval publishing.'

For sure, this tallied with some of what Filligrew had told me.

'He refuses to print anything,' said the Observator, 'yet it is his own works that are poor, not these of mine. In truth, he wishes only to deflect blame from his own person.'

Another thought entered my mind. 'If Flamsteed is withholding the works, how did you come by them? Did you steal them from the Observatory?'

'No, no, they are mine by rights to give to the world,' he insisted. 'They are paid for by the publick purse, after all. I desire only to see them in Navigators' hands. When I fell out with Flamsteed, he turned me penniless from the Observatory, casting me aside after a lifetime's service. I freed the observations from their captor. They lie aboard here now, as we speak.'

'They are back in Sir Thomas's safe keeping then,' I said, 'while you sound like a Catholick spy and may be bent on sending them to France.'

'That is merely my night ranting. I have faith in the tables and only wish to see their commercial and politickal value benefit England. *Inter alia*, many lives may be spared from drowning at sea, both Catholick and Protestant.' He leaned close. 'Filligrew is the traitor. He will sell to the highest bidder, to whoever pays the handsomest price, of whatever faith or nation, whether to publish them or to keep them hidden. Even to destroy them.'

I shook my head. 'The commodore knows Flamsteed. He'll return the observations to Greenwich.'

'Not true, not true,' said the Assistant Observator. 'It is I who knows Flamsteed, and Filligrew who claims the honour. Sir

81

Thomas is a liar – a master of politicking and trickery.'

'The trickery I have seen myself,' I said, abashed.

'Then accept my story, sir.' Spatchears' face loomed unpleasantly close. 'You must help me get the observations to England. Take them to England, sir, O please take them! You owe it to your fellow Navigators and seamen.'

'I cannot go to England,' I said, pushing him off. 'I'm a wanted man, for all I know already condemned by the Admiralty Court. If I set foot in the country, I shall be arrested and hanged by the Navy.'

'They must never go to the Navy,' said Spatchears, his head waving from side to side. 'Not the Navy, for they would pass them to Flamsteed. The tables must go to my patron, a Fellow of the Royal Society, the Curator of Experiments, who would publish them directly, and for all to use.'

I cocked my head. 'Isn't Filligrew himself a Fellow?'

'More lies and falsity,' said the astronomer. 'He shall never be elected, for his ideas are stolen from others.' Now Spatchears was clutching at my shirt. 'O sir, how perfect it is. Take my tables to the Royal Society and my patron might use his influence to your benefit. His name is Robert Hooke, Esquire, most highly regarded in Court circles. Think of it – the tables need only save a single one of His Majesty's barks to release the Sovereign's unbounded gratitude.'

Spatchears' words echoed Filligrew's of a day or two earlier, of how the tables would win favours and prestige and influence.

'Do you think, Observator Spatchears,' I said slowly, 'your tables might be worth a free pardon?'

'O, free pardons for ten murderers would seem a nothing! Listen, my good sir, you must break out straightaway and escape to England.' He let his voice drop to a whisper. 'I know where he hides the tables. And the keys.'

I sat back and considered our condition, captive and chained. The old astronomer babbled on about the commodore's keys and drawers as if escape were the matter of a moment's thought.

Even if I could break out of this cell, to where would I run?

'Perhaps your madness does come in daylight, sir,' I said miserably, briefly succumbing to a wave of desolation and despair.

Then I spied two figures passing in the passageway outside, one of them a deck-officer of Filligrew's. He was in close conversation with none other than Seth Jeffreys. So he was already ensconced aboard, no doubt dragging his daughter in his wake, and speedily making himself indispensable in the commodore's commercial affairs. The merchant spied me the same instant I laid eyes on him. He hesitated a moment as if he weighed going on or stopping, but the chance of tormenting me held sway. On his sharp features as he approached the barred door was a smirk of gratification at the turn of events.

'Why, if it is not Captain Loftus,' he said delightedly. 'Or should I say, former captain?'

He spoke all unaware of how he altered the workings of my mind. Within the time it took the *Prometheus* to surge along the blue Caribbee Sea no more than her own length, desolation flew like a bird from my shoulders and in its place came a will to act, to strike back. The deck-officer caught my black look, but not Mister Jeffreys, who ploughed on quite unaware.

'I trust your quarters are gracious enough, commanding as you do a space suited to a single fat porker. And your servant here – does he attend you well, and not spit into your food?'

He gave out his high laugh, the one he used in Whitby to inform a collier-master that the payment on his owings had risen by ten shillings the month, knowing it spelt the man's ruin. Or telling a sixpence-a-day bargehand that the Justice in the courthouse had cut the wage rate and there was nothing to be done but accept starvation as a Fate from the Good Lord.

Before the laugh was fully out of the merchant's throat, I was at the cabin door and in a flint's spark had reached through and got him by the collar.

'Traitorous snake!' I shouted into his blinking face, but before

83

I got another inch with my revenge, the officer's boot came between the bars and struck upwards into my low belly. It was a vile place to kick a man, but a first-rate defence for Jeffreys. The air left my chest with a groan and I let the merchant go, sinking to my knees with my hands between my legs.

The officer lifted his sea-boot once more and drove it on to my chin. The blow clacked my jaw-bones together and threw me backwards. I slumped sideways on to the cabin floor, shrinking away from the flailing boot still thrashing between the bars.

'Beat him!' I heard Jeffreys cry. 'Flog the rogue till he begs for relief!'

Pressed in the cell's corner, I hoped the officer's kicks could no longer reach. But with poor timing, the ship gave a great roll and sent me sliding helplessly down towards the bars. I braced for renewed blows, yet the kicking never came.

It had been no ordinary ship's roll. The *Prometheus* lurched violently and heaved her stern about in a sickening manner. From above came a cacophony of gear clattering aloft and sails going aback, mingled with shouts from seamen and cries from the poop. Alarmed, the officer forgot about me and promptly disappeared up the companion. Jeffreys, left unprotected, slunk off to the Great Cabin.

'The dam' schemer,' I muttered, ejecting a mouthful of bloody spittle as the ship yawed about.

'What's happening?' cried Noah Spatchears. 'Are we attacked?'

'It sounds,' I said through swelling lips, 'as if we've brought up all standing. I shouldn't be surprised if we lose a spar or two. Who's running this blasted ship?'

From the multitude of shouted orders and cries of alarm reaching us from above, a distinct voice called imperiously down the companion.

'Bring Loftus on deck this minute.'

It was Sir Thomas's command. There came a commotion in the passageway, and a band of men entered the cell in a rush.

84

7

SIGNALS OF DISTRESS

Moments after Filligrew's call, I was hustled from the cramped cell and manhandled, shackles and chains and all, bodily up the steps to the quarter-deck. Swaying and dizzy, blinking in the unaccustomed blazing light of a full Tropick noonday, I stood on the high stern of the *Prometheus*. Before me was laid out a scene of pure chaos.

The weather-deck was alive with seamen running this way and that, swarming up the ratlines and out on the yards. The topsails flogged noisily, shredded and torn, broken and snapped lines dangled everywhere, and from the foremast flew a parted shroud, endangering the mast's very stability. The sixty-foot wide maincourse had been forced aback, putting incalculable strain on the standing rigging. Sheets and braces had been let fly everywhere in a desperate attempt to avert further destruction. Seamen battled aloft to tame the flapping and booming sails as the airs filled and emptied them. The *Prometheus*, having lost all way, lurched awkwardly on the slop of the sea.

Going downwind with all plain set, the ship had been brought up all standing – steered through the eye of the wind and hove to while still braced and sheeted for running. It was an act no master would risk unless driven to it by extreme and immediate peril.

Filligrew, ignoring the tremendous commotion above our

heads, stood by the wheel glaring ahead through his spy-glass. He spoke without lowering it.

'Loftus, every available officer must fall to and help. That's why I had you brought on deck.'

I followed where he directed the tube. Ahead, about half a league downwind, one of the flota's barks was stopped dead in the water, her canvas all loose and shivering in the breezy tradewind. For an awful second, it looked like the *Saskia*, until I whirled round and saw – thank the Lord – my ship a good league safe astern and tramping slowly towards us under topsails, no doubt with Captain Gamble observing proceedings intently from her quarter-deck – my quarter-deck.

Some little distance to our larboard side, not moving but hove to, with her rig in disarray like ours, was the *Willingminde*, which Captain Sprang had been forced to bring up all standing in common with the flagship. So the vessel ahead of us had to be the twelve gunner, the *Hannah Rebacka*, Filligrew's third bark. Half her sails were in tattered shreds, she had taken on a slight lean, and she did not roll on the swells. It was plain what had happened, for there was no land in sight and we were in the open sea. She must have been going at full tilt when the disaster came upon her. The culprit was a hidden reef, upon which she had hurled herself. Now she was being pounded to pieces by the heavy swell.

Sir Thomas eyed the stricken bark almost as though watching a pageant of sail and remarking on the cut and set of the rigs on parade.

'I would like to think we could get her off before her frames break,' he said, and offered me the spy-glass.

I snatched it up and saw, dancing in the blurred image, dozens of men running about the *Hannah*'s decks. Twisting the tube to focus, I could see boats being lowered. Many fellows thrashed about in the sea.

Why had the flota been running so fast? The Caribbee Sea is strewn with unmarked shoals and coral banks, and in unknown waters masters make it common practice to run their barks under prudent half canvas. Scanning around the distant horizon, I spotted a fifth ship, a stranger, not part of the flota. She was hull down and disappearing fast.

I looked at the commodore. 'Has there been a chase, Sir Thomas? That's damm'd risky in these waters.'

'It's your seamanship I want, Loftus, not your opinions,' he snapped. 'Every available boat is to assist, but I cannot allow all officers away at once. You are to take the Great Launch.'

'Unchain me,' I said, looking round for the guards. 'I'll go off at once.'

'Bear in mind, Loftus, there is nowhere to escape to,' said Filligrew, and ordered the shackles released. To my relief I stood once more without the anklets and chain.

'I'll save as many of those fellows as we can fill the boat with,' I said, setting off towards the break.

Sir Thomas called out after me, 'The ship – save the damm'd ship! Take a tow – pull her off.'

In minutes, four boats were stroking towards the *Hannah Rebacka*, two each having been lowered from the *Prometheus* and the *Willingminde*. With me in the Great Launch were twelve strong fellows at the sweeps, sending us surging downwind with plumes of spray splattering their sweating bodies. Nearing the scene, we began to hear cries of alarm and fear.

'Come on, lads, there's not much time,' I encouraged.

Each time a wave foamed against the *Hannah*'s sides, she swung further broadside on to the reef and rolled horribly, first one way, now the other. She had piled on to a submerged coral mountain, and hung balanced on the seaward edge. She might be driven higher on the reef and lie there for years until the last of her timbers rotted away. More likely, the building weight of water in her hull would drag her off the reef and into the depths.

The rescue boats were in line abreast, the rowers' faces set as they stroked onwards. Another large wave struck the *Hannah* and she gave an overloaded lurch as if she were filling fast. At only half a cable distant, it was clear the attempt to lower her boats had failed, for the tackles would not run out evenly. Two launches hung over the topsides. One had its stern under the water and its bow in the air. The other swung clear, loaded with men clinging to the gunnels. Suddenly, the *Hannah* rolled and hurled it against the hull at the main rigging channels protruding from her topsides. The boat split asunder, casting bodies into the water as if they were no more than ants tipped off a leaf into a stream.

'Look – the maintop!' came a cry from the *Willingminde*'s launch nearby.

The *Hannah*'s violent rolling had caused the main-topmast to crack at the cross-trees. It fell, crashing into the rigging, where it hung brokenly in a welter of shrouds, blocks and torn canvas, arcing back and forth across the weather-deck with every heave of the sea. It struck and felled seamen where they stood, and swept more than one man clean overboard.

My oarsmen had stopped rowing. It looked too dangerous to go any closer.

'There's no other way, fellows,' I urged. 'Stroke on and take us right in.'

We came under the dark side of the doomed bark, where the water was strewn with debris – barrels, ropes, boxes, sails, broken timbers. Amongst these were the bobbing heads of men, shocked faces peering up, arms waving feebly. Those who could swim struck out for the launches and soon a dozen clung to our gunnels. We reached over and hauled them bodily aboard, exhausted and distraught. Some were too stunned to speak, others wept. A few were beyond even saving themselves.

I called to one young lad not more than a fathom from my grasping hand. His eyes were wide open in surprise and he thrashed his arms yet went under all the same. Resurfacing a second later, he tried to call out but his mouth filled with gagging seawater.

'Your hand, man!' I bellowed for all I was worth. He shook his head as if to say, no matter.

I stood up ready to jump in but caught the shadow of something falling across the water. Next second, a jumble of massive spars and canvas – the whole fore-topgallant assembly – crashed down from high above. A rope or a block caught me a blow across the shoulder and sent me thudding into the bottom of the boat. When I raised my head again and peered over the gunnels, numbed and breathless, the lad was gone, borne under by the mass of wreckage.

More men crowded at the *Hannah*'s rail, clutching on as she rolled, calling to be saved. By now, she had been driven sideways, broached to the seas, fully beam on, grinding her underparts on the reef. Wave after wave struck, sending her careening over to steerboard far enough to expose the strakes and the masses of green weed and barnacles clinging to the blackened timbers, streaming seawater. Then she came upright again, dwarfing our launch with her huge bulk. Every time she cranked over, barrels and boxes and cordage and slimy oils disgorged from the broken holds and then, before she rolled away, tuns of water gushed into the ten-foot tear in her hull. Its sheer weight was dragging her off the reef's edge.

We were too close in. We had come right in under her sides and filled the lurching Great Launch with men, sprawled all about the ribs, crying and terrified. But the launch was down at the gunnels and taking a slop of water aboard with each roll. The need to get clear became overriding.

'Take up your sweeps!' I cried.

Some of the oars dangled in their locks, swinging loose. Others had been shipped but were lying under our cargo of half-drowned sailors. Shoving aside a groaning sailor with blood pouring from a gash to his temple, I grasped a sweep and got it into the lock. A few other fellows did likewise, and together we heaved on the unwilling oars, fighting to get purchase in the water. The blades struck floating timbers and half-sunk spreads of canvas, impeding our strokes. Hardly had we opened a gap of three or four boat lengths from the ship when there came a rending noise, distinct above the pounding of the sea on the bark's hull, above the shouts and pleas of the seamen in the water. The dark topsides slid sternwards then in a single sickening tilt the *Hannah* lurched back fifty, sixty feet or more. Her stern hung over the deeps, the tunnage of sea inside making the end inevitable. She was going down and likely to take us with her.

'Pull for your lives!' I yelled.

My shout was all but lost in the sound of the ship tearing herself off the reef. She fell over to larboard with her stern drooping and the bowsprit lifted high in the air. At such a tilt, she revealed to me her entire weather-deck, the foc's'le and the beak – the catheads, anchors, windlasses and all – as if I were at the main-top looking down. The heavy guns broke from the tackles and hurtled backwards on their carriages, smashing through the rails and taking mangled bodies as they went. At that moment I swear the ship was set to topple over and crush us.

With a sudden lurch, she slid backwards, heading down and off the reef. Her stern parts plunged under the waves and the pressure inside blew out the upper windows of the Great Cabin. The main hold covers in the waist were forced open and lifted clear off the hatchways. Plumes of spray burst like smoke from every opening. Some of the men still left aboard threw themselves into the water, getting fatally entangled in ropes and shrouds. One or two seemed unable or unwilling even to jump off, but stood, fixed to their stations, clinging on as the angle increased, losing their footing and clawing for handholds.

We were pulling like madmen against the suck of the sea. Half fascinated, half witless with fear at the evil gurgling sound of the rushing, exploding water, I watched the sea claim the *Hannah Rebacka*. With an enormous, animal exhalation, the bark gave up the struggle, drawn relentlessly down under the waves until nothing but her decorated beak was left. Then only the bowsprit remained, standing near vertical, poking up from a hissing sea that frothed with bubbles of air.

90

The proud bark that had borne men on adventuresome voyages, carried stores and animals abroad, fought battles and taken prizes, was reduced to that single, forlorn spar, ridiculous and heart-rending. An unworldly silence fell, as every one of us still alive, stroking with our sweeps to hold off the reef or gripping the gunnels in shock, reluctant to comprehend, gazed at the *Hannah Rebacka*'s bowsprit pointing heavenwards. Then, without a murmur, that final spar slipped quietly away. The waters closed as it vanished, as though the bark had never been. All that was left were barrels and sails and other wreckage – and bodies, dozens of bodies floating everywhere.

We were near to tipping over and going down ourselves, grossly overloaded with forty or more fellows bundled aboard a launch for twenty. Two other boats were close by.

'Can you pick up more men?' I called, and when they nodded their ayes, I directed us to stroke upwind and regain the flagship. Soon we came under the *Prometheus*'s topsides and were disembarking the half-drowned men on to boarding nets.

'Loftus! Here man! Here – by the quarter.' Sir Thomas's head appeared above the high rail aft. 'Quickly, take the launch away,' he cried. 'Over there to the south.'

I did not understand. 'Commodore, there are still men by the reef,' I called up. 'Soon as we've dropped off these fellows, I've got to go back.'

'Take your launch to the south, dammit!' swore Filligrew, waving distractedly. 'Go and order her captain to bring up.'

He was pointing, but we were unsighted behind the vast bulk of the *Prometheus*, tucked in under her topsides. Order whose captain to bring up, and why? Had we not all stopped?

'What about signals?' I called back. 'Send a signal.'

'I've given you an order,' he shouted. 'Obey it or face the consequences.'

What consequences could be worse? We had wrecked a bark and lost scores of men, yet now he ordered me, a prisoner until a few minutes ago, to tell off one of his own captains. Perhaps he had become temporarily deranged by the loss of his ship.

'Push off there,' I said as the last of our rescued sailors got up the nets.

We stroked clear, pulling forward of the great bow. Still Filligrew waved and shouted from the quarter-deck, pointing to the south. As we came clear of the stem and passed under the flagship's beak, we saw what the matter was. The oarsmen ceased rowing and gaped. I was up on my feet in a flash, fairly screaming my lungs out.

'Bear off!' I shouted. 'For the love of God, turn to larboard!'

It was the *Saskia*. She was two or three cables distant and sailing straight towards the reef. Though her courses were bunted up, she ran on at half speed under topsails. What in all the Saints' names was she doing?

'Stroke towards her, fellows,' I begged, and the oarsmen closed up their mouths and set to at the sweeps. It seemed an age before we had covered half the distance when, to my utter bemusement, a row of signals rose up her flag haulyard. Signals? I gasped. What could she be signalling for? Why did she not bear off and save herself?

We raced on across the sea, ignoring the flotsam and jetsam of the wreck, perhaps even cutting across floating bodies, though I could not bring myself to look. At last within hailing distance, I stood in the sternsheets and bellowed across. All of us were up and shouting. A handful of faces appeared along the rail, seamen awaiting their orders, not understanding what was happening.

'Ahoy, *Saskia* – you're standing in towards a reef!' I bellowed.

On the quarter-deck, gesticulating and agitated, stood three or four officers, strangers to me, doubtless brought in by the new commander. A terrible argument raged. Another figure, in captain's dress of long-coat and calf-boots, stood near the wheel, erect and immobile, his back to the officers as if refusing to hear them out.

92

'Captain Gamble!' I bawled. 'The reef stretches across your path. Alter your heading to larboard.'

He continued to gaze straight ahead.

'The reef!' I shouted. 'It's only a cable off. You must turn the ship!'

Two officers stood directly in front of him, red-faced and frightened. Snatches of the exchange reached us across the water.

'The signals are incomplete,' I heard Gamble say, and something about disobedience.

'Take the boat alongside,' I ordered.

The oarsmen pulled at the sweeps and in half a minute, I was at the waist calling for a boarding rope. When it came snaking down, I swarmed up the topsides and over the rail without pause. Some seamen came forward as if to try to stop me but when they recognised their former captain, they instinctively stood aside. I ran to the break and charged up the steps to confront Gamble on the quarter.

'Captain, turn eight points to larboard and heave to,' I panted, 'or you'll see this bark wrecked.'

He did not even glance my way. His officers seemed dumbstruck. With a nervous glance at Gamble, one of them addressed me.

'What about the signals?' he said with imploring eyes. 'The signals were unclear.'

'Dam' the signals!' I cried, and pointed off to leeward. The backs of the swells heaped up not a hundred fathom distant. 'Look – you're running her on to a blasted reef.'

'There'd have been a clear and proper signal,' said Gamble, addressing his officers. 'This fellow is the commodore's prisoner. He must have escaped. I want him put in irons.'

The officers hesitated. Suddenly I spotted a familiar figure in the ship's waist. How had I missed him before?

'Youssef!' I yelled, running to the break. 'Put her on a reach. Brace up on larboard. Hurry, man – move!'

It struck me later he simply responded to my voice out of

habit. From where he stood, he could not have seen the reef nor any breakers, for they were barely visible from the height of the quarter-deck. Yet with the merest glance my way, he instantly began issuing orders.

'To the sheets! Brace up on the larboard tack!' he called.

Gamble was trying to say something, but too late. In seconds, dozens of seamen swarmed to the belays. I caught a glimpse of Jakob Tosher amongst them, then more of my seamen from the old steerboard and larboard watches, Edward and Nathaniel and Luke and the others. They ran to their stations, responding as of old, well practised at their skills, drilled into harmonious effort, calm and collected. It was as if I were captain again.

I turned to the seaman at the wheel. 'Come eight points to larboard, steersman.'

'Obey that order,' said Captain Gamble, swinging round to the wheel, 'and I guarantee you three hundred lashes.'

Looking helplessly from me to the captain and back, the poor helmsman was torn. It was Henrik Gannes. Suddenly he decided and, without further hesitation, spun the wheel over.

'Good man, Henrik,' I breathed. 'Don't worry, I'll see you right.'

For a few seconds, the *Saskia* failed to respond, wilfully keeping her head on the same bearing. She wanted sail.

'More canvas,' I called into the waist.

Instantly, the sailing-master shouted for courses to be set, and a dozen men sprang up to loose out both main and forecourses. On deck, more jack-tars sheeted in as the big sails filled, taut and straining in the stiff tradewind. Pulley blocks groaned, the braces came home and the great yards cranked round. The *Saskia* heeled, dug in her bows and bore off, picking up speed.

I ignored Gamble's spluttering protests and went to the steerboard rail, shading my eye, trying to pick out the line of the reef. Just ahead, the seas broke and hissed over the reef's edge a matter of a few fathoms away. The current and the leeway were pushing us relentlessly closer. The *Saskia* foamed along, still

94

turning, now broadside on to the line of the reef. Come round, I urged her, come round further.

A shudder shook the bark's timbers. A dull rumbling came from deep below, and the rail trembled. She had struck. Yet there was no crashing stop, no tearing sound of the keel striking hard coral. Somehow the *Saskia* kept moving. She came a little more upright and bore onwards. It must have been a glancing blow. She was still sailing, thank the stars.

'Steer up two full points, Henrik,' I ordered, then called out, 'Come close-hauled, sailing-master.'

Youssef's commands rang out across the weather-deck and the tars leapt again to the belays. Slowly, the *Saskia* hauled herself to windward. The breakers receded and the waters ahead lay smooth and unbroken. She's grazed the corals and stripped the pitch off her bottom strakes, I thought, and bounced off. What a strong ship she is!

Now Captain Gamble advanced on me, his bland face suffused with pink. If he was intent on debating the proprieties of countermanding a captain's orders, for my part the urge was to strike him dead on the spot with my bare hands. But the arguments could wait, Gamble could be dealt with after, and I would be back to see it done. If any seaman struggled still in the waters near the *Hannah*'s going down, he was my first obligation. I leapt off the quarter and down into the waist to find the Barbar.

'Good man, Youssef,' I said, grasping the boarding rope and heaving myself on to the rail. 'Stand off to the south and heave to.'

'Captain Mattoo,' he began, wonder spreading across his brown face. But I had already sprung over and dived headlong into the launch, falling in a heap amongst the surprised oarsmen.

'Pull away hearty there, lads,' I said, gripping the gunnels of the rocking boat, 'back to where the *Hannah* was.'

They all said, 'Aye, sir!' and the launch swung clear.

The great gilded stern of the *Saskia* receded, lifting and yawing as she bore briskly away across the swells. After two or three cables, and reaching safe water, she rounded into the wind, clewed up the courses and lay easy under the backed main-topsail, fore-topsail drawing. Youssef, then, had obeyed again and carried out my last order, surely recognising the wisdom of it. Like the good seaman he was, he had hove her to, no doubt against Gamble's protests. In the crisis, the Barbar had responded as if I were still commander. In more auspicious circumstances, I mused, how much further might he go in my cause?

Faint cries rose from her quarter-deck. It sounded as if the arguments had resumed. Swearing under my breath that if the Lord gave me the means, I would have Gamble's insides strung out to dry, I halted the launch.

'Hold off, fellows,' I said. 'Oarsmen, be still a moment.'

The launch slowed and we rocked listlessly on the swells as I cocked an ear, straining to catch the drift. There were alarmed shouts but the words were too indistinct to make out. I stood up, balancing on the thwarts the better to squint over. For sure, men were aloft, out on the yards, swarming along the bowsprit, and moving about her decks, settling her down after the sudden turns. Otherwise, the *Saskia* looked in fine trim, perfectly whole, quite serene and upright.

'Help – O help me!'

The cry was no distance away. A hand lifted from the waves. Without an instant's hesitation, I ordered the launch stroked round and we set off to pick up yet another half-dead seaman, floating amidst the chaotic aftermath of the sinking.

An hour later, the Great Launch bumped alongside the *Prometheus* once more, laden with our haul of pathetic specimens, the last of the half dead survivors of the *Hannah Rebacka*. Some had suffered injury from falling spars and guns breaking loose, their feet and hands crushed, bones splintered, skulls caved in. Others were deranged by shock, white-faced and incoherent. We struggled, too, with fellows refusing to relinquish their grip on the gunnels, rigid with terror at the prospect of being thrown from their fragile refuge.

As soon as the injured were taken safely aboard, I followed up the rope and marched straight to the break. Sir Thomas stood with spy-glass raised, surrounded by his coterie of officers.

'Permission to approach the quarter,' I demanded and, without waiting for a nod, stamped up the steps ready to confront the commodore and demand that Percy Gamble be immediately stripped of his command. Surely Filligrew could not argue with that.

'Commodore, Captain Gamble appears to have lost his reason,' I began.

He cut me off. 'Loftus, the *post mortem* can wait. A misunderstanding over signals, that is all.' He spoke wearily, as if the last hour had aged him greatly. 'There are new messages from the *Saskia*. Signalsman, there.'

The fellow stepped up. 'Just hoisted and read, sir. She's cracked her strakes and broken a plank below the waterline. Both chain-pumps working at full stretch, and the level rising.'

O Lord, not the *Saskia* too. 'I'll take the launch back,' I said at once, 'and get more work done at the pumps, get the men pulling together. I'll cover the damage with a sail and stretch it tight.'

'Wait.' Filligrew turned to the signalsman. 'How long does Gamble say she's got?'

'Water's rising in the holds at six inches the hour, sir,' he said.

'She'll fill to the waterline in twelve hours,' I said, calculating rapidly. 'She must be beached as fast as possible.' I whirled round, but of course there was no shore to be seen. Barring the proximity of that dangerous reef, we were in the open sea. 'Commodore,' I asked, 'how far is the nearest land?'

Filligrew shrugged. 'Perhaps twenty leagues. We are somewhere south of Cuba Isle.'

Gazing to the north, where the horizon lay distant and empty with no hint of land, I remembered studying Filligrew's sea-

97

charts the night of my downfall. The great Cuban island's southern coast was a treacherous maze of reefs and cays, sandy shoals and hidden rocks, but there was no alternative.

'She can do it. At six knots an hour, she can get there in time. Tell her to make sail at once, Sir Thomas. For the love of Neptune, give her a course.'

'There is a difficulty,' the commodore said, waving the tube vaguely towards the *Saskia*. She lay motionless in the water with no outward sign of the turmoil inside her wooden walls. 'I am quite uncertain of our true position. We were chasing a Spaniard – a small galleon, loaded to the hatch covers with gold for certain. We were overhauling her fast and would have fallen upon her in another hour.'

There had been that sail disappearing over the horizon as I came on deck. All at once, it dawned on me that she had made her escape by luring the flota towards the reef.

'The fact remains, Loftus,' Filligrew went on, 'if we'd had a first class Navigator on deck none of this need have happened.'

'What?' I said, disbelieving. 'Do you imply this is somehow my fault?'

He frowned. 'It certainly shall be if you continue to make difficulties. You must Navigate for me now, establish our latitude by the sun, make use of my Spanish sea-charts. They are of no proven worth, but nonetheless all we have. You might find a safe approach to the shore.' He fixed me with a steady look. 'It must be done quickly, Loftus.'

Forgetting rank and station, I took a pace forward and gripped the commodore's arm. 'Let me go back aboard – let me captain her to safety.'

'You? Captain the *Saskia* again?' He brushed my hand off his sleeve. 'You had your chance, and threw it away.'

His dismissive air angered me beyond measure. During those few moments aboard the *Saskia*, I had resumed command as if by right. Yet I had instantly relinquished it again to follow a greater duty towards the drowning men of the *Hannah*. If only I

98

had clamped Gamble in irons and seized control there and then. With most of my crew still aboard, there would have been little or no resistance. Those seamen would have responded to my call to action.

The Great Launch was still by the boarding rope, the oarsmen ready. Without a word, I turned and ran off to the waist. Shouts rang out from the commodore and men moved to cut me off. I got as far as the top of the steps at the break before they took hold of me and dragged me back before Filligrew. He sighed, letting his gaze wander past me momentarily towards the *Saskia*.

'Your hotblooded ardour, Loftus, were better directed towards finding the safe passage inshore,' he said, and then spoke to his officers. 'Signals to the flota. Turn north for the Cuban shore. The flagship shall keep station astern of the *Willingminde*.' He glanced over and held my eye. 'The *Saskia* to forge ahead in the van, under full canvas and at her best speed.'

The signalsman and officers went smartly off to their work, while Sir Thomas wore the detached air of one who knows he is about some nasty work.

'What do you think of my plan, Loftus?'

'You might as well condemn the *Saskia* to the shipbreaker's,' I muttered through clenched teeth. It would be madness to close such a coast with no notion of our true position.

He shot me a sly look. 'She's sinking anyway. At least when she strikes, we shall know where not to follow. On the other hand –'

'You've made your calculation, commodore,' I said, choking with rage, 'and you may go to Hell on it.'

He smiled benignly, as if he knew a secret. 'Have you forgotten, my friend, who is aboard the *Saskia*?'

'Aye, Youssef and most of my men, dammit.'

'I'm not sure you give a dam' for the Barbar's life,' said Filligrew, 'but what about your pretty miss?'

It stopped me dead. 'No, she's here,' I answered. 'She's aboard the *Prometheus*. Why, I've seen her father, and –'

Filligrew just gave a sad smile, shaking his head. 'Her father is here, but Miss Abigail chose differently. Something about discussing with Captain Gamble her plans for the bark's future. She'll be in the *Saskia*'s Great Cabin now, working on her books, no doubt.'

I fell quiet. Trying hard to shut out the vision, I saw the *Saskia* hurling herself on some unseen coral reef or rock in the blackness of night, being pounded into pieces, her masts toppling, seamen crushed under their weight. And Abigail on the tilting decks, terrified as wave after wave boarded the broken-backed ship, the rising waters dragging at her skirts.

Filligrew was saying, 'Such a tiresome, wheedling fellow, the merchant, to have so sweet and personable a daughter.'

The commodore looked into my face, and in that instant he knew he had his Navigator.

8

Pincered Claws

The day descended into a drawn-out agony as the full hazard of Filligrew's plan unfolded. In tight formation, the flota forged across the seas, reaching under all plain sail along the train of the swells, the three barks in line astern, braced up on steerboard tack for a north-northwesterly course. Beneath the blank horizon lay the rocks and shoals of the southern Cuban coast, and it fell to me to Navigate a passage through these little-known waters with only a few unreliable charts. After that, there was little more than hope and a latitude.

The *Saskia* led the way, with the *Willingminde* keeping close station and the *Prometheus* bringing up the rear. Astern of her was an empty sea where once the *Hannah Rebacka* would have sailed. Each vessel had set every scrap of canvas she could bear, with studding yards run out and stunsails set outboard of the courses and topsails. The flagship, like the others, carried such a cloud that she rolled her gunnels under and left a broken wake, ploughing onwards in a wilful dash into danger.

At first the *Saskia* went along well. Every spare man aboard manned her pumps and made up parties for bucket chains. Breaking out her strongest sail for heavy airs – a storm-canvas fore-topsail made of the stiffest cloth – they had carried it right forward to the beak and sent ropes down to sling it like a hammock under the bowsprit. Then they had hauled the canvas

101

down the stem and under the keel to cover the damaged underparts and wrap the hole. Bringing the clewlines to the weather-deck capstan, they sweated the cloth as tight as drum. Yet still her signals told us that the water poured in. With each league that ran off beneath her keel, the unwanted cargo of seawater increased, and she wallowed visibly.

In the *Prometheus*'s Great Cabin, in a lather of sweat, bent over the sea-charts and instruments, I worked up our position from the sailing-master's logs and any scrap of the dead reckoning that came to hand. During Filligrew's reckless chase, attention had gone from the log and the minute-glass and the compass course, and even the best estimate was going to be no more than a guess.

Sir Thomas had accepted my plea to commission into the effort any man who might contribute, so at the chart table sat old Noah Spatchears, fretting with the latitudinal calculations, muttering and scratching at his columns, bemoaning the poor quality of the angles we sighted. And when I went up on the quarter-deck, there was Adam Pyne, brought from the confinement in which he had languished since loyally refusing to serve under the commodore after my removal. He stood with the cross-staff raised, sighting the lowering sun as it arced towards the sea-horizon, calling out the angles of its descent to a notetaker at his elbow.

'When you carry those sights down to Spatchears,' I said, loud enough for the attentive Filligrew, standing a little apart, to hear, 'tell him the hour's run was two and one quarter leagues by the log. Instruct him that we kept a good course by the card, with a half a point of leeway showing in our wake.'

'Aye aye, sir,' said Adam and opened the instrument case to fold it away.

I took one end of the long cross-staff and helped him guide it into the open box, whispering, 'Spatchears knows where the armoury keys are. And don't forget the boarding axes.'

Without a nod or any indication he had heard or understood,

he calmly closed the instrument case, latched its lid and placed it gently beside the binnacle before heading for the companionway. I remained on the quarter-deck, watching as the minute-glass was flipped, hovering at the taff-rail as the log-line ran out, then following the sailing-master's hands as he reeled it back in and counted off the knots. By the wheel, I craned over the steersman's shoulder to see the compass card yaw about uncertainly.

'Keep your eye on that card,' I said to the helmsman. 'Two spokes only, if you will.'

He nodded, twirling the wheel this way and that, feet planted apart against the rise and sway of the *Prometheus*'s great stern as she bounded onwards.

Filligrew sauntered over, his hands stuck into the broad, tooled belt of his briches, with the air of one whose barks were at no more risk than on a breezy afternoon sailing in the Thames between Wapping and Gravesend. It struck me his confident look might sometimes be a cover.

'He's the best steersman aboard, Loftus,' he said, mildly reproving.

Ignoring him, I bent to the sea-charts and pilots laid out on the deck-boards, their edges held down by rounded beach stones. Time and again, I studied my rules and markings, measuring off the sea-miles to the Cuban coast, keeping in my head our course made good, a reckoning of our speed, an amount of leeway, a notion of the current, the wind's heading and the distance run. It all changed by the minute and by the turn of the glass, and still we could not know for sure where our ships were in that sea.

'Bring the flota half a point to the wind, commodore,' I told him.

Filligrew craned up to scan the broad, lofty sails, watching every nuance of their set and trim, keen to spot the slightest hint of a luff.

'No closer than that, Loftus. We shall pinch.'

'Aye, but we must arrive a little upwind.' I drummed my fingers on the taff-rail. 'We should spy the land before sunset, but quite when or how far off it might be, I can't say for sure.'

'I have the fullest confidence in your skills,' he said, the eyes turning on me again.

Soon the Cuban shore appeared, at first sight no more than a smoky mark on the horizon, then spreading like fingers either side until it lay all across our heading. Surveying the sky in the west, I reckoned there was barely more than an hour's light remaining. The lookouts, from their hundred-foot vantage, called down that they could distinguish no features such as an entrance or indent, but in the further distance, they saw a range of mountains lurking in the failing light.

'How do they bear?' I called up.

'A point off the steerboard bow.'

'What description can you give?'

'Two peaks of equal height and close paired,' called the lookout, swinging his spy-glass back and forth. 'A third mount, lower – perhaps a league or so to their east.'

When this floated down to me on the breeze, I quickly knelt by the sea-charts. There they were – three mountains as described, marked on the chart three or four leagues behind the littoral. The name of my chosen carenage stared back from the sheet. By some stroke of fortune, or the guiding hand of Fate – or even by dint of my Navigation, I allowed – we had come nearly dead upon the only possible anchorage for leagues around. All I had to do was get us through the entrance.

Bahia Delgado, read the chart, in curving letters along the shoreline of what appeared at first sight to be a wide open bay. Below the name were a few pilot's notes, handwritten.

'The Bahia Delgado,' they declared, '*is a tenable anchorage protected at the eastward side by the Cabo Delgado, a low ground of rock and reef that breaks the prevailing swells.*' So far so good, but as I read on, the hairs tingled down my spine. '*On approach, first find a reefy spit thrusting four or five cables southwestwards, consisting of rock and coral of sharp character. Immediate to east is a reef of like kind which closes upon the other to not more than one cable apart. Both are unseen from seaward, so that the way in lies like a great crab, ready to pincer the unwary between its doubled claws.'*

'Well, Loftus?' said Filligrew.

I faced him squarely. 'No one in his right senses would run in on such a shore with night coming on. You might as well order the *Saskia* to round up and scuttle herself while we watch.'

He shook his head in mild irritation. 'What should her course be now, Navigator?'

'The *Saskia* must follow my orders to the closest degree,' I said, 'and read her signals aright.'

'Aye, Loftus,' said the commodore, unsmiling at the reminder of Gamble's gross error at the reef, 'but what course do you give?'

Still I hesitated, knowing that the moment I obliged, he would order her to plunge blindly on and bear down upon the shore regardless. Yet there was no alternative but to press onwards, and we both knew it. My heart was in my mouth when I said, 'Steer northeast by north.'

'Signal the *Saskia*,' Filligrew called briskly over his shoulder, 'to steer northeast by north and press on without shortening.'

My eye fell on the *Saskia*. She was down by the bow, but continued to push through the water, taking heavy seas over the beak. She reminded me of a hunting hound, padding along with her nose to the ground. We were going in, heedless.

The surrounding land, low and featureless, gave nothing away, no point on which to fix and let us pivot round the Cabo Delgado and find the gap. Already, across the sea away to the west, the sun was barely ten degrees above the horizon, and the cotton-wool clouds of day were clumping together and spreading low across the evening sky. While Adam swung the cross-staff to sight the land for any features on which to hold a passing bearing, I put up the spy-glass and raked back and forth. At last a flash of white foam appeared – the southwestern reef, the barrier of stone and coral that lay across our course. The more I examined it, the more terrifying it looked.

'Sir Thomas,' I called, pointing, 'the reef's edge and the entrance beyond.'

He nodded and raised his tube.

'Aye, I have it.' He sounded pleased.

'Ease half a point to larboard,' I told the steersman, and watched the signal go at once to the *Saskia*. Then I reached over the binnacle to spin the minute glass. I had to check our progress minutely, watch the speed and estimate for current and leeway or we would miss that impossibly narrow entrance.

The commodore went off to oversee the flurry of signals that flowed as I made rapid course alterations. He had an elaborate code peculiar to his flota, for privateering ships kept their intentions close and their signalling secret from that of the King's barks. This time, the *Saskia*, three or four cables ahead, rapidly acknowledged her orders and altered course.

The night was coming in fast. As the gloom thickened, there appeared at the *Saskia*'s stern quarters a row of lanterns, hung in a line from the taff-rail. They shone red, blue, green and white, the colours produced by various smoked or clear glasses. Meanwhile, at the beak of the *Prometheus*, a matching chain of lamps was lit and strung out along the spritsail-topsail yard and a like one at the stern. Between the two barks, the *Willingminde* arranged her own rainbow of lamps. For me, the scene took on the shape of a dream. When the sun had quit the day altogether, the barks themselves became nothing more than silhouettes, only their ghostly sails standing out in pale, drifting shapes lit all around with the bright-coloured lamps. Before us and after us, the rows of signal lights blinked and rocked as our plunging ships rolled and swayed along.

Somewhere in the blackness ahead, perhaps standing on the quarter-deck, or sitting at the table below in the *Saskia*'s Great Cabin, was Abigail. How much did she understand of the danger? Was she prepared to leap over and swim, or jump down into a launch, if the *Saskia* ripped into the reef and went down in a rush? At six or seven knots of speed, it would happen so fast few strong men could save themselves, least of all a slight girl never taught to swim.

Having no means of warning her, I extinguished such grim visions and instead filled my head with the plan of the bay, the extent of the reefs, the angle of the wind, the direction of the wave-train. From the wheel, I watched the compass and checked the entrance's position by the minute. The vague white sails half-lit in the signal lamps' glow were all we could see of the *Saskia* as she careered onward, and there was nothing to be done but call the course and trust our signals to be read aright.

'Ease her another half point to larboard,' I said, and tipped the glass again.

'Aye aye, sir,' called the steersman, and the signals were a-hoist in an instant.

In the lamp-glow of the compass binnacle, I caught sight of the sand grains running through the glass. The stream of falling powder fluttered each time the *Prometheus* raised her stern to the sea and swayed down into a trough, yet the regularity of the flow never altered and the conical pile built below. Then I thought of the *Saskia*'s headlong progress. She must be passing through the gap itself by now. The splash of surf on the reef's edge looked alarmingly close either side of her dim shape. Before the grains ran through the little glass this thousandth or ten thousandth time, I knew, the fate of the *Saskia* would be done.

'She's luffing!' came a seaman's cry.

'Has she struck?' shouted another.

My heart hammered against my ribs. The *Saskia*'s sails flogged, her spread of canvas slack and loose as the speed came off and she slewed round. Had she come to a dead stop, stricken on a reef?

'Look, she's turning,' came voices from aloft. 'She's hauling up to windward.'

Now we could see her courses quickly bunted up, her yards coming round and the topsails holding their wind.

'From the *Saskia*, sir,' said the signalsman. 'She's safely through.'

A great hurrah rose into the warm night breeze and was carried aloft into the sails. The *Saskia* had slipped into the bay like a nimble yawl.

Now it was up to us to follow exactly her track, and not a fathom either side. Only half a ship's length away, the water creamed white and broken where it streamed over the outward edge of the reef.

'Rocks to steerboard!' came a cry from aloft.

'Come off a point,' I ordered.

Excited shouts rose from the larboard rail, where another line of jagged coral broke the surface, and the bark yawed and closer and closer. Disbelieving, staring at the gap through which I had just sent the *Saskia*, I saw it was far, far narrower than ever I had imagined.

'Steady on the helm,' I managed to call.

Suddenly, we careered past the foaming reefs and surged free into flat water. We had done the impossible and steered through the menacing pincer claws of Bahia Delgado.

'Let fly courses, clew up main and fore,' the sailing-master sang out. Seamen ran out on the bowsprit to hand the jibsails and spritsails, others clambered aloft and began running the stunsail yards back in.

In our headlong rush to beat the sunset, we had bent on every scrap of cloth the *Prometheus* could carry, and now it was the work of forty seamen scrambling aloft to the yards and out on the sprit to reduce her sails. But the deed was done with perfect harmony of action, and the big ship soon slowed. The wash of water along her sides died to a burble and she heaved no more on the swells, lapsing instead into an easy canter.

While we drifted gently forward, fetching along under fore-topsail alone, still the *Saskia* drove ahead with topsails set and drawing, eager as a thirst-stricken fellow in a desert on seeing a well. She rolled like a hog until she gently grounded twenty or

108

thirty yards off the sloping beach. Her gear flailed about aloft as she came to a stop, then the hull tilted a few degrees to one side, like an old woman on market day, worn out and propping her head in her hand to rest. But the *Saskia* was beached, and safe.

She quickly put her launches down to set out a kedge anchor and stop the stern swinging. In the glow of her lamps, shadowy figures moved about the quarter-deck. One of these, I knew, must be that misguided pedant, Captain Percy Gamble, who had idiotically risked his bark over the conventions of signalling. But beside him, was there a glimpse of a white-clothed girlish figure at the taff-rail?

Swivelling round to check our own quarter-deck, I found all eyes intent on their tasks, the steersman bending to squint at the compass, Filligrew scanning the shore ahead, the signalsman busy with his lights. From the waist came the shouts and answers of the sailing-master and seamen as the course changed and the trim altered to suit. Then came the cry I was looking for.

'Let go the cutter with a leadsman!'

The leadline party went over the rail and into the cutter – the leadsman with his sounding gear, followed by a pair of oarsmen, a youngster and an older man. They stroked off to find a deep water anchorage for the *Prometheus*'s greater draught. Adam moved silently to my side as the flagship rounded up and stopped.

Even in the dim half-light afforded by the *Prometheus*'s signal lamps, Pyne's uncertainty was apparent. Like me, he knew this was hardly the perfect moment, yet it was our only chance and we had to take it. When would we be let free to roam the decks again, and with such preoccupation all around us? The *Saskia*'s men, I reasoned, knew full well who had saved the bark from Gamble's stupidity, and from a far worse fate on the reef than the one she had suffered. Soon they would discover the second salvation I had wrought, that of bringing her to the shore before she foundered. Rallied behind me, they would throw off the most honourable Captain Gamble, tilting the balance of power my way. We had to get aboard now, for though she might lie careened on the shore a few days until her broken planks were mended, the *Saskia* was our fortress. Even the commodore would balk at the price of storming her, the cost in blood and men and destruction. Then, all repairs completed and Abigail on my arm once more, I would command her as part of the flota. But this time, I swore, it shall be on my terms, and not Sir Thomas Filligrew's.

'Six fathoms found!' came the leadsman's call as the cutter nosed out ahead of the flagship.

'Ready to let go bower,' sang out the sailing-master in the waist.

All around, the ship was a-buzz with the business of coming to anchor. The rigging resounded with chantying as busy jack-tars hauled up the canvas folds and bunted them to the yards. The main bower was loosed from its cathead stow and a few links of heavy chain run out in readiness for letting go. The officers, the sailing-master, the bosun, the mates, all were preoccupied, and Filligrew had his spy-glass trained towards the vague outline some way astern that was the *Willingminde*, watching her track us through the gap. I stood near the break with Adam at my side, boxes of instruments and sea-charts under our arms, watching the bustle.

The sounding cutter returned, coming all but unnoticed under the towering hull. The leadsman balanced in the thwarts while he shouldered the coils of knotted line calibrated by fathom markers with its lead weight at one end. Then he reached for the boarding rope while the two oarsmen held the boat steady. I touched Adam's arm. The time was now.

In unison, we hefted ourselves on to the rail and swarmed down the boarding rope. One-handed, clutching my precious instrument box, I barely touched the sides, my feet scrabbling for grip, and all but fell into the boat, knocking the leadsman back into the thwarts. He gave a muffled grunt as he tumbled in a heap, then let out a ripe curse, scrabbling about in the rocking boat. In a second, one of the oarsmen rose up and lashed him tight with his own leadline.

Adam stepped nimbly aboard and I took the cross-staff box from him, stowing it roughly alongside its brother.

'Push off, lads,' I hissed.

'Aye aye, captain,' the oarsmen responded, and rowed off with a will.

'Well done, Adam,' I said. It was he who had found the key to release my two rebellious fellows from the commodore's prison cells. Without missing a stroke, Eli Savary and the Dutch boy Gaspar grinned back. Their blades dug in, churning the sticky salt waters of the Bahia Delgado into a froth of pale green luminosity, and after a dozen strokes we were clear. I bent to open our boxes and reveal their treasures. There were six brace of pistols, along with shotbags, powder horns and boarding axes.

We pulled towards the head of the bay and minutes later the grounded *Saskia*'s great stern, beached at an angle, loomed from the darkness. There was a tremendous noise and commotion on her decks high above, orders called and acknowledged, the clack and groan of lifting gear as the yards were sent down before she was careened to expose the damaged underparts. Above all this came the regular chant of the chain-pump parties. With so much confusion and activity, there could hardly be a better chance.

We stroked in under the steerboard quarter and bumped alongside. With pistols at our belts and an axe in each hand, we were ready. Eli's hard-muscled swing brought an axe-blade into the bark's timbers a few feet above the waterline. It bit well, and he tied the cutter's painter round its head.

'No point losing a good little boat,' he rasped, then glanced at the tightly bound leadsman. 'Nor leaving this poor fellow adrift.'

'All right, lads – up and over,' I said, and lunged from the boat, at the same moment swinging a boarding axe in a high arc. It struck the wood and held, the blade's solid clunk telling me its bite was good. Clinging to the one axe, I raised the other and

111

swung it yet higher. Thunk! Likewise, it bit and I was up and half out of the water, swinging the axes in tandem, first the right and now the left, my bare feet scrabbling at the turn of the bilges where green weed and sharp barnacles grew. Through my leather slippers, the soles of my feet became cut and torn, but with another heft or two of the axes I had gained height and was away up the wooden wall, past the sternlights, now gripping dry planks with better purchase. I heard Adam's and the other fellows' double blows following close behind. At the tumble-home, the topsides leaned away from the vertical at last. Pausing under the mizen channels, hidden from above, I stuck one axe in my waistband and waited till the others joined me.

A multitude of noises reached my ears. As when we left the *Prometheus*, I counted on every man aboard being busy at his tasks – men aloft and alow, moving across the decks, into the rigging, stowing sails, pumping out, laying out anchors ahead to keep her ashore. All attention would be on the business in hand.

Together at my signal we progressed upwards, moving more freely now, scrambling past the deadeyes and up the shrouds. I reached the rail in a flash, with Adam, Eli and Gaspar barely a step behind. With one final heave, I swung over and planted my feet on the quarter-deck of my own ship.

There was no sign of Abigail. I trusted she was safe below in the Great Cabin. Only ten feet from the mouth of my levelled pistol stood Captain Percy Gamble. He turned at the sound of our arrival, and his doltish mouth fell open like a landed fish.

'Loftus, you bloody oaf,' said the man who had driven my bark on to a reef.

I could have shot him there and then, and perhaps it would have been better that way. As it was, I left him to my fellows and bade them take him captive. They fell on him as he stood there gaping while I went straight to the break of the poop. The *Saskia*'s men would rally when they saw who it was, and this time there would be no polite and gentlemanly bargaining with the commodore. From now on, safely back in my hands, she would sail on my terms and under my captaincy.

'Fellows of the *Saskia*!' I thundered. 'This is Captain Loftus. I am taking command of the ship.'

Every man stopped what he was doing and stared up. No one moved.

Then I heard Gamble's strangulated shout.

'Soldiers! Guards! On deck!'

To my utter stupefaction, twenty fully armed marines burst from the main hatch, their weapons clattering and jangling, boots clumping on the deck-boards. At once, the seamen fell back to the rails. Muskets pointing at the ready, the soldiers advanced on the quarter-deck in a rush.

9

Bad Blood

Days passed before I laid eyes on the sun again, during which my below-decks prison became a Hell of isolation and torment, cut off from all commerce with my fellows.

Alone for so many hours on end, I had little to do but self-recriminate. Over and over again, the events of that night plagued me with the ill-humour of regret and humiliation. The searing memories came tumbling back, hot and bloody in my mind – Gamble's astonished protests as we took him prisoner, my address to the men and their blank uncomprehending faces. Then had come the onslaught by the soldiers, the tang of burnt powder filling my nostrils as the high-blooded Adam loosed off a futile shot, the shouts and cries of resistance from one or two loyal fellows, more shots. After that, the ignominy of surrender, insults, captivity and beatings.

As soon as the *Saskia*'s repairs were completed, the flota got under way and already several days at sea had passed. There had been plenty of time for me to rue not seeing that, from the moment Gamble stepped aboard to take command of my bark, he had installed a hidden force of his own marines.

Dam', dam', dam'! The harder I struggled to restore my position, the worse a fist I made of it. What now, when any remaining faith Filligrew might have held in me had been so rudely shattered? I fought against an upwelling of bitterness that

114

so few of my erstwhile crew had risen up in support, not least the treacherous Barbar, the demon Youssef. Bile rose again in my throat at my condemnation for crimes I did not commit, and at the innocent Adam being dragged into the same pit of troubles. A pox on Filligrew and Gamble, a plague on the Navy. If only I could get free, I would wreak a vengeance on them all.

Two decks below the *Prometheus*'s Great Cabin, I was chained in a compartment deep in the nether reaches of the sternparts, far below the comparative comfort and civility of the cell I had once shared with Noah Spatchears. In better guise, this new prison had been a bread or grain store. Its chief advantage for the gaoler lay in the single point of entry – a hatch in the deckhead – and the impossibility of escape. Only the grain-rats had easy passage, scuttling about, whiskers a-twitch, searching corners for the slightest morsel.

Twice in the day, the lid of my hutch was thrown open, letting in a draught of air and light. It was the cook's apprentice, bringing me a bowl of scrap vittles at the dawn and at the dog-watches, occasions when I relished the fleeting few seconds of noise and bustle of the ship and its people reaching me from the far distant weather-deck.

So it was that I sat awaiting the bells struck for the dog-watch, anticipating that brief moment of engagement with the outside world, albeit in the unsatisfactory form of the cookboy, when at last the footsteps came and the lid was lifted back. I scrambled to my knees – the cell was too low to stand up in – and held up my hand for biscuit and saltfish.

'What news is there, cook?' I called. 'Have you told the commodore I must see him?'

As ever the foolish boy kept silent, afraid to taint himself with anything of the disgraced captive. To my confusion, when there came an answer, halting and uncertain, it was not the cookboy who spoke.

'O – it smells so,' said a soft voice.

In the gloom I caught sight of a slender shape framed in the

115

square opening. An agonised shiver ran through me. I was disgusted at my condition, not because of the foul and airless nature of my imprisonment alone, but from the shame of failure.

'Are you well, my love?' I mumbled, not meeting her eye.

'Well in body, if not in spirits,' she said with a sigh.

My mouth was hard and dry when I spoke. 'I did it for you, Abigail, and would again.'

She was silent.

'Well, what of my loyal fellows,' I said, 'poor Eli and Gaspar and Adam? Henrik and the others who rose up?'

'Alive but subdued. I have tended them in their imprisonment, while Sir Thomas considers their fate.'

'I'll do anything to mitigate their punishment. Did Filligrew send you?'

'I came of my own will, but he remains adamant. You are too dangerous to be released.'

Despite the chains, I managed to stretch up and catch her hand. She did not withdraw. I stroked her palm, hungry for its softness.

'Tell him, Abigail. Say I shall Navigate the flota, lead him to his prizes, take him to whatever shore he wishes, help him raid and plunder and enslave. Nothing for myself, no pleading my own sake, if he will only free those good fellows and let me be with you.'

'It is too late. I have tried, but he stands firm.' She sounded heavy of heart. 'He hoped for such a profitable partnering with you, but you dashed it away. He is a proud man, angry when defied.'

Of a sudden I remembered something. 'Have I destroyed everything for you as well, my love? The work for you and your father as his commercial assistants?'

She hesitated. 'There is more, now, Matthew. Sir Thomas has grown respectful of father's commercial skills and has promised us a plantation.'

'A plantation? I am happy for you then,' I said miserably, and

116

cast my glance downwards. 'I would come ashore with you, Abigail, if the Fates could arrange it, abandon the sea, farm the land, arrange the labour, toil in the fields. Whatever you and your father desired.'

She shook her head. 'I proposed it but Sir Thomas refuses. And of course my father –'

She trailed off, and I patted her hand comfortingly. 'I shall do nothing more to jeopardise that future for you. I know you can make it a successful venture.' I paused, thinking of the gulf that now lay between us. 'Where are your plantation lands to be?'

'On Cuba, when the flota returns there after some business in the Lesser Antilles,' she said. She guessed what I would be thinking, and went on, 'The Spanish have lost their rights to the land. It shall be done in the name of the King's Navy, with proper seals and letters. It is quite an ordinary plantation – tobacco, sugar-cane, molasses perhaps. We shall have to work very hard to turn a profit.'

'If only we could sail away somewhere, Abigail,' I said sadly. 'Find ourselves a small bark, make our life together.'

Her voice hardened a touch and she withdrew her hand. 'Ships, the sea – I almost believe you care more for them than anything. They're all you ever think of.'

I was contrite. 'My love,' I said, 'I only wanted to command the *Saskia* again.'

At this, her frustration came to the fore. 'O, you're foolish! You wished yourself into believing the crew would rise up at your bidding.'

I bridled. 'Some of them did, and it was only the soldiers that stopped the rest. The seamen want me back. The bark would have been sunk without me, and they know it.'

'No, it was Captain Gamble who got her safe ashore. He told me how he did it.'

'Him? Saved the *Saskia*?' I was outraged. 'For all the blood in Rome, Abigail, I did it for you! Filligrew lied to me that you were aboard.'

Her eyes were wet. 'You only say that now, when you've thrown it all away.' Her voice shook and she became more inflamed. 'You've spurned every chance – command, trading, prizes, everything! Even me!'

Suddenly she threw a cloth bundle down on my head and was gone. I heard her leather-heeled shoes clattering up the steps back into the broad, open world of the ship and the sea. A guard came over and dropped the hatch, slamming the bolt across.

I collapsed dejected at the bottom of my cell, not even calling out after her. Though my belly rumbled with starvation and a smell of fresh roasted pork and warm sourdough loaf filled my nostrils, I ignored the contents of the cloth bag. Instead, I sat miserable and tormented, wondering at how we had grown so apart. I burned at the thought of her going to sit at dinner with a triumphant, sneering Gamble and the mendacious Filligrew, passing the wine, expounding on their exploits and reckoning up their prize monies while that snake Seth Jeffreys simpered in his chair.

My misery grew as I understood that perhaps Abigail saw how my hot-headedness had led to defeat, not restoration. Lord, I muttered, why must I suffer this double agony, that although my actions are aimed at bringing her back, all I do is drive her further away? How much longer might she tolerate such foolhardiness?

From then on, alone and unvisited, I spent the dragging hours concentrating on what could be gleaned from the ship's movements, figuring out her course and direction. The Lesser Antilles, Abigail had said, was the first destination. The *Prometheus* tacked to windward, then anchored for stretches, and I reckoned she must be sailing only by night when the tradewind softened, all the while keeping inshore, where the contrary current is weaker, as she headed east along the southern coast of Cuba. Then we pressed on into the open sea, the heel of the bark and her halting, irregular motion telling me she was close-hauled, the unmistakable strain and work of a hard beat against the tradewinds.

118

Either it was in my dreaming, or sometimes truly I did hear, raised above the enscmble of all the bark's voices, the single wavering tone of a madman's chant. Could it be Noah Spatchears in the fury of his counting and the derangement of his logarithms? In my confinement, I counted too, and for the same reason – to keep hold of sanity. I numbered the days of my imprisonment by noting the ship's watches as rung by the bell and rigorously marked thumbnail scratches on a timber of my wooden cell, a nick for each of the six full watches and a crossed notch to mark the day's completion.

Thus I knew it to be the ninth day of our passage when I awoke, entirely unrefreshed, to find the motion of the bark changed yet again. She eased sheets and braces and reached along for a while, then came distant shouts from men aloft as the canvas was shortened. Soon, the seas flattened, the ship rolled and yawed no more, and the launches were lowered. We had arrived at a destination. By one means or another, I reckoned, it must signify an end to my present condition.

Sitting expectantly in the black hole of my prison, head resting against my knees, unstretched limbs aching and the stench of my own filth overpowering my senses, I heard steps above. The hatch flew back. A big fellow reached down into my box and unlocked the manacles from the ringbolt.

'Up and out of it,' he said, hefting me through the opening with a single hoist of his beefy arms and bearing me away up the steps.

To my wretched shame, I found myself on my knees, dirty and unable to stand upright, dumped in the passage leading to the Great Cabin, surrounded by the well-shod feet of several officers and the bare ones of a brace of seamen. In the cell, I had resolved to go to my death with the bearing of an officer, a Navigator and former captain. At the very least, I admonished inwardly, get off your blasted shins and think of all the learning and Navigation that is about to go to waste when they hang you from the cross-jack yard.

119

Through physical weakness I failed even in raising myself to an abject crawl. The big arms scooped me to the steps and shoved me bruisingly up the companionway, planting me ignobly on the deck-boards, but at least I was on my feet again. I stood reeling in the unaccustomed brightness of the late afternoon glare.

Sir Thomas Filligrew broke away from a group of his officers and sauntered over. With the fast declining sun behind him, his face in shadow, he looked me up and down as if I were a fish or perhaps a squid landed from a hooked line, and not much of a prospect for a commodore's supper.

'Well, Matthew Loftus, Navigator and sea-captain,' he said, 'you have managed to destroy yourself and your career.'

Leaning on the rail, giddy but upright, I blinked and squinted in the harsh light.

'Sir Thomas, those trusting fellows of mine,' I mumbled, my mouth slack from disuse. 'They only followed their captain. Show them mercy.'

He shrugged. 'Your fellows shall suffer a month or two in irons until they agree to serve, by which time they shall have quite forgotten Matthew Loftus ever captained them.'

'It's Gamble you should punish,' I managed to retort. Despite my resolve to show dignity, I grew more heated by the second. 'He's the ship wrecker. He ignored your signals.'

'There are two sides to that.' Filligrew cleared his throat. 'The *Saskia* was erroneously not included in the signals, for I was somewhat less mindful than I should have been. The *Hannah Rebacka*, you see, was my first command, and named after my lately deceased wife.' His eyes were full on me, large and wistful. 'Gamble was signalling for further clarification. He's a Naval man, time-served in the King's fleets. Obeying orders to the letter is dinned into him.'

'If he's a Navy man,' I protested, 'how can he run as a privateer?'

'He remains in the service, but in peacetime many officers are

120

left to rot on the beach. Having him in my flota helps win letters of marque, commissions from the King for protection of trade and suchlike. Gamble has connections.' Filligrew smiled wanly. 'You have a deal to learn about the art of politicks, Loftus.'

'Sir Thomas, I am politick now.' I spoke very quietly. 'I stand ready and willing to Navigate the flota, to lead you to prizes at sea, direct you to villages and settlements ashore – whatever you may wish.'

'Too late for that.' The conciliatory tone was gone. 'You have shown yourself too wilful by far. I have determined a suitable fate.'

'Admirable,' I said. 'An admirable progress. Hang me, and let's get it done.'

'Lord save us, a privateer doesn't hang his fellows if he can help it!' cried Filligrew, chuckling. 'Where you might have held a vote, I have taken soundings amongst the men, many of whom remain respectful of you. Of your seamanship, if not your leadership. Would it gladden your heart to know what they think your destiny should be?'

I shrugged. 'Flog me, confine me, keelhaul me. I no longer care.'

'None of that. They want to see you given a privateer's chance.'

He stretched out an arm and swept it in an arc ahead of the ship. For the first time, I saw in the soft light of the dying sun that we were standing off a cove at a barren, inconsequential island, no more than perhaps half a league in length. The towing launches kept the *Prometheus* on station, with the bark tailed into the wind in the lee of the land, and it was clear that no anchor was going down. Filligrew did not intend to linger a second longer than necessary.

'Few mariners know these islands' whereabouts,' he said conversationally. 'We stumbled on them this afternoon. Luckily it was daylight or we might never have seen them. One of our native guides recognised the archipelago, says he used to come here to fish. Be that as it may, they most fortuitously provide for your punishment. There's shelter, a little sustenance perhaps, not much else. In the boxes, you'll find the necessaries for a rudimentary life – knives, nets, fish-hooks, medicines and the like. You'll survive, as your seamen wish.'

He contemplated the view as if to confirm his good fortune in finding islets so well-suited to the purpose in hand.

'The Witness Islands,' he said, 'or Los Testigos as the Dagoes call them. Either way, bollacks to it. They're small and insignificant, not even marked on the sea-charts.' Then he faced me, saying, 'You, Matthew Loftus, by order of Commodore Sir Thomas Filligrew, for the misdemeanours of disobedience and the disruption of the flota's purpose, are hereby marooned. May the Lord be with you.'

He tilted minutely from the waist.

Stunned, I was barely able to match the courtesy. Filligrew raised an eyebrow, then simply turned his back, the audience terminated. Two soldiers manhandled me to the rail, where my foot-chains were released and bindings lashed at my wrists instead. Below, a cutter waited with two oarsmen and a collection of boxes and bundles in the thwarts. I was suspended at the rail, between my ignominy aboard the *Prometheus* and my fate on the barren rocks of Los Testigos.

'Matthew!' It was a girl's voice. Abigail ran over and caught my hand. She kissed it, her lips soft on my skin, her cheeks wet, her touch trembling and fragile.

'Can you forgive me?' I muttered, shame-faced.

'You've cut yourself from me,' she mumbled through the tears. 'The love that was between us is dead.'

'Abigail – no!' I cried.

But she was gone, flying away across the deck. At the same time, the seamen shoved me off the rail, sending me in a tumble down the boarding rope to land with a crash in the thwarts of the cutter. Struggling up, stunned by the fall, hampered by the wrist-bonds, I got to my knees and looked back up the full height of the flagship's looming topsides.

Filligrew's big head leaned over, arm pointing. 'Away, lads.'

Other faces appeared at the rail, silently watching, ashamed perhaps of my public agony, wondering how they might face a marooning if it came one day to be their own fate.

Just as the sailors were about to push off, a figure hopped on to the rail, swarmed lithely down the rope and took up a seat. It was the Barbar.

'Youssef has come across to flagship to speak for you.' His face was impassive, a carving in glossy brown stone.

'Let me go back and see her,' I pleaded.

He nodded at the oarsmen. Their sweeps clacked in the locks and we stroked away, leaving the *Prometheus* behind.

I glared. 'Why did you not fight, Barbar? Why did you fall in with the soldiers? Coward! Traitor!'

He showed no anger, but just said, 'Mattoo's mouth is full of bitterness like chicory. He leaves behind a heart that is broken in pieces.'

'Don't even speak of her, you insolent Arab!' I shouted. 'Let me go back aboard. I'll prostrate myself before Filligrew, beg his pardon, do his bidding.'

Youssef shook his head. 'Barbar already try. Miss Abigail try. Everyone try. No good now. Commodore finished with Mattoo.'

The oarsmen kept to their work, stroking on into the cove, faces averted, until the stem of the cutter grounded in the sand. Carried ashore and planted on the beach like a sack of oakum, I sat there, disbelieving, staring at the world through blurry eyes. Youssef oversaw the unloading of my miserable assortment of boxes, and when it was done he came over. I held out my wrists.

'Untie me, take me back,' I pleaded. 'I've got to see her.'

'Mattoo can survive here,' he said baldly. 'Shelter, some food, maybe water.' He placidly surveyed the grim, uninviting landscape.

'You make it sound like a kitchen garden,' I said. 'At least will you tell her I love her?'

'Allah shall protect you,' said Youssef. 'Fishermen and buccaneers may pass this way.'

'You may tell Allah my gratitude is unbounded,' I muttered, 'but this is a sentence of death.'

From his deep-set eyes there came what might have been a flicker of regret.

'None aboard wants it so.'

With that, he strode into the water and leapt aboard the cutter, bidding the fellows pull away sharp.

'What about untying me?' I cried, holding out my wrists.

'You find knife in boxes,' he called. 'And keep small case dry – Filligrew does not know.'

When the boat was no more than half a dozen strokes distant, he twisted round and studied me briefly, gazing down that long, bony nose, the Arab head tilted haughtily. Then he faced forwards and did not turn back again.

10

IDLE HANDS

Filligrew's flota displayed an undue degree of haste to leave. By the time Youssef's boat had left the strand, the *Prometheus* – standing not two cables off – had already loosed out topsails to depart into the gathering dusk.

Suddenly I could bear it no longer. Fumbling with my hampered wrists, I fell upon the boxes and tipped them open, one after the other, searching for a knife. Finding one, holding the handle down by my foot, I bent down and drew my hands back and forth across the ropes. Panting from these urgent, clumsy efforts, I looked up to see the Barbar's cutter no more than a diminishing brown lozenge on the fading blue of the sea as it approached under the *Prometheus*'s bow. Astern of the flagship lay her faithful escort the *Willingminde* and some distance off, the *Saskia*, already under way.

Frantically working at the stubborn lashings, the sweat pouring and my heart banging, I ripped and sliced through those damnable manila strands until they gave up. Throwing the junk-ends away, I pelted down to the water's edge and plunged in, making fifty, sixty frantic strokes and more before my efforts became laboured.

Already, Youssef's launch was hoisted in the tackles, the capstan bringing it aboard. Falling away from the yards, one by one the courses billowed out and were sheeted home until a

125

bubbling wake appeared under the barks' sterns. The far-off wind-borne shouts of sailors working aloft to loose out canvas grew ever more distant. With the *Saskia* in the van, the flota paid off and scudded along to clear for the sea, picking up a breeze and making four knots or more. Defeated, I stopped swimming and trod water.

As the barks disappeared into the deepening night, hauling offshore to find the full weight of the tradewind, a faint clamour drifted back, something like a fuss raised up, a cry of alarm and a chorus of voices in unison. I pricked my ears but the noise soon faded. The sun dipped beneath the horizon, spreading gloom over the isles, and the barks' hulls merged indistinctly with the sea leaving nothing but their sails glowing whitely in the last of the light. I turned back to shore and dragged myself dripping from the sea.

Shoulders drooping, arms hanging loosely by my sides, I crossed the strand. It was no more than fifty yards in width, and ten between where the wavelets lapped the sand and the main shore behind. A line of six coco palms bordered the encroaching vegetation. I sat down under the spreading fronds and listened, eyes half closed, to the busy hum of insects and the swishing breeze in the palmtops.

It was long past sunset. I leant back against my palm tree, taking long breaths to rid myself of the suffocation of my recent confinement and the rawness of that unbearable, regretful parting from Abigail.

The love that was between us is dead, she had said.

I tried to reckon whether any real will to live remained within me. To live for what, I heard myself ask aloud in the stillness.

Dumbly, I gazed about. Across a narrow strait lay a second isle, smaller than my own but equally barren and unwelcoming, a rise of scrubby hillside a hundred feet in height, and bereft of life. Perhaps these empty islets set in the desert ocean were all I would ever know now. What a lonely, desolate place to die.

I had to stir myself, to replace despair with action. I got to my

126

feet, thinking to go down to the shoreline and porter my half-emptied boxes a safe way up the strand. In the morning, I would examine their contents and calculate my chances of survival. Just then there came from seaward the dull blast of a distant shot. Another discharge followed, this time quite distinctly the breathy roar of a long-musket, and then together a volley of shots. I ran to the rocks bordering the strand and clambered up a fathom or two to gain height. There was nothing to be seen in the gloom, for the flota had vanished, gone forever from the Witness Isles.

The breeze of day had died and the rustling of leaves at the palms' tops fell away as absolute night settled on my Tropick prison. Miserably, I gathered palm-fronds for a palliasse and lay down to sleep. Soon, a hundred thousand tree-frogs and a million crawling beasts in the bushes set up such a racket as might never be heard aboard ship.

How many hours passed, as time and again I rolled over to find comfort on the bed of fronds and relief from biting insects inhabiting the sand, I shall never know. In my half-sleep, a persistent, low moan intervened, like a wind wailing in the shrouds of a bark at sea, portending a gale and a rough passage. When at long last it broke through the veil of fatigue, I was brought to full alertness. The night was windless, so what breeze made these groans? Or what animal? Above the incessant trill of insects, there came only the gentle lap and froth of water at the shore. Otherwise, all was still. There was nothing but the black sky above, no Moon, only a starlight from the heavens.

The cries came again, muffled by distance, a mournful sound like the grey seal's warning if a fishing bark approaches its rocky hideaway. But there were no seals in these latitudes. Was I raving with a fever already? Sitting up like a corpse tightening from the open coffin, I held my breath and listened.

There it was again, a moan just like a human voice.

'Ho-oo,' it groaned.

Half thinking there would be nothing more than a brown booby lying on the shore with a broken wing, I scrabbled about

127

for a simple weapon. My hand fell on the knife and I set off towards the source of the sound, padding low across the strand in my bare feet. After two hundred paces, the voice cried out again, distinct enough to send a shiver of fear through me.

'Ho – Lord help me,' the voice said.

The cry was surely that of a man. Running onwards, panting, my lungs tight, I crossed the entirety of the strand and gained the flat rockbed on its southern side. My feet skittered on the surfaces, sharp barnacle shells cutting my flesh as I cantered on. Pausing to cock an ear, I caught not a sound except the wavelets lapping the rocks where they fronted the warm sea. Then, peering into the near distance, I made out a pale form lying across the stones, a man's body – a young fellow, tall and willowy, a mere youth with nothing on but a pair of torn briches. Gasping, I dashed over, all caution gone.

'How the Devil – ?' I cried, bending to him. 'Are you hurt?'

He moved his head, revealing a deep mark across his temple. Feeling into the bloodied gash, I found a path dug into the flesh, but no bone cracked. A musket ball, clearly half spent when it struck, had caught him a glance before arcing clean away. He was barely awake to my ministrations, shivering so his teeth clattered in a constant tattoo, his limbs shaking in a maddened dance. He must have languished, struggling in the water, for hours before gathering the last ounces of strength to drag himself ashore.

'Up, lad,' I said, lifting him tenderly. 'We'll get you to shelter. Here, on my shoulder.'

Dazed, he leant on me and we stumbled and staggered back across the rocks to my little bower. I at once ran about to open the boxes, hoping to find the essentials for saving life. Filligrew had been as good as his word, the honour by which private seamen gave the marooned a chance to live, for I quickly discovered bundles of seaman's slops, a flint-box, dry stores of rice and flour, and casks of small beer and sweet-water. I wrapped him in swathes of clothing, then foraged for leaves and wood to get a fire going. Perching him close the flames, I set about to warm some beer in a cook-pot, heaping in a handful of rice to make a filling broth.

In Tropick climes, though the sun is vividly hot and even the night air is warm as an English summer's day noontime, yet a man cannot endure long in the waters of the Caribbee Sea before his heart and liver chill, and he dies of a lack of warmth. So I vigorously rubbed the lad's back and chest to stoke up the bodily heat, then stretched out his legs and beat his thighs to make the muscles pump the life back through. Slowly, the fire's comfort seeped back into his bones and my hopes rose.

'Take this broth,' I said when the rice had softened enough, helping him spoon it down.

When he had eaten, he stopped shivering and lay back. I broke open a sweet-water cask and bathed the wound until in the flames I could see it was clean, then tore up a strip of cloth and bound it tight to cover it from the steamy air and the flies. He did not resist or make complaint, but his eyelids drooped towards the extended slumber a body demands when death has been near.

'Tell me,' I said softly, 'why in the Saints' names did you jump?'

'You are wronged, sir,' whispered Adam.

And with that, his lids closed. He let his head fall into my hands and I lowered him on to the pillow of leaves. He slept soundly, his chest rising and falling regularly, and I let him be.

For many hours, I tended the fire, now and then going off to gather dry sticks and twigs. Night long, the smoke rose in a column from the blaze and, as I piled on the fuel, the hot coles of the burning branches issued a reviving heat that bathed my friend in warmth as he slept. And when a breeze ruffled the smoke and curled it towards me, stinging my eyes, I wiped them dry, but still the wetness ran down my cheeks.

Two more nights ensued during which Adam's life hung in the balance. I drifted from sleep to wakefulness and back again, longing for the first glimmers of dawn. My dreams were peppered with regrets, wheeling through my head in black flocks like birds of carrion, consuming the corpse of my hopes, attacking the marrow of my will. Over and again, I cursed Filligrew and the greed that brought men to the Antilles in search of gold, sugar, tobacco, to plunder or to build fortunes on the bent backs of slaves – enrichments that demeaned their seekers, spoils that ruined lives.

When at last the third morning came and the sun sent shafts of light between the leaves of the shelter, I stirred once more to face the struggle for survival.

'Lord, the night never ends,' croaked Adam. My ailing companion lay sprawled across the fouled remains of his sick-bed. His gaze was blank and fixed, the face gaunt and hollow-eyed.

'It's dawn now, Adam,' I sighed.

His youthful features creased with concern. In a voice hardly stronger than a crow's dry cough, he said, 'Sir, am I blinded? Has the sickness corrupted my eyes?'

I thought, what can I do? I lifted up a half coco-nut full of precious water.

'Here, drink.'

He groped clumsily for the shell, his lips touching the woody nutshell rim, and swallowed a mouthful, then another. Exhausted, he lay back, his ragged breaths sounding like a galley-cook raking the morning's dead fire before six bells rang. He looked near death. There seemed to be a presence crouched over his wasting body, the assayer of men, drawing a life ineluctably towards its reckoning.

Perhaps I had missed something in the boxes of stores. Surely, amongst the paucity of implements and provisions we had been left, there should be a medicine chest? Frantic, I tore at the hampers one by one, emptying their contents on to the sand and rummaging through. There were hooks and knives, fishing nets, small bags containing line, trennels and other assortments. I found hand tools – axes, a hammer, chisels and bradawls, even a

130

sailmaker's palm and needles. Then I unearthed a cross-staff, a worn and well-used example, its dull brass scale all but unreadable. I threw it down, disgusted. What did he expect, that I should practise the Navigation here? To go where? I muttered rancidly.

At last, I came upon a closed case buried at the bottom of a box where it lay snugly. It was about fifteen inches by twelve, the size of a travelling apotheckary's chest of wares. In the red-tinted dawn as the sun lifted into the day, a word lettered in gold shone from its front: *Physick*. The case was locked. Snatching up a bradawl, I fumblingly forced open the lid. Inside, instead of stoppered miniature bottles and blue phials, there was nothing but a single large book with a blank cover, filling the interior, fitting nicely. My fingers slipped at the edges as I grappled angrily to lift out the volume. What use was a damm'd book of medicines and healing without the substances themselves? I threw down the empty case and flung open the pages.

To my astonishment, here was not a book of Physick but instead only row upon row of numbers, page upon page of nothing but columns of figures, all in manuscript, enscribed in ink with an even, practised hand. Familiar star names headed the pages – Altair, Aldebaran, Betelgeuse, Sirius and the rest, the mariner's guides. It was a common almanack of the stars! What twist was this, that we two Navigators should be cast ashore with hardly the means to survive, but only this dull and useless record of the heavens to mock us in our captivity? Sickened, I threw down the volume and resumed my search.

Now I came upon another case, the size of a captain's armoury box. Once again, I braddled open the lid. Still no medicine but at least there was a more useful contents than the almanack, for inside lay a brace of fine pistols, new flintlocks, along with three dozen of ball, a sealed horn of shot powder and its partner, a littler horn of flash. Well, this is no deception, I said aloud, and wondered who had secreted such a treasure. Then I remembered Youssef's words, as he left me on the beach, that none knew of the small box.

Carefully, I closed the lid and set off to find a safe, dry hiding place. If any buccaneer or fisherman called at the isles, these beauties would be the means of taking our freedom. As I stepped back up the strand, my foot caught on the old handwritten almanack. Cursing roundly, I kicked out and sent it flying into the scrubby undergrowth, damning the lunatick who had substituted such a dead article for the vital medicines of life.

Adam did not die. With Tropick downpours, I learnt to catch the rainwater running off our knocked-together shelter and, with plenty to drink, his sight returned. Over the next days and weeks, as our provisions dwindled to nothing, in growing desperation I rooted about in the bushes for nuts or berries and tried to boil grass and seaweed to glean nourishment for our bony bodies.

Still Adam endured distressing agonies. Attacks of cramp woke him from a near permanent coma of exhaustion, doubling him over, head into his knees and gasping. Violent voiding made of his palm frond palliasse a stinking bog of wet leaves. He lay back in the mess, distraught and exhausted, while I set about my work, wondering that a man's body might emit such quantity and remain a substantial thing. After clearing up the soiled fronds, I went outside to gather fresh ones, then gently ease up his body to carpet the sand with new green leaves, letting him sink down with their cool smoothness against his naked back.

Whether he must have taken a spiny urchin's dart into the sole of his foot and got the rot in his blood, who could tell? But I longed for the sickness to claim me instead.

'Forgive me, Adam,' I muttered, 'for condemning you to this.'

He smiled weakly. 'I came by my own wish.'

'Good fellow,' I murmured, and patted his arm. When the sun broke above the horizon, bathing our island world in golden light, I padded out on to the strand, where the blue-green sea lapped the shore's edge. Already, so soon after sunrise, the furnace beat fiercely against the whiteness of the beach and the sky was as pale as washed canvas. All around seemed lifeless and desert. Rag-headed and clothed in nothing but torn slops, I loped away to seek the means of our survival.

The lonely Witness Islands were no more than rocky outcrops rising from the wastes of the Caribbee Sea. Of these four isles, shaggy-topped with sparse greenery, the largest was less than three quarters of a land mile long and quite narrow in breadth, while the smallest amounted to nothing more than a sheep-field's worth of low ground. Yet here was a strand where the ghost crabs ran all about, idiot creatures with a whitened, translucent shell that made them nearly invisible against the glaring sand. They scuttled away faster than a man could run, yet if he came upon them by stealth they did not escape but dug half a hole and sat, claws up, stock still as a squirrel. Then they could be plucked out and carried away in a cloth bag.

To gain the beach on which the crabs clustered I had to swim three cables' distance to the second islet, a stretch of water I named Crab Strait. Here the swells rolled into the gap and the currents threatened to bear me out to sea. Hours later, fatigued from the effort of the chase but with a bag of half a dozen claw wavers tucked inside my briches, I would plunge into the waters and recross the strait. Crawling, dripping and breathless, up the beach, I would bear the booty at once to Adam and bid him eat his fill. He knew nothing of my endeavours, falling hungrily upon his ghost crabs to devour them. Cracked open, they yielded a portion of raw meat enough for a mouthful or two, and the juice that ran from their shells tasted sweet and reviving. Lord knew, there was little else to sustain us and my reward was to see, by each day, death's advance thwarted.

One afternoon, some weeks into our marooning and exhausted by these labours, I rested in the sun on the smooth rocks nearby, warming and drying, falling fast asleep. When I next awoke, the sun had dipped stealthily beneath the rising land beyond Crab Strait and darkness was descending. The brief reddish glow of the Tropick dusk infused the day and within a half a glass more the sun was quite gone. The evening sky showed the first brilliant lights of the night to come, and soon the canopy glittered with stars. To keep my mind alive, I picked out the familiar mariner's guides and named another score of the twinkling signallers. The pale yellow orb of the Earth's great satellite rose in the north and climbed gracefully higher, her disc curving in a parabola. I soon became absorbed in the Moon's progress as she rambled amongst the diamonds and sapphires of the night sky, passing before the stars, splitting constellations and outshining the planets.

I sat up with a start, suddenly alert. The Moon, her distance from the other stars, her progress through the universe – why had I not thought of it before? At once, I unfolded my cramped and stiff limbs and set off along the shore.

With careful steps, I searched the ground, zigzagging back and forth, quartering the terrain, until my foot scuffed against something that was not a stone or a root. Bending, groping in the dark, I laid my hands on a soft, rectangular object. The downpours had soaked its leather cover but, wiping the sand off, I opened the volume and found the vellum dry inside. There was a title page. Holding the leaf up to catch the shining moonlight above, I could just distinguish what was written there. My temples pounded in excitement.

A New Catalogue Of The Moon and Three Hundred Stars. The subtitle was wordy but had a ringing clarity to it: *With Systems And Tables To Achieve The Necessary Calculations For The Lunar Distance Method Of Navigation.* As if confirmation were needed that I had been bequeathed his great treasure towards the Longitude, underneath the title was an inscription. Again, I held the page up to capture the silver light mixed with the fainter beams of the Milky Way, and what they illuminated was this: *Author and Deviser, Noah Spatchears, Chief Assistant Observator.*

How stupid of me to have thought it an ordinary mariner's almanack. In the late tremors and uncertainties, I had quite forgotten my encounter in the private cells aboard the *Prometheus*.

Somehow the old man must have secreted his precious works for me to find.

Brushing aside the weariness of near starvation and fatigue, I sat balancing the almanack upon my knee and studied the pages. The volume of tables was a work of the most marvellous character. There was beauty in the simple regularity of the columns of figures, the thousands of recordings of the Moon's progress around the heavens and of the three hundred observable stars which nightly swing across the canopy as the Earth revolves about its axis. I resolved to observe the diamonds of light until I could name a hundred stars or more, in twenty constellations, simply by means of reckoning their position one against the other. As a Navigator, I was familiar with the twenty or so brightest stars mariners use for their angles, but now I promised to add diligently to my exploration of the star-map. One day, I swore, my skills must again steer a bark's course by the lights of the night sky. If nothing else, the practice would serve to sustain hope in the face of despair.

Yet there was more. A greater purpose lay in my hands, encoded in the figures and numbers covering those dense pages. That purpose was the finding of the Longitude, the key to Navigation, the unlocking of God's machinery regulating the Universe. The sinking of the *Hannah Rebacka* had brought me face to face with the sailor's nightmare – running hard upon a hidden reef, crashing on to the grinding rocks, his bark breaking in pieces under his feet, hearing the awful cries of drowning men. That great fear, of coming upon the shore after a passage with no fix of the land, would be banished forever once we had the Longitude.

I sighed, aware how valued such an advance would be. Surely all the Sovereigns of nations, all the admirals in all the Navies of the world, all the commodores of privateering flotas, would give a ransom for these tables. They would fight, and make war, and lay waste to men and ships, just to grasp the solution and enrich themselves.

Weary from hunger, I drifted into an exhausted sleep rich with swirling, jumbled scenes. I saw the Merchant Jeffreys in a long-coat and high sea-boots, raising a cross-staff to the twilight sky, now steering at the ship's wheel, now standing on the quarter-deck like a commodore directing his flota into battle. Then appeared a strutting captain in peacock finery whose officers cravenly bowed, yet it was not Gamble's face I saw beneath the fancy tricorn but Noah Spatchears' pallid, shrunken countenance, lips moving in endless incantations. And I dreamed of Abigail, cradling a leather-bound manifest ledger in her arms, but when the covers fell open and nothing was revealed but logarithms in dense rows, she threw down the book in annoyance.

When I awoke, sticky and oppressed, all these remnants faded like a sea mist on a summer's day. Sitting up, with the heavy volume still in my lap, it came to me with renewed force that if I could only put this treasure of knowledge in the right hands, then here was my chance – of pardon, both for myself and Adam, of a life beyond forever running from the law, of freedom from living in fear of the hangman's rope. Somehow, we must live, and escape, and prove the tables' worth.

By degrees, day by day, Adam revived. Soon he rose from his sick-bed, weak but with the will to live unbroken, and at once we set about enlarging our food and water supply.

We fished on the reef, the one driving a school of snapper, mackerels or small barracuda towards a net held out by the other, yet we hardly ever caught more than a single fish. We stalked boobies where they roosted on the low shore, slow-witted birds reckoned an easy catch, yet only once or twice did they tamely walk into my arms as Adam shooed them. He was never strong enough to cross the strait to Crab Beach, where I herded ghost crabs and pounced on them until my legs barely held up. Sometimes, returning at dusk from a sortie alone gathering the scant fruits of the isles, I might find Adam with a fire well-lit and a minute, half-grown reef fish grilling. Then I would lay down my sorely-won handful of nuts and berries and set to pounding them into a paste, stirring in a spoonful of coconut milk to make what passed for a creamy sauce. Feasting, we would bemoan the lot of mere seamen, for we persuaded ourselves that though this starvation fare might be meagre it was tastier than a ship-cook's mashed down biscuit and salt-beef.

Yet it was a lie, and we were losing the battle for life. A morsel of food once every few days was not enough. Our bodies wasted away with infinite slowness, Adam's more so than mine. We had shrunk to little more than bones, kindling sticks hung together on strands of twine. If we had the will, we must get free before we starved.

Thus, hardest and longest of all, we worked on our departure. With axe and knife, we cleared the ground for a makeshift shipyard. With a stick in the sand, we carved out the lines of our preferred design. From the windward shores, we brought drift-wood, the bounty of breeze and current, dragging great boughs and lesser pieces across the hillock to lay down a keel, if any mere raft can have such. We cut bush and tore up weed, and tramped a little rope-walk up and down, Adam holding one end while I twisted up the creepers and vines towards him, to make the rigging and the stays. With these home-made lashings, we bound tight both the sea-whitened logs and the few boughs of green wood the isles offered, held together by planks broken from our store-boxes. We stepped a dwarf mast to rise from her weather-deck, stayed fore and aft with cap shrouds to the outer logs. Then we stitched spare slops and briches into a single square sail, run along with a line of eyes and pennants for a reef when the wind got up. Piece by piece, she took shape on the shoreside, a rude craft to a shipwright's eye, but to ours a handsome ocean voyager that was our last hope of salvation.

'I name this ship *Sovereign of the Seas*,' I said, bearing a nutshell aloft with a precious drop of coco milk in it, while Adam held the raft steady in the water, 'and may the tradewinds fill her sails and send her across the swells and between the reefs safe into her haven.'

'And how shall we Navigate, sir?' said Adam.

'Not by the cross-staff,' I grimaced, 'but by the sun, the wind and the current, as men have always done since boats first touched their keels in the sea. And by old Eli Savary's way, which he calls the first compass of all.'

'What way is that, sir?'

'Why, Adam, by the swing of his bollacks.'

We laughed in an over-hearty way, the nervous levity of seamen who fear the voyage ahead, knowing how vast and ominous the ocean is and how frail their vessel.

Her sea trials were a disaster. We attempted the crossing of Crab Strait, where the waves were low and the distance narrow. Not ten fathoms from launching, the rudder paddle slipped adrift of its lashings. Then a breeze swept the strait, filling the sail before we could free it and springing the mast from its step. Struggling to save what we could, we let the rig and rudder go by the board and leapt into the water, swimming and towing the raft behind us. With Adam's gaunt face growing fearful as his strength ebbed, I ordered him to abandon the exercise and save himself. Soon I too was forced to give up and swim for my life. I followed him on to the strand of our marooning with a heaving chest and seized muscles, all but done in. I lay for minutes on the beach, arms covering my head, my face buried in the hot musty sand, until Adam came and helped me back to the shelter. Too drained to forage for sustenance, we retired to our palliasses of palm fronds where, night long, I tossed on my damp bed, fretting on past mistakes and fitful in my dreams of thwarted departure.

But by morning, quite to the contrary of expectation, our lonely isles had become all too crowded and dangerous a place.

138

11

Jewel of the Sea

It was just after dawn. I was shaking Adam into wakefulness after running pell mell from the rocky cove where I had gone early to catch a reef fish.

'We're no longer alone,' I panted. 'There's a vessel riding at anchor.'

Open-mouthed, he sat up, still half asleep. 'A bark? Where?'

'In the hidden cove facing Isla Pequena – the one we call Idle Bay. She's a little schooner, a trader of sorts. And only three fellows aboard, as far as I can tell.'

He struggled visibly to comprehend.

Then I said, 'Get up, Adam. We must take her, or die trying.'

At once we made ready for an assault, all or nothing. We cleaned and charged the two precious pistols Youssef had secreted in the boxes, uncountably glad to find the horns had kept the powder good. The weapons were of finest manufacture, the kind that would fire when asked. Together with the pieces, we took up two short knives and an axe each. These were all the weapons we had.

'Ready?' I asked.

With a pistol a-piece and spare horns and balls, we set off into the low scrub. Two advantages presented themselves: our knowledge of the lie of the land, and surprise. Yet as we loped through the undergrowth, it was a puzzle why such a schooner might fetch in here. The Witness Isles could hardly be reckoned as worthwhile stopping points between trading posts, where a ship might wood and water. Mariners would be sorely disappointed to find the hillsides all but bare of trees save for the few coco palms. As for water, we had only what we caught from rainstorms, for there was no spring or pool. Thus there would likely be no such visitors again until after we were long dead. This must be our one and only chance.

Reaching Idle Bay, we topped the rise above the cove, keeping well hidden. The schooner was moored with an anchor out from her bows and a stern line to a rock. Her launch was still stowed on deck, so the interlopers must have chosen to swim the short distance ashore. The three of them were on the narrow strand, occupied in tending a fire, with their backs to a straight rock wall behind. Reckoning themselves safe, showing no sign that they had an inkling of our presence, they were off their guard.

'They're devoted to that fire,' I whispered.

Two were youngish fellows, dark, with bushy beards sprouting from their chins and their loose clothes colourful but filthy.

'Spaniards?' breathed Adam.

They were Dagoes for sure, and carried a pair of pistols each. From the bloodied remains on a nearby rock, it was clear they had used knives for cutting up the large fish now roasting on their fire. The third man was an altogether contrasting figure, not bearded but grey-haired, lighter-skinned and a deal older in years, sitting detached from the others as if uninterested in their doings, staring moodily at the fire.

I rested a hand on Adam's arm. 'They're better armed than us, and stronger.'

'I'm as ready as you are, sir,' he said without hesitation.

'Good man. Go off to the south and get down from the high ground into cover. When I show myself from this side, you present from yours and we'll have them by surprise. I'll next see you when we are victors, and owners of that schooner.'

He took up his charged pistol and, with hardly a rustle of the

140

dry bushes, was gone. I moved down the slope to a position not twenty yards from the party, above them where they could not spy me behind the rock face, but with a good sight of the schooner and clear across the bowl of the bay to the rising ground opposite. The interlopers had paid no attention to their surroundings as we approached in stealth, confident they were alone, intent on cooking their fish. After a few minutes, Adam's raised arm appeared low in the scrub across the far side, not more than fifty paces off our targets. I lifted my own arm in acknowledgement. Our moment was now.

With my pistol raised and cocked, I was on the point of breaking cover when one of the darker fellows began kicking the older man. Cursing in his own tongue, the Dago made him get up on his knees and bend forward. The man moved with difficulty – not through age, I saw at once, but because his hands and feet were bound. His captors fell to beating him and he kept his head bent low, for he could not resist their blows or defend himself.

Then this grey-haired fellow suddenly said in clear tones, 'Now's the time then, boys?'

To my astonishment, he had spoken in English. The Dagoes each drew out a heavy pistol. One of them deliberately cocked back the lever and levelled his barrel at the back of the prisoner's head. Plain to see, there was about to be an execution of the most unjust and barbarous nature.

I stood up at the lip of the rock wall and took a two-handed aim at the chest of the would-be executioner.

'Throw off your weapons!' I shouted.

Two faces swivelled upwards and the Spaniard's pistol swung my way. I tripped the flintlock and the pan flashed, sending sparks all around. The charge fired and the pistol bucked. The fellow did not go down with the shot but seemed to fling himself against the rock wall. The ball thudded into the beach where it kicked up a shower of sand. Dammit, missed altogether – and at fifteen paces range. But at least he had let drop his pistol.

Adam broke cover, running on to the beach and kneeling to take aim at the second fellow. The ball struck the Dago's legs, throwing him to his knees. He dropped his piece and writhed on the ground.

Now they still had a pistol each left to fire against nothing more than our short knives and axes. The fellow I had missed leapt up and grasped the Englishman, manhandling him to his feet and holding him as a shield. As he fumbled for his second pistol, I saw his hand was a mess of blood. My ball had caught him after all. Nevertheless, he brought the muzzle of his piece up and pointed it at me.

I launched myself from the rock two fathoms above. The pistol barked, spitting sparks, and the ball snatched at my briches. Passing through the rising smoke of the discharge, I landed on the two, catching the bearded one full on the neck. With a snort, he crumpled, breaking my fall, and we rolled on top of his prisoner. I was quickly on the Dago's back but he managed to whip out a knife from his belt before I could pin his hands. I bore down on his wrists, the flashing point inches from my face.

The Spaniard Adam had wounded went for his fallen weapon, but Pyne reached him first and struck a blow with his axe. The man staggered and they fell upon each other, fighting.

Tussling with my own opponent, sensing his much greater bodily strength, a sheer will possessed me, the urgent craving to get charge of that vessel, the stark knowledge that if we failed now death would be mighty quick. As if in a formal dance, though with grunted oaths rather than politenesses, we each worked towards getting an arm free enough to strike.

'*Fuego de Diablo!*' cursed the dark-bearded interloper.

My face was buried in the back of the Dago's head, my mouth full of lank hair. The fellow was well-muscled and I could not raise my pistol butt to administer a felling blow. Without warning, he jerked back his head, clacking shut my jaw so that I nipped my own tongue.

'Hell burn you,' I spat.

142

Something caught under my feet, almost overbalancing me. It was the Englishman, struggling under both our weight. His hands were groping between the Dago's legs. The Spaniard yelled in pain and let go his grip on the knife.

'*Cojones de Dios,*' he groaned.

My pistol butt came down from high and cracked across the back of his skull. He collapsed like a sack on top of his former prisoner. Neither fellow moved as I grabbed up the loose pistol.

Adam too stood victorious, legs planted astride the crumpled figure of his opponent, and breathing in snorts of triumph.

'Bind your man up, quickly now,' I said, tearing off a cloth band from the Dago's waist. I tied his wrists and ankles, then dragged him aside. Relieved of this weight, the Englishman sat up and ejected a mouthful of sandy spittle.

'Teeth and armpits, it's a wonder what a man'll do when you cradle his plums,' he said, flexing and unflexing his grip with some difficulty due to the wrist bonds. 'But the Saints thank you, my good fellow.'

'I thank you in return. But are there any more?' I said, panting. 'Aboard the schooner?'

'The three you see is all,' said the Englishman. He was perhaps fifty and spoke in the tones of an educated man, if not a gentleman. 'Two done in and one whole, though it was intended to be the other way about.'

He wore sailcloth briches with ropes for shoulder straps, no shirt against the sun, and his horny, calloused feet were those of a common sailor. I bent over and touched his belt and pockets for a knife, but there was none.

'Who are you?' I demanded.

Beside where he sat, upright but at a tilt, its base dug into the sand, stood a black bottle. 'Pass me that,' he said, 'and I shall tell you my story.'

I shook my head. 'That can wait. How do you come to be their prisoner?'

'That's a tale worthy of the printer's attentions.'

'Then it'll have to stew a while yet,' I told him, 'and you stay tied.'

Adam came over, pointing at my thigh. There was a burn hole clean through the loose folds of my briches where the Spaniard's ball had passed without touching flesh.

The Englishman let out a whistle. 'I see I am not alone this morning,' he said, 'in coming close to getting a ball in a bad place.'

We dragged and carried our prisoners to the base of the rock, where we sat them down, backs against the wall. One remained as still as if dead, though I saw that he breathed. When I splashed seawater on his face, he revived, though his hand displayed a ragged gash to the thumb. Adam's victim was muttering and rolling his eyes, holding his right leg, blood spotting the sand where a ball had gone clean through the calf. When these wounds were bound the bleeding stopped.

Both Spaniards had fairly bristled with arms. Not only did they carry two pistols and two knives a-piece, but they had cutlasses, hand-axes and a pair of long-muskets propped against the rock wall. I gathered up the spare pistols and offered one to Adam.

'We'd better recharge these,' I said, 'and be sure the powder and spark are good.'

The Englishman looked alarmed. 'If you're going to finish us all off, lads, will you hear my confession first?'

'We're not bent on killing anyone,' I said. 'All we want is the boat.'

'Everyone wants my *Diamond*,' he said. A smile broke over his features, but his eyes were sad. He was half-drunk. 'Let me have a free hand to grasp that dam' bottle, there's a good fellow.'

'No rum till we haul away off these blasted isles,' I told him, going over and checking his bindings as well as the Dagoes'. Then I straightened and cast an eye across the waters of Idle Bay. 'Adam, it's time to go and survey our prize.'

As if by signal, we turned to each other, smiling, and danced the steps of a jig around the beach, so pleased were we with the prospect of our release from the Witness Isles. With whoops of triumph, we ran to the water's edge and, a pistol each held dry above our heads, swam out to the *Diamond*.

The schooner's topsides were painted black at the gunnels and varnished brown to the waterline. The full hull rode easily on the water and her black-pitched bottom showed every time she rolled on the slight swell. At her waist were a couple of boarding steps, by which we clambered to the rail together and peered over, wary of attack. Nothing moved, so we scrambled quickly up and stood on her decks for the first time.

She was about forty five or fifty feet in length – not including the sprit – with a flat run from right aft to right forward, and must have been fifteen foot broad with plenty of beam carried towards the bow. As a schooner, she boasted a foremast and a mainmast, with a long boom extending aft to right above the taff-rail. To my eye, she had a fast rig and a hull for speed as much as carrying. There were two light guns bowsed down either side, two-pounders I reckoned, with a half-pound swivel at the bow and one aft for the stern chase, so she was well enough armed to defend herself.

At the quarters was the long tiller-bar, with a compass binnacle by a hatchway which led below. We ducked into its low entry and dropped down to find a captain's sleeping cabin, a day room and a bread store. The below decks space ran forward under the waist to a small galley-furnace just aft of the foremast. She was well-used but cared for, and smelt of new wood and pitch from recent harbour work. There was a carpenter's table right forward where the anchor cables dropped into a chain locker from the windlass, a sail-room midships, and hammocks slung along either side. All these quarters were quite empty of people or animals. Under the sole boards, we discovered stores of supplies in kegs, barrels and sacks stowed in every cranny and running the length of her keel between the ship's frames – dry stores enough for months at sea. The hold beneath the captain's

145

quarters was locked, but finding a key we opened the lid to reveal an armoury and powder store, jammed with muskets, shot and sacks of powder.

Back on deck, we reckoned her to be in fine trim, as if just fresh from a refit. Her standing rig was all of a piece, well tarred and tight, the running rig neatly coiled and the sails – as far as we saw at a glance – patched but in good order. The mainsail was roughly folded on the long boom, the staysail crudely brailed up to the foremast, and the jibsails loosely lashed on the sprit.

'If those Dagoes only knew how to stow a sail.' I shook my head. 'But this is a bark any sea-captain would be proud to take into harbour.'

When we swam ashore, the two black-beards were awake and scowling, mouthing in their Spanish tongue, blasphemies, like as not. The Englishman directed his mournful gaze at the fire.

'That kingfish is well past roasted,' he said.

Adam and I were giddy with our sudden deliverance from the solitude of marooning. The aroma of the fish's scorched, thick body charring on the flames was seducing. It was a beauty of two feet at least, more than a double handspan around and surely caught offshore, being of a size and variety our island prison had never offered. The fire was near its last and the skin was crisped brown and the flesh steamed white inside. With my knife, I speared the prize and cut it into pieces, whereupon Adam and I fell on the steaks, desperate to satisfy our ravening appetites. It might have seemed an uncommon scene, two fellows by a fire greedily eating and scorching their tongues while three others, all of them bound up and one half drunk on rum, sat quiet, stewing in the Tropick furnace. We cared nothing for that, for the fish filled up our bellies and gave us strength and refreshed our spirits. When we were done, Adam and I each took a long pull on the rum bottle.

'Is it resistance to talk?' said our English prisoner, his sad eyes on the bottle.

'No, speak up, man,' I encouraged. 'Tell us your story, if you like.'

'My name is Will Wrack, skipper of the *Diamond*, that lovely moored behind us here. Everyone in the island chain knows me and my ship, yet just a little time ago I thought that none should ever see us again. For these two Spanish here, having taken my vessel and slaughtered one of my poor and innocent crew and put the rest off, had granted me a death by shooting. It was to be followed by their feasting on this roasted fish. They allowed me that bottle of sugar-rum to ease my passage out. A ball through the back of the head was their preferred way.'

'Aye, Mister Wrack, we saw it,' I said, putting a juicy portion of the intended execution meal into his outstretched hands. Pulling on the bonds, he lifted the food to his mouth and champed open-jawed, like a dog.

'Where did they seize your boat?' I said. 'And how?'

'In Grenady, just off the Grande Anse,' he mumbled, spitting shreds of flaked flesh. 'Surprised us, coming up in the dark in their rowing boat. Wanted my schooner to go fishing, they said, but fishers need good hands aboard and they landed off all my fellows at Prickle Point. They had no call to slit the throat of my most companionable friend – Pauley, my blackamoor mate and a freeman. These Dagoes are piratickal of nature, no doubt of it. They took me along to steer them safe to the Spanish Main, yet when we passed the isles here, they had me haul in, saying they'd seen enough of how to sail her and could do without me.'

'Your schooner's too well-armed for a fishing boat,' I remarked.

'Armed for her own defence,' he said. 'And right enough in these waters.' He sighed. 'I take you for lawless men, do I? Pirates? What's your cause to be on the Witness Isles?'

I shook my head. 'Private men, marooned here. Starved of good meat for too long. But first things first.' I got up. 'What do you say, Adam, that we take Mister Will Wrack with us to help sail the bark, and leave the Dagoes here to live or starve as we have done?'

147

'Aye, it's fair,' he said, then with a shrug and a smile added, 'there are crabs and fish, and rainwater to collect.'

I shaded my eyes to squint at the schooner. 'She's a fine little bark, and well stored up. She'll take us where we want to go.' I turned to the bearded Spaniards. 'Right, *señores* – up with you.'

We escorted them back aboard their one-time prize, lashed them at the rail and swam ashore to loose the stern line off its rock. Taking Will Wrack between us this time, we stroked the distance, climbed aboard and set him down in the waist, tied to the rail opposite his tormentors.

'Don't leave me like this, boys,' he said. 'Bring up my tobacco pouch and clay, there's good fellows.'

'You'll have to wait,' I said, though not unkindly, for he had a likeable way about him.

'Let me help sail her,' he insisted. 'She's my bark – I know her best.'

'You may sing out, Mister Wrack,' I grinned, 'if we work her poorly.'

But we did not. We raised up the big jibsail, leaving it unsheeted while we went about the business of getting her anchor. It was hard labour, the two of us working at the windlass, for the bower had gone down into near ten fathom and we were hardly the fittest of men, but up it came at last. Adam sheeted home while I ran back to the quarter and grasped the long tiller-bar. We let her drift clear of Idle Bay until we caught the breeze, then steered round towards our encampment, the jibsail alone carrying us along at four knots or so. She seemed a lively bird on the water, and my heart sang. We had fallen upon luck the Devil himself might envy.

Hauling round the headland, we approached the strand of our marooning with some confidence, knowing the waters well and the depths too, with our weeks of swimming here in search of morsels of fish and shell. After splitting out a small portion of the boat's stores, we left the Dagoes, that cursing pair of brigands who deserved nothing, with rice and beans enough to last a week, as well as the necessary vitals of survival that Filligrew had granted us, such as hooks and lines and small knives. They were fortunate enough, I reckoned, to benefit from that code of honour between privateers, when they had been about to execute a man.

Soon, the breeze swung our bows towards the strait and Adam sweated in the sheets for the short reach through Crab Strait towards open water. Beneath my feet the *Diamond*'s deck-boards trembled as she heaved to the swells and I breathed deeply, savouring the tang of salt sea air which I loved almost beyond anything. For the first time in god knows how long, the fresh ocean breeze brushed my face. Bracing against the thrumming tiller-bar, sensing the rush of water over the rudder blade as the schooner gathered speed, I thrilled unashamedly at the prospect of steering this little bark free across the seas.

Secure below in a secret locker of the captain's cabinet was the apotheckary's Physick box with that most precious, irreplaceable volume inside, left for me by Observator Spatchears in hopes of my delivering it into safe hands. It was our chance of freedom, and a pardon. Now the fates had given me the means to win that prize.

They had sent me the little *Diamond*.

12

WRONGFOOTED

With difficulty, tied as he was, Will Wrack struggled to gain his briches pocket and at last held up a battered baccy pouch. It was empty.

'Captain, permission to light a clay?' he pleaded.

The *Diamond* was ploughing merrily across a deserted sea. I sent Adam to the cabin lockers for pipe and tobacco, and when he returned Mister Wrack arranged himself more comfortably under the rail. Moving awkwardly in his bonds, he filled the pipe, lit it and settled back. I had given him leave to beguile us with the rest of his tale.

Wreathed in smoke, Will Wrack duly unfolded his life's story. He had inherited a small family firm in London many years ago, married and settled to a quiet, commercial life. Then one misfortunate day on an outing to Portsmouth to buy materials for the business brought in at the docks there, he was caught in an alehouse by the Navy impressment. After seven years at sea abroad, he returned to find his wife and children all dead from a fresh visit of the plague – an aftermath of the great disaster some decades earlier. He sold what remained of the firm's assets and took ship to New England, where he bought the *Diamond*, refitted her and headed south to become an island trader. Yet in the end he had tired of the Tropick heat and the lawlessness of the Caribbee, and had stored up for a voyage to start again.

150

'That explains,' I said, 'why the *Diamond* is so well stocked. Where were you headed?'

'Before I got diverted,' he said, 'north to Newfoundland for the salt-cod trade, where the English are making great profit from the Grand Banks fishing.' By this time, his clay had gone out, so he refilled it, saying, 'Now, captain, don't you likewise owe me your tale?'

Adam listened from the tiller as I sparingly gave Mister Wrack the bones of our story, that we hoped to win our pardons by somehow returning safe to England an object of immense value, one that could not be allowed to fall into Naval hands.

Will Wrack, his teeth clamped around the bit of his long clay, sucked on the stem, making the bowl glow richly and said, 'And what might that object be?'

'It's an almanack of the stars,' said Adam eagerly, before I could stop him. 'Tables for finding a Longitude.'

A loud crack was followed by a shout of pain. Mister Wrack had been taken so suddenly he had bitten clean through the stem, sending hot coles of burning baccy cascading down his belly and into his lap. He wriggled about, awkwardly batting at his legs until the fire was out.

'The Longitude?' he roared. 'Are you quite mad? Why, that's no more than a lunatick's notion! Even a common fellow like myself, who skippers nothing more than a schooner, knows the Longitude cannot be found at sea.'

I gave him a fierce look. 'Well, now you know about it, sir,' I said, 'let me persuade you that it most certainly can be done. Not by time, of course, for as any learned man knows, time-pieces cannot be made accurate. It's done by measuring the Moon's distance from the stars and planets.'

He saw I meant it and at once took on a more serious demeanour. 'Well, well. And you say you have an almanack that can do this? Lord alive, an almanack! It makes me think of Wimpole-court. I'm transported back to my little firm in London, by the Fleet. I spent half a life printing books – texts for study, schoolboys' books, treatises on Mathematicks and the like.' He looked expectantly from my face to Adam's. 'It was Wm. Wrack & Son, Cheapside, a most respected name for two decades.'

Adam and I both shook our heads. The name meant nothing to either of us.

'Did you never publish anything nautical?' I asked. 'Maritime studies and suchlike?'

'Never,' he said. Then as if remembering something, he looked heartbroken and went on, 'I added the "& Son" when after six girls in a row my only boy was born.' A minute later, he brightened. 'But tell me all about this almanack of yours.'

After explaining something of the Lunar Distance Method, and how important an advance the tables represented, I paused, for there was a matter that had been troubling me ever since I had discovered the Spatchears volume and begun studying its secrets.

'You know, Mister Wrack,' I said, 'I've been trying out these tables, back there on the isles using an old cross-staff, yet I cannot seem to get an accurate result, even on land. I am a taught Navigator, but still they seem Devilishly difficult to fathom.'

'Nothing ever comes easy in the business of Navigation,' he said consolingly.

'I shan't dispute that,' I replied, nodding.

Suddenly Adam shouted, 'Look – a sail!'

Holding the tiller-bar steady with my leg, I raised the spy-glass. She had appeared suddenly not far off to windward, the westering sun picking out her sails against the sea.

'Let's get more canvas on, Adam,' I called, anxiously eyeing the strange vessel.

'Hoist up my ensign, lads,' said Will Wrack peering under the rail. 'There's no need to fear this one – she's only an island trader.'

I barely heard him, too intent on the rapidly approaching bark. How well did the *Diamond* sail? She seemed handy and

152

fast enough, but in truth Adam and I hardly knew her ways. Worse, we were two weakened fellows aboard a schooner that wanted five strong hands to work the best from her. If only there had been a chance to rack out the deck-pieces and practise a shot or two, but as it was – short-manned, fatigued from the marooning, unfamiliar with the weapons – we could never hold our own in a fight.

The stranger closed, revealing herself as a carrying bark of a hundred tuns burthen, with patched and tattered sails set on masts rough-hewn from the tree. Her decks were crowded with dark figures.

'She's the *Savanner*,' called Will. 'Fly Will Wrack's own standard and she'll present you no trouble. Raise up the Frenchy standard too.'

I sent Adam to rummage through the flag locker. A minute later, the boy returned and unrolled a yard-long standard of unfamiliar design. It had a white background on which was embroidered in the centre a large black 'W'. Then, not without a hint of distaste, he held up the flag of King Louis of France.

'Let the Wrack colours fly,' I said, 'but not that damm'd Bourbon rag.'

'Hoist it,' said Wrack, tugging at his lashings, 'otherwise they shan't be sure it's me.'

There was no choice but to believe him for we had let the stranger, running with the wind, come close. Still, it seemed a traitorous thing to have the Fleur de Lys billowing from the taff-rail.

The trader handed her courses and rounded up, fore-topsail aback, main-topsail drawing, while we went about on to steer-board, the staysail aback, jibsails drawing. Hove to, the *Diamond* lay easy on the water, riding the swells like a duck, not more than ten fathoms separating the two vessels. A throng of men lined the trader's rail, dozens of black faces looking our way. Adam and I drew our loose shirts down to cover the brace of pistols we each wore at the waistband.

I hailed across, 'Bring up your captain to speak.'

The Negroes showed no sign that they understood. They were wild-looking men with unkempt bushes of hair and smooth but formidably manly chests, and brass or gold rings around the upper arms. Others, paler skinned and more Indian in appearance, were stockier though every bit as fierce in countenance. Each one bore knives or cutlasses at their waists. No slaves I knew of were allowed such privileges.

'They speak patwah,' chuckled Will. 'Part Africk, part Frenchy, morsels of English and Spanish. And the captain's right there on the quarter.'

A small-built Negro man, as untamed a figure as the rest, stood in the obvious position of command.

'Who are they, Mister Wrack?' I said. 'Slaves?'

'No, free Saint Lucy men, headed for the Spanish Main to sell dried fish, pork on the hoof, and all the leathern stuffs their women make.'

'Aye, but to what nation do they owe allegiance?'

'To none but themselves. The French tried to drive out the Carib people and put in Negro slaves on Saint Lucy with white overseers, but the Indians and the black men combined and expelled them. Saint Lucy's easily defended – few landing places, steep mountains and dense forest. The French let them be, and wisely, I'd say.' He tugged at his bonds. 'Release me. I shall speak to them.'

The instant he showed himself at the rail, the blackamoors greeted him with foot-stamping, grins and waves.

'Find out, Mister Wrack,' I said, 'what barks they have spied, such as warships or privateers.'

He chattered out a stream of foreign words, receiving an excited babble in return. Then he turned to me with a solemn face.

'They've seen an English ship, a Navy cruzer of twenty guns. Only a couple of leagues to windward.'

Dammit, that kind of luck could only be of Satan's own

design. I said grimly, 'I've untied you, Mister Wrack, and now you're going to show us how to sail her.'

He raised an eyebrow. 'Not to haul up towards the Navy?'

'The other way,' I said.

He gave me a wry grin. 'So you're on the run, eh boys?'

I ignored it and sent him off to work with Adam.

The blackamoors paid off their bark. We returned their amicable *adieus* as the distance opened and soon had the *Diamond* bowling along on a beam reach. She goes well on this point, I thought, reckoning our speed by studying the sea foaming past at the waterline. We sailed on in watchful silence for another hour.

'Sail ahoy!' cried Adam, from high in the shrouds, for the second time in the hour. 'A league to windward and four points off the steerboard bow.'

The spy-glass showed the bark to be a cruzer, no doubt of it. She had the weather gauge and it was still a good two hours before the cover of dark. Blast it, our only chance was to turn downwind and stay out of range, in hopes of losing her with the nightfall. When I lowered the tube, Will Wrack was watching me intently.

'Hoist the topsail,' I called over to Adam, 'and we'll run off free. That'll give us her best speed.'

'Not with the *Diamond*,' said Mister Wrack, shaking his head.

I gave him a searching look. 'What would you do?'

'Forget the topsail. Bend on the smaller staysail and reef the main. Then work up to windward close as she'll go.'

'To windward?' I said. 'You're off your head, man. Do you want to bring us under her guns?'

He looked out across the sea. 'That's a heavy cruzer. Her best sailing is a point or two aft the beam. If you turn downwind, with her longer waterline she'll catch us in an hour, two at most. But if you head up straight towards her, she'll have to pinch. She'll slow.'

It seemed a madness to close the English warship. I hesitated.

'You'd best look sharp about it,' he insisted. 'Haul hard to windward with that bit less canvas on her – she'll go better. Given luck and a prayer, we'll pass across her bows a few cables clear.'

All my sailing instincts screamed against the notion, yet I could see plain as daylight that he was right about running off downwind. She was bound to catch us.

'What are you thinking?' said Wrack. 'That I might want to see you in the Navy's hands in hopes of a recompense and getting back my bark?' He fixed me fiercely with his eye. 'Never. Never shall I see my *Diamond* delivered to that bastard assemblage. Not after what they did to me.'

Perhaps I had to trust Will Wrack.

'We're coming close-hauled,' I called to Adam, pushing the tiller-bar. 'Mister Wrack, show us how she goes.'

'Give me the steering,' said Will. He centred the bar and, as the sheets were hauled, he let the schooner find her groove.

'She's balanced now,' he said, letting go of the tiller. 'See?'

Sure enough, the *Diamond* kept her course, working slowly up to the point just before luffing, nodding away a little freer but then resuming her course. In the waist, the three of us worked quickly, slackening off the haulyard, easing down the mainsail to tuck in a full reef and hauling the luff tight again. When we dropped the big staysail, the *Diamond* perceptibly lost way, but no sooner was the second staysail bent on and hoisted and the sheets sweated home than the schooner picked up speed like a willing colt.

'Back to the tiller, Mister Wrack,' I ordered, and he sprang away, keen as mustard.

Even with this smaller spread of canvas, now she was hard on the wind the *Diamond* kept her speed, tilting along with a palpable sense of urgency. I returned to the quarter and checked all around, eyeing the sun's position, sensing the breeze on my cheek and studying the train of the swells. There was no doubt about the schooner's going, and the compass confirmed she was making three points into the wind – where a cruzer would rarely make half a point. And we had gained a knot of speed. She was sailing like a Dutch jacht – like a Prince's fancy pleasure boat with fine lines and a deep, long keel.

Will Wrack's countenance betrayed no amazement. He steered on, stony-faced, humming a low tuneless song to himself, giving the tiller a touch here and now a tweak, intent on the sea ahead, forever seeking the flatter water, sending the schooner along the line of least resistance. The fellow had a true steersman's eye. He crouched by the long tiller-bar like a cat, legs braced apart, both hands gripping the smooth bar, his glance flashing from the luff of the jibsails and back to the bounding bowsprit

He caught my gaze and said, 'I'll see her in anyone's hands but the King's Navy.'

Taking up the spy-glass, I saw the cruzer's sails looming huge in the tube, yet it was plain we had forced her on to a close reach in order to keep a crossing course. She had already lost speed, no doubt of it. Still everything urged me to free off make our escape, yet here we were working ever closer.

The regular crash of the *Diamond*'s bows as she met the seas with her plunging head, the swish and gurgle as each wave broke and passed along the leeward topsides in a swirl of foam, the creak of the sheets reamed in taut through the blocks and the groan of the masts every time the boat dipped headlong into a trough, all these became a chorus of voices joined in harmony. The stiff breeze sang in the shrouds, whistled in the gaps between the jibsails and thrummed the edges of the canvas. Yet the schooner never faltered or shied as a bark so often does when close-hauled. Instead she left a foaming wake that hissed away astern as we leapt forward into the very path of the warship.

'Signal shot!' came Adam's cry.

A puff of whitish smoke rose from the cruzer's bows, followed by a dull report.

'Stand on,' I commanded.

157

Instead of obediently hauling over, we continued to close the gap. Mister Wrack looked quite pale but kept on steering.

'We're going well,' I said encouragingly.

'She's firing!' cried Adam, scrambling deckwards from his vantage at the shrouds and taking cover under the rail.

Two black smoke-clouds issued from swivels at the cruzer's bows. A double boom thudded out across the sea, with the whistle of shot an instant later. Not a quarter of a cable off, a pair of huge spouts lifted a tun of seawater high into the air. The *Diamond*'s bows lurched and she staggered.

'Hold your course, Will!' I cried.

The heavy three-masted cruzer bore relentlessly onwards, a full-rigged ship of three or four hundred tuns burthen, with a broadside of ten guns, six-pounders in all likelihood, a size and weight of ball capable of smashing open our sides like eggshells. Yet to bring those guns to bear from this position, the cruzer had to bear off downwind. Now I saw the windward edges of her courses lift and flap, and the weather-deck got busy with seamen running to the belays. Far from paying off to range the guns, she was trying to haul up closer to the wind, just as Mister Wrack had predicted. And all the while the schooner was making ground to weather.

Again, two puffs rose from the swivels at her beak followed instantly by their booming reports. This time it was all too close. The first waterspout rose up a boat's length ahead of our bow, a ten-foot high gout of seawater that reared high and fell away with a great whoosh, leaving a hissing maelstrom of foam on the sea's surface. The second fell right off our windward side. Whump! A tun of water burst from the sea and towered above us. Adam threw himself flat to the boards and the seawater crashed down, exploding on deck before gushing into the scuppers.

The *Diamond* lurched over, putting her rail hard down, and faltered. The sails banged above our heads and she slowed, for the massive spout from the shot had taken the wind from her staysail. But an instant later she shook herself upright, the tiller-bar trembled under Will's grip and she plunged ahead making six or seven knots just as before.

'Are we struck?' I shouted. 'I heard a crack.'

No one replied. Off to steerboard, I saw the cruzer's aspect changing. Until this point, she had shown us her steerboard side with a fearsome row of heavy gun barrels poking out along the curve of her sheerline. Now her bows were dead on and, as I watched half disbelieving, her larboard topsides appeared, showing another row of deadly black snouts. All at once I realised how far we had overhauled her.

'Hell's flames, we've almost done it,' I breathed. Another minute and we would be clear.

Adam shouted, 'She's turning!'

Now the cruzer did bear off. Even at this distance we heard her yards groaning, blocks and braces rattling – and those dark muzzles, ten of them in a row, were suddenly ranged directly at us.

'Tack ship!' I bellowed, flinging myself on the belays.

Will Wrack shoved the tiller across the quarter. The *Diamond* lurched upright and swung her bows. There was a great commotion aloft, of canvas flogging and loosened sheets cracking in the wind. Fighting to get her going on the new tack, Adam and I were yelling together, red-faced and cursing, mouthing profane words in sheer fright. Heeling over, the little schooner leapt away, going as if she knew the chase was on. Staring over the rail, breathless, I expected at any moment to hear the roar of those ten cannon, the English six-pounders loosing off their deadly weight, the balls whistling their ghostly way towards us.

Yet the cruzer's high quarters were showing and the fearsome muzzles were pointed uselessly at an empty patch of sea just a few lengths astern of the *Diamond*. Our lightning fast tack must have quite outwitted her. The English officers, reckoning they could no longer range their guns, had borne off, giving up the chase. The Navy still had their stern swivels though, and puffs rose from the cruzer's quarter-deck. The spouts frothed up harmlessly two cables off our beam, but we were clear and they knew it. The cruzer turned with grace back to her beam reach, as if to say, the game's done and good luck to you. Disbelieving, we pounded on another minute or two, quickly getting half a mile upwind.

'Mister Wrack, you were quite right,' I said, as the three of us gazed astern watching the distance open. 'And the *Diamond* goes on the wind like no other bark.'

'She's in good hands, captain, I'm happy to say,' he said from the tiller-bar, smiling broadly. 'Just keep her out of the Navy's clutches.'

But when he turned to face ahead, the smile froze. Adam too, standing in the waist with a half-coiled line in his hand, was transfixed. Heart leaping, I followed their gaze. It was unbelievable. How had we missed her?

All gold paint and decoration at the bow and stern, gleaming white stripes along her twin gun-decks, a bone in her teeth as she forged through the swells running fast downwind, there was no mistaking such a vessel when she was this close. Unseen, she had come up on our blind side and we had fallen right under her guns. It was a massive and powerful French frigate from which there was no escape.

I whirled round towards the cruzer. We had outpointed her for sure and she would never have caught us. Yet it was as plain as a holystoned deck-board that the English had just as much given up on sighting this newcomer and seeing how heavily they were outgunned. But why? There was peace with the French and no reason for warships to engage on the high seas. Or had we, during the chase, strayed into the territorial waters of France?

The sharp report of the frigate's signal gun crackled across the surface of the sea, no more than a cable or two separating us.

Will Wrack spoke flatly. 'She wants us to haul over.'

'I can understand plain signals, Mister Wrack,' I said through clamped jaws.

'Aye, but don't forget that,' he said, with a jerk of his head towards the taff-rail.

My eye caught the *Diamond*'s flagstaff, and the twin colours it carried so boldly. Beneath the 'W' standard of Will Wrack's schooner, we still wore the Bourbon colours.

I took up the tiller-bar and heaved it across the quarter, sending Will Wrack to help Adam tend the sheets. We came round through the wind and tamely hove to before the mighty man o'war. Blast it, we had escaped falling into English hands only to drop like ripe manjoe fruits into the lap of the French.

'They've signalled that we are to await a launch,' said Will, intent on the frigate and the bustling activity aboard. 'And they seem uncommonly jumpy.'

'Mister Wrack,' I called, 'do you speak the Frenchy lingo as well?'

'O aye,' he replied airily.

'Then you're going to help me talk our way out of this.'

With a cacophony of clattering belays and rattling blocks, the frigate began her slow manoeuvre to wear round and heave to, with what must have been nigh on a hundred jack-tars springing to work, bunting up the courses then scrambling aloft to furl the topgallants. The topsails were let go aback and jibsails left drawing, whereupon she forereached quietly within hailing distance. Meanwhile a launch was readied and lowered, with six men at the sweeps and a brightly uniformed boy in the sternsheets.

When it came alongside, riding the swells, Mister Wrack and this French youth engaged in an exchange. We learnt that the frigate's captain, on his way to Martinique, requested us to follow him there as he had good reason to believe the French Navy would requisition the *Diamond*, though at present he had no powers to do so himself.

'Are we under arrest, Mister Wrack?' I said, perplexed.

161

'Not in so many terms, Captain Matthew,' he replied, with a sardonic shrug towards the warship.

Then I told him what he was to say. He listened carefully, eyes widening. When he spoke to the French youth, the midshipman, or whatever rank he held at the age of no more than sixteen, laughed openly. It must have been the sheer neck of it that tickled him. To my amazement, Will banged the rail and fulminated, at which the boy suddenly touched his cap, bowed slightly and sheered his cutter away back to the mother ship.

'Sharp tyke,' snapped Mister Wrack. 'Reminded us we might soon be in the formal custody of the French Sovereign and said we had as much chance of having such a request met as he had of marrying his grandmother. Changed his saucy tune when I gave him the Governour of Martinique's name and all his titles, and the whereabouts of his birthplace. And his connectedness to the King himself.'

'And that swayed him?' I wondered.

'In France, you must always know a gentleman's kinship and provenance. It's a country charmed by rank and birth and position.'

'And England isn't?' I said.

When the cutter returned, the boy politely said the captain sent his apologies for inconveniencing one of his nation's own vessels – we were after all wearing the French standard – but in the circumstance he wished us to know that nonetheless we were in custody and our future was now a Naval matter. All decisions rested with the fleet commander, Admiral Honoré Chamblaire, at Fort de France.

Martinique lay some leagues to the south, a beam reach of several hours. With the French man o'war shadowing us astern, the *Diamond* frothed along towards her destined port. So soon after gaining our freedom, we had become captive again, being taken under armed escort into King Louis' Antillean capital, the very heart of his nation's Naval power in the West Indies.

Will Wrack seemed comfortable enough after finding a new

162

long clay and getting it going with a merry crackle. My misgivings were hardly relieved when he began enthusiastically describing the fortified and protected Naval station to which we were reluctantly being escorted.

'Sounds as though you've visited Fort de France many times,' I remarked, not hiding my suspicion.

'I've traded there more times than you've eaten roasted snapper,' he puffed, as if it were the most ordinary thing for an Englishman to frequent French soil.

'How do I know you're not a damm'd spy, then?' I accused. 'You seem more content in French Naval hands than in English. Perhaps I should shoot you out of hand.'

He bridled. 'I'm no blasted spy! You should learn that a man can be loyal to his country without loving its military.' Then he calmed, drawing thoughtfully on his pipe. 'And what would you do – make a run for it? You'd be blown to splinters.' He exhaled a curl of smoke. 'Just as you would have been if I hadn't shown you how to outsail the cruzer.'

I made no answer, but seethed inside.

Will Wrack glanced at the frigate. 'You sowed doubt enough in that captain's mind,' he said, 'but how exactly is this notion of yours going to work?'

'You shall hear no more till I'm ready,' I said curtly.

13

PUISSANCE

Tall, graceful window lights with mullioned panes and a walking gallery stretching the full width of the Great Cabin towered above as I passed under the stern of this splendid and imposing three-decker. Amongst the golden decorations that climbed in gilded waves up to the quarter-deck fully thirty feet away arched a wood-carved banner proclaiming her to be the *Joyeux de La Rochelle*.

Tying off our little cutter at the ship's waist, I glanced apprehensively up the boarding steps over the bulging curve of her huge topsides, wondering what awaited me on deck. I mounted the gangway in trepidation, past three rows of gunports – all of them open, with the giant guns run out for extra room tween-decks in harbour – and on past the great ironworks of the channels and chainplates bearing the enormous rigging loads. I had never ascended to such a leviathan, never even set my foot on the decks of any Navy vessel. Now here I was going aboard a French admiral's flagship, expecting somehow to treat for my bark's freedom.

Early that morning, closing the blue-grey streak that resolved slowly into the coastline of Martinique, the frigate had signalled us to bear off. We let the *Diamond* run along in a gusty breeze under high cliffs until the rocky coast sheered away. There opened before us an expansive bay, the Rade de France, stretching two leagues wide at the mouth. As we entered, with the frigate in close escort astern, the swells eased down, the gusts and flaws steadied and the schooner came upright, creaming along in smooth water.

The sight that greeted my eyes I could hardly credit. Such a host of sail was riding here that even these vast, open roads appeared crowded. Between the clustered vessels ran great numbers of wherries and sail-rigged cutters, dozens of longboats and launches too, plying busily across the waters. On the high land, towering behind and above the ships' masts, there stood monumental fortress works – bastions, ramps and gun emplacements – commanding the whole of the roads beneath. We must have been under the minutest observation from the hundred or more ships at anchor, and from unknown numbers of look-outs and spy-glasses ashore.

For a country that went by display and ostentation, this was a true exhibition of martial and Naval might. There was an abundance of not just the shipbuilder's artistry but of the carpenter's poetry and the gilder's munificence. These French barks were tall-sided vessels, high at both bow and stern where gold-painted castles rose above the weather-deck. With two and three decks of guns carrying thirty and forty pieces – I counted one with fifty – they were sea-going fortresses, and made an English cruzer look like an ordinary lightly-armed merchantman. Yet these great French sea-castles were over-burdened, hindered by their own weight and unbalanced, top heavy from waterline to weather-deck but with stunted rigs and the stoutest masts imaginable. They're nothing like the handy, fast sailing warships that come out of Dutch and English yards, I mused, and a world away from our flashing little *Diamond*.

We brought the schooner to anchor in six fathoms. When the frigate's launch came over once again, Mister Wrack, following my instructions, insisted we were free sailors under the French flag and refused leave for anyone to board. He handed down a note for the captain and a letter for the admiral of the fleet. The

165

boy gave a shrug, as if to say, you cannot escape anyway, and bade his men stroke back to the frigate.

My letter had its effect and I was peremptorily summoned to the admiral's vessel. Now, alone – at their insistence, for they had an English speaker aboard, they advised – I gained the rail of the foreign warship, my heart pumping not from the exertion of climbing her impossibly high topsides but from fighting the instinct to fling myself over the side and swim for dear life.

The *Joyeux*'s weather-deck stretched away fore and aft, stacked with stores and barrels and garland racks and coils of rope. A brace of formidable capstan heads occupied much of the midships space, barely leaving room for passage about the deck and for men to work the belays. As for the deck-pieces, even the *Cornelius*'s six-pounders were puny toys by comparison, for these well-blacked guns measured ten feet from barrel to touch-hole and rested on four-wheeled carriages with hefty running-out tackles permanently rigged. People were everywhere, men and women going about their business or sheltering under awnings from the day's heat. The fellows were mostly in the uniform of gunners and musketmen, soldiers rather than sailors. The jack-tars stood out in their unmistakable blue slops and, unlike the landsmen, ran barefoot.

Signals had been sent in advance and a Naval officer from the *Joyeux*'s complement stood waiting to receive me. He wore a splendid fancy rig which by drawing so much attention to his figure served only to exaggerate his portliness and lack of height, a combination which proportioned him exactly like a water barrel. Beside him stood a younger man, lesser decorated, thin faced and decidedly edgy. Both men considered me, in my borrowed clothing rig-out from Will Wrack's own store, with something approaching distaste. Nevertheless, I made them a formal bow.

'Captain Matthew Loftus, the schooner *Diamond*,' I announced.

The junior officer, holding my letter, acknowledged me in

workable English delivered in hideously contorted accents. Then he introduced his pompous companion as fleet Secretaire to the admiral.

'Captain, your bark is well known to the authorities here,' the young man said. 'As you are wearing the Royal standard of France, your vessel is to be requisitioned without further delay.'

'Requisitioned?' I said, appalled. 'Why, that's illegal –'

He cut me off. 'You are also ordered to hand over any items of value to the Sovereign, such as those mentioned here. The tables for the – ah – Method of the Lunar Distance?'

He waved the letter Will Wrack had carefully enscribed in French while I dictated. I repeated my demand that the *Diamond* be allowed free passage, without threat or action, in return for the item in question, whose immense military and strategic value the admiral himself had undoubtedly recognised.

'The Secretaire admonishes the impertinence of your request to an audience with Admiral Chamblaire,' said the thin-faced young man, 'and informs you he considers your assertion of the item's value preposterous and incredible. Where, he demands, is your proof of its nature? Without such, the admiral orders your vessel to be boarded forthwith and you placed under arrest.'

As calmly as possible, I reached inside my weskit and withdrew two folded pages of parchment. 'Be so kind as to show these to Admiral Chamblaire. That's your proof.'

They snatched the sheets – with torn edges where they had been removed from the volume's binding – from my grasp and examined them. There was much muttering and shaking of heads, for the two pages displayed nothing but row after row and column upon column of handwritten numbers. There was no doubt the Frenchmen were soundly impressed.

'If the admiral has an interest in seeing the rest,' I said, tilting forward the minutest degree, 'will you advise him that, regrettably, he has only a few minutes in which to act?'

The thin fellow took a step forward, thrust his face close and stared up at me.

'A few minutes? Preposterous!' he spluttered. Then he tilted his head, keeping his eye on me like a cockerel examining an approaching fox. 'Why do you say this?'

'Because the volume in question – of which you have two sample pages – may become unavailable for future use by the French Navy or indeed any other Navy. It is rolled up, tamped into one of my deck-pieces, and wadded tight against a full charge of powder. If I do not return unmolested before the half-hour glass has run, my men have orders to fire the gun.' Ostentatiously, I brought from my weskit a pocket-clock – Will Wrack's, and a poor time-keeper, he admitted – examined it and said, 'I estimate that only twelve minutes remain.'

The two of them exchanged a few rapid sentences. I had called their blustering attempt to cow me and they knew it. The portly Frenchman, holding the papers, turned quickly and headed aft towards the admiral's quarters.

'If any boat, Monsieur le Secretaire,' I hailed after him, sharply interrupting his progress, 'other than my own cutter with me alone in it, approaches the *Diamond*, the deck-piece shall be touched off instantly.'

This time I made sure my bow was of the sincerest nature, a dip from the waist with my eyes lowered. The thin man gabbled a translation to the Secretaire, who promptly marched off again. When he returned a minute later, red-faced and perspiring, he barked out a series of instructions so fiercely that his junior flinched.

Before the half-glass could be turned, I was back aboard the schooner with the anchor hauled up and the *Diamond* under way, a foaming wave at her bow. We were headed for sea with an armed French sloop in close company off our beam. When we reached the heads of the bay, well out of range of the shore batteries or any anchored bark, both vessels hove to and a minute cutter was lowered from the sloop, in which the *Joyeux*'s thin-faced officer was rowed across by a single pair of oarsmen. Stepping aboard, damp about the briches, a touch of green to his cheeks, he staggered as the *Diamond* lifted to a lumpy swell, clearly happier aboard a three-decker on an even keel in the roads than on a schooner bouncing in the swells by the harbour heads.

'Show me the tables, if you please,' he muttered.

With a silent prayer, I handed over the leather-bound volume, tightly rolled and tied with a ribbon, the cover somewhat distressed from having been pressed into the barrel of a gun and then dragged out again by a drawstring. The Frenchman grasped the book and opened it flat to its spine. I winced as he brusquely turned the pages, licking a finger and flicking over the leaves as if it were nothing more than a politickal tract, or a prayer-book.

'It seems to be entirely in manuscript,' said the Frenchman, 'as were the sample pages. Thus, it is prior to any publication?'

I nodded.

'And this is the author – the astronomer, one is to presume – who has signed his name on what would be the frontispiece?'

I bowed.

Satisfied, he closed the book and handed me a parchment. It was written in good English, signed 'Chamblaire' and sealed with a handsome mark. It purported to guarantee the *Diamond* free passage from the Rade to the high seas beyond French waters. Balancing one-handed at the rail, with the precious volume tucked under his arm, the officer paused.

'Sir, I trust you have noted,' he said, 'the admiral's explicit provision that if met by our warships on the high seas and running under any other colour than the King of France's, your bark shall be arrested – and sunk if you resist.'

I gave another bow, and said, 'It is well noted, as is the illegality of such a threat.'

He looked surprised. 'O no, sir! Not in time of war.'

Will and Adam gave a simultaneous sharp intake of breath.

The young man's thin features cracked into the hint of a smile. 'Captain, word reaches us that England has been at war with France for more than a two-month.'

My mouth was dry. I performed my practised bow with as

169

much dignity as I could muster, and he turned for the boarding rope. Without a word, the *Diamond*'s crew got her under way in scrambling haste. I twisted nervously round half expecting to see a frigate weighing and coming after us, or to find a dozen shots whistling over to smash us to pieces. But the sloop was passing peacefully back into the roads and in no time we found ourselves quite alone on the wide waters of the open sea, the Rade de France a mere dim outline astern.

Adam came back to the quarter with something in his cupped palms.

'Sir, this mud in my hand,' he said deliberately, 'came up on the anchor flukes. It is French soil.' He gathered the cheeks of his mouth and gobbed juicily on it, then threw it on my feet.

'Adam, you misunderstand –' I began, but he turned on his heel and marched off to the beak to stand gazing seawards with his back to Martinique.

'And neither shall I ever forgive you,' put in Will Wrack sternly.

With that, he dived for the hatchway and disappeared below leaving me alone at the tiller, mulling over what had happened. Wrack emerged moments later bearing a heavy black bottle. Pulling out the cork, he sniffed at the bottle's mouth, savouring the sweet aroma of sugar-rum.

'We'll drink to our freedom,' he said, taking a long swig and handing the rum to me, 'and to my loss.'

I pulled lustily at the sugar-rum bottle, smacking my lips as it seared down my gullet. 'Forgive me, Mister Printer Wrack, but it had to be done.'

'Aye, and the bone-headed Frenchies fell for it like a bonito taking the baited hook.' He simpered, and adopted an accent. "This is the astronomer's signature, I take it?" says that Frenchy, observing the proud name of Wm. Wrack, and upon a mere Mathematickal schoolbook at that.' He drank down two fingers of rum. 'Ah, Captain Matthew, how could you? My last memento of all those years in Wimpole-court – the only old manuscript I ever kept for sentiment.'

I grinned sympathetically and swigged from the bottle. 'Has is it occurred to you, Mister Wrack, that we are now on the run not just from the English Navy but the French Navy as well?'

'That's new for me,' he mused, 'but hardly uncommon for pirates.'

'Take the steering,' I said, handing him the tiller-bar. 'Poor Adam's convinced I'm England's greatest traitor.'

The boy's anger was hard to assuage, until I took him below and showed him the precious Spatchears volume, still safe aboard though minus two pages. Then Adam too took a couple of pulls off the bottle and matched our smiles, his grin disappearing only momentarily when he remembered how long we had enjoyed his misery before disabusing him.

The friendly night came down upon the four of us, three sailors and the little *Diamond* tilting along beneath our feet. We fell to imagining the portly Frenchman berating his thin-faced junior, then ducking into the Great Cabin to cower before the admiral's wrath. How would he explain giving a trio of English rogues and their handsome bark a free passage in exchange for nothing more than a handwritten school text, the manuscript of a book published twenty years ago and as useless as the time of yesterday's tide?

Later, when darkness was fully upon us and the *Diamond* left a frothing wake glowing astern in a greenish and sparkling trail, while Mister Wrack was below rooting through his stores for salted fish and rice to feed up my crew's appetites, Adam all at once called from the pump brake at the forcmast. 'Sir, I just got two hundred strokes of water before she dried!'

Then I remembered how the English cruzer's closest ball had grazed the *Diamond*'s strakes, perhaps loosening the caulking or, worse, splitting a board. Will stuck his head up from the hatchway and I shot him a questioning look.

'Aye,' he said at once, his eyes wide, 'she's taking on water, and pretty damm'd badly.'

14

Reef Encounter

'If only I were back in Wimpole-court, I would publish the volume myself,' said Will Wrack, sitting on the quarter with the Spatchears tables open on his knee. 'That would solve all difficulties – keeping them out of Flamsteed's hands, and the Navy's.'

The *Diamond* rode sweetly in ten fathoms at full stretch of the anchor's cable in a deep, little-known pool, into which the printer from near the Fleet had steered the leaking schooner. Dashing in through a secret gap, we found protection from the swells, for all around an invisible sill broke the power of the rollers, reducing them to a mere chop. Yet there was no land to be seen, only the wide sea all around, stretching west all along the Colomby Coast to the Darien, and east for a thousand leagues to Africka. Riding in Culpepper Pool was like nothing so much as being moored in the ocean itself.

We had struggled with the damaged planking at the turn of the bilge, the growing inrush keeping us at the pumps for half of every hour. By the end of the second day, we had sistered in a new timber, strengthened the nearby frame and caulked it all as tight as a tar in a rumshop. At last relieved of pump duty, Will Wrack and I lay exhausted on the quarter-deck in the last of the evening sun while Adam slept below. Soon we would be benighted and safe in the pool till daybreak, for certainly no

172

vessel would brave the difficult entrance in the dark. Only under the high sun could the reefs and the channels be seen, the dangers revealed by the colour of the sea, blue for deep, green for shallow.

I had told Will Wrack the whole tale of the Spatchears tables, my desire to deliver them to the Royal Society and see them published, and how we were wanted men bent on acquitting ourselves of false charges. Now I sought his help.

'Mister Wrack, as you know manuscripts, will you examine the tables? Perhaps you can offer a clue to where the flaws might lie.' I leaned across and tapped the open page. 'Take this star here – Aldebran. When I practised with the cross-staff on Isla Grande in the Witness Isles, I could never make the figures come right.'

He laughed. 'I know little of the proper Navigation. But I confess I am hardly surprised there are flaws, for so many scribblers leave errors in their works.' He cradled the volume, running his hands over its cover. 'But it's an excellent example of the binder's art. Good weighty parchment, fine-grained too. And it's enscribed in the best of inks, written in a strong hand – steady, flowing and well-worked, most probably not the author's own. Look here in the *Introductio*.'

I had been unable to tackle the *Introductio* because it was in Latin.

'This is grave and long-winded stuff,' he said, 'written by a pedant who obfuscates the simplest of matters, a failing common amongst many learned folk or academicians who come to the business of writing.'

'Aye, I'm sure, but do you read the clerical language, Will? What does it say?'

'It's a preamble to the main text. Most works of Natural Philosophy would have something of the like.' Delicately, he leafed the pages over. 'Here, the author declares, *inter alia*, his tables to be true and accurate, designed for the mariner to use at sea, a most important progress towards the astronomer's ambition of finding a fix at sea, *et cetera, et cetera*. That sort of notion.'

'But they're not true and accurate,' I protested. 'The predictions don't work.'

Night after night on the Witness Isles, I had raised the worn cross-staff towards the heavens and taken star sights and Moon sights by the hundred. Yet though a simple noon latitude seemed right enough, when I consulted Observator Spatchears' tables for fixing a star's position my results had never tallied and the intricate calculations always worked out wrong. Not just by a degree or so, but by an intolerable margin. If the columns could not predict the stars' movements, they could never produce accurate fixes for Navigation. Yet Spatchears had insisted he had proved his predictions, journeying to Tropick latitudes for that express purpose. Were the tables, then, nothing but a fantasy of his troubled imagination?

'It's not all fine writing, though,' said Will, peering close. 'This marginal note in the *Introductio* is altogether in a different hand from the chief enscriber's, much shakier and less certain than the well-crafted quill work.'

I craned over to see, for it was something I had missed altogether. The note was versed and in plain English:

> *The sun and stars above revolve,*
> *As if to circle through the Universe;*
> *Yet Copernicus alone the truth can solve:*
> *'Tis Earth doth spin, the heavens reverse.*
>
> *Now is the riddle of the Moon's errings*
> *Written here in column and table;*
> *Yet the cogs' and wheels' whirrings*
> *Want a key to set them stable.*

I studied the writing. Could it be Noah Spatchears' own feeble hand?

'Well, now,' said Mister Wrack. '*The riddle of the Moon's errings* and *the cogs' and wheels' whirrings* – that's plain enough. It must mean the complexities of the events described in the tables, as I see them laid out here – the motions of the Earth round the sun, the observations of fixed stars and the predicted positions of the Moon, at all points in the lunar cycle, year on year, and for certain determined latitudes. But now,' Will went on, '*Want a key to set them stable*. Perhaps the versifier's saying they cannot work without a code of some kind. To adjust the readings and return them to accuracy.'

'Do you mean they are deliberately falsified?'

'That's the idea,' he said. 'A system of errors that only the key or code can put right.'

'Why would they contain such errors?' I said.

Will sucked the end of his long clay. 'For security. To render them worthless to anyone without the correction.'

'Where is this code, then?' I demanded. 'Somewhere in the volume? Have you looked right through?'

'There's nothing,' he said with a shake of his head. 'Perhaps he left it somewhere else for you.'

There had been no other books or papers in the Witness Isles stores, I was sure of that. Starving, I had ransacked every box and bag and sack of the rations left us. Why did the old astronomer fail to leave the key? It must have been an enormous risk stealing the tables back from Filligrew and spiriting them into the stores. Why leave out the vital part?

'To Hell with Spatchears,' I muttered, inwardly cursing his unreliability. 'He declares his tables true and good when they're quite useless.'

If the old astronomer held this key or code, then my hopes of securing an influential pardon were vanishing as fast as the Tropick day was fading into night in Culpepper Pool. How could I possibly reach the old man? Where would Filligrew's flota be now? The Antilles? Cuba or Jamaicka perhaps? Did Spatchears remain locked in the cells or had he been sent back to

175

England? More likely, I thought grimly, the poor chesty old fellow might simply have expired.

Suddenly, Will Wrack was half on his feet, the volume almost slipping from his hands.

'Lordy, I don't believe it,' he said, pointing with the stem of his pipe.

A bark approached from the north. Dammit, I had let our vigilance slip. Fumbling with the glass, I saw she was a topsail schooner very like our own though a deal bigger, better than sixty foot on deck and armed with six pieces. Her gunports were open, and she slouched along under half canvas, clearly seeking the tricky gap Will had guided us through, trying to pick her way amongst the reefs and strong currents.

'She'll have to be lucky in this light,' observed Will.

If the bark got in, we were there for the taking. We watched in trepidation tinged with some admiration as she did just that, creaming in through the gap in the last of the evening's glow. A crowd of figures lined her rails, many spare men idling while others busied about to get her hook down. She dragged three or four times on the smooth, scoured bottom before settling back, well caught in.

'I'll be damm'd – she looks like the *Goodenough*,' said Mister Wrack, squinting across. 'I knew her captain once, a long while back. Who has her now, I can't say.'

I ducked below to hide the Spatchears' volume and rouse up Adam to prepare hand weapons. When I came on deck, it was to see a boat being let down from the newly-arrived schooner. A party embarked to row the cable or so of chop between us.

'Take a pistol each, fellows, primed and charged,' I told Adam and Will. 'We've no choice but to hope for a parley until we see how things stand.'

We let the boat came alongside. There were four oarsmen, naked to the waist, with two better-dressed officers seated in the stern. One of these, cutting a well-made, youngish figure, with a shock of fair hair gathered at the back in a pig-tail, stood up and respectfully requested the party's permission to come aboard.

'Two of you only,' I said, making sure they could see the pistol at my belt. 'The boat to stand off.'

The young pig-tailed officer hung back to let the older man board first. A rugged cove of perhaps forty years, with a wary look in his eye, he was dark-bearded, bow-legged and wearing a short jacket-coat over a loose cotton shirt. As his companion followed up, swarming over the rail, the fellow stood before me on the quarter.

I stepped forward. 'Captain, welcome aboard the schooner *Diamond* –'

He jerked his head and said rudely, 'Here's the captain.'

Only three paces off, this young person made the most striking appearance, being remarkably well dressed in a fine loose white shirt and smart crimson weskit cut tight around the waist, blue briches of good serge and soft black calf shoes the like of which were more often seen only on gentlemen officers' feet. To set off the fine dress, gold rings shone on the fingers and there was even the flash of a diamond at the earlobe. Embarrassed, I realised I was staring, and shifted my gaze to meet cool, blue-grey eyes, crinkling at the corners.

'Welcome,' I thought the figure said.

It was an odd thing to say when stepping aboard a stranger's boat. Something about the person struck me as off-kilter. The briches fitted snug and accented the shape of the legs, and the folds of the linen shirt drew attention to the outlines beneath.

'Captain Wellcome, the schooner *Goodenough*, private bark,' said the newcomer, hands on hips, grinning broadly.

'Matthew Loftus,' I mumbled, quite put off, 'of the private schooner *Diamond*.'

As I offered my handclasp and the palm touched mine, realisation dawned.

'Bess Wellcome,' she said, laughing, and showed clean white teeth.

A woman captain! I was covered in confusion. But Will Wrack was beaming.

'Why, I knew your father, Jeremiah Wellcome,' he said, bowing and introducing himself.

She returned the salutation, saying, 'Then we are well met. I heard my father speak of you, Mister Wrack.'

Instantly, the tension lifted. Perhaps, I thought, we need not be enemies after all.

'Captain Wellcome, I propose a parley,' I said, 'here on the quarter, with drink and vittles.'

She bowed and we agreed the rowing boat should lie back on a line from our stern, in view of all, while we decided how to proceed. The pair from the *Goodenough* arranged themselves under the awning to enjoy the cool of the breeze and I sent Adam below for bottles and tumblers.

'My companion here,' said this Bess Wellcome, settling down to relax like a cat on a window-seat, 'is Robbie Macfarlane, master of the *Doughty*.'

'One-time master,' he said, in Scots accents. He had a mistrustful air and threw searching glances from my face to Will Wrack's and back, trying to work out how things stood. When Adam returned with the drink and a lantern, for dusk had quickly fallen, I poured generous fingers of rum and handed round the mugs, fully regaining my composure.

'So where's the *Doughty* now?' I asked.

Macfarlane swallowed heartily, then studied the pewter mug.

'Remarkable good stuff, man!' he declared, smacking his lips.

Will, who had a magnificent clay sputtering and sparking merrily in the sudden Tropick twilight, breathed out a cloud of smoke fit for a signal gun and said with some pride, 'It's Ron Lapido, from Hispaniola.'

'Ach, it's a fine rum.' He licked his lips, then directed his gaze at me. 'So you're curious about my bark? She's sunk, that's where she is. Caught by an unlucky shot. Or should I say, an unlucky encounter. With a private flota.'

178

I sat up too quickly.

Robbie noticed, his eyes gleaming in the lamplight before he resumed. 'They were working up the island chain, hauling over every bark. I ran straight into it. The privateer took arms and stores off me in exchange for our free passage, then the two-faced bastard stuck a shot on me.'

'Why?' I asked. 'There was no need if you'd given him what he wanted.'

'Ach, I insulted his pride. As he sailed off, I ran up my favourite colour – red ground defaced with white death's head over crossed bones. A *Jolie Rouge*, the Frenchies call it. Means "Pretty Red" – for blood, no quarter and all that.' He grinned darkly. 'I hoisted it topside down. Then it says, "I bugger you". That single jibe cost me my bark.'

'How so?' I said.

'He loosed off a shot,' replied Macfarlane. 'Damm'd mis-fortunate. Got us by the garboard strakes. Had to beach her ashore on Dominica, on a strip of sand six feet wide. That blasted island rises sheer up from the sea, hardly a shelf any-where to claw an anchor on to. No way to save her, and the *Doughty* was done for.'

'Do you know who this privateer was?'

His tone was surly and dismissive. 'Ach, man, what do you think? He did not exactly introduce himself.'

'He raised no flag? No colours to declare himself?'

'None at all. Never hoisted a scrap.'

'Did you go aboard his ship?'

Robbie's eyes darted from side to side. 'Never even saw the man himself. He sent over some dam' functionary to oversee the plunder of my stores. Weaselly little fellow.'

Lord alive, I thought, lifting my pewter and slugging back a mouthful of warm, sweet rum. Then I said, 'Do you know why this flota was hauling over vessels?'

The Scotsman shrugged. 'Looking for something or someone.'

'And he didn't say what or who?'

'Not you, that's for sure,' scoffed Macfarlane. 'He's after bigger fish than your little model ship.'

Thinking this man's weakness for cutting jibes might one day cost him not just his boat but his life, I bit back my annoyance and asked, 'Did he give any clue where he's headed?'

'The functionary talked about a plantation. Said that was why they wanted my stores.'

I leant forward. 'What plantation? Where? Cuba?'

'I've no idea, man.' The Scotsman leant back defiantly. He clearly knew more than he would tell.

I gripped his arm. 'What's it to you, Macfarlane? Tell me what you know.'

He roughly swiped my hand away. 'I've said enough.'

We were an instant away from dropping all civility in favour of exchanging blows.

'All right, Robbie,' cut in Captain Wellcome, 'that's enough.'

'Ach, Bess,' said Macfarlane sheepishly. His tone softened, and he smiled at her with a sly look. 'Luck of the Irish, eh? After the *Doughty* sank, who should come along but my good Bess here. She plucked us off like ripe manjoes. You're a warm-hearted lass, are you not?'

Captain Wellcome, sitting cross-legged as I had seen no woman do before, laughed roundly. 'Robbie, you tell it as though I were a Saint.'

He chuckled. 'You're comelier than any Saint in his Catholick niche, and keener on coin than a Puritan preacher in a new-built kirk.' Looking round the company with a grin, he said, 'Before she'd let us aboard, she lifted gold pieces and silver dollars from each and every man's pocket, like a verger.'

With the rum, Macfarlane had shed his nervous aspect, yet still he would not meet my eye. His glance darted this way and that, taking in the *Diamond*'s fittings and rig deck-pieces and her general state.

'So now, Captain Wellcome, it appears you're shipping all the *Doughty*'s men as well as your own,' I said. 'You must have five and twenty fellows aboard.'

'Aye, fifteen of mine and eleven of his,' she said. 'A stinking, lusty mob they are, who can't let me toilet in privacy.'

My face grew hot, perhaps from the Hispaniola sugar-rum. Never had I heard a woman – a girl, indeed, and a pretty one despite her weather-tanned skin – speak of lustiness, nor of her toilet, nor of men's glances.

'We've too many fellows,' she said. 'That's why I want to parley. Are you three alone aboard?'

She could see we were. We were open to a night boarding by stealth, or a plain assault in the broad day which we could never resist. Moreover, the *Goodenough* lay between us and the only passage out. The question needed no answer.

I leaned forward and said, 'Why did you haul in here?'

'To wait,' she said simply, 'for our quarry.'

'What quarry?'

She cast me a sharp glance. 'That, Captain Loftus, is the *Goodenough*'s affair.' Then she smiled and said, 'Let's get to our business. You're short-manned. You lack a few good hands, that's the issue.'

Macfarlane butted in. 'Aye, you must hardly be able to sail her in a press.'

I bridled. 'We outsailed an English cruzer, dammit.'

Captain Wellcome reached forward and patted my knee. 'Keep your briches on – I believe it. But how do you fight the ship?'

'Aye, that's it,' said Macfarlane, 'where are your gunners?'

'That's not our purpose,' I retorted.

'Then what is?' said the Scotsman, leering.

'Robbie, let's get on with what we came for,' said Captain Wellcome. She shifted her limbs and sat up. 'I shall come straight to it. Will you take on a few of his fellows?'

'Surely with both your crews together,' I suggested, 'you can sail and fight your schooner very handily?'

She chuckled. 'We can barely fight for falling over each other's feet. We'd have three powder-boys and four rammers squabbling over each piece. We'd be blown apart before we agreed who aimed the gun.'

She put her head back and laughed. It was infectious, and I smiled with her. Relaxing, the rum lightening my spirits, I looked at her more and more, her glow drawing me like a beacon. She charged the talk with a life and amusement that I'd never imagined in a woman.

'Men we have,' she said, 'yet we're short of powder and shot. Any shot. And dry stores. What can you let me have?'

Will Wrack had stored armaments and dry goods a-plenty aboard the *Diamond* for his trading voyage. On the other hand, we sorely lacked a couple of strong fellows to man the boat and fire the guns. I was ready to bargain.

'I shall take two fresh young fellows on, and give you twelve of iron roundshot and ten pound of powder. I can spare you three sacks each of grain and rice, all in return for twenty dollars.'

'Take five men,' she said, 'including Robbie.'

'Three I'll take, but not Captain Macfarlane.'

The Scot made as if to speak but she silenced him with a raised hand. After a pause, as she weighed my reply, she said, 'Take Macfarlane, and I shall guarantee you get out of the reef.'

So that was it.

'No deal,' I said. My hand was on my pistol, plain enough for the two pirates to see. 'Send your oarsmen back to the *Goodenough*.'

Macfarlane made a move but Adam pounced and had his firearm away in a flash. Will had surreptitiously laid aside his glowing clay, and now held a pistol too, with the lock sprung back. Captain Wellcome sat stock still.

'Your pistol, if you please,' I said levelly. 'By the barrel.'

She pulled back her weskit deliberately, removed the belted pistol and handed it over.

For half a minute, no one moved or spoke. Night had fallen as

182

we talked and we sat in a circle, faces lit by the glow of the lantern's flame flickering in the dying tradewind. We had come to the crux of the exchange. It was me who broke the silence.

'We're all private seamen here,' I said carefully, 'and can come to an agreement without a fight. You, Captain Wellcome, remain here tonight, and that's our guarantee against boarding. In the morning, I shall take the *Diamond* clear of the Pool without any trouble from the *Goodenough* or they never see their captain again. Is that understood? Your boat can pick you up outside the entrance, to give us a head start.'

Stillness reigned as everyone weighed the new circumstance. At last Captain Wellcome spoke.

'Robbie, tell the fellows to take the boat back.'

I breathed again. 'I admire your good sense, Captain Wellcome. After dawn, if there's been no trouble, you may call your boat over to stand off with six fellows and no arms. I'll pick the three I fancy for the *Diamond*'s crew.'

The deal was agreed. The *Goodenough*'s captain called softly to the oarsmen, who brought their boat back alongside and took off Robbie Macfarlane. They argued briefly with Captain Wellcome, asking if she was held or free. Free enough, she replied, and they rowed off with ribald laughter, making coarse jokes about the fair sex, and a woman who was a captain too. When she rejoined us, I said she was to be made comfortable on deck and the *Diamond*'s fellows would each take a watch in turn guarding her.

'How civil you are to a guest,' she mocked.

'To a hostage,' I countered.

I split the watches between the three of us and the night passed in peace until I came on deck four hours before dawn to relieve Will Wrack. Half a cable off, the *Goodenough* rode quietly under the stars, the faintest low hum of chatter and talk drifting across from her crowded decks. By our own rail, I saw in the lamp's glow Bess Wellcome curled up fast asleep, a picture of feline repose.

When the eastern sky showed a glimmering at the horizon, I roused her and we breakfasted together on dried fruit and warm flat bread. A half hour past dawn, as agreed, a boat put off from the *Goodenough* and stood by while I surveyed the six seamen. Three looked very well-used – rough jack-tars hardened to a life of privateering and pirating. As well, there were two youngish fellows of sixteen or eighteen and another of about thirteen, all of whom looked to have fresher spirits, untainted by years of disputes and quarrel-making.

'You there, stand up,' I said to the first. 'Let me see you're whole in limb, and your back is strong.'

When I had assayed all three one by one, I called, 'Fellows, don't you want to stay aboard the *Goodenough*?'

'No fear,' said one.

'Too damm'd crowded,' said another, grinning.

I chuckled. 'Aboard the *Diamond* you get your bread and biscuit, plenty of seamen's work, not much pay and a hammock each below.'

'We'll join with you!' they chorused.

We let the three young fellows aboard, Will and Adam checking for weapons. They possessed nothing but the slops they stood in and showed themselves glad to be on a deck with space to move about. We set them to work lowering round shot for the *Goodenough* into the boat along with a ten-pound powder bag and six sacks from our stores. The boat put off with instructions to unload and follow us out through the entrance to pick up their captain as soon as we were clear.

Our three new seamen were Hap, a Scot of seventeen, Bart, the youngest at thirteen and English, and Jan, a fellow about sixteen with a Dutch father and a native mother. While the rest of us made sail, I sent them forward to haul the anchor, which they set about doing with a will.

Very soon we creamed past the *Goodenough*'s stern, the new boys waving their farewells, then reached through the break in the reef and stood into the swirling waters of the escape channel.

There, we hove to, drifting on wind and current between the Culpepper and its neighbouring reef while the *Goodenough*'s boat made its approach. Captain Wellcome and I watched the boys dodging eagerly about, finding the belays, tidying lines, running up the ratlines for a vantage at the maintop.

'Look at those lads,' I said. 'Do you think I chose well?'

She gave a rueful grin. 'You might have done me a kindness and taken the surly ones. And Robbie too.'

I laughed, letting my eye linger on her face a moment. 'I do regret, Captain Wellcome, treating you a little rough, but we had no choice.'

Almost imperceptibly, she inclined her head in graceful acknowledgement. 'You kept to your bargain, Captain Loftus, and I admire that.'

'Aye, well. The pity is we did not meet in easier circumstances.'

She smiled with true warmth. 'One day, perhaps. Who knows?'

There was a shout. The rowing boat came plunging down the swells and in moments was alongside. Without further ado Captain Wellcome clambered over the rail and then she was away to regain the *Goodenough*, the sweeps pulling against the current running hard between the reefs.

'Pay off to steerboard,' I called, centring the long tiller-bar. 'Square the boom and let her run straight.'

Instantly, the *Diamond* bore off downwind and picked up way, escaping the trap of Culpepper Pool and heading for the safety of the open sea.

The open sea! I was discovering just how crowded and well-sailed these Antillean waters were. There were pirates and brigands seeking prizes. There were armed merchantmen and wild Saint Lucy natives stalking the islands. There were Navy patrols of many nations prowling up and down the Lesser Antilles chain. Somewhere beyond the horizon was a perhaps greater threat, the flota that did for Macfarlane's *Doughty*, a powerful privateer looking for someone or something. Was it

Filligrew, and was that where I would find the key to the tables?

I twisted round to study the foaming wake behind, reckoning we had got six knots of speed. Then I lifted my eyes to the rowing boat, already half a cable distant, plugging laboriously upwind against the current. Bess Wellcome's face was turned towards me, and then her hand lifted in a simple gesture of farewell.

15

Fair Exchange

'By all the Saints that ever lived,' I muttered from my stance high in the shrouds, 'I believe she has the legs of us.'

We were less than half a day out from Culpepper when we encountered a sail reaching south on a crossing course. This was a well-armed bark, about two hundred tuns burthen, with four in the broadside, twice our firepower. Like a hunter, on spying us she had altered directly to intercept. Once again following Mister Wrack's sailing advice, we shortened canvas and tried to work our way up to weather, but this time it made no difference. We tacked and beat to windward, tacked again, and then again. No matter which way the little *Diamond* dodged, no matter how sharply we put her about from steerboard to larboard and back, still we could not lose the bigger vessel. With her much longer waterline she had a speed we could not hope to match, let alone outpace. She steadily gained ground until less than half a league of open water separated us.

I scrambled down the ratlines and rejoined Adam by the tiller, where Will Wrack had the tube raised.

'Lord alive,' he said, 'she's hoisted up a Spanish colour.'

I glanced at the taff-rail. 'What about the French standard?' I said. 'Catholick Spain allied with France in the last war.'

He looked uneasy. 'Aye, but treaties made in Paris count for little in the Caribbee.'

'Let's see if she might parley, then,' I suggested.

He shook his head. 'Not if the Dagoes think there's an easy prey on offer. And they're ill-accustomed to taking prisoners, even Catholick ones.'

'Very well,' I breathed, 'if we can't get away, then she's at least going to have a fight on her hands. Mister Pyne, steer straight for her bows.'

Going forward with Will Wrack to prepare for gunnery, I assembled the new crew members. As yet, the boys from Bess Wellcome's *Goodenough* had had no chance to prove themselves true, so they were allowed no tools, neither seaman's knife nor marlinspike, and forbidden to come aft of the mainmast. We had fed them good rations and small beer and set them to work, which they went about with a will – serving and whipping sheets and pennants and bracelines, tearing old rope into junk ends for caulking, falling on to the anchor cable to scrape barnacles off, and a hundred other sea-boys' tasks. Now it was time to see how their gunnery went.

'Fellows, can you load and fire these two-pounders?' I said.

'Aye, captain,' said Bart, eagerly. 'We practised it well enough with Robbie Macfarlane on the *Doughty*.'

'We've seen action, captain,' said Hap, the keen young Scot.

I left Mister Wrack in charge as gunner, and turned my attention back to the Spaniard. She bore steadily onwards, plainly intending to close and turn for her broadside. Likewise, we stood on, heeling hard on steerboard tack under a full press of canvas, our deck-pieces that side aiming their snouts high into the sky, the larboard ones pointing into the depths.

'Keep on for her bows, Adam,' I called.

We had to avoid her main guns at all costs. All the while, closing until the gap between our two vessels had narrowed to gunshot range, I kept bow aiming at bow. The Spaniard had to swing one way or the other, yet in doing so she exposed herself to our weapons. Puny they might be in comparison perhaps, but by God we would give all we could muster.

I was still hoping to close and offer a parley of some sort when her single forward gun flamed red. The shot whistled overhead and plunged far astern. One of the gunner boys – Bart, I think – raised up a mocking cheer. But Will Wrack and I, following the ball's arcing travel, saw plainly the Spaniard was only getting her range.

'Whichever way she turns, Adam,' I ordered, 'aim for her bowsprit.'

Still she did not turn but fired again, another shot from that powerful forward swivel. This time it was ranged well. In truth, it was ranged dead right. It happened so fast I had no time to duck or even flinch.

The roundshot struck our steerboard side level with the foremast, shattering the rail into hundreds of sharp, flying splinters. The ball angled across the waist and smashed into the carriage of the larboard aft deck-piece. Under the impact, the gun flew clean off its tackle. Something exploded – perhaps the powder bag tucked behind the piece – hurling charred, broken timbers in every direction. Shards of iron and wooden splinters sprayed around, wreaking their toll, singing past my ears, thudding into the rail behind.

In the waist, the three boys and Will Wrack were felled all together as though swept by the whirling blade of an axe. Blood spattered high into the air and the droplets blew into my face. At my shoulder there came a sigh of despair and Adam crumpled like a sack on the deck-boards, a red wound on his forehead. The tiller-bar swung loose and arced across to leeward. Instantly, the schooner began to round up into the wind. Half stunned by the shock of smoke and noise, I flung myself across the quarter, got behind the tiller and pushed it up to weather. Come on *Diamond*, I urged.

The distance between our two barks had diminished to less than a cable. If I veered away, the enemy would loose off her side guns point blank. We had no weapons to answer with, for my crew were laid flat and, for all I could tell, dead and dying.

Already, it seemed as if the end game had come upon the *Diamond*.

The helm answered and she swung into her groove, charging forwards oblivious to the carnage lately spread over her broad decks. Through a veil of stinging wetness in my eyes, I made out the stooping figure of Will Wrack, stumbling over to crouch by the steerboard deck-pieces. He was alive! And Lord, two of the boys were back on their feet, staggering over to help. We would not surrender yet to these Spanish.

The *Diamond* bore relentlessly onwards. The attacker closed, her hull and rig swaying and dropping on the swells. Spanish faces were turned my way, hands raised, pointing in alarm. Their helmsman threw his weight on the long unwieldy tiller-bar, but I steered on. The enemy bore up into the wind and the mouths of those heavy guns swung our way. The gap came down to a boat's length. In seconds, the linstocks would go to the touch-holes, the four black mouths would blast their heat and flame, the carriages would snap back on their chain-tackles against the force of the discharges, and a storm of destruction would descend.

Fire first, I thought dully. With a great cry I hauled the tiller-bar with all my strength. On the instant, the *Diamond* swung her bows three points to leeward. She came upright and levelled off her gun barrels, aiming at the enemy's beak.

'Fire!' I cried.

Will's arm came down. Both steerboard deck-pieces blasted in unison at point-blank range. The roundshots passed clean through the Spanish bark's rails right forward, shattering them into pieces and lifting the swivel gun in its mountings. Half a dozen men dropped where they stood.

The *Diamond* bore onwards. We were so near the Spaniard I saw fresh white grain showing where wood had been shattered, glimpsed flecks of blood on her greasy deck-boards, saw terror-stricken Spanish faces only feet away. I hauled on the tiller, the *Diamond*'s onward rush seeming unalterable.

Ram her. The words dinned into my stunned mind, above the

rattling blocks and straining sheets and the froth at our plunging bows. Strike her, hurt her, it's all that's left. Smash alongside, strip off her chainplates, derange the snouts of her guns. I gripped the tiller and stood on. The enemy's seamen suddenly understood and tried desperately to dodge to the larboard side. The Spanish gunners ran back from the rail, dropping their matches, scattering for their lives. As their ship luffed, she slowed, but the *Diamond* forged on. Ten fathoms, five fathoms.

With mighty force, our steerboard bows struck the enemy amidships. Eighty tuns of speeding, heavy-timbered schooner crashed into the Spaniard's hull, sending a tremor along our own decks that pummelled the soles of my feet. The standing rigging thrummed like the strings of a viol, the masts trembled, the deadeyes groaned in protest. I grappled with the wayward tiller-bar, hanging on to the rail for purchase, trying to get the *Diamond* to pay off. She drove on, smashing along the Spanish bark's topsides, tearing and ripping at her mizen chainplates. Channels, chunks of planking, ripped shrouds and deadeyes all flew into the air and rained down about me. Not ten paces away, the enemy's quarter-deck ranged past so close I looked right into her officers' shocked faces.

We passed through a cloud of smoke and suddenly ahead was clear water. I whirled round. The Spaniard was recovering, bearing slowly off on to a reach. Now her quarter-deck was crowded with figures, lining the rail, levelling their weapons.

'Down!' I screamed, and flung myself flat to the deck-boards.

The musket shots arrived half a second later, the balls spitting angrily into the topsides, scything through the sails and whirring off into the distance. There was a blow to my thighs, a hard punch, and when I struggled up to take hold of the tiller-bar my left leg was a numbed, dead weight. Lost, the *Diamond* hunted her wind. I grasped the bar and wrenched it to windward. Thank the Lord, the helm answered. We ran off and opened the distance to beyond musket ball range.

Somehow, we had survived the first encounter. Dazed, I tried

191

to take stock. Adam lay a pace or two away, quite still, an ooze of blood from his head staining the boards. In the waist, Will Wrack was doubled up by the steerboard rail, moaning lustily. Beside him sprawled Bart, the English boy, face up as if dozing in the sun on a summer's day. Then I looked again. His body was twisted and broken. The entire torso lay open, red and gaping, ripped apart. A foot-long shard of timber protruded from between the exposed rib-bones.

Near Bart lay two figures, barely moving.

'Jan! Hap!' I cried, my mouth dry as a beach.

Slowly, they struggled to their feet. They gave an uncertain wave and moved unsteadily past Bart's body to help Will Wrack.

Fearfully, I scanned round to see where the Spanish bark was. She lay less than a cable off. Her mizen stood crooked where the shrouds had gone, ripped away in the desperate ramming, and her progress was slow. Yet she was wearing ship – with difficulty, but still it was plain to see what she was about. She was turning to come back.

I sensed a terrible weariness and my thoughts were a confused jumble. Could we reload and fire again? With at least one tackle broken, we had only three working guns. Bring off another ramming then? In truth, I doubted we had any prospect left but to be blown out of the water. Striking down our colours in surrender meant capture, then torture until we swore to their Pope, probably to be shot for our pains. Or perhaps to face a slow strangling on the rope's end, to weaken and die of salt thirst hanging in the sun's glare. Or be thrown overboard to struggle in the water a few last hours until lurking beasts below smelled out a living prey.

No, we would fight to the last. I looked again over my shoulder, hating the enemy bark. She seemed a ship of death bearing down to finish us off.

Just as I turned away, bringing curses down on their Dago heads, something caught my eye. Beyond the Spaniard was an approaching shape, a distance off, riding down the swells.

Straightening, my bloodied leg dragging, I twisted round and saw it was another sail, well astern of the enemy. Every man aboard both barks had missed it – the *Diamond* engaged in a fight for our lives, the Dagoes intent on us, their weaker adversary. If she was another Spanish bark coming to aid her companion, then we were doubly done for.

The arriving vessel fairly creamed down the swells, charging into the fray with her ports open and guns run out. Blinking the salty sweat and drying blood from my eyes, I stared again, hardly giving credence to the sight. She was a topsail schooner, bigger than the *Diamond* and much more massively armed. I squinted against the sunlight, uncomprehending. She was the *Goodenough*.

Reaching the trader on the windward quarter, the schooner squared off to run alongside. Cries of alarm went up, carrying across the water as the Spanish – too late – saw what was happening.

Time ran slow, as though the clock's hands ticked through molasses, the seconds lengthening and laggardly. My hands were clamped so fiercely around the tiller-bar it was later an agony to release them. I forgot my insensate leg, the Dutch boy's ripped corpse, Adam's awful stillness beside me. All was driven out as I watched the *Goodenough*'s lightning assault.

With a roar, her larboard broadside spoke, the guns blazing in unison. Four spurts of grey smoke streaked with red flames gouted outwards not ten fathoms from the quarry. All four shots found their target, raking across the Spaniard's decks. Debris and broken spars and lumps of ragged limbs spewed into the sea off to leeward, carried away by the wrecking force of the balls. Tatters of rig flew in the air, the spreading canvas crumpled, stays were torn out by the root. With a sharp crack, the mainmast split a man's height above the deck and crashed over, sagging into the sea. Faltering under the weight of all this gear dragging in the sea, the Spaniard slowed.

The *Goodenough* ran three lengths past and put about in a fast tack. Sails snapping and flogging, she spun round, hauled sheets, got a bone back in her teeth and pounded upwind. Breasting the enemy, she bore on to a reach and levelled off her steerboard guns. The booms echoed over the water, plumes of smoke fumed upwards, and a second fatal mass of flying metal punched into the wounded vessel.

The *Goodenough*'s crew hardly paused in their gunnery work, their naked backs bent sweating over the hot mouths as they rammed and sponged and recharged. She ran on past, turned again and put a third broadside into the Spaniard. This merciless barrage finished the matter altogether. The Spanish bark's rig was gone, her fore-topmast hanging brokenly, the main a mere stump, the mizen leaning crazily, nothing left aloft but the rags of her sails. Her decks showed jagged-edged holes in the upper works and smoke poured from the waist. She had no colours left flying to be hauled down. Across the water came the sound of a lusty cheer from the pirate schooner's crowded decks.

'Thank you for that, Bess Wellcome,' I croaked under my breath. With the last of my strength, I shoved the tiller-bar to leeward and lashed it to the rail. The *Diamond* heaved herself reluctantly into irons.

'Boys, pin the staysail aback,' I managed to call out. 'Let the main boom fly.'

They moved dreamily after the shock of battle, as if half asleep, but the work was done. The *Diamond* settled herself in the water, hove to and lying easy. Meanwhile, the victorious *Goodenough*, with armed men lining her rails, crashed brutally alongside the Spanish vessel. Driving hefty boarding axes into her upperworks, they pinned the vessels together and swarmed across with cutlasses and pistols and whoops of triumph.

I lowered a sea-bucket over the side and splashed water on Adam's face, dropping on one knee to bathe the wound. He groaned and opened his eyes. There was a rounded, lumpy bruise rising from his skull-bone.

'I shall fight,' he said haltingly, his head ranging from side to side.

'It's over, Adam – the fight's done,' I told him.

He made a futile effort to rise up. 'The Navy . . . all of us, fight for the Navy, lads . . .'

'Adam, you're safe,' I said. 'Safe aboard the *Diamond*. Not the Navy.'

I left him sitting there dazed and set off for the waist but after a few steps, my leg collapsed. Gingerly, I dragged up the loose slops to expose a two-inch wound where either a musket ball or a wood splinter had ripped back the flesh. It was clean and not deep, but the thigh felt as though it had been beaten with a plank. I tore my shirt apart, bound the gash tight and limped off forward.

The bloodied remains of Bart lay spread across the weather-deck in a gruesome parody of a human figure. I hobbled past, my stomach urging. Mister Wrack's lamentations had grown louder, but he was half-sitting, hands clasping his belly, eyeballs distended in pain. At each gasping breath, he released a long and mournful howl.

'Can you speak, Will?' I said. 'Where's the hurt?'

'Ribs,' he gurgled. 'Winded.'

'The gun drove back, sir,' explained Hap, wide-eyed.

The two-pounder sat at a lopsided angle to its gunport and by the carriage lay the chain which had parted, allowing the piece to leap back as it was fired. With one smashed carriage and one broken tackle, we had been left with just two guns and no chance unaided against the Spaniard.

'Make him as comfortable as you can, Hap,' I said. 'Fetch palliasses up here and spare slops to put behind his head. Do the same for Adam. I'll get sweet-water and beer.'

Hap ran off at once, but Jan stood transfixed. He was staring at the gory remnants of Bart's pulped body. I got up, balancing against the rail to support my leg, and put my arm around him. At once he fell on to my shoulder, sobbing convulsively at seeing the life blown out of his friend, warm flesh and blood turned to butcher's meat. I held him for a few brief moments. He had seen what no man, let alone a mere boy, should ever witness.

Half a glass later, we paid off and sailed slowly up to the *Goodenough*.

After the boarding, victor and vanquished had stood off, lying easy a few boat lengths apart. The Spanish trader's decks were alive with pirates from the schooner, the rails lined with captive and bound Dagoes. Steering up to weather of the *Goodenough* to heave to, I saw, standing upright on the quarter, Captain Wellcome in parley with the Spanish vessel's defeated master.

Spotting the *Diamond*, she broke off and called across. 'Are you well and whole?'

'One dead,' I replied. 'Some wounds, but we shall live. What of you?'

'Plenty of dead, but only the enemy,' came her cry. 'You've taken a beating, by the looks. Haul up to Tyrrell's Isle. At the northwest corner there's a broad bay with a high rock tower on the north hand and a low islet to the south. It's a safe enough place and there's a strand for beaching – this Spanish scrapwood is sinking. Be there tonight!'

We got slowly under way and set our course for Tyrrell. Glancing back, I saw Bess Wellcome marching about the quarter-deck, tall and commanding, her back straight and her head high, the blonde locks cascading down to her shoulders. She looked a magnificent beast of prey, glorying in victory, revelling in the battle won.

Some hours before dusk, when we had found Tyrrell's Isle and were a league off in deep water, I brought the schooner to. Jan and Hap balanced a hefty bundle at the rail's edge. Like all free seamen, eschewing any priestly sentiment I spoke to comfort the living, saying that no life was ever spent in vain. Remembering words of my father's, I told the *Diamond*'s company that the sea and the sky were the source and replenishment for all the elements and minerals that made humankind.

Then I said, 'Let him go.'

His friends allowed Bart's mortal remains to slide overboard, bound in spare slops that passed for a shroud, the shoulders and feet weighted with stone shot. We bowed our heads as a young man's corpse went to its grave amongst the fishes.

'Revenge, then,' said Captain Wellcome, not taking her eyes off me for an instant. 'That's your purpose.'

'Aye, revenge,' I lied.

It was night-time, and we sat together on the *Diamond*'s quarter-deck. Our two schooners were anchored off a curved beach bordering a wide, calm bay on the sheltered side of Tyrrell's Isle. Not long before sunset, the *Goodenough* had towed in her prize and run the stricken Spanish trader's bows hard on to the strand. The prisoners were put off, hands bound and feet shackled, and the victors fell on the trader like ravenous ants over a decomposing carcass, stripping her of every armour piece, all powder and shot, her dry stores, any fitting or bit of rig that was left.

Below decks, the *Diamond* had become a sick bay. Will Wrack lay in my cabin, with the hatches propped open to catch any cooling breath of air. His belly was a single dark and angry bruise, and at every breath he endured a stab of agony. Adam's head wound had unhinged his mind so far he thought himself a Navy midshipman again, and I ordered rest and food, with small beer and rum so that he slept as sound as a babe. When we had washed the boards clean and replaced the steerboard gun tackle's chain, I left Jan and Hap to tend them below. Shortly after nightfall, Bess Wellcome had rowed over.

She found me nursing my own wounded leg, and helped me salt and bind the gash with clean cloth. Then we laid aside our pistols and our suspicions and drank rum under the riding light, letting the day's noise of battle and bloodletting fade into a distant jangle. From the *Goodenough*'s decks rose discordant carousing and rummy songs.

'Aye, I'd like a revenge,' I was saying, 'on the man who took my bark, and I'm damm'd sure it's him who sank the *Doughty*. Macfarlane could tell me more if he was minded to.'

'As far as Robbie's concerned, the sooner someone gives that privateer a bloody nose the better.' She gave a ripe chuckle. 'Somehow, he can't see it's going to be you who does it.'

As I poured us generous fingers of sugar-rum, she took out a small clay, fingered tobacco into the bowl, lit it, and settled back to smoke. In the ghostly gloom and the still of the night, her pipe glowing and sparking, she puffed and exhaled contentedly, exuding the air of one completely at ease.

'Here's to the *Goodenough*,' I said, raising up my mug. 'We were all but done for. That five of us still live is a matter of your timely arrival and nothing else, Captain Wellcome.'

'By the Lord,' she laughed, 'can't we be Matthew and Bess?'

I smiled. 'To Bess, then.'

'Matthew,' she answered. Clinking our pewters together, we drank deeply. The lamplight illuminated her grin as she said, 'It's you I've got to thank. We were more than a league off and quite unsighted. We'd have missed the quarry altogether unless we'd heard the gunfire. You drew us down – and kept her busy till we got there.'

'For my part, I would have left her alone,' I grimaced.

She sat up and gave me a prod in the ribs. 'Matthew, we've got ourselves the prize of a lifetime.'

'Why, what does she carry?'

'She's in ballast – stones, old timbers, logs.'

I drank some rum, and waited while she relished keeping me in suspense. Then she giggled like a young woman, which, for all her mystery and her wild crew and her fighting, she very much was.

'Our Spanish friends,' she said, 'were on their way to Isla Margarita for trading. So instead of being loaded up with blankets and cloths, tools and knives, even cloth stuffs and animal skins – all the poor goods they bring back from there –

all they carried was the means to buy.' The pipe-bowl glowed red as she drew hard, sucking lustily at the smoke. 'Just the means to make purchases for trade, Matthew. Thousands and thousands of pieces – dubloons, eights, dollars, marks. Gold, silver, even pearls. Maybe three thousand in dollars.' She flashed the rings on her fingers – rubies and emeralds. Her ears were pierced with diamond studs, and her man's weskit was fringed with a row of pearls at the collar. 'Think of the jewels I shall purchase now!'

'Bess,' I said, 'for all the golden prize money in the world, I'd sooner have that poor fellow Bart still living.'

She stopped pulling on the clay and stared at me. 'He's the dead one? That little turnaround tyke? Good riddance.'

'You're too hard,' I protested. 'He showed himself a good, eager fellow.'

'Eager for a man's lust,' grinned Bess. 'Matthew, he's taken more pricks than a sailmaker's sewing palm. The fellows were forever fighting over him.'

Feeling a touch foolish, I slugged back a large shot of sugar-rum. Into my mind's eye had flashed a memory from aboard the *Cornelius* – a row of smiling, youthful faces, the sea-boys, bright and alive, brought from Amsterdam, and the looks that passed between them and the older men. It was the seaman's way, after all, when there was not a woman to turn to.

Bess's tone softened. 'You fought well today. And more than that, you kept hold of your bark back there in Culpepper Pool. It's not always that free sailors come to agreement without a fight.'

She brought out a small knotted hessian bag and held it up. I caught the clink of metal as it swung.

'A hundred silver dollars, Matthew,' she said, 'one thirtieth share of the prize money. A divvy for helping secure the prize.'

So here was prize money, the very thing – or rather its lack – that had brought me to grief on the *Cornelius*.

'It'll speed you on your chase,' she smiled, and the coins jingled softly in the dangling bag.

I reached out and grasped it, letting it rest in my palm a moment to judge its bulk, then tucked it inside my briches, saying, 'Aye, a privateer never refuses silver. And it shall help us in our cause.'

Her eyes glistened under the starlight. 'Will you tell me that cause, Matthew?'

I refilled our mugs, the thick brown sugar-rum gurgling into the pewters. An unmistakable feeling of friendship had sprung up between us. Leaning back, letting the liquor slide warmly down my throat, I told her something about the Navigation and how I had hoped to win our pardon.

'I suppose it seems a nothing to you,' I said, 'the Navigation and all of that. Plying between the islands, never far from land, all these sights and calculations are no use to you, are they?'

'O no,' she said vehemently, her jewellery flashing, 'we often get a latitude from the sun or Polaris. It's one of the secrets of my success. I can dip out of sight to leeward of the Antilles chain and still find my way back to land. Keeps us out of sight of patrols. My father swore by it, and taught me how to use the cross-staff and reckon the sight.' She chuckled. 'It's a fine thing for a woman, isn't it, skippering such a schooner? The *Goodenough* was his, and now she's mine. My father was a privateer turned pirate because, he used to say, it's better to stay beyond any nation's law or flag. They change their rules and alliances and start wars all too often for a poor mortal seaman to keep pace with.'

'Aye, I've been caught by it myself,' I grinned sheepishly.

'What's your story, Matt?' she said. 'Are you off the big ships? A one-time Navy man?'

All at once a longing washed over me to unburden myself and share a few secret thoughts. 'I hardly know you, Bess,' I said, 'yet somehow I believe we can trust each other. Can I tell you how I came to leave England?'

The white oval of her face was turned full on me. 'England,' she repeated with a sigh, savouring the word. 'I've never been, but – perhaps one day. Tell me everything.'

I settled comfortably and recounted my boyhood days in Whitby, how I grew up aboard the colliers that plied between there and the Tyne, my long nights of study to learn the Navigation, and the gale-ridden day I was picked up, near drowned, by the *Cornelius*. I told her of my adventures aboard that fastest of flyers until, at the last, I came to Filligrew, Spatchears' tables and the problem of the code, and my whetted desire for a pardon.

Whether it was the rum, or the easy conversation, or the still beauty of the moonlit night after the terror and blood of battle, I cannot say, but we found ourselves sitting close, murmuring together and sharing quiet thoughts. Then our limbs touched, her leg warm against mine. I quite forgot the aching wound and faced her with a smile. When our lips met, it felt as though we had taken each other by the hand and leapt off the heights, a plunge we could not retreat from, a delicious and secret adventure in which we risked everything. A-tingle, I opened her shirt and spread back the cloth folds, hungry for the rounded flesh. Her hand found my briches, groping for the urgent shape beneath. We could not quickly enough fling off our confining clothes and when we were naked we savoured everything we saw and touched, and drank in the newness of each other's bodies. The smoothness of her skin tantalised my senses, for I was ravenous from the absence of a woman's caress. Her sighs and gasps as I stroked and explored each fold bespoke her own want of tenderness and feeling and pleasurable release.

There, on the quarter of the *Diamond* resting serene in that broad, quiet Tropick anchorage, the waters slapping tamely at the bark's sides, our naked skin bathed in moonlight, we made love, revelling in the sudden passion and the irresistibility of our coming together. And when at last we lay back, sated and aglow, and saw our two pistols lying where we had so carelessly cast them aside, handle to handle, barrel to barrel like two lovers, we laughed and kissed again at the oddness of it all.

After a long spell, silent and intimate, she said quietly, 'Matthew, shall I tell you what Robbie Macfarlane knows?'

16

POOR HOLDING

What a dispirited air this place displays, I thought, surveying the drear aspect of Cala Arena. It lay on Cuba Island, five days' fast downwind run from the Antilles, and presented a depressing view even for sailors eager to sight land. When we brought the *Diamond* past the headland and fetched slowly into the anchorate, we found no vessel riding in the bay, the harbour empty of barks, the roads deserted. Rather, there hung overall a palpable dread reminiscent of the clammy touch of a Whitby fog. My crew went about their tasks in an uncommon, monkish silence, making ready the bower, hauling down the canvas, tidying up the belays until, with just the *Diamond*'s big jibsail still drawing, we rounded up into the wind.

'Let go anchor,' I called. Even my own commands seemed muted in the oppressive silence.

Will Wrack, still sore though fit and able after resting on the run down from Tyrrell's Isle, tripped the pawls for the cable to run free. When the schooner settled back and the flukes had bitten soundly in almost twenty fathoms, an eerie tranquillity fell over the scene. The anchor cable graunched as the *Diamond* lifted to the slop and heave of the open bay, rolling and lollopping in a constant motion that rattled the lockers, sent haulyards slapping and the booms clattering. Each time the bark swung on the surge and snapped taut her cable, the hook threatened to relinquish its precarious grip amongst the broken shell and smooth rock of the sea's floor. It was poor holding for an anchor, yet it did not have to keep us here long. If nothing else, I felt certain of that.

That night at Tyrrell's Isle, Bess Wellcome told me what Robbie Macfarlane had refused to divulge. Before his boat the *Doughty* was sunk, he had gone aboard the privateer's flagship to treat. As I surmised, the commodore of the flota was Sir Thomas Filligrew.

I had listened, hardly breathing, as Bess told me how in the Great Cabin, Macfarlane encountered a young white woman, an English wench who was Filligrew's scribe, scratching out agreements in a neat hand on clean white parchment. The functionary was her father, a merchant. Passing back through the stern quarters by a cell, Robbie saw an ancient, desiccated fellow with a mad look in his eye, who wailed and pleaded not to be put ashore but to be taken back to England. Filligrew had laughed and said he was to become a landsman again, not to study his books but to be a planter of untamed acres on the Cuban shore.

Macfarlane had discovered that the flota sought a renegade called Matthew Loftus. Sir Thomas must have tortured poor Spatchears to elicit a confession that he had left the tables for me on the Witness Isles. Of course, after our encounter in Culpepper Pool, Robbie had harboured hopes of getting a reward from the privateer for my whereabouts.

Bess went on to relate that, not long before, her own *Goodenough* had hauled over a Porto Reeka trader bound for Venezuela loaded with salt-cod brought down from Newfoundland. All the coast, the traders said, knew and feared Filligrew's flota, which was headed for Cuba bent on raiding a Spanish plantation on the southern coast. The settlement was to the west of a great promontory known as Cabo San Francisco, beyond which lay a foul and disease-ridden land where the Dagoes had made their settlement.

Did Bess know that this news would break us apart? Perhaps.

At any rate, she listened sympathetically enough as I explained how Noah Spatchears held the key to the tables, and thus to our pardons. In all this, I never once mentioned Abigail's name, yet with every sentence of my story, her vision kept floating to the front of my mind. Within a day, with my crew barely recovered and our repairs incomplete, I left the *Goodenough* behind in Tyrrell's Bay and took the *Diamond* to sea.

It was five days' fast run downwind before the schooner closed the shore. Cuba Island, though in the hands of Spain, was subject to English, Dutch and French forays into the territory and attempts to settle its rich lands, and the channel between Jamaicka and the Cuban shore was commonly patrolled not only by Spanish warships but English cruzers too. We came upon a pair of native *canoas*, little vessels hewn from a single log, out fishing a league off the coast. Five dark men were aboard each one, and Will Wrack hailed them in rough Spanish. They told of a settlement beyond Cabo San Francisco attacked 'some Moons past' by a flota of three English sail. Many white Spanish had been killed and the remaining planters sent away, replaced by other Europeans – white men and women speaking English – along with a dozen slave Negroes. This was at a place called Cala Arena. We sailed on, rounding the headland of Cabo San Francisco until, not without trepidation, we had come upon the desolate bay of that name.

Now, raking the shoreside with my spy-glass, I saw nothing stir, no European people nor slaves, no animals nor carts, no movement nor any sign of life. No signal answered ours, no boat put off to offer exchange and commerce. A haze of blue woodsmoke hung above a straggle of low wooden huts ranged along the strand. Behind was a more substantial clapboard structure two storeys high, a works or manufactory of some sort. From the smell of sickly sweetness drifting from the land, I guessed it to be a sugar-cane press and molasses factory.

On the rooftop of the works was mounted a single swivel gun, a meagre enough show of defence. On rising ground further inshore, amongst cleared and planted ground, stood a white-painted brick house with a commanding prospect. And that, I was sure, would be the headquarters of the Jeffreys Plantation.

Yet otherwise, my mind was in turmoil. What would it be like seeing Abigail again? How would she receive me after all that had happened? In truth, I no longer knew whether I had come here for the astronomer's secret and the road to pardon, or another thing altogether. Did I seek something with a stronger pull, a yearning to rejoin my first love?

I sent down the launch ready to go ashore, leaving Jan and Hap on anchor watch, for Adam was still lost in his mind. Armed with cutlasses and two pistols each, and loading three long-muskets into the boat, Will Wrack and I set off warily to approach the landing-place. As the boat grazed the beach, it was plain our forebodings had been well founded.

On the foreshore we came upon the smouldering remains of a large native *canoa*. All around lay the ruins of its cargo – sacks of yams and herbs, clay pots and cloth bags, not plundered but smashed apart and destroyed on the spot. Then we stumbled nearby on a far more gruesome aftermath. Strewn along the littoral lay the bodies of a dozen men. They were natives, going by their olive hues and red-painted tattoos, come from along the coast to trade their wares. Each and every one had had his throat slit right around below the jawbone, half the neck cut clean through, the heads left hanging by the cords.

With growing revulsion, I backed away from the corpses and made to run up the hill towards the brick house. Mister Wrack held me back, counselling that we should beware lest the perpetrators of the savagery lurked close by. Holding our pistols and cutlasses, we moved carefully through the ruined village, house by house, hut by hut, fearful of coming unprepared upon further ghastly sights. It was not long before we unearthed a band of Negroes huddled in their cabins.

'Where are your masters – the Europeans?' I asked the slaves.

At first, frightened witless at the sight of us and our weapons, they were too terrified to speak, and showed the gaunt looks and yellowing eyes of sickness and poor vittles. When we encouraged them with kind words, they told us the plantation's owners, a merchant called Jeffreys and his daughter, had established themselves in the brick house, the Casa Blanca. But the planting had gone poorly, for the cane crop was sown in thin soil. The goats and mules had fallen sick. The kitchen garden had failed and no blacksmith had been landed to fire up the forge and repair implements. All in all, the plantation's prospects were meagre. Many of the English people, particularly the craftsmen and the chief planter, had boarded the first trading vessel to call in and had left for Jamaicka. Food became scarce and illness crept into the village, while the overseers spent their efforts on fortification before agriculture, forcing the Negroes to labour long into the night building ditches and ramparts. That sounded so typical, I thought bitterly, of Seth Jeffreys.

In the end, though, it was not the fever and starvation and despair stalking the fields and byways of Cala Arena that had done for it. A warlike tribe of Cuban savages, the Negroes said, had descended from the mountainous interior, a band of three or four hundred warriors armed with spears and arrows. They had arrived outside the palisades of the settlement and demanded that a Cuban native be brought forward to conduct a parley. They wanted their territory rid of the interlopers and enslavers – the bringers of disease, the stealers of fruit, the killers of game animals, the enclosers of land. If the settlers agreed to depart peaceably, every last man, woman and child would be spared. But there was no vessel to embark them, for the flota had sailed away, leaving Cala Arena unprotected.

The overseer, said the Negroes, condemning out of hand the very notion of treating with such barbarians, had fired the first shot, killing the savages' spokesman with a single musket ball to the head. At once, the Cubans attacked, throwing themselves carelessly at the palisades against such ragged fire as the white men could muster from behind their flimsy shelters. Overwhelming this puny resistance, the natives swarmed past the fortifications and marauded indiscriminately, murdering every living being they encountered, whether half caste or white, defenceless or armed to the teeth, wizened with age or mewling in a cot. They slaughtered the domestic animals too – the mules, goats and dogs transported from Europe or brought in from Jamaicka – intent on being rid forever of all white bloodlines, whether in man or beast. When the natives' *canoa* had beached, come to trade and all unaware of the carnage, the mountain tribesmen fell on them and cut their throats, saying that the fellows were traitors for giving succour to the oppressor.

The murderers passed over only the Africkan slaves, sparing them because they knew them not to be free souls but brought in chains from a far-off land across the sea.

Had all the whites been killed? I asked with growing trepidation. The Negroes nodded grimly. Heeding no further warning, I ran off up the hill, my pistols raised. Will Wrack caught me up and held back my headlong rush, insisting on a more watchful approach along the path towards the mansion. So we took stock and checked our weapons before moving stealthily towards the silent and brooding house. And there in the Casa Blanca, we encountered the most nightmarish scene of all.

First the silence, the absolute stillness that told us what the blacks had hinted at. Next, the stench that permeated the house, for each room – the floorboards themselves, the very walls – exuded a sickly odour of corruption. Then the low hum of a million feasting blowflies and crawling things. Finally, the sight that confronted my unwilling gaze, and that every night since invaded my sweating dreams.

With a single sweeping glance I took in a sorry heap of flesh and bone, little more than a pile of torn and crumpled clothes – the unmistakable merchanting garb of Mister Jeffreys' green long-coat, the once-white silken hose and the shiny patent buckle shoes now growing mouldy at the uppers. Hardly sensible in my

207

mind, catching sight of another human form nearby, cast down as if thrown there, I saw patches of untanned soft white skin, patently that of a young European woman. My reluctant eye fell on the mud-spattered frock and then, lying apart on those blood-stained boards, a familiar linen bonnet.

I escaped from that house at a run. The intolerable sights and smells all but deranged me. Down the twisting path, I threw myself on a rocky ledge high above the bay. Clawing at the ground, ripping plants and foliage with my bare hands, I cursed the sky and the sea and the bloody ground itself.

Will Wrack left me alone and I lay on the outcrop, sometimes muttering oaths or prayer-like utterances, at other times berating the Devil for his cruel designs. Now and again I held off my ranting and drew a few sobbing breaths, gazing out over the Cala in despair. If only I had stayed with her, abandoned the sea and gone ashore to work the plantation. If only we could have settled together, perhaps befriending the native peoples and letting them live amongst us and prosper. If only I had been there when the savagery came. If only, if only.

My eye fell on the bewitching little *Diamond*, riding non-chalantly at anchor, her beauteous lines a poignant contrast to the hideous butchery ashore. Suddenly, my consuming enchant-ment with ships and the sea bore down on me like an intolerable burden. How does a simple thing of wood and canvas and pitch and oakum clutch at a man's heart and catch his eye, at the cost of so much else? Abigail had seen clearly, like a lit beacon on a night hill-top, how I adored all too keenly a splashing stem, a spread of tall canvas, a prosperous breeze and the open sea. I hung my head. Perhaps we had always been destined, the sailor and his sweetheart, to drift apart like flotsam caught in a current. Now that separation never could be bridged, for here on this dismal shore, in a brief shock of blood and terror, all had ended.

There came a soft tread behind and a hand rested lightly on my shoulder. Will Wrack's tones were muted.

'They're ready to go in the ground, skipper.'

208

Heavily, I got up, saying, 'It was kind of you to spare me the worst.'

Together, we walked up to the rising land behind the house, Will's hand on my shoulder. Grimly, we did our best to consign the shrouded bodies of Abigail and Mister Jeffreys to their God, Will Wrack mumbling half-forgotten phrases over the freshly turned earth. We marked the graves with rough wooden crosses, then solemnly turned to go down the hill, heading for the strand, passing by the house of death with our eyes averted.

Mister Wrack halted and pressed a hand on my arm. 'What was that noise?'

'I heard nothing. Let's push on.'

'Wait – there it is. Sounds like chanting.' He raised his cutlass. 'Might be the savages come back for more white blood.'

I listened hard. There came a distant rattling cough, as of a sick man heaving his very last breath.

'Or some poor cove who needs help,' I said, raising my pistol.

The two of us struck out for the house, moving close under its brick sidewalls. From somewhere behind the main structure, I heard the noise again. Creeping round to the mansion's rear, we found an arrangement of minor buildings, sheds and storehouses built of clapboard. From one came the faintest murmuring, with no more weight in it than a breeze through the treetops. Gingerly, I got down on my haunches and crept over to peer in through the paneless window. On a crude bed lay the husk of a human figure, barely impressing the palliasse, so weightless did he seem. His hands were clasped on his chest and, except for the lips, he lay unmoving on a filthy straw bed, a shrunken old man near death.

'Four, seven, eight, two,' came the whispered words, followed by a drawn breath. 'And the next integer, two decimal nought nought four, thus: eight and five and three –'

I ran quickly inside and approached the deathbed, softly laying a hand on the bony shoulder. The counting ceased and a pair of sunken eyes turned on me for a passing moment. Then the numbers began again.

'I must count, and reckon, and calculate – *nil desperandum*!' His mutterings were interspersed with wheezing, painful draws. 'Nought decimal two, six –'

I lightly took hold of his wrist. It was as thin as a kindling stick and when I lifted him – the sole European survivor of the massacre at Cala Arena – he weighed no more than a half-bag of corn.

A hand clutched bird-like at my shirt. 'England – home to England?' he croaked.

'Aye, we shall get you to England, Observator Spatchears,' I said, and at once the shivering, frail body relaxed.

His life hangs on no more than the threads of a whipping twine, I thought, and when he expires his secrets die with him. I bent to whisper a question into the colourless dry shell of his ear. His eyes were closed and his body utterly still. Like a baby, cradled in my arms, he had dropped instantly asleep. Will Wrack took up his legs and we set off, bearing his reedy frame out of the house and down the hill to our launch.

Back aboard the *Diamond*, I made old Noah half comfortable in a bunk below and ordered the anchor up at once. It took all five able-bodied men – Will, Jan, Hap, Adam and me – to haul the bower and its cable from those deep, languid waters. We worked on in silence until the dripping anchor broke surface. Even then in the lifeless still of the late afternoon, the schooner seemed reluctant to get under way, oblivious to the repugnance I felt for the place. My voice trembling in shock from what we had found there, I sent the three boys out in the launch to tow the *Diamond* seawards, then helped Mister Wrack sweat up the big staysail, hoist the main and set two jibs.

Evening clouds had gathered on the western horizon. When the sun ducked behind the hills, the day's heat instantly diminished but still the sails hung slack. Then a breath of wind crept silently from the sweltering shore, and the staysail shivered like an old sleeper wakening from a doze.

'Wind coming,' I called to the tow as the *Diamond* picked up way.

The land breeze strengthened, shaking and rattling the loose folds of the staysail. The canvas bellied for an instant, went limp, then swept upwards and outwards until the sheet snapped taut and the sail bulged full of wind. The *Diamond* heeled, the tiller-bar trembled in my hand and the schooner answered her helm, slowly spinning out a turbid wake. She crawled across the pool of melancholy that was Cala Arena and at last began to haul clear.

'Ahoy! Hold on there!' came a far-off hail.

A boat was approaching, though more than a cable distant. The oarsmen were pulling like swimmers chased by a shark. I snatched up the spy-glass and brought it to bear, seeing two white Europeans, an old man and a boy together, waving agitatedly.

All at once I cried, 'Haul over, lads – heave her to!'

The *Diamond* slowed to let the rowing boat pull alongside. With shaking hands, I reached over before anyone else to grasp a gnarled wrist, hauling the old fellow aboard. Quick as a flash, the youngster leapt up after him and there they were, standing on the deck. I pulled them to me and hugged them like the long lost friends they were.

'By Mary's blood, captain, I thought you must be dead,' breathed Eli Savary. He was skinny and hollow-cheeked, on the edge of starvation.

'We only saw it was you at the very last minute,' said the Dutch boy, Gaspar Rittel, panting from the exertion of their desperate rowing.

'But how do you come to be here?' I said, smiling stupidly, aware of the crack in my voice. 'How did you escape the slaughter?'

'We refused to do Filligrew's bidding,' Eli explained, 'so he put us off with the planters, though not before he'd had us lashed. Between him and them unChristian savages ashore, we were dam' near done for.' He performed his trick of gobbing spittle in an arc high enough to clear the rail while barely moving his head. 'Mister Jeffreys sent us working one day at the palisades beyond the far field, and we never went back. Been hiding ever since, captain, living rough in the bush for weeks past.'

'We came back once looking for scraps of food, sir,' put in Gaspar, 'but all we found was bodies, so we ran away again. We were afraid when the schooner came in, then we saw it was you coming down the hill from the big house.'

Eli was busily casting his seaman's eye over the *Diamond*'s decks.

'You've come upon a good little ship here, captain,' he said. 'All she needs is a bit of care and toil. Soon as you give us a bowl of broth to fill our bellies, I shall set these boys to work and bring her up to Dartmouth trim.' Getting no response from me, he paused. 'Captain Matthew? Sir?'

Something had happened to the workings of my jaw muscles. They refused to respond. I grasped the old salt's hand and would not let it go. He chuckled, embarrassed, looking round at the other fellows, and I fell on his shoulder.

Bless his heart, Will Wrack quietly gave the orders in my place.

'Sheet in and let's steer away to sea, fellows,' he said. 'We're leaving this place.'

At last relinquishing my hold on Eli, I let him go off to help get the *Diamond* under way. At the rail, clutching the warm smooth wood, staring vacantly seaward, I stood silently watching the land fall astern. In minutes, the Tropick night descended, wrapping the sea in darkness and extinguishing all sign of Cala Arena.

In the *Diamond*'s stifling cabin, I put fresh manjoes in a wooden dish and offered Noah small beer to sip. He had revived enough to become aware of his new surroundings and greedily drew the liquid into his mouth, some slopping over the rim as the schooner moved along in a lively sea.

'Am I on a ship?' he croaked. 'Are we bound for England?'

'First, Observator Spatchears, we must get you well and whole,' I told him.

He stretched out a skinny hand and rested it on mine. 'Is it the young Navigator?'

'Aye. Remember how we talked all those nights? The Longitude, the predictions, the Royal Society, the Greenwich Observatory?'

'Take me home to England! Home, home, home!' He fell into a hacking cough, chest gurgling as he drew hard for air.

'Calm yourself, sir. You shall go home, I promise.'

He looked startled. 'But I must see the conjunction! The arc of the orbits!' he babbled. 'The trajectories! The calculations!'

'Rest easy, Mister Spatchears,' I soothed. His suffering at Cala Arena must have further enfeebled an already damaged mind, for the infernal numbers and strange ranting plagued him worse than ever.

'Early in the third month, the fifth of the ides,' he raved. 'How shall I know the truth? Not the fourth and the sixth, but the third and the fifth.'

Disheartened, I went up on deck, wondering how we would find the code, or even if it existed, or indeed whether there was any hope the old lunatick would live long enough to divulge anything at all.

It was the pitch of night, and we coasted west a league or two off the Cuban shore, running with a warm, soft wind at our backs. Eli, champing on a plug that Will had lent him, was steering.

'I'm sorely worried about that young Mister Pyne, captain,' he said, nodding towards the foc'sle where Adam stood, wraith-like and motionless. 'Never even recognised Gaspar and me! First imagines he's aboard a Navy warship, then all at once he's a babe crying for his mother's nipple.'

I sighed, and went up forward. When I touched him on the shoulder, Adam turned with a start.

'The officers shall call the roll at noon watch,' he said in clipped tones. 'Then it's gunnery practice.' Suddenly, his face crumpled, like a child's, and he wailed, 'Today at school, I could not learn my alphabet. The master beat me.'

He was lost, wandering in a world of his own. I patted his hand, offering calm words, and when he spoke again he sounded more like himself.

'Sir, there's something troubling me.' He frowned. 'My name, sir. Adam, yes, but my family name – I don't know it.'

'Why, my dear boy, your name is Pyne – Adam Pyne, private seaman and Navigator of the schooner *Diamond*.'

Still he said nothing, so I tried to revive his damaged memory.

'You once were Midshipman Adam Pyne of the warship *Success*, a two-decked fifty gunner of the King's Navy.'

At once he straightened, standing stiffly, his countenance fixed and staring. 'Aye aye, sir,' he said, heels snapping together. Up came the right hand towards his brow in a Naval salute. 'Midshipman Adam Pyne, of the *Success*, reporting for duty, sir.'

I took his hand down. 'No need for such forms any longer, Mister Pyne.'

'Ready to take the next watch, sir,' he said, as if he had not heard. He lifted up his head, put his shoulders back for the first time since his wounding in the Spanish action, and marched off.

17

Native Wit

It was the second morning of our coasting along the Cuban shore when we sighted the fishing *canoas*, eight or ten foot in length. Each carried a pair of fellows, their red-painted bodies strong-muscled and their skins two shades lighter than the Saint Lucy peoples.

Eli gave me a worried glance. 'They'll likely kill us and eat our hearts,' he said, 'and fix our heads on poles to dance around.'

'These are not the same people who did the slaughter at Cala Arena,' I reminded him. 'And Observator Spatchears needs medicine and succour. He's near death.'

I gave the order to haul sheets and close the natives, whereupon they instantly made off for the shore in a fury of splashing paddles. Will Wrack hailed them in Spanish but they stroked on. When he tried patwah, they eased up and turned their *canoas*. They seemed to recognise a handful of words, then their natural curiosity drew them in. After further gestures and signals, they understood we had a sick man aboard and wanted medicines and herbs, and would give coin or stores in return. They pulled into a huddle.

'What do they say, Mister Wrack?' I said anxiously.

'I believe they want no coin,' he said, 'but we must show our sick man for scrutiny. White men have brought great ravages – poxes, red-spot and the like.'

'Let's bring up the poor old cove, then,' I said. We gingerly lifted Spatchears up the steps and laid him on the deck-boards in the waist. The chiefest of the fishermen brought his *canoa* alongside. Standing to see over the scuppers while his mate balanced the rocking craft, he peered at Noah's damp straw-tinted skin, then stretched out a leathery hand and stroked the old man's perspiring cheek. After this, he bade us bring the whole crew – Eli, Gaspar, Adam and the boys – to the rail. With steady brown eyes, he studied us each one in turn, the skin of our limbs, our hands and our hair, and gazed piercingly into our European faces.

Suddenly his face opened into a broad smile showing an astonishing row of straight white teeth, and he beckoned us to follow. We had survived the inquisition.

The fishermen paddled briskly away and the *Diamond* tramped along after. Quite suddenly the waters turned pale green either side of the schooner. We were being led into a maze of narrow channels at the edges of which appeared reefs of coral less than half a fathom beneath the surface. Even this far out, still a league clear of the land proper, the shoals stretched all round, invisible until we were upon them.

The passage twisted first this way, then the other. Glancing astern to survey our track, I saw our way back out was lost in a field of glinting ripples where sunlight made the waters unreadable. The *canoas* went at a great lick, drawing further and further ahead, until at length we closed a low headland and quite suddenly the native craft all disappeared. When we cleared the head minutes later, anxious not to lose sight, the sea was empty; every one of them had vanished.

The shore lay two cables distant. Though we scanned it for signs of life, there was nothing. It was low, rocky ground near the water's edge covered in bushy Tropick plants, rising behind into thickly vegetated foothills, then forming higher and higher slopes until in the far distance beyond rose a range of blue mountains. I raked the near view back and forth with the tube, seeing nothing stir, no sign of habitation, no indication of an entrance for a cove or lagoon. It was if the natives had been spirited away by the hand of gods in the sky, or clawed under the waves by baneful spirits from the deeps. They had drawn us in amongst the reefs and abandoned us with no hope of finding the passage out.

'Look!' cried Hap from his vantage high in the ratlines.

A single *canoa* was emerging from the background of the shore as if it were sliding out from the very rock itself. The fellows in it were so struck by the amusement of this game that they almost rolled their tippy vessel. They laughed and clapped their hands as we crept cautiously closer under jibsails. Getting up with them, we saw an impossibly narrow cleft, perfectly hidden from the seaward approach until a bark was hard upon it. With such a labyrinthine reef barrier covering the approaches, combined with the blind entrance, these natives might have dwelt here a thousand years undiscovered.

The channel could not be attempted under sail, so we hove to and tackled the launch over the side. The three boys pulled away with the towline while I conned the *Diamond* through the gap, Will and Eli sighting at the bow. We brought out long sweeps and poled the schooner off the sides until, after a cable of this work, the channel broadened and debouched into a broad clear pool where the air smelt fresh and the water clean. Apart from a patch of narrow strand, it was entirely circled by mangrove trees and dense vegetation behind, enclosing it like a secret hideaway.

A few fathoms down was a hard sand floor into which an anchor could firmly bite its flukes. The boys swung the *Diamond*'s bows round and over went our bower. I had them row out a kedge from the stern so that we were moored fore and aft, with the bark lying at an easy angle to the southeast trade-wind, and head on to the slight swell that lopped in from the sea.

Great excitement greeted our arrival. The whole village emerged from huts invisible amongst the foliage from all but the most discerning eye, set back from the white strand where many

217

canoas were drawn up. The crowd scampered up and down the beach shouting and waving. There was no distinction between the demeanour of the men and women, the maidens and youths, the children and the old folk – every one of them whooped and yelled and danced about. They were a fine figured people, not tall but straight-backed, both sexes little clothed, the men clean chinned but some with locks of straggling hair to their shoulders, the womenfolk smooth limbed and full breasted. Their skins were dark olive rather than black, all painted more or less with the red colour we had already seen, in patterns and intricate designs that in some instances covered their bodies entirely. These people were quite unlike the Caribs from Saint Lucy, lighter-skinned and not so well-made, but much less fearsome.

'They're welcoming us,' I said. 'Let's get ashore and have them see to the astronomer. Eli, you're in command.'

'Aye aye, sir,' he said.

Will and I clambered down into the launch and the boys lowered the old lunatick down. We stroked off to a chorus of voices from the shore, the villagers waving and beckoning. As we gained the strand many hands at once took up the astronomer's wasted body and bore him away towards the village. An elder tugged at my arm, jabbering.

'He's the *cacique*, the leader who'll take us to the healers,' Will said.

Passing into the village, where huts made of timbers and bark and grass and leaves stood in no particular order, we were bidden enter the largest, an oblong structure of twenty paces in length and ten in width. We stooped inside, finding a cool shaded place with wall openings that let the breeze rustle the palm frond roof and grass-hung sides. Ten or a dozen women and men squatted here, smoking leaf-rolls, mixing substances in clay pots, murmuring softly to each other. Its ambience was of calm, an equilibrium I had never sensed anywhere else.

Noah was laid on a straw bed at the centre of a group of

women. Their hands fluttered over his body and one old crone with a deep-lined countenance encouraged him to sip from a shallow wooden bowl. I wondered whether any mere native treatments could save a man so close to his end.

At the elder's bidding, I sat down with Will, and the natives passed a calabash for us to drink. The milky liquid tasted so sour I choked at first, but it warmed my throat and I sipped again.

'Cassava,' said Will Wrack, smacking his lips after taking a mighty pull. 'Puts you at ease in company.'

Surrounded by friendly faces, we nodded and smiled to cover the gaps when language failed. An easy atmosphere reigned as Will's conversation with the *cacique* progressed, and the more I sipped the cassava the more a sense of peace and serenity washed over me.

I slipped into a sort of half doze, transported into a confused world of ever changing scenes both ashore and at sea, seeing great barks and smaller ones, now with guns firing, now quiet. Abigail's face floated past but to my anguish dissolved into the features of Mister Jeffreys. Soon I was lying with Bess under the moonlight, then we were sailing free in our schooners across the white-topped ocean swells. After a while I dreamed I was leader of a fierce tribe of Indians, who fell upon the shore and vanquished a lesser people, and we killed their men and boys and feasted on their privities to make us strong and potent. We took up their women and settled their lands and paid homage to their gods and ancestors, who bade us make peace instead of marauding in our war *canoes*. I learned that I was descended not from my father but from my mother, and that when I died the new leader would be not one of my own sons but a son of my sister's. The ancestors, I understood, said that though all things appeared to spring from the bursting forth of the seed of the plant, as in a man, in truth they burgeoned from the woman, the bosom of the earth that nurtured the roots.

For a long while, I basked in these visions and dreamy

sensations. Then the images faded and I blinked open my eyes. I was back in the native hut. My throat was dry and a dull drumbeat thudded in my skull.

'Water,' I croaked, and Will, laughing, handed me a coconut shell. I swallowed the liquid and held it out for more.

'I had a most fantastickal dream,' I said, coming back to my senses.

He grinned. 'Cassava's powerful stuff, Captain Matthew. I've been hearing the tribe's history and translating it for you.'

'Then what I dreamt is true?' I said, half disbelieving.

'How do I know what you dreamt?' chuckled Will.

Then I saw Noah. He was sitting up, quite alert, studying the hut with interest. Scrambling to my feet too quickly, I got a little dizzy, but went to his bedside.

'By the stars,' he murmured, 'am I in England?'

'Not yet, Observator Spatchears. Do you feel better?'

He passed fluttering hands over his nearly hairless skull, as if unsure it was still there. 'O *ita vero*, yes indeed. I do believe my mind is improved.'

The women moved silently away and I bent to touch his forehead. It was cool and dry. The hollow rattle of his chest had died to no more than a tremor. What miracle is this, I wondered? Can they have cured his fever in two hours, the same disease that kills Europeans in their droves? Mister Wrack came over to peer into the bowl Noah had drunk from and, sniffing it and inhaling deeply, gave voice to my own half-formed thought.

'My, what I'd give for the recipe of this medication. We could sell it for a thousand guineas.'

A girl trod softly up and put her hand on the bowl, gazing at Will. When he relinquished his hold, she slipped away to rejoin her sisters and aunts.

'It strikes me they're peaceable enough until the white man tries to take their secrets,' I said. 'Why should we steal the fruit of all their learning? We should recompense them for saving this man's life.'

The old astronomer, becoming more bright-eyed, was struggling to speak.

'The tables – my lunar and stellar predictions.' He grasped my hand. 'I secreted them. When you were marooned – at the Witness Isles.'

'I've got them,' I said. Was he well enough yet to give any rational answers? I bent over and said, 'Sir, we worked out the riddle's meaning. There's a code of some kind, isn't there?'

The astronomer's eyes narrowed. 'What is your intention with the works?'

'I want to see them published by the Royal Society, as you wish. That's why we came after you.'

He smiled faintly, his eyes a touch watery.

'And is there a code, Mister Spatchears?'

'Most certainly. I protected the tables by falsifying the numbers.'

'Thank the Lord,' I breathed in relief. 'Now, sir, where is it – the code?'

He closed his eyes. 'Filligrew has the copy of it.'

Aghast, I put my head in my hands. Dammit, I should have known.

'Why?' I muttered. 'Why did you leave the code with him? Why secrete the tables without the code?'

'I could not retrieve it,' wailed Noah, chest wheezing.

'We've run half across the Caribbee,' said Will unhappily, 'only to find you haven't got the damm'd thing.'

'O, please listen,' said the astronomer, distressed. 'You see, the commodore has the tables.'

I raised my eyes to heaven. 'No, no, Observator Spatchears, I have the tables.' It seemed my whole plan was crumbling, lost to the incoherent ramblings of this ailing madman. 'And since you've just said he's got the code, it's a stalemate.'

'The other tables. I meant the other tables.'

A numbing shock went through my veins. I gripped his arm. 'What other tables?'

221

'The second copy,' whispered the astronomer. He put his hands up to his temples and rubbed them. 'Aboard the *Prometheus*.'

What confusion was this? My head spun. It was a crushing enough blow to learn that Filligrew had the code all along. Now it turned out he had a second copy of the tables too. What was left?

I stood up, reeling from the cassava and the heat. The women were smiling shyly and giggling in the corner, and a few native men sat contentedly nearby, nodding and laughing in my direction. Wordlessly, I took a few shaky steps to reach the entrance. There was a touch of breeze outside, and I gratefully drank in breath after breath of the languidly moving air until I revived a little and my head cleared. Then I strode back into the hut.

Noah was sitting up, gazing with interest at his surroundings. The rapidity of his recovery was almost beyond comprehension, but so was the mystery locked inside that ancient, rambling mind.

'Observator Spatchears,' I said sternly, 'you say Filligrew has the code and another set of the same tables. How has all this come about? And if it's true, why then is he chasing me?'

'O please, Captain Loftus,' wailed Spatchears, 'do allow me to explain. I promise to keep hold of my reason.'

As the astronomer began his story, around us the sounds of the villagers going about their daily tasks receded into a background murmur against the turmoil in my mind. I forced myself to pay attention as he meandered through his tale, pausing once in a while to let his chest clear and the breath come easy again.

At length, and with much digression and pointless detail, he related how he had laboured at the Greenwich Observatory to have made in secret, unknown to John Flamsteed, the Astronomer Royal, or anyone but the lonely clerk he bribed for the task, two identical fair copies of the tables scribed up from his notes, after which he had burnt every scrap and jot of his original observations and other writings. It was a necessary secrecy, he explained, for many men including eminent gentlemen of distinction and courtly provenance coveted the works and sought to spirit them away from Greenwich for their own purposes; while others, Flamsteed included, would refuse to publish them at all and thus keep the advances hidden from mankind. As a further measure to disbar those of wrong intent, he had worked long into the night for a year to devise a system of errors solvable only by a key or code of great complexity. Thus, whoever got hold of the tables without authority would find the predictions useless and unworkable without the correct solution.

Then Spatchears spoke of his voyage to the Caribbean and how he had proved his predictions worked in the relevant latitudes. He had brought to the West Indies both copies of the tables in case one should be lost. But Filligrew had seized them and then, to the astronomer's consternation, discovered the code too. Old Noah managed to retrieve one copy of the tables, which he put in the box for the Witness Isles, but he could not find the code. For obvious reasons, the solutions and the tables had always to be kept apart. Filligrew had therefore secreted them separately and he – Spatchears – had been unable to find the code's whereabouts.

At last, he sat back, fidgeting, brows fretting, eyes roving, nervously fiddling with his garments. '*Mea culpa, mea culpa,*' he wailed. 'I have led you along a pointless path. I intended to leave you the code along with the tables, but I could not.'

'Wait,' I said, 'you just said the solutions were always kept apart from the tables. Solutions, plural?'

He became instantly agitated. 'Did I say that? O, yes – the solutions.'

I leant across. 'Do you mean that, like the tables,' I said, enunciating very carefully, 'you had more than one copy of the code made?'

'No, by all the precessions, not that!' he cried, burying his head in his palms. 'No, no, no, you can't have it.'

I gently lifted his hands away to reveal his lined old features distorted in distress. 'Observator Spatchears, is there another code?'

Exquisitely discomfited still, he nodded. Thank the stars for that! Now at least there was a chance. I patted his hand encouragingly.

'So where is it? Have you got it with you?'

'Woe, woe,' he trembled, hands flapping, 'I have nothing, nothing at all. I might as well be a monk.'

He moaned and cried long and loud, as if again on the brink of tipping into incoherence. When he calmed and his breath came regularly at last, he explained that fearing thievery or loss, or treachery at Greenwich, he had decided it was too dangerous to get his scribe to write down the second copy of the code.

'Then you wrote it down yourself?' I asked patiently.

'Not at all.' He sounded almost affronted, as if it were beneath him. Then he said very softly, 'No one wrote it down.'

Frustrated, I cried, 'How can there be a second copy if no one wrote it down?' Even as I said it, a ghastly notion entered my mind. Reaching out, I grasped his palm again. 'Then where is it, Observator? Where?'

His face was tortured. 'I committed it to memory. I learnt it by rote – *memoriter*.'

'You memorised it,' I said stupidly.

'Did I? Yes, so I did.' He nodded vigorously, close to tears.

I shut my eyes in despair. Here was a half-sensible ancient fellow, deranged after years of toil in a dark cell, unbalanced by his momentous adventure into the Tropicks, beaten at the hands of Filligrew and finally starved and enfeebled at Cala Arena. Sometimes he could barely remember his own name, or mine, or what had happened to him yesterday. The code was surely lost.

Then I thought back to when we had first met.

'Observator Spatchears,' I said slowly, 'when we were aboard the *Prometheus*, did you not recount and recite many numbers in your head?'

His reply was almost inaudible. 'Indeed, yes, I might have done. It helps my mind.'

224

'What were the numbers?'

He looked shifty. 'Is there more medicine?'

'In a moment,' I said, none too kindly. 'Was it the code that you recited?'

'The numbers are gone, quite gone.' There was a brief silence. 'I can recall nothing since my fevers, neither the numbers, nor their correct order.'

'Yet you once held the entire code in your head, committed to memory in every detail – each number, every integer, all the figures and logarithms?'

'In my head, my poor frail head. So long ago.' His eyelids were screwed tight shut, his breast rising and falling tremulously like a pigeon's.

I leaned close. 'How long is this code? What might be the extent of your task in remembering it?'

'Remembering the code *in toto*? O, impossible! Why, it must run to five and twenty pages folio. Thirty, perhaps. Numbers by legion, rows and columns, ranks and ranks of integers.' Then he whispered, 'The code must be exact, or it gives false predictions.' At once, his melancholy turned to indignation and he rounded on me. 'Young fellow, are you quite mad?'

I drew a long breath. 'Tell me, does Filligrew know about the existence of your memorised code?'

He shook his head. 'No, he does not.'

'So he put you ashore at Cala Arena thinking you were of no further use?'

Spatchears nodded. 'The commodore made much of my night ranting in the cell, claiming it disturbed his work and his sleep.'

'Indeed, I understand. Now, Observator Spatchears, listen carefully,' I said. 'As soon as you are fit enough, you must start work on remembering this code, every last number. I am sure you can do it.'

Spatchears' face was that of one who has seen a spectre. 'O declinations!' he cried. 'Integers and logarithmicks! My infinite numbers – four five seven and six!' Flecks of foam formed in the corners of his mouth. 'Magnitudes and variations – eight one six five!' His voice rose to a shriek. 'Jupiter's moonlets are multiple and Saturn's ring's a singularity! Venus is the second and Mars the fourth!'

'Medicine here,' I called, signalling for the native girl to bring the bowl. The old man sipped at the miraculous beverage until his equilibrium returned, but he was plainly exhausted. I sat down opposite, rocking on my haunches, staring at his quivering face and reduced body, wondering. Though stronger, he remained little more than a vestige clinging to the remnants of life. And in this faltering man's damaged memory was buried the code and all my hopes.

Later, resting in the torrid heat of the *Diamond*'s little cabin, with the rustle and slap of waves at her waterline and sunbeams cast by the windows floating across the white-painted walls as she chafed and twisted to her anchors, I lay listening to murmured chants coming from the bunk next door where we had settled the astronomer.

If the commodore had a set of both the tables and the code, then why seek me out for the second tables? Why not just sell them to the highest bidder, or deliver them to the Navy and get his reward in commissions? Then it occurred to me that in time of war with France, the man who brought the tables back to England claimed the glory. But if another volume – even one without the code – arrived in London first, Sir Thomas Filligrew's triumph would be greatly diminished. Hard on the heels of this thought, another notion struck home. If my volume reached London after Filligrew's, then it would be worth nothing – no reward of money, no glory.

It would not even be worth two common seamen's pardons.

'O *misera, miserae*. Captain Loftus, I beg you, it is the most wonderful chance.'

'There's not the time,' I insisted.

In the *Diamond*'s cramped day cabin, where the miniature

table was strewn with papers covered in his scribbles and jottings, Noah Spatchears' eyes gleamed with fervour. He no longer wheezed and hacked all day long, for his constitution was in the rudest health, all but matching the condition of his memory – *mens sana in corpore sano*, as he put it.

Safe in Tranquil Inlet – the natives had no name for their hidden lagoon so I had chosen one of my own – the astronomer had laboured long and diligently at his half-remembered code. Adam Pyne, trained in the Navigation and knowing something of Mathematicks too, slowly regained his wits enough to become Spatchears' valued scribe. Passing the cabin, I saw them bent over the work, the astronomer chanting numbers and Adam duly writing them down, then waiting as the old man pored over the written figures. On occasion Noah, angry with himself and his forgetful mind, scratched out a whole column but patient Adam, without so much as a sigh of regret, would dip his quill and begin again.

By degrees, column by column and integer by integer, the old astronomer laboriously reconstructed the greater part of his code until he declared that better than three quarters of the work was done. Though he found the effort harder and harder, and complained bitterly that the Tropick climate might yet do for him entirely, he was confident that in the end the code would be all but complete.

'After such work and sacrifice,' pleaded Observator Spatchears, 'can we not wait just a little longer?'

'I've explained the urgency. I must get you on your way to England before Filligrew can act.'

'Even though my observation of this forthcoming astronomickal event shall aid your cause and mine? To show the tables' immense powers?'

'I thought you'd already proved your tables,' I said sharply.

He gave me a haughty look. 'Young man, as with all else in celestial observation, a definitive, incontestable proof – *sine dubio* – is the best riposte to the scepticks.'

Leaning over to examine his papers, I said, 'Well, what exactly is this event?'

'An unusual transit,' he said quickly. 'Most fortuitous to find ourselves so near the correct Longitude, or what I believe to be the Longitude. This event is purely a matter of place and time, to see one of the Lord's most glorious works of all. By serendipity, we alone may observe the phenomenon in its full and proper glory, for the path of observation is narrow in the extreme. To predict it correctly, with the necessary exactitude of time and place, would make a most emphatic demonstration, such that would dish the qualms of those disbelieving Fellows and Observators. Why, not even John Flamsteed himself could fail to acknowledge it.'

'But what transit is this?' I insisted.

Scarely able to get the words out in his excitement, the old man explained the event in all its astronomickal detail. As he spoke, not only the wonder of it but its full import stirred my mind, and I longed to witness it. But was there the time?

'When precisely do you predict the event to take place?' I demanded.

'The sixth ide of the month, the sixth of nones.'

'What day of the month is that, for a common seaman?'

'O dear, habit, habit, habit. The Royal Observatory goes by the ecclesiastickal calendar, and I still fall into it. The sixth ide of November is, let me see – the eighth day of that month by the Julian calendar.' Bubbling with enthusiasm, he added, 'That is just one week hence!'

'So you have remembered enough of the code to make such a prediction?' I asked.

'For the transit, certainly,' he said eagerly, then made a thoughtful pause. 'For the Navigation at sea, not quite. Not yet. But I shall, I shall.'

'Then I suggest you devote yourself to that,' I told him. 'If you've got most of the code, then you're going home to England at once. As you're well, we shall set sail for Negril Cove on

228

Jamaicka's western point. The packet ship for England passes there and I plan to stop her and put you aboard. She drops her Naval escort after clearing Port Royal, though I grant there may be English patrols about. Now listen, your voyage is not such an arduous affair. The packet continues northwest for the Yucatan Channel, then beats east with the Florida Current fair under her keel until she bears north along the treasure-ships route for –'

I trailed off. The astronomer was not listening to a word of it. His cheeks had drained of colour, as if the worst of his madness was about to return.

'When must we depart?' he whispered, his eyes wandering around the cabin.

'Tomorrow. At dawn.'

'I shall miss the event. Why so soon?'

'Because I want you in England before Filligrew.'

'Filligrew? O dear, O dear!' he said agitatedly.

I watched him closely. 'Observator Spatchears, are you sure you've told me everything?'

The old man's skin was pale, hanging slack and leathery from his cheekbones, and the veiny eyeballs started from the hollows of his haunted face. It was another seizure.

'Adam,' I called, 'bring his medicine – quick, lad.'

The astronomer took a draught, and revived a touch.

'Observator Spatchears, does it help to know,' I said gently, 'that Negril Cove is due south of here? On the very same Longitude?'

He brightened instantly. 'Perfect, perfect, *ne plus ultra* – the perfection of the universe,' he babbled, getting up and spinning merrily round. It made him giddy and I had to grab his arm before he fell. 'If we are there for a week, I shall still be able to make my observations! O perfection!'

'I hope we are not there a week,' I said, thinking of the dangers, and quitting the cabin to prepare the schooner for sea.

At first light, and with a *canoa* to guide us out through the reefs, we hauled our anchor and left Tranquil Inlet.

229

18

Out on a Limb

The dawn seemed an inordinately long time in coming. On the beach where he had erected his equipment, Noah Spatchears fiddled and fussed in the pitch dark. A few feet away, I sat on a rock warily scanning the deserted cove and, beyond, the black and empty sea-scape.

The *Diamond* was anchored in a far corner of Negril Cove, riding in deep water off the steep-to shore, hard by the only rising ground the landscape offered and hidden almost under the Tropick forest canopy itself. From there, she would be difficult if not impossible to spot from seaward. I had left the schooner in Mister Wrack's charge, with instructions to send the boys high into the shrouds at first light, straining to be first to spy the packet. If we missed her passing this time, it meant hiding from the English patrols another full month.

Away to the southwest, the low swamplands of the Great Morass stretched endlessly into the Jamaickan interior. For now we remained under the cloak of darkness, but in half a glass more the dawn sun would lift herself above the low-lying swamplands. At least, I thought, that shall give my lookouts, watching like sea-gannets spying a shoal of fish, a longer view beyond the bay and out to sea.

The cutter was drawn up on the foreshore where I had rowed us to our morning's work, for I had elected this day to relieve

Adam Pyne of his onerous duties as astronomer's assistant. Observator Spatchears, oblivious to the dangers of our tense wait for the packet and eager to continue observations in the days leading up to his predicted event, busily tended his apparatus. He glanced up at the still dark sky and studied the arrangements above. Venus rode low in the west, shining stronger than all the stars around her, but I caught him muttering about an azimuth.

'O dear, I anticipated catching the sun's rise,' he wheezed, 'to get a horizontal angle.'

I chuckled, for the ever-impractickal student of the skies had forgotten to check the chart to see if he would have a view of the sea horizon to the east.

'Not in a west-facing cove, sir,' I smiled. 'But look – the sea it's lightening a touch. You'll catch an excellent sight on Venus.'

Spatchears bent to the cross-staff and muttered numbers under his breath, noting down the altitudes of planet and stars. He had arranged a most impressive wooden scaffold to keep the cross-staff steady while he completed his observations – no use at sea, but an admirable notion for terrestrial sightings.

The sun burst from behind the land and bathed the scene in a golden light. I narrowed my eyes, watching the *Diamond* swing peacefully to her anchor. Any day, any hour, and the packet would pass offshore.

'Thirty two and a half – no, thirty three.' Observator Spatchears, scribbling and jotting furiously, fiddled with the pocket-clock – Will Wrack's less than perfectly reliable piece – and sighed, 'O for a Longitude.'

I caught a faint noise and sat up straight. 'Quiet – what was that?'

There it was again – the rumble and clank of an anchor chain. I squinted at the *Diamond* and saw two figures at the bows. What in blazes was Will at now? Anchoring practice?

A single pistol shot crackled across the width of the bay, echoing off the forest behind me. It was the signal for trouble –

two shots for the packet, one for danger. Scrambling up at once, I pelted down the foreshore, shoved the cutter off the sand, hurled myself bodily in and set to rowing, the astronomer and his works forgotten. I had pulled no more than a cable's distance when I saw the lads coming aft from heaving home the anchor and start hoisting sails.

An instinct made me spin round. At the southern headland there appeared a large bowsprit, jutting beyond the rocks. Then came jibsails, set and drawing. Into full view sailed a powerful schooner, cruising fast, and a deal bigger than the *Diamond*. She must have measured seventy feet on deck, and showed three open gun-ports along her topsides. High at her truck flew the Cross of Saint George. She was a six-gun Navy schooner, armed and ready to fight. With the ripest of oaths, I bent once more to the oars, urging myself to keep the strokes regular or lose my breath altogether.

The Navy schooner was no lumbering, unhandy warship weighted down by her armaments and stores and decorated carvings, barely able to sail on a reach without falling off, such as the English bark we had escaped off Saint Lucy. This new-comer was in the mould of our own vessel, or the *Goodenough*. Taking their cue from buccaneers and pirates, I reckoned, the Navy must have begun to commission handy and nimble barks rigged with enough fore-and-aft canvas to make them go a point to windward. With a longer run of waterline, this schooner had more natural speed than our *Diamond*. She was well-manned and could be sailed to her best ability. She had twice the firepower, and five times the men to load and aim the pieces. She had every advantage that our schooner lacked, bar the weather gauge.

Lord, I breathed, when she fires a signal shot, we must haul over and bluff our way out, otherwise we shall all be blown to Kingdom Come, every man jack of us. And what would be the point of that? When next I twisted to look, thinking the *Diamond* must reach the same conclusion, I saw that she had

232

come about. Far from shortening sail, preparing to heave to and admit defeat before such overwhelming odds, she carried all plain sail still. She had gone on the other tack, heading toward the Navy bark. And she had opened her gunports.

'Blast you, Wrack,' I panted aloud, 'what the Devil do you think you're about?'

The Navy bark cleared the headland and bore off downwind. With the snouts of her guns run out at the ports, she fetched into the bay, bearing down on her prey. The *Diamond*, heeling on larboard tack, creamed up from the opposite point of the compass. Foreseeing a single chance to alter the outcome of this unequal encounter, I threw myself at the oars with demented vigour.

The gap closed. Gasping for breath, I brought the boat between the two charging schooners and, keeping station with the oars, fixed one eye on the *Diamond* – on the anchor in its stow right forward at the catheads on the steerboard side – and the other on the advancing bows of the newcomer. Then I prayed that the gunners might hold their fire a few moments more. Like so many other last-minute submissions, this one too went unheard.

Cannon fire cracked across the width of the bay. Instinctively, I ducked as the ball whistled overhead, yet no gun smoke rose from the Navy bark. Idiots! It was the *Diamond* who had fired first, loosing off her forward swivel.

Then I saw another sail. Clearing the headland in stately, unhurried progress under topsails came a two-decked thirty gunner, all carved decorations at the beak and stern, men by the hundred crowding her decks, the guns ranged and ready. High at the truck of her main fluttered a three-yard English standard. Lord alive, a warship!

'Bring up!' I shouted, 'Will Wrack, I command you!'

They were too far off, out of earshot, and intent on the Navy schooner. Had they even seen the warship yet?

Crack – crack! The double shots, all but simultaneous, were

233

let off by the Navy gunners at the schooner's bow. I crouched low in the launch, ridiculously, for the balls flashed far overhead in an arc, one landing a boat's length off the *Diamond*'s steerboard side. To my utter disbelief, the second ball caught her amidships. A spray of splintered wood flew upwards from the deck. By its heavy thud, the shot must have struck full force, yet the little bark ploughed on with hardly a pause.

The *Diamond*'s bows forged ever closer. With a few urgent strokes, I threw my boat across the narrowing gap. Seeing me at last, Will Wrack tried to turn aside and pass. He knew the instant she slowed to pick me up, the schooner would be a sitting target, but now he was pinching her, sailing too close-winded. The *Diamond*'s jibsails luffed, snapping angrily, until he was forced to straighten his course to keep up speed.

The dark, planked topsides loomed overhead. With half a dozen strokes, I brought my boat right into the foamy crest under the schooner's hissing stem. The bow wave lifted the cutter's prow. I sprang for the great flukes of the bower and closed my hands around the anchor's rusted ironwork. I clung on, ignoring the smashing sound of the launch's frames and ribs splintering as the *Diamond*'s stem bore into it amidships. Flung bodily against the bows and winded by the jolt, I held on and swung my legs on to the anchor stock. With one heave I got over the cathead and fell panting on the foredeck. Through the scuppers, I saw the remains of the shattered rowing boat whirling past, waterlogged and sinking.

I stumbled into the waist, taking in a scene of broken rigging and splintered planks. Eli, Gaspar and the other lads were crouched by the guns, intent on their work.

'Heave to!' I panted. 'That's an order.'

Hearing my shout, they turned, startled. Aft at the tiller-bar, Mister Wrack stared ahead as if nothing in the world existed but the enemy. Then I saw the forward deck-piece had been bodily struck backwards from its chains and planted askew to the rail – or to where the rail should have been, for a great hole gaped there. There was already a man down, flat on the deck-boards as if flung there from the mainyard.

It was Hap. I dashed over. He lay face up, pale and limp, his body quite still. One arm was tucked behind his back, for he had fallen awkwardly. Reaching down to touch his neck, I felt the life still pumping, but my hand came away wettened, dark with his fresh blood. Where was the blood coming from? And then I saw he was not lying with an arm twisted under him. The limb was gone. It lay a foot or two away, crooked but unbloodied, torn off by the ball's passing.

'Blast you, Will Wrack,' I shouted. 'You'll have them all killed.'

Eli had a lighted linstock in his hand. I flung myself across the lurching deck and shouldered into him with full force, knocking him over. The fallen taper lay smoking on the deck-boards until in a fury I stamped it out. Then I lunged aft.

Will Wrack was transfixed, registering nothing until I was a yard away. He let go of the tiller and put up his guard but I struck his hands aside. The tiller-bar crashed against the stops and the *Diamond*, like a riderless horse, turned her bows into the wind and luffed. The noise was tremendous, the cracking and flogging of the sails mingled with confused shouts from the boys.

'Close up the ports!' I yelled, 'Stand away from the pieces — we're surrendering!'

Someone was grabbing my arm, wrenching for control of the tiller, shouting that we must never give in.

'Why did you fight, Will?' I shouted hoarsely, trying to fling him off. 'We can't win this!'

His grip remained tightly closed around mine on the tiller-bar, as if he still hoped to alter things.

'Don't give up now, Matthew,' he said, his eyes pleading. 'Don't let the Navy get her.'

'What are you so concerned for? Your precious bloody bark?' I snapped, 'You'll see us all dead at this rate.'

235

Angrily I shrugged him off. He fell back a pace, his mouth open as if starting to speak. What happened that next instant, I shall never properly know. Heat seared my eyeballs and a fiery wind whipped at the hair on my head. An overwhelming, deafening report dinned into my skull. The hot gale took the breath from me and a shower of warm wet stuff drenched my whole body. I was aware only of being down on my knees, still futilely gripping the bar one-handed, eyes tight closed, ears ringing, my mouth and nostrils clogged with something sticky, smelling of charred flesh.

I clung dizzily to the tiller, blinking through painful eyelids. From head to toe I was covered in crimson, flecked with sharp white splinters and small lumps of greyish matter. Had I been hit? Where was Will? He had been standing there on the quarter, only a pace away. Now he was nowhere to be seen.

I was spitting foul greasy lumps from my mouth, trying to say his name. Then it came upon me. I remembered an instant's vision of a man's body exploding, the torso swelling and bursting, an erupting spray of blood and shattered bone. It must have been a hot shot, an iron ball heated red, a direct hit. In the merest flash of time, it had shredded the man whole and sent his remains clean overboard into the sea. Of Will Wrack, I realised in horror, there was nothing substantial left.

The Navy schooner was a hundred feet away. My senses were in turmoil. Somehow, I had to strike or see every last one of us blown into boiled meat. The boys and Eli were still in the waist, hunkered down before their guns, blank faces staring at the mess covering the quarter-deck. I waved my arm in a side-to-side gesture, trying to say, it's over, it's all over.

Staggering across the quarter, shoving on the tiller-bar, slipping and sliding on the gore-wettened boards, I brought the *Diamond* round. She bore up, passed through the eye of the wind and slowed. Reaching blindly for the belays, I managed to fling off the main sheet, letting the boom swing loose until she lay quiet, hove to.

236

At last, coughing and retching, I drew breath and found my voice.

'Pin the jibsheets,' I said hoarsely. 'Let the staysail run free.'

Eli and the boys obeyed, moving slowly. An eerie silence had fallen. The guns no longer spoke. The Navy schooner was shortening sail and coming round, showing her broadside. For an instant, the three bulbous snouts were ranged across us displaying their open black mouths.

'Strike down the colours,' I ordered.

At once Jan ran to the haulyard and fumblingly pulled them down in a heap. Even so, another shot boomed out and a smoke cloud rose at the schooner's bows. Yet this time she had only fired a signal. Haul over, the Navy's shot commanded, and that is what we had just done.

Now the big English two-decker stood into the bay, not a cable off. Jack-tars crowded the yards bunting up the topsails, and more sailors swarmed out along the bowsprit handing the spritsails. On the weather-deck, soldiers lined her rails in their dozens, while others stood in the fore- and main-tops, forty, fifty or more muskets trained down upon us. A minute more and the *Diamond* would have been raked from stem to stern with musketry.

Wiping my eyes, I loped over to tend Hap. Ragged muscle and splintered bone hung from the upper part of the limb, so I bent down to tie off the stump. He moaned as I tightened a torn strip of shirt into a binding.

'You need a surgeon,' I muttered, 'to get you grogged and pitched.'

The loose arm lay two feet away, and next to it was a vicious piece of split wood, the amputator, its jagged end bloodied. Picking up the useless limb, queasy at the feel of the soft, still-warm skin and slack, yielding muscle, I flung it over the side. Let the sharks and piranhas have it. Hap had no further use of the thing.

The others were whole, but in shock. Eli rubbed his sore

shoulder, while Gaspar came to bend over Hap, helping him sit up.

Adam gazed fixedly at the approaching schooner, then said briskly, 'Sir, a detachment is ready to pipe the officers aboard.'

He raised up his arm to salute, but I pressed it down by his side, hissing, 'Don't say who you are, man!'

There came a hail. 'Ahoy, schooner,' called a voice through a speaking-tube. 'Have you struck?'

I went to the rail and called across that we had.

'Very well, then you are in the custody of His Majesty's Navy. Disarm and present yourselves for arrest.'

I told them we had a severely wounded man requiring attention. Back came the cry that we were to be boarded, there was a surgeon at the warship, and the injured would be attended to. A minute after, we laid down our arms before a horde of boarding marines.

Dimly, it dawned on me I had done the very thing poor Will Wrack had pleaded against with the last breath of his life. I had delivered his *Diamond*, and all her crew, into the hands of the English Navy.

19

JURY RIGGED

'Adam, Eli!' I called, but my throat was dry as parchment. Against the noise of the great Navy two-decker all around my cell, I heard only the drum of a hundred feet on the deck-boards above, the chantying of the sailors, the rap and rasp of their work at the rigging and the armaments, the busy ferrying of stores and the mustering calls for repast.

Lacking light and the sustenance of proper food, I was chained immobile in a closed box stretching only four feet by three. My elbow joints pressed painfully against the sides and the lid crushed down on my head. The heat was of such stifling fierceness that every breath was a hard won effort to live a minute more. I suffered an intense craving for water, relieved only by the drops of salt sweat dribbling over my lips or by dint of twisting my neck to lick the perspiration-soaked walls of the cage. Miserably, I sat in my own soil.

Letting my chin drop forward and the ache of my legs recede into numbness, gratefully I submitted to a semblance of sleep, a disjointed nightmare of half-remembered things in which time ran endlessly on towards a distant emptiness. Hearing shouted voices, sensing a blaze of light and an inrush of fresh, salt-scented sea air, I dismissed them as nothing but the ravages of delirium. The dream became a sweet relief in which my limbs were laid out straight, and cask-water was poured between my lips. I gulped, choked, then swallowed, marvelling that a fever could so faithfully impart the sensation of liquid bathing my swollen tongue and flowing down the gullet. Then I opened my eyes. It was no dream.

I lay stretched flat on wooden boards in a low tweendecks space where the large bright squares of open gunports let light flood in. A half circle of faces surrounded me, then someone swung his arms and a bucketful of seawater washed over my body. I sat up, gasping for air as the water ran down and soaked into my slops and shirt.

'He stinks,' said a voice. 'Look at the filth.'

'Smells like the flesh-rot, First Mate.'

'Strip him down, lads,' said the mate. 'He mustn't go up top like that.'

They laid me against a massive culverin's wheeled carriage and brought hot pottage and a piece of biscuit, which I consumed greedily but with difficulty owing to my cracked lips and dry throat. Within minutes, I was manhandled up a broad gangway which led on to the open weather-deck. The two-decker's spaces, unlike the cramped quarters of the *Diamond*, allowed the rapid passage of men in great numbers. Sailors ran about everywhere, carrying tools and spare rigging parts, toting buckets and cases, while commands were shouted in a continual barrage. Through this welter of confusion, I was marched to the break of the poop. On the broad raised quarter-deck, beneath a boomed awning of patched cloth slung from the lateen yard, stood a knot of uniformed officers, busy with their spy-glasses on the shore. We were anchored still in Negril Cove.

'Permission to bring the prisoner to the quarter-deck, sir,' called the mate.

The officers put down their tubes. How youthful they appeared – one was little more than a boy – but the captain was a fellow of perhaps my own age, dressed in full Naval rig-out, an attire hardly less elaborate than the Frenchman's aboard the *Joyeux* at Martinique. While the officers wore loose white shirts, baggy briches and leather slips on their feet, this captain had on a black tricorn hat, dark blue long-coat with tails and embroidered borders, weskit and plain shirt underneath, tight pantalons, silken hose and calf-boots. In the Tropick heat, it was an absurd display of peacockery.

'Bring him up here, First Mate,' said the captain.

He spoke in the smooth drawl of a gentleman. His face was pink and round. It was Captain Percy Gamble.

'Good God alive,' I burst out.

'Be silent,' snapped an officer. 'Await the captain's permission.'

'Well, well, Loftus,' Gamble said in languid tones. 'My presence here should hardly surprise you. War is such a boon to us Naval fellows for, like barks, we are soon commissioned back into service.' His companion officers chuckled obediently. 'Not long since, I called at Cala Arena, on patrol, you understand. A terrible scene of needless waste, such a pity the Navy was unable to protect the settlers from savage attacks. Yet we learnt from the Negroes that you had taken the astronomer away. Speak.'

'How did you know where to find us?' I muttered.

'It was clear that you might attempt to rendezvous with a packet. As there are only two routes from these unwholesome waters, it was no great effort to scour the coves and bays of this particular coast. It relieved the boredom of endless sea patrols. Speak.'

'What have you done with my men?' I demanded.

'The no-goods off your miserable bark are in custody. The astronomer, whom we found wandering on the beach, has descended into lunacy and is confined for his own sake. We are quite civilised, Loftus.' He paused, then drawled on, 'One of your fellows has been persuaded, after a little racking, to give us your story from the Witness Isles onward – refusing to obey a Navy command to stop, entering French waters, and consorting with pirates. Speak.'

'Release my men. They've done nothing.'

241

The lieutenant fidgeted with a parchment, catching Gamble's eye.

'Ah, indeed, Lieutenant Botterel,' said the captain, taking up the paper. 'One way or another, you all face punishment. Now hear this. You and your brother criminals are made captive by Captain Percy Gamble, of the sixth-rater, the *Bounteous*. My commission is to discover you and bring you to justice. You shall be sent to Port Royal to face trial before the Admiralty Court for the murder of a Naval officer and for stealing the English private vessel, the *Cornelius*, also known as the *Saskia* and presently commissioned into the Navy. Speak.'

'These charges are quite false,' I blurted. 'For a start, the *Cornelius* is Dutch owned. I shall defend myself vigorously in open court, and I demand that your ill-treatment of my men and myself ceases forthwith.'

'Ill-treatment?' said Gamble. 'When arrested, you made foolish demands and refused to subject yourself to Naval authority. Insubordination aboard the *Bounteous* is rewarded by twelve hours in the meat-box.' He nodded for me to speak.

'To Hell with your authority,' I retorted.

'You do nothing to aid your cause, Loftus. On the other hand, you might somewhat ameliorate matters by the return of the stolen valuables – an "appendix of numbers", I am given to understand.' All at once, the captain took a few steps across the quarter, twirled round and came back, his eyes small. 'Sir Thomas Filligrew seems very whetted about this item.'

Appendix? What did he mean? I was angrily suspicious. 'What's Filligrew's part in your coming here?' I demanded. 'Where is he now?'

He smiled charmlessly. 'The commodore is hard by Sint Maarten, watching for you on the other packet route. He was most astute in reckoning you might appear at one or the other. Speak.'

Something was going on that I could not fathom. I said incredulously, 'Is the Navy on the same mission as Sir Thomas?'

'That is hardly any business of yours. Now, I assume the item

242

is hidden aboard your bark – the *Diamond*, is it, Lieutenant Botterel? It would save a deal of trouble if you were promptly to reveal its whereabouts. Speak.'

I glanced under the sides of the awning and saw the little *Diamond* riding nearby. She was crawling with men carrying iron lever bars. Someone had given away much of our story – perhaps under torture – but no one could reveal the tables' hiding place. Only I and Will Wrack knew that.

'You've no right to wreck her,' I said. 'She's not commissioned into the King's Navy.'

'O, but she is, for I have just signed the papers. And it is the Queen's Navy now, Loftus. The King has died on his horse and the war is done in the name of Her Majesty Queen Anne. Speak.'

'What Filligrew's after is not aboard,' I said.

'What Sir Thomas is after, my dear man, is justice. This "appendix" business is a minor affair. The astronomer Spatchears – such an odd name – has admitted stealing the item in question and shall be taken to trial, if he lives. Speak.'

'I repeat, not one of my fellows has committed any crime.'

'Far from it, Mister Loftus. Your schooner has traded at Saint Lucy – legally French territory – and plied in for commerce at Fort de France, all during time of war.' Gamble clucked his tongue. 'The man William Wrack is, I understand, beyond reach of the law. However, at least two others of your men – an old man and a Dutch boy – are deserters from the *Prometheus*.'

'That's absurd. Eli and Gaspar were put off by –'

'Silence! And the other seamen of your band, answering to – what was it, Lieutenant?'

Botterel consulted his paper. 'Called themselves Jan and Hap, sir. No other names admitted.'

'One refused to be pressed, an offence in wartime, and when his sentence is done he shall serve as an ordinary seaman howsoever the Navy sees fit. The amputee is of no use to the service and is to be sent ashore after a flogging, with a bill for the surgeon's attentions. And the last one, Lieutenant?'

'Midshipman Adam Pyne, late of the *Success*, sir,' said Botterel briskly.

The poor, dear dimwit. In his befuddlement he must have given himself away, and by the sounds of it the rest of us too.

'Pyne is a murderer and a deserter,' said the captain.

'It's a lie,' I protested.

'Quiet!' snapped Gamble. 'For murder, Adam Pyne should under usual circumstances appear alongside you, Loftus, in the Admiralty Court. However, as a deserting Naval officer, he may receive an immediate declaration of sentence here and now. Full muster, Lieutenant Botterel, if you will.'

Captain Gamble walked a little way off to join his officers, while the lieutenant went to the break and gave a string of orders. The entire crew assembled noisily in the waist, more than two hundred souls, boys and youngsters and older men alike, some in leather aprons or carrying tools – craftsmen and idlers like the carpenter and surgeon – and many sailors in white slops and blue shirts. By contrast, the scores of soldiers wore red. Others, in smart calico, were the numerous petty officers Navy ships required to watch over all these numbers and keep them subordinate.

At a shout from forward, the crowd of seamen stood aside. A party pushed through bearing up a broken figure. He was roughly brought to the break of the poop, struggling to stand, head hanging down, spots of blood showing on the filthy shirt. His legs barely carried him. Like me, he was hampered by heavy foot-chains.

'Stand to attention before the captain.'

A petty officer struck his calves with a baton. With difficulty, the fellow straightened as best he could and stared fixedly forward. It was Adam.

The captain took the paper from Lieutenant Botterel, surveyed the assembly of seamen and officers, then cleared his throat.

'*Adam Pyne, Midshipman, lately of the Warship* Success,' he read, '*you are charged with Desertion and found guilty* in

244

absentia *by the Court-martial sitting at the Bahama Isles. For such an heinous and awful Crime –'*

Gamble stopped and turned to Botterel. 'Is that the accepted phrasing, Lieutenant? *Heinous and awful?* It strikes one as flowery.'

Botterel stiffened. 'Aye aye, sir. It is the exact form of words as prescribed in the Admiralty's Rules of Conduct During Warfare, newest edition.'

'Ah, good. Conformance to procedure is so important. To continue. *For such an heinous and awful Crime during time of War, I, Captain Percy Gamble, the* Bounteous, *have imposed the mandatory Punishment.'*

Gamble looked up from the paper, enjoying the rapt attention of his audience.

'*The second and further Charges, murder of a serving Officer, and failure to aid a Superior while in command of the Longboat, stand without Requitement on your Record. The Charge of Desertion takes Precedence in War and the Sentence is required to be carried out on the Day of this Proclamation.'*

As the inevitability of what was to come penetrated my dulled mind, I saw how profoundly Gamble relished the moment.

'*Therefore, I hereby declare that on this Day, Monday the Fourth of November Anno Domini Seventeen Hundred and Two, before the full Company of the commissioned Warship the* Bounteous, *Midshipman Adam Pyne shall be taken upon the Foredeck at the due Time, where a Rope shall be put around his Neck and he shall be hanged.'*

'He's innocent!' I shouted. 'He hasn't had the chance to defend himself. This isn't justice, it's murder!'

The seamen thronging in the waist shifted uneasily, murmuring amongst themselves. Lieutenant Botterel strode forward to the break and commanded silence. Wrestling free of my captors' grip, the foot-chains clanking, I lunged forward and tore the paper from his hands, ripping it down its length. The marines guarding me quickly recovered their wits and forced me down flat, pressing on my back and legs.

'Gamble, you win,' I panted from the deck-boards.

The captain took a step back, looking as if he had just avoided a turd on the pathway. 'What infantile nonsense is that – Gamble, you win? Do you think this is some variety of a game, Loftus? Speak.'

'I call your bluff,' I said. 'Withdraw your wretched threat.'

'Bluff? Threat? The proclamation just read has the full legality of the Admiralty Court itself. As post-captain, at sea on commission, I have powers to carry out the death sentence. Speak.'

'Stop the hanging,' I pleaded. 'I'll give you what you came for.'

'I would hang you too, Loftus,' he said thoughtfully, 'but the pity is you are not in the Naval service and I am thus obliged to transport your carcass back to Jamaicka and have it hanged there.'

What was the matter with the man? Did he want the tables or not? Perhaps he had not heard.

'For pity's sake, you bastard, don't hang the boy. I said –'

'Silence him!'

The crack of a belay pin across the jaw sent a jarring shock into my skull and I tasted blood in my mouth.

'Have the condemned man taken below and fed, Botterel.'

Adam, trying to stand straight, his gaze distant and unseeing, saluted before being marched off down the gangway into darkness.

Captain Gamble's colourless, tones drifted over.

'And Lieutenant, instruct the bosun to use a three-inch cable tomorrow. It is kinder on the neck and thus prolongs the spectacle, making it a more memorable occasion for the men.'

Giddy from the blows and the heat of the sun, I heard Gamble's level tones addressing his officers. Then he turned his attention back to me.

'Loftus, we are disappointed not to have found the commodore's valuables in your little bark. While I am minded to haul anchor without delay and take it as a pitiful prize to Jamaicka, my fellows here maintain this appendix might be of some import. I disbelieve them. What material does the book contain? Speak.'

Still pinned to the boards, I managed to shake my head. 'You know what it's all about, dam' you.'

'You'll have to do better than that. Something to do with the Lunar Longitude, or so Botterel maintains?'

'Let me up,' I said, and at the captain's nod, the seamen allowed me to rise. I stood before Gamble's over-dressed figure, wondering what the Devil he was playing at. Did he truly not know what the tables represented? Perhaps if I convinced the idiot of their value, he might see sense and call off the execution.

'The Lunar Distance Method,' I said. 'You must have heard of that.'

He gave his stilted laugh. 'The Navy has Navigators for these impossibly tiresome tasks. I cannot trouble myself with such a thing. A Navigator is a mere craftsman, such as a carpenter or surgeon. Speak.'

'Don't you understand? It's the greatest advance for years in finding the Longitude.'

His false laugh rang out. 'The Longitude? Think you've found the Longitude, do you, Loftus? Where is it, marked on the sea with a chalk piece?'

A few paces off, Gamble's officers stood in a gaggle, and at their captain's cue duly made their deferential chuckles.

'The principles of Natural Philosophy,' I began, 'may be beyond your understanding, but –'

'Hold your noise,' he snapped. 'I did not say speak.'

Gamble took another mincing turn about the quarter-deck, hands clasped behind his back, head down, examining his neat footwear. The polished boots fitted tight, and must have caused him great misery. Every other soul on board – officers, craftsmen and common seamen alike – went about barefoot or in leather slips, for the Tropick heat was a sure promoter of the foot-rot.

Bootsore or not, the captain came to some conclusion.

'Lieutenant Botterel, have the next subject brought up for Loftus's inspection, will you?'

Within half a minute, two marines appeared on the quarter, dragging between them a second human figure, even more battered than poor Adam. Head drooping, he shuffled along in the attitude of an old man.

Gamble, his features contorted with disgust or delight at the sight, said, 'Botterel, have the guards make him present himself properly.'

Grabbing the grey hair, a marine yanked him back by the hair to reveal the bloodied and bruised face of Eli Savary. He had been beaten to within a whisker's breadth of his life.

'Blast it, Gamble, what's the point of this?' I raged. 'He doesn't know –'

'Silence! Have the grace to speak only when commanded. No wonder that most delicately well-mannered young Miss Abigail found you coarse beyond measure.'

Percy Gamble knew how to cut a man. The unnecessary cruelty of his remarks left me speechless, but Eli Savary straightened, making an effort to hold his compact, hard-muscled old body erect. He fixed the captain with an intense stare, like a fox on a rabbit.

'Inside them fine togs,' he said savagely, 'you're coarser than a whore's armpit.'

'Be silent!' snapped the captain. He rubbed the end of his nose as if offended by a stink. 'Loftus, this loathsome specimen who insults even the title "jack-tar" is to undergo a punishment worthy of his own debased existence. Keelhauling. Amusingly simple in design, convenient in execution and astonishingly efficacious in result. It requires only –'

'Dammit, Gamble, the fellow's over sixty.'

'Do you want your fellow keelhauled or do you not? Speak now.'

'Dam' your eyes, I'll give up the volume.'

248

'Don't do it, Captain Matthew.' It was Eli, standing stockily between his captors, his shark-like eye still on Gamble. 'There's not much left he can do to old Eli Savary.'

'The tables aren't that important, old fellow,' I said miserably. 'I shan't let him harm you any more.'

Gamble took his little turn again around the quarter, hands tight behind his back. Completing the tour of his miniature kingdom, he faced me once more.

'You are, Loftus, from the same mould as Filligrew – a Longitude lunatick, struck on an absurd and unattainable notion. Nevertheless you are prepared to sacrifice any amount of your precious beliefs when necessity demands. So, where is this appendix?'

His eyes were shrunken black discs, unblinking but penetrating. He knew damm'd well the tables – appendix, as he so mis-named them – were of vital import, even though he appeared to give them no credence.

'If you want it,' I said levelly, 'you had better hear my terms.'

'What an impudence, that you even think of bargaining with me!' He nodded towards Eli, whose unblinking stare fell on the captain as if he was putting a curse on the man's very soul. 'Particularly when your fellow here is about to bite the barnacles off the *Bounteous*'s bottom. It is a grand game, you know. The subject is lowered over the stern and hauled underwater the full extent of the keel, some one hundred and thirty feet in the case of the *Bounteous*. The prisoner is thus taught how to hold his breath for a spell, an excellent moral discipline. Further, the rough and sharp barnacles infesting the bottom are cleared somewhat by the action, thus improving a ship's speed through the water. Pity that the barnacles must suffer so in tearing themselves against the subject's skin, bone and teeth, but sacrifices must be made. Speak.'

He was playing for time, I felt sure, working out what was preferable in the twisted Percy Gamble order of priorities – to inflict a gratuitous misery on an already half-dead seaman, or

249

achieve a small gain in his career advancement. At least he must now see he could not do both.

'I shall tell you where it is,' I said slowly, 'on one condition.'

He took a turn about the quarter. When he came back, his rat's eyes were keen. He was reckoning up the cost to his career.

'You may as well name it, Loftus,' he said.

'Reprieve and a pardon for Adam Pyne,' I said, 'and for my other fellows likewise.'

Captain Gamble pushed his face into mine. 'There is, Mister Loftus, as much chance of me reprieving that deserter as there is of a common seaman like yourself becoming post-captain through learning the Navigation.'

He began to laugh, caught up by the humour of his own remark.

'You can have the blasted appendix,' I cried. 'Let Filligrew reward you handsomely. Don't you understand?'

His reply was near inaudible, all but swallowed by his bitter mirth.

'I give a rotten fig for your damm'd appendix. Filligrew is as deluded as you. The Navy needs order and correction, not astronomickal fantasy.'

'Free Adam – why won't you free the boy?' I said, raising my voice.

'No such crime goes unpunished,' he said. 'The deserter hangs.'

'For pity's sake, the boy's innocent!' I cried.

'You are a fool, Loftus,' laughed Gamble, openly contemptuous.

Then I saw the truth, that he relished punishment beyond anything. He would rather flog a man's back raw than feast at table. He would keelhaul a jack-tar before caulking a seam on his leaking ship. He would hang a loyal seaman sooner than take off his boots in company. No mere advancement of Astronomy, no petty understanding of the workings of our Universe, could ever fulfil such twisted desires. He wanted a fellow's neck, and nothing else.

250

A roaring noise dinned in my ears, the blood pounding. All of a sudden, it came to me what must be done.

'Then condemn me instead,' I pleaded, choking. 'For the Lord's sake, hang me in his place.'

Gamble was red-faced, lips drawn back, mouthing something I tried not to hear.

'Too late! Too late!' he cried, advancing, heels tapping on the boards, a finger pointed at my face, his countenance mocking and twisted. 'He'll be dead at the dog-watch!'

He tripped. The ridiculous boots picked out a poorly sanded deck seam and got the better of his footing. He staggered forward a pace or two, off balance, arms windmilling, and ended up half a yard from where Eli Savary stood, back straight, head high, and still with that awful bead fixed on the captain.

Confined by chains, hands bound behind him, Eli somehow found the strength to throw his captors off balance, if only for the briefest instant. In the space of a single second, he got one foot out ahead so that Gamble's face, puce with righteous rage, was a foot distant. Then he leaned away, bending half over backwards and – using every muscle in his broad old back, his beefy shoulders and thick neck – swung violently upright. From the backward roll to the forward lunge, the grizzled head described perhaps fifty degrees of arc. A living man's skull with its blood and brain intact weighs about fifteen pounds, the mass of a doubled roundshot in a medium gun. This blunt instrument of well-tempered bone and hardened ivory, this cast-iron kettle laden with its brainy organs, curved on an arcing trajectory, all its weight concentrated behind the forward momentum. The entire corpus of Eli Savary's upper body, tough as old scrimshaw and brass, bore onwards until his forehead met the middle of Gamble's face.

It was a mighty, murderous blow. Some call it the sailor's nod.

Gristle, bone, snot, hair, teeth, all ground together under the impact. Gamble's nose, the softer, pulpier parts, gave way until Eli's skull moving violently forward met the framework of the

251

captain's face at rest. Driven backwards with such force, Gamble's body lost all tension, as the wind empties from a sail. Limbs akimbo, he crumpled flat aback on the boards.

Men and officers ran forward. The captain lay inert, quite still, lifeless as a corpse, as though Eli had knocked the very brain from its fixings. A knot of officers bent over the stricken captain. There was shouting, and wild commotion all around.

'Is he dead?' cried a voice. It was Botterel's.

'No – look, he's moving.'

They peeled back. Gamble sat half up, then fell sideways. His face was unrecognisable – reddened, misshapen, bloody. There was no nose. His open mouth was a scarlet hole, from where a piece of gristle hung, the portion of tongue he had bitten clean through. His jaw was working, and gurgling sounds issued from his throat. Drops of red frothed out.

He was still trying to give orders.

20

KNAVE TO PLAY

In the endless dark of the meat-box, night and day were one. The beating administered after Eli's bloody but futile revenge on Gamble had rendered me all but insensible. Beyond the merely physical aches, a sense of vague, all-encompassing despair overwhelmed me. Time lengthened and my mind wandered. The distant shouts of a mob penetrated my mind, then the noise of piping fifes and the hubbub of a crowd gathering. I was transported back to my Whitby childhood, when I had stood agape in the courthouse square on the morning of a fair-day to witness a vagrant flogged or a mule thief hanged. Reeling from a dead faint to bouts of confused awareness, I could remember neither where I was nor why.

At last, there came the thud of approaching treads and the trap of the box was flung open. Again, buckets of seawater dashed in my face left me gasping but half conscious. Dizzy and fearful, I was bundled along a gun-deck passageway, registering only a blur of red-shirted and blue-coated figures. Light flooded in through gunports and hatches, relieving the below-decks gloom. It was still daylight. The afternoon sun. Surely not yet the dog-watch, then. What was important about the dog-watch? Then it came to me. 'He'll be dead at the dog-watch' – the last words I had heard Gamble speak.

Please, let it not be the dog-watch yet, I found myself begging.

My own life's worth nothing, let me die in his place. I gave out a cry, pitched something like that of a gin-trapped animal.

'Lively now we're out of the box, aren't we?' said a seaman, laughing throatily.

With kicks and shove, the marines rudely bore me along the low, tweendecks passageway, full of stale smells. Through a doorway, I glimpsed a white-painted room with a scrubbed table of bare wood, shelves lined with apotheckary's jars, iron tools and implements racked along the walls, a storehouse of clamps, leather straps, tenon-saws and cleavers – the surgeon's quarters, equipped as much for dismemberment and boning as for mending and repair. Torture, then, I thought dully. But our party hastened past, emerging into the bright sun and crossing the length of the weather-deck towards the quarter. Another interview with the monstrous Gamble perhaps, but I had already offered my own life for Adam's. What had I left to say or do to stop the man?

But I was not conducted up to the quarter. Instead we ducked through the officers' doorway below the break of the poop and into the stern quarters, a warren of small poorly-lit cabins. There was a door at the end of the passage. The guards knocked and a voice said, 'Enter.'

Hauled into a large, airy space all painted white, blinking against the blaze of daylight pouring in from three full-height mullioned windows at the far end, I found myself in the Great Cabin. Someone bade me be seated. My guards were obliged to help me slump into a chair, exhausted, giddy, soaked in seawater yet sweating like a carpenter. The manacles were removed from my wrists, although the foot-chains remained in place.

'Leave us, sergeant,' said the unfamiliar voice, and the guards departed.

The speaker was the only other soul in the room. A polished table stood between us and his face was obscured by the windows' glare until he got up to draw a curtain half across. He was distinguished of bearing, in a high ranking officer's silk shirt and smart briches, a man perhaps late in his sixth decade, still erect though heavy at the waist, with white hair tied back in a pig-tail by a miniature red velvet ribbon. Signet rings flashed as he moved and buckle shoes tapped on the deck sole. From above pudgy cheeks shone alert, keen eyes.

'Captain Loftus, I offer a most sincere apology for this appalling treatment.'

Apology? I could not think straight enough to respond.

'Drink, sir,' said the gentleman. 'Take wine if you will – arrack, in the old-fashioned way they call it hereabouts. There are manjoes and sliced breadfruits there, and the juice of limes squeezed into sweet-water, a most reviving beverage.'

Shakily, I fumbled with the mug he offered. When it met my lips, the sharpness puckered my mouth and the lime-juice coursed coolly down my throat.

The gentleman spoke again. 'I am Vice-Admiral George Pitchbert, of the flagship *Forbearance*. I'll be frank with you, Loftus. Wrongs have been done aboard here.'

Struggling to unscramble my mind, I mumbled, 'The hang – . . . the hanging.'

'Quite, quite,' he said. 'Not due till the middle of the dog-watch, at five of the clock this eve.'

Thank the Lord for an answered prayer. The room blurred and I blessed the fates in giving me another chance.

'The keelhauling – and the rackings,' I croaked.

'All stopped for now,' the vice-admiral said. 'But I cannot override a captain's authority for long.'

'Was the piping I heard,' I said thickly, 'to mark your coming aboard?'

The vice-admiral greedily swallowed wine from his goblet, nodding. 'As soon as my flagship hauled into Negril Cove, I came over.' He leaned across the table, eyes narrowing. 'Loftus, we must come to an agreement on this business of Filligrew's damm'd appendix.'

As Pitchbert took up his wine again and drank, the

significance of his presence began to sink in. A vice-admiral, no less, had arrived here with the keenest of intentions about the so-called appendix, by which must be meant the tables. Even in the swamp of my confusion, that much was clear.

'The item in question,' he said, 'may be the most vital single piece of Philosophickal advancement in existence.'

'Philosophickal advancement?' I repeated numbly, and took another sip of the refreshing juice. 'Is that why Filligrew's so struck on getting it back?'

'Tosh! It's his career at stake, dammit.' Pitchbert irritatedly reached round and tugged at his queue to smooth it, muttering as if to himself, 'Why else would he promote this expedition?'

I straightened, blinking. 'Filligrew sent the Navy after me?'

The vice-admiral gave me a pitying look. 'After you? No, to retrieve the appendix, Loftus. For Her Majesty's Navy. Though it's purely – because of war – a Naval matter now, yet we sometimes put privateers under Navy command and vice versa.'

I remembered that Gamble had run with Filligrew's flota to enhance the commodore's Admiralty ambitions. Now the same Percy Gamble was, apparently unwittingly, doing his dammedest to impede them. The vice-admiral had been obliged to come and put things right.

Pitchbert looked at me over the rim of his goblet. 'My mission is for the appendix, this business of the Lunar Distinction Method. Good God, Loftus, do you not understand the importance of finding a Longitude? Imagine if the solution fell into France's hands. For the love of Saint Peter, we are at war!'

I was mystified. He had just misnamed the Method. He might know what it signified for war and commerce, but did he know anything of the matter itself? Perhaps Commodore Filligrew called the tables 'an appendix' in order to hide something from the ignorant Naval men. My mind was spinning with possibilities, yet first and foremost came Adam. All I wanted to do was save the poor lad's innocent neck. After letting a long draught of lime-juice slide gorgeously down my throat, I spoke slowly.

'Did Filligrew describe this appendix, vice-admiral?'

'Why do you ask?'

'We both need to be sure we are discussing the right piece of work.' I coughed and swallowed hard. 'The appendix you refer to is the vital missing part to complete the commodore's Lunar Distance Method. Is that correct?'

He pursed his lips and said, 'Aye, exactly the thing – the Lunar Distance Method.' Then he drummed his fingers impatiently. 'The point is, Loftus, the first man home with this appendix wins the plaudits of a grateful nation. Need I say more?' Pitchbert rubbed his hands together in a blur, like a seaman about to clamber aloft on an icy morning. 'You can help me Loftus, and in return – well, let us see, shall we? No promises. Are you going to tell me where it is?'

I frowned. Had Gamble said nothing about my offer to give up the tables? About my plea to hang in Adam's place?

'Captain Gamble told you I would not reveal its whereabouts?' I asked cautiously.

Pitchbert gave a snort. 'That stiff-jointed drummer-boy! So obsessed with rules and procedures, or the prospects of his next command, he cannot see the end of his nose.'

It passed through my mind that after Eli's blow, he might not have a nose end to see at all. Then I took a deep breath and said, 'I have the appendix, sir.'

He leaned forward. 'Where? Where is it?'

I held up one hand. 'You cannot expect something for nothing.'

'Quite, quite,' he said, withdrawing a little. 'Go on.'

'First, the hanging must be stopped.'

'Already postponed.' His reply was instant.

'Not postponed,' I said, my voice rising, 'but stopped altogether.'

'That can be agreed, too.'

He had barely hesitated. It was done – the hanging was off! Relief coursed hotly through my veins.

'Now, where's the appendix?' he demanded.

Already he was pushing ahead too fast. 'I demand pardons,' I said, measuring my words, 'for all my men, regardless of what crimes they are falsely accused of. Including the astronomer of course, and pardon for myself likewise.'

'A tall order, Loftus. Do you understand that?'

'Aye, but a vice-admiral may sign such documents. I want pardons, written, signed and sealed,' I said levelly, 'or you'll never clap eyes on that appendix.'

He ran his hands over the back of his head until he came to the pig-tail, which he stroked thoughtfully. 'It's going to be difficult to justify in London, Loftus. Very difficult indeed.'

He had not said *no*. I pressed ahead. 'More difficult than explaining why you failed to get hold of the vital piece?'

His jaw muscles worked silently, as if he were rehearsing the point. 'Your fellow is due to be hanged, you know. I could apply the rack to the others – and to you. Gamble would approve. I'd soon find out where it is.'

I met his eye with an unwavering stare. 'You just agreed to stop the hanging. If there is the least chance of it going ahead, vice-admiral, then understand this: you'll get no appendix. If one fingernail is pulled from any of my fellows' hands or one thumb crushed, no appendix. If a single bone is wrenched from its socket on the rack, no appendix. I trust I make myself clear?'

He studied me intently for a few seconds. 'Perfectly clear, and I believe you mean it. Very well, I shall arrange the pardons immediately.' He leaned forward, his expression hardening. 'But likewise, no appendix means no pardons and no reprieve. Either you deliver, Loftus, or you and your fellows go, one by one, to the gallows.'

I did not flinch, and replied in level tones, 'I agree to deliver, vice-admiral, if you do the same.'

He sank back into his chair, exhaling deeply. 'I do agree. So that's it, then. It's settled between us.'

At last, I thought, and heaved an immense sigh.

'Now, where is it?' In his eagerness, Pitchbert knocked over his goblet of wine. 'Where?' he said, pulling a large linen cloth from his sleeve and dabbing at the running liquid. 'Where do I find it, Loftus?'

'It's hidden, vice-admiral. At quite some distance, and difficult to find. Only I can take you to it – as soon as I see a written agreement and pardons as promised.'

'Very well. I'll call Gamble's scribe in to draw up the papers.'

He got up a little unsteadily and marched to the door shouting for Lieutenant Botterel. When the scribe came in, the vice-admiral fussily asked about inks and parchments and sealing wax, all of which Botterel had with him in plenty. I drank wine to steady my nerve while the lieutenant laboriously prepared in copper-plate the heads of the agreement, until at last he was poised to record the exact terms.

'Now, Loftus, describe the whereabouts of the volume, if you will,' said the vice-admiral, 'for the lieutenant to scribble down.'

'Clearly, sir, I can hardly divulge that in advance. I shall have to Navigate you to the hiding place.'

Pitchbert studied me with keen interest. 'Why on Earth should you want to do that?'

'The place is unknown to the English Navy,' I said simply. 'You could never find it. It would be like seeking out one particular barnacle from the millions on the bottom of your flagship – the *Forbearance*, was it not? You must let me and my men go back aboard the *Diamond*. I'll Navigate her to the place of hiding. Your vessels follow, of course, then I hand over the item and you let me go free.'

He stood up, angry. 'Preposterous! You may direct my ships to the place, but not go off in your own.'

I shook my head. 'It's the only way you gain possession of that volume.'

'Gamble would have grounds to put me in the Court-martial,' he retorted. 'You would have only to free sheets and run away. Don't take me for a fool, Loftus.'

'Never, sir. The point is, we might give your heavy warships the slip but the *Diamond* can't outrun Gamble's fast schooner – the one that captured mine.'

'You mean the *Charity*?'

'O aye – an excellent companion for the *Bounteous* and the *Forbearance*,' I said. 'Consider it from my view. Once I hand over the appendix, what assurance have I that we would not be instantly recaptured? This way I have a sporting chance that you'll keep to your word and let us go on our way with the pardons.'

He shook his head solemnly. 'Dammit, you're a wanted man. You shall have a detachment of marines aboard, with an officer.'

'Not the marines,' I said, 'but I agree to an officer. Unarmed.'

'He would be a hostage. The Navy might never see him back alive.'

I nodded. 'That's the idea.'

There was a pause as Pitchbert drained his wine. At last, he put down the empty goblet. 'And when you've collected the appendix, what guarantee do I have that you'll deliver it and release your hostage?'

I shrugged. 'Our agreement. I have the honour of the Navy's word, you have the honour of mine.'

'There speaks the private man!' He laughed, then his demeanour became more serious. 'So let's be clear, Loftus. Three Navy warships – my flagship, Gamble's sixth-rater and his fast schooner – shall sail in company with your little craft, able to bring it to the point of destruction at a moment's notice. Is that not so?'

'Exactly so. The *Forbearance* or the *Bounteous* can overwhelm her with firepower, while the *Charity* can outrun her on any point. It's a copper-bottomed arrangement, unless I chose to commit suicide through trying to run off.'

'Very well. Write it all down, lieutenant. Shall we drink to it, Loftus, while the agreement is made up for signature and seal?'

I raised my glass. The arrack-wine, tasting of fruit and flowers, sent a stream of heady delight running into my veins. At last, after the carnage of Will Wrack's desperately heroic resistance and the ghastly sentencing, the tide was turning. Adam's life spared, pardons for us all and freedom in the *Diamond*. Despite the discomfort of a sore jaw, I smacked my lips.

'You approve?' said Pitchbert happily. 'A Frenchy beverage, embargoed in wartime from the shores of England, but I took a small prize last month. She was laden with wine, so now I have a case brought with me wherever I visit. Promotes good understanding between men.'

The vice-admiral prated on while the soothing wine passed into my throat, until at last the scribe had done.

'Read away, Botterel, if you will,' he instructed.

The lieutenant straightened and began to recite the terms colourlessly, as if they were about a tunnage of sisal or manila ropes, or bales of flaxen sailcloth, instead of a treaty that saved men from death. I sighed inwardly and leaned back, eyes closed.

'. . . *and further that the prisoners be freed forthwith into the hands of the said Matthew Loftus, and put aboard the schooner* Diamond, *a captured prize of Captain Percy Gamble, and* –'

'You can scratch that out,' I interrupted. 'The *Diamond* is not going to be a prize, remember. Not for anyone, and least of all him.'

Pitchbert frowned. 'Yes, yes. Delete it, Botterel, it's hardly worth jeopardising our bargain over one barely presentable little schooner.'

I was a touch put out at that, but Botterel just frowned, scratched it out with his quill and pressed on.

'So to the crew list. "*The schooner* Diamond'*s complement is to be as follows: Matthew Loftus, master; Eli Savary, mate; Gaspar Rittel, ordinary seaman; Hap, ordinary seaman (wounded); Jan, boy sailor; and Noah Spatchears, landsman.*"'

I leaned over and tapped the parchment. 'Lieutenant, you've omitted the name of Adam Pyne.'

Botterel glanced up sharply at Pitchbert, who slowly replaced his goblet on the table, brows furrowed. Something was wrong.

'What's going on?' I demanded, half rising. 'Sir, are you reneging so soon?'

He cleared his throat. 'There appears to be some misunderstanding, Loftus. About this Pyne fellow, I mean to say.'

'O no, he was always part of our agreement.' I flushed angrily. '*All* my men, I said. Pardon and freedom for every dam' one, most particularly for Adam Pyne.'

The vice-admiral shifted uncomfortably. 'It cannot be, Loftus.'

'Why the Devil not?' I cried.

He and the lieutenant exchanged glances.

'Loftus,' said Pitchbert, 'I had no idea that you were unaware.'

'Unaware of what?' I demanded.

'The hanging this eve was to be of Eli Savary.'

I stopped. 'What do you mean? Then where's Adam?' I was on my feet, banging a fist on the table. 'What have you done with him?'

'Permission to speak, sir,' said Botterel. 'I believe Captain Loftus passed a night longer in the meat-box than he realises.'

Pitchbert looked uncertainly at me. 'O dear,' he said. 'Yester eve, before the ship's company, and in accordance with a legal proclamation by Captain Gamble – O Lord, this is a poor business.' He shook his head, then gathered himself. The words burst out in a rush. 'Yesterday, at two bells of the dog-watch, Adam Pyne was hanged to death.'

I slumped down in the chair, the whole world reeling.

'You Devils,' I muttered. 'I curse you and your damm'd Navy to Hell. I dam' you with all my heart.'

I fell into a long, stunned silence. Images of Adam's prolonged death flickered unbidden into my mind. Dear Lord, I thought, first Will, now that poor boy.

'Loftus, what can I say?' Pitchbert spoke agitatedly. 'I only came aboard this morn. Perhaps you heard the pipes. Midshipman Pyne was already – well, the sentence had been carried out and the body consigned overboard. With proper

Naval formalities, I might add.' He passed a hand across his brow. 'It appears that Captain Gamble has been a mite over-zealous. Of course, your fellow Savary would be dead too at this five of the clock, if it were not for our agreement.'

'Our blasted agreement is worthless!' I bellowed, rising suddenly. Dragging at my foot-chains, I reached over and snatched up Botterel's ink-well, then hurled it across the room. With one stroke of my arm, I swept all the parchments and quills and seals off the table.

'Guards! Guards!' I heard someone yelling.

There was a great deal of shouting and the thump of heavy steps. In another moment, the soldiers had lashed me firmly to the chair. The vice-admiral was adjusting his shirt and smoothing down his briches, running a hand through his grey locks and patting the pig-tail to make sure it remained in place.

'Good God, Loftus, you're an angry man,' he said, resuming his seat opposite. 'Still, I see your point, perhaps. Here, take some wine.'

Restrained, I could no longer move my arms. With a shaky motion, he filled a goblet and then drank it off himself.

'The Navy shall never get its vile hands on that appendix,' I whispered.

'Look, my dear man, this has been the most terrible misunderstanding,' said the vice-admiral. 'How could I have prevented the hanging?'

I remembered my last spell in the meat-box, the sounds of a full muster on the deck-boards above, the piping, the singing and the jeers. Now I knew it to have been the nervous excitement of men watching a fellow dance on the string of death.

'Look, Loftus, I have no wish to sound callous,' Pitchbert was saying, 'but what difference does this make? Gamble's bent on pursuing his path. He's found a cause now to hang another man and no doubt can find reason to hang a few more, yourself included. Not even the prospect of Filligrew's ire deters him. But you may still save the rest of your fellows. Think at least of that.'

I barely listened. Only yards from my prison box, that innocent, loyal young man had died, strangled slowly by a thick rope in true Navy tradition. Why, even the good Justice Lynskill in Whitby Town had sent condemned men and women to their Maker with a high drop from the mounting-steps by the court-house, their necks being broken before their tongues flopped out and their bodies spasmed and let go their waters. Not so for Adam.

The vice-admiral spoke again. 'What's the point of more executions? Let our agreement stand. Save yourself.'

'Never,' I blurted out. 'As long as I live, you shall never get it.'

There came footsteps along the passage and the figure of an officer entered, his countenance somehow misformed, out of shape. Scabbed weals covered the middle of his face. When he spoke, it was in cadences I recognised only too well.

'With the greatest respect, vice-admiral,' mumbled Captain Gamble, surveying the scattered writing things and papers that Botterel was busy gathering up, 'but I was always of the opinion that this ruffian Loftus was a violent and unredeemable murderer. I have prepared a whipsman and a grating for his punishment, so if you'll allow me –'

'Gamble, the Lord only knows you wreak havoc wherever you go,' sighed the vice-admiral. 'You've lost us the one thing we came for.'

'Hardly, sir, if I may say so. One criminal has already met his proper end, and the next shall go at the dog-watch this eve.'

'I forbid the execution,' said Pitchbert flatly.

'Sir, with the utmost respect,' said Gamble, with his unctuous but disrespectful bow, 'as post-captain I insist upon it, and must point out that –'

'That in matters of shipboard discipline, a vice-admiral may not overrule a captain who is not under his flag at the time? O aye, indeed, Captain Gamble, and doubtless your reports shall make this most explicit. Well then, hear this. Stay of execution is now an order from your new commodore of the fleet. Haul down

264

your colour from Filligrew – dubious authority, anyway – and haul up this one in its place.' From a satchel by his feet, Pitchbert pulled a rolled bundle wrapped in the coils of its own lanyard, unknotted it and spread it with a flourish. 'Hoist up the standard of Vice-Admiral George Pitchbert. From now on, Captain Gamble, you run under my flag.'

Gamble's misshapen jaw fell open. 'Vice-admiral, I urge you to reconsider. Sir Thomas shall be most discomfited if you remove his flag.'

'To Hell with Filligrew,' snapped Pitchbert, wagging a finger right under Gamble's broken nose. 'And hear this. If I do not get the appendix, his flag shall never fly above the court-house at Port Royal either.'

Gamble looked taken aback. 'The commodore's appointment, sir? But I understand you are obligated if he produces this Method for the nation.'

'Save your arguments for the Admiralty.'

'May I point out, sir, the Court at Jamaicka cannot –'

'I refer to the Admiralty in London, dammit,' snapped Pitchbert. 'After this business is done I am bound to England for an audience with the Sovereign herself.'

Gamble jerked his head up and stared ahead. 'Aye aye, sir. God save Her Gracious Majesty the Queen.'

'Aye, sir,' said Pitchbert, mocking. 'You know dam' well your career's directed by the Admiralty in London, not by the secondary courts of the colonies. You and Filligrew may cheep and trill from that perch in Port Royal until you fall off, but it shall make no difference in London.'

Their voices droned on, the machinations and ambitions of these murdering, callous fools angering and fatiguing me in equal measure. Filligrew appointed to the Admiralty Court at Port Royal? It did not matter to me, only to those poor innocents he would hang in bunches from the gibbet. My heart was filled with bitter regrets, thinking how I had hauled over the *Diamond* and surrendered when Will Wrack launched his insane, hopeless, brave attack against insurmountable odds. Perhaps I should never have struck our colours, never have delivered my seamen into Naval hands. Perhaps it were better to have fought till the last man dropped, as poor Will wanted, and to have let Adam die in battle rather than on the yardarm.

'Gamble, you've done your dammedest to ruin everything,' the vice-admiral was saying. 'I want that appendix and, let me remind you, so does Sir Thomas, no matter how many prisoners and prizes or hanged men's corpses you may deliver. You'd best not appear in Port Royal without it. Think on that.'

'Sir, I shall have the man Savary brought back on to the surgeon's table for examination,' said Gamble defiantly, 'to ascertain the whereabouts of this wretched appendix before he dies.'

Pitchbert breathed out a lungful of wine-ridden air. 'You may try, but I have no hopes of it.'

I lifted up my eyes and met the vice-admiral's gaze.

'There's no need for more torture or strangling,' I said, speaking so low he had to crane forward.

'What are you saying, Loftus? Again, if you please.'

'You've taken Pyne's life, and nothing can change that,' I said. 'There's no merit in letting this murderer torment my fellows any more, or hang another innocent. If our agreement stands, I will take you to the appendix.'

Pitchbert all but overbalanced in his eagerness to catch my words. 'The agreement stands, does it? Despite the hanging? Loftus, answer me – it stands as before?'

'Aye, it stands,' I said, holding his eye, 'but for one detail.'

'Detail? What detail, Loftus?'

I took a breath. 'I shall nominate the officer who accompanies us unarmed aboard the *Diamond*.'

Pitchbert blinked. 'What the Devil difference does it make who – ? Ah, wait, I think the light dawns.' The vice-admiral closed his eyes, the flicker of a smile illuminating his features. 'You want Captain Percy Gamble for your hostage.'

The captain's eyebrows were as high as a crosstree. 'Vice-admiral, what agreement have you made with this criminal?'

'Close up your hatch, captain,' said Pitchbert.

I was solemnly shaking my head. 'If Gamble were to step aboard the *Diamond*, he'd be a dead man.'

In the short, intense pause that ensued, only a feeble spluttering issuing from the astonished captain's mouth could be heard.

Then Pitchbert snapped, 'What are you aiming at, Loftus?'

'You, vice-admiral, are the hostage.'

He shut his wine-lipped mouth with an audible click, and sat back.

'A gentleman of your rank is worth more,' I said quietly, 'than the carcass of a miserable post-captain.'

Captain Gamble exploded, barely able to get his swollen tongue to form the words fast enough. 'Vice-admiral, I do not know what conspiracy has taken place but what I hear is quite beyond reason. What precisely has transpired? You go aboard the *Diamond* unarmed, with this fellow? An act of reckless lunacy. I forbid any collaborations with ruffian elements. This man is the most wanted criminal in the Caribbee Sea.'

Pitchbert recovered his composure and looked blackly at the captain. 'For pity's sake, Gamble, can't you read men in the least degree? You've executed one of Loftus's fellows and you're planning to hang or torture the others. His fellows do not know the volume's whereabouts, and it's as plain as a bung in a barrel that he himself would never concede it. Not now you've killed his friend.'

He cast a glance at me, as if seeking confirmation. I held his gaze and kept silent, and he read it for himself.

'Aye, indeed, as I thought.' Pitchbert put his fingertips together and tapped them one against the other. 'Very well, Loftus. I go aboard to get this appendix and you get your freedom – it's a plain deal. Lieutenant Botterel, write out the contract again and all those pardons, ready for my seal.'

267

Botterel took out another sheet of parchment and self-importantly dipped his quill. Percy Gamble stood, his horribly mangled mouth open, staring from one to the other of us and back again.

'And Gamble, assign Captain Loftus to the First Lieutenant's cabin.' Pitchbert's orders rapped out in quick succession. 'Put Savary and the others in good quarters and feed them up. And if you lay the tip of a cat or the touch of a stave against their flesh, I'll have you in the Court-martial.' The vice-admiral looked me up and down. 'Fit by morning, Loftus?'

I nodded.

'Then we weigh at dawn. Write this down, Botterel. The schooner *Diamond* goes in the van. Her captain shall be Matthew Loftus, with Vice-Admiral Pitchbert aboard same. The schooner *Charity* to keep close station, the *Forbearance* and the *Bounteous* within gunshot and in line astern. And the flota goes under my flag.'

'Sir, you realise that I am obliged,' said Gamble, stiff-backed, 'to record this travesty in my reports.'

'Scribble what you dam' well like, my good Percy. It'll be nothing to what I say about you.' The vice-admiral rose. 'The prisoners are under my protection from here on. I'd advise you for your own sake not to go near Captain Loftus. Dismissed.'

Gamble, after a cold, lingering glance at Lieutenant Botterel and his quills and inks, marched wordlessly out.

Pitchbert stood straightening his weskit. 'Just one thing, Loftus. What guarantee do you give not to kill me out of pure revenge on the Navy, once I'm aboard your *Diamond*?'

I moistened my lips. 'The best guarantee you'll get, vice-admiral,' I said slowly, 'is that your name is not Gamble.'

268

21

RAY OF HOPE

Under a press of sail and fairly flying, the *Diamond* lurched along in the van of the Navy's flota. Braced at the taff-rail, cocking the tube of the spy-glass up, I raked the sea-scape. To a sailor's eye, and even a landsman's, this company of fine vessels made a grand sight, yet only bitter regretful notions filled my mind. How Will Wrack would have enjoyed the spectacle of the Navy lumbering along in the wake of his little bark. And how poor Adam's heart might have swelled with misdirected pride at the sight of such a convoy.

The *Bounteous* and the *Forbearance*, a magnificent brace of warships, rolled heavily along the tradewind swells on a beam reach, the decks and rails thronged with sailors and fighting men, a dozen officers and midshipmen poised on their quarter-decks. For now, they had shortened canvas to run with topsails and forecourse, yet I had only to turn the *Diamond*'s bows to windward in order to leave those heavy vessels standing. Half a cable off, astern and to windward, ran the six-gun schooner the *Charity*, altogether a different matter. Carrying two big jibsails, but with mainsail reefed and staysail brailed up, she chafed like a short-reined horse just to keep station. Light on her feet, quick to turn, longer at the waterline – on any point of sailing from running to beating, she had the speed of us.

I glanced up. Rounded, cottony clouds pocked the blue of the sky. Even in the brilliance of daytime the Moon showed herself, but only in the thinnest of crescents imaginable. No more than a sliver of ghostly white, she floated above the sea waning her last on the long path from Full to Change. This was a secretive Moon, risen solely by day and now departing the scene altogether before her invisible return as the New Moon. Every time I looked up, I wondered again about Noah Spatchears and his Lunar observations.

We surged along in a small gale of wind, the brisk south-easterly on our steerboard quarter – a soldier's wind, they called it, for the motion was easier on their landsman guts. Tell that to our nauseous vice-admiral, I grimaced.

'Keep your course,' I said to Jan, and stepped down the hatchway. In the stern quarters below, above the slosh and rattle of the *Diamond*'s progress, the familiar rapid, urgent mutterings of astronomy issued from the cell-like space between the captain's cabin and the steps where Spatchears was bent once more over his papers. Peering round the doorway of my own quarters, I saw the generous figure of Vice-Admiral George Pitchbert spilling off the bunk, eyes tight shut and a sheen of sweat covering his face, the shirt clinging stickily to his underarms. He stirred, passing an arm over his brow, but did not open his eyes. The cabin stank richly.

'Sir, some fish soup for you?' I suggested.

He groaned.

'A bowl of porridge with chicken fat, then,' I offered.

'Urrrggghh.' Swaying back over the edge of the bunk, he vomited with force, spattering a colourless liquid across the deck-sole.

'To settle the guts, my mate Eli Savary swears by a little sweetened sugar-rum with melted pig's lard in it,' I said. 'You have only to let me know.'

He retched again. I left him and went forward, crouching low, heading for the midships quarters. Debris lay all around – smashed panels and broken drawers, busted locks and prised up deck-boards, the aftermath of Captain Gamble's careless search. Where the mainmast ran up the forward side of the athwartships bulkhead was a cabinet of lockers for small stuff – seizings, light blocks and the like, a bosun's hoardings. It had been all but torn from its fixings around the ten-inch thick mainmast, and every part of it was exposed like a raw wound. Will Wrack's refitting of his schooner had been the labour of love, yet now it lay in ruins. With a whispered apology to him, I picked up an iron lever and forced the remains of the cabinet off the cylinder of the mast. Then, feeling around at the base where it went through the sole, I located a finger-hole and scrabbled inside the mast's hollow centre.

The tip of my middle finger touched something smooth and leathery, the cover of a book, tightly rolled and with a line running to the masthead. At Tranquil Inlet, it had been tricky enough to remove the mast cap to reach the sixty-foot hollow, but worth it for such a hiding place. Groping with my fingertips, I touched a scroll of parchments resting on top of the book. With some difficulty, I drew out the rolls through the minute hole, crumpling them only a little. By now severely cramped, I gratefully straightened and, careful not to rouse the vice-admiral in his malodorous bunk, tiptoed into the adjoining cabin. The old calculator was startled, protectively concealing his papers.

'It's me, Observator Spatchears, and here's the code,' I said, handing him the fruit of his labours at the native village, which included his transit predictions.

'Marvellous!' he said, taking them at once and smoothing them on the table. 'I shall rework all my figures.'

I frowned. 'You said you had done the necessary calculations.'

He looked affronted. 'Indeed, but a careful astronomer reviews and tests his work constantly. *Per ardua ad astra* is his motto. As a result, I have recalled even more lines of the code.'

'But you're sure of the day, now?'

He started to cough, chest lifting and drawing. He jammed a cloth into his mouth and I gently banged his back.

'As certain,' he breathed, 'of the date as an astronomer can be. After all, the calculations are derived from my own observations.'

'Aye, and what about the latitude?'

'My back-staff work improves by the day,' he said with what was almost a shy look, adding, 'I admit to being as pleased as a jack-tar on a liberty boat, as your Mister Savary might express it. Practickal Navigation aboard a bark is a most challenging exercise.'

'No *malady mer*?' I enquired, for the man had spent a lifetime confined in the dusty corridors of study. 'A bark's sway and roll may make a Navigator lose more than his fixes when he's below with his eyes on numbers and charts.'

'Not a whiff,' he retorted.

'You'll make a seaman yet,' I said, encouragingly. 'What about the time, then?'

He shook his old head irritatedly. 'As to timing, well, the path is narrow and if we miss it, it all amounts to nothing.' He sniffed – a wetly rattling sound – then lowered his voice. 'If only we could get the Longitude exactly. My good captain, are you sure you can find the right place?'

I shrugged. 'Near enough, I trust. My memory for coastlines is good, and the latitude helps, but I shan't know until we see the lie of the land. The region's quite uncharted.'

'Then we must hope,' said the ancient star-gazer, 'that the Universe obliges – *Deo volente*.'

'Aye, and God willing, your memory of the code is as good as your observations,' I said, turning to go.

At dawn, we hauled sheets to close the coast. The smudgy outlines sharpened into low hills and gained both colour and features until we crested the curve of the sea and picked out rocky headlands and a forest of vegetation. The Tropick sun lifted higher and from the deck-boards rose a warm woody smell. We slanted along under a press of sail, watching for the blue-black hue of the deep sea to lighten and take on the paler hue of soundings.

Spatchears appeared briefly and wordlessly on deck to take sunsights, then dropped below to figure his numbers. Brushing the damp sweat from my eyes, I gazed into the sky. Unlike yesterday, the sun was now quite alone in her canopy. Without even the waning Moon visible, I could not rid myself of misgivings. There were so many chances for miscalculation.

Perched at the main-top, Gaspar Rittel called down that the sea's hue had altered some distance ahead. Four or five cables off, the water took on a lighter shade, and further beyond showed the pale, insipid green of shoal water – the start of the reef field spreading across our path, as daunting a barrier as any moat and mound protecting an old-fashioned castle ashore.

'Shorten sail, Eli,' I called.

The *Charity* matched our speed by lowering jibsails, while the two warships, keeping station well astern, bunted up their top-gallants. I called down the hatchway to request the vice-admiral's presence on deck. Tottering out, wiping the corners of his mouth with a stained linen rag, he squinted against the fierce sunlight.

'Welcome, sir,' I said, 'to one of the least known and most dangerous coasts in the Caribbee Sea. Would you care to study the approach?'

He took the spy-glass from me, holding it unsteadily. 'Can't see a blasted thing. Just some little fishing boats.'

Pitchbert handed back the glass and lunged for the rail. He leaned over, shoulders heaving, but all that came up was a dribble, for his guts were empty and likely sore as blisters from his night-long purging.

The tube showed me a host of small *canoas*, mere insects at this distance, their occupants paddling furiously, melting away into the indistinct coastline. If only I could tell them that their secret cove was safe, and might be safer yet after today. I closed up the spy-glass.

'Sir, we must stand off to ascertain our latitudinal line. The reef field extends fully two leagues out from the land, and the warships can progress no further with us.'

'Aye, Loftus,' gasped Pitchbert, dabbing with his linen, 'but the *Charity* follows.'

'She must dog our track as close as she can, sir. It's a tortuous passage between the reefs.'

The gut-wracked vice-admiral looked around. 'The sooner I go back aboard the *Forbearance*, the better. Do proceed with haste.'

'With caution, sir,' I suggested.

Green-faced, he was beyond caring. After an exchange of signals, the warships ran off a little south, well clear and to leeward of the reef field. I descended quickly to the cabin, where the astronomer brought out a sheet of rough drawn plans.

'Captain, your pilot's sketch, which I kept with the code sheets,' said Spatchears, and resumed work on his figures.

The plan was crude in execution, hastily drawn in a rocking *canoa* while I was at Tranquil Inlet, yet it gave me the lie of the reefs.

'What of your sights?' I whispered. 'Have you worked them?'

'O, I am sure of my back-staff angles,' declared Noah, 'yet in using the instrument, I find its deficiencies legion, and have become intent on creating a new design. Example: take the brass scale –'

'We shall design back-staffs and cross-staffs later. What of the event?'

Giving me his most offended look, he elaborately cleared his throat. 'My sightings confirm that we have the day. The hour is much more problematickal. Under ordinary circumstance, I should never publish such a prediction. It exposes one to such possibilities of ridicule and –'

'Aye, but what's the predicted time?'

He blinked at the sharpness of my tone. 'Twenty four minutes before the zenith point of the sun's diurnal arc. Or local noontime, as a Navigator might have it.'

'And how good is the pocket-clock, from yesterday's time?'

He reached into the pouch of his weskit and pulled out that

274

handsome time-piece of Will Wrack's. Ever since Tranquil Inlet, old Noah had been following and recording its errors by sighting the noon meridian altitude, then adjusting his figures to allow for its daily gain or loss.

'It is a wonder to me,' he mused, wheezing softly, 'that there are yet men who would believe the answer to the Longitude lies in man's inventing instruments to measure Time accurately enough to –'

'By all the stars in the sky,' I rasped, 'how is the piece keeping time?'

He stiffened as if about to argue, then recomposed himself. Gazing at the watch's face, he said, 'It has been gaining *per diem* between six minutes and forty one and six minutes and forty nine seconds. With little change in the patterns of daily temperature movements hereabouts over the period, and my estimation that humidity has not deviated beyond the usual twenty four hour differences, I subtract an average of six minutes and forty five seconds from all timings. That allows for the error of the time-piece and should give accurate time relative to local noon here.'

Lord, he was long-winded. 'Then how long is there to go?'

'O, *tempus fugit*! Local noon is but an hour and thirty minutes away.'

'Time might fly for you, Observator, but not for me. If your prediction is for twenty four minutes before the zenith, there's still over an hour to wait.'

'Allowing for a margin of error in the workings, yes indeed.'

'What margin?'

He tapped the time-piece. 'Minutes only.'

'Very well. Be ready to take another sight if I call you.' I left him and went up the steps, sorely troubled. How could I procrastinate another hour? The more I delayed, the more it would arouse Pitchbert's suspicions.

On deck, it was at once clear the *Diamond* had drifted quite a distance closer to the reefs, yet the vice-admiral remained as impatient as a jack-tar at the muster for rum rations.

'Loftus, why can we not go in now?' he demanded.

'It's very hard to determine the entrance, sir, and the current is driving us west at a good rate,' I said, anxiously scanning the scene. 'One last fix, and we'll take the plunge.'

I called for the Observator and Spatchears appeared bearing Will Wrack's handsome three-foot long walnut instrument case. Placing it carefully on the deck-boards, he sprang open the locks and took out the back-staff. Glancing round for the sun's position, he unfolded the instrument to its fullest extent and steadied himself against the rail, back towards the sun. Then he sighted down the scale to see where the orb cast its shadow, adjusting the transom back and forth, muttering numbers and repeating them rapidly. For an unnerving moment, I feared the madness had returned. Pitchbert looked mildly surprised at the astronomer's chanting, but showed no interest in the sighting itself.

'The shore,' I said, pointing, one hand on the vice-admiral's shoulder, 'offers nothing useful to the mariner, nor indeed to the settler or planter. It's rocky and barren. The vegetation is impenetrable. Above all, there are no harbours or coves, and barely even the most tenuous of anchorages.'

'Dammit, Loftus, this is chatter. If you are certain of the place, I am minded to order you to sail in at once.'

'A rash thing, sir. This could be the wrong point on the coast altogether.'

'You must know the place, dammit. You hid the appendix here.'

'Aye, but one part is indistinguishable from another until we approach right close.'

'Well, well, I suppose so.'

'Nor do the reefs give any indication or feature by which I can identify them.'

'Indeed.'

'And I haven't a good measure of our Longitude.'

'Of course, of course.'

'The astronomer here, vice-admiral, is working out our latitude to the smallest degree.'

'I can see that for myself, Loftus,' snapped Pitchbert.

Old Noah was busy repacking the instrument in its box. 'In a few moments,' he announced, 'I shall confirm a latitudinal line, and further be able to say that the timing –'

'Very good, Observator Spatchears,' I cut in, guiding him rapidly towards the hatchway. Clutching the walnut case close to his chest, he stumbled down the steps. Under the tension of the moment, he began to mutter those infernal numbers again.

'Four five two six,' I heard from below. 'Eight eight nine nought, then five one three and again three.'

Now the vice-admiral looked concerned. 'Do you rely on this fellow? Is his mind quite whole?'

'The man is a brilliant astronomer and deviser of Mathematicks, sir.'

'Indeed? He seems deranged.'

'Madness may be close to genius, sir.'

Eli's urgent cry interrupted this discourse. 'Captain – the reefs!'

Not a boat's length off at the larboard side lurked the indistinct, brown shapes of huge coral heads, spaced unevenly at intervals of several fathoms apart, sprouting from the great reef banks that lurked below. The current swirled ominously. With the New Moon and its unusual conjunction, the tides were the highest of springs and their pull the strongest for years. On steerboard side lay a similar field of coral equally ripped by currents. The channel had closed in around our bark.

The *Charity* slouched along astern, trying to track our course closely. Her sails, like ours, were filling and slacking in the fickle breeze. Lord above, I thought, this is going to be a deal harder than expected. And how long to go now?

We reached a pool of clear water, free of coral heads and not far off the shore.

'Make ready the bower,' I said.

Eli swung the *Diamond*'s bows into the wind, and right forward Jan let go the anchor. The schooner's head fell off, went broadside, then the flukes bit, the cable tautened and she swung back straight. The *Charity* rounded up and anchored three or four boat lengths off. Going below, I returned with boots and a bundle of sailcloth, and began pulling on the footwear and tying thick leggings to my calves.

'What the Devil is this, Loftus?' said the vice-admiral, gesturing in annoyance at the trousseau.

'I'm going ashore now to recover the volume, sir. The scrub behind the strand is infested with snakes and poisonous crawling creatures. The natives are undoubtedly watching from cover nearby. They tip their arrows with a venom fierce enough to kill a large pig in half a minute.' I stood up in my improvised rig and grasped a boat-hook. 'And since you cleared all weapons off the *Diamond* and allow me no cutlass, I am obliged to fight my way into the vegetation with this in order to reach the cache.'

Gaspar and Jan lowered the *Diamond*'s new launch, a handsome item of Naval equipment and in fact the *Charity*'s spare boat, generously commissioned to us by the vice-admiral the better to expedite recovery of the lost treasures. Eli and I got in and stroked away.

Out of earshot, he leaned over and whispered, 'Captain Matthew, excuse me, just an old salt and all that. But by the Virgin's hairs, what the Hell are you about?'

'The difficulty, my friend, is that there are still thirty minutes to go.'

'Thirty minutes?' he scowled, stroking on. 'You mean half a glass, I shouldn't wonder. What use are minutes to a seaman? Measure the day in ship's watches or not at all, I say. My advice, captain, would be to junk-end all those clocks and time-pieces and just go by the sailor's way.'

'The sailor's way, Eli?' I said distantly, casting a worried glance skywards.

'A peep at the sun or the stars tells a sailor when it's time to rouse up for vittles or a change of the watch,' he huffed. 'The only thing it can't tell him is when it's time to sit at the heads or go in the piss-dale.'

Ashore, Eli stayed with the boat while I forged into the scrub and pretended to root about, swishing at the bushes with my boat-hook, disturbing the many scuttling creatures infesting the Tropick growth. Evil black caterpillars with shiny and segmented bodies dropped from the leaves, twisting and writhing as I stamped on them. Gingerly I pushed forwards, brushing overhanging branches aside and peering between the fronds, keeping hidden from view.

In the far distance, low down on the horizon and in bright sunshine, ranged the topsails of the *Bounteous* and the *Forbearance*, cruising unhurriedly back and forth, waiting. The *Diamond* lay off the strand with the *Charity* riding just beyond. I mooched about in the undergrowth, well aware that both the vice-admiral and the officers on the *Charity* would have me under constant observation. How much longer might I draw this out? At what point would my entire subterfuge collapse?

All at once, I saw a number of red-shirted men moving about on the *Charity*'s decks – armed marines, assembling at the rail as for a boarding party. So Pitchbert, as I guessed, had not after all the minutest intention of honouring his agreement.

If only the prediction would come right. Everything was in place except the crucial occurrence, and all hope of escape was slipping away. So too was my chance to avenge Adam's and Will's deaths. I wanted the Navy to suffer a defeat and loss that would make the laughter ring all around the Courts, the officers' clubs, the Greenwich cloisters and the Chatham yards. The ambitious Vice-Admiral George Pitchbert was to be brought down from his pedestal, humiliated in the eyes of the whole officer class of the Navy. Most particularly, it was Percy Gamble I desired to see shamed, his career dished, the captain demoted to an ignominious end as a penurious dud.

Sweating in the intense heat, puzzled and angry, I hacked and

279

lashed at the undergrowth to vent my frustration. Far from disgrace and failure being heaped on the Navy, on the heads of Gamble and Pitchbert, it was falling upon me. The sun continued to throw its infernal heat down from almost its fullest meridian height, unrelenting, merciless and uninterrupted. Dammit, I had delayed and extended to the utmost. Twenty four minutes before the zenith, Spatchears had said. Like everything to do with the mad astronomer and his works, it was a terrible error. I needed no cross-staff, nor quadrant, nor telescope, nor any blasted tables and columns, to tell me it was past noon. The time had come and gone. The prediction was nought.

A hail came from Eli and I ran to the water's edge. He was pointing agitatedly in the direction of the *Diamond*. Fifteen or twenty figures now moved about her decks, the raised barrels of their long-muskets visible in the clear bright day.

'Dam' you,' I cried into the sun's face.

How ludicrous to curse the sky. I fell to my knees on the hot beach and beat my fists, throwing up showers of grains into my face from the countless numbers there – as many, the philosophers said, as there were stars in the heavens.

Eli sat slumped in the launch, staring out to sea. The boat's prow was buried in the sandy shore, its stern rocking as wavelets lapped past and broke, hissing, on the damp strand. In the harshness of the Tropick heat and the startling blue of the sea under the noonday sun, I raged and raged, my anger incontinent. How could I have expected a conjunction of heavenly events to intervene on my behalf?

The muffled report of a musket-shot shattered the stillness. A puff of smoke rose from the *Charity*'s decks. The ball, half spent, whirred past and crackled into the undergrowth.

'Impatient cussed tykes,' said Eli, and spat.

22

FAITH AND CHARITY

As Eli and I stroked in alongside the *Diamond*, I counted a dozen soldiers with long-muskets crowding the weather-deck, some standing at ease or lounging at the rail, smoking. Near the fore-deck sat Gaspar, Jan and the one-armed Hap, downcast, prisoners again.

As we hauled ourselves dispiritedly over the rail, a voice barked, 'Arrest these men.'

The rig of tricorn hat, blue serge jacket-coat and fastened weskit, with a brace of pistols at the belt, was unmistakable, even without the newly-deformed jawline. Captain Gamble came down from the quarter, polished calf-boots clicking on the boards and cutlass drawn. I was instantly grabbed by two burly marines, while two more manhandled Eli away.

'Gamble,' said Vice-Admiral Pitchbert stepping forward, 'you're making things worse. Did I not explicitly order you to remain aboard the *Bounteous*? Consider yourself on a charge of insubordination.'

The captain bowed insolently. 'For rescuing an admiral from the hands of a vicious and determined band of pirates? For that matter, my lieutenants shall swear no such command was given and my scribe Botterel can show there were no written orders.' He adopted a conspiratorial smile and lowered his voice. 'Do not forget that I have removed and placed into my own safe keeping those dubiously legal pardons of yours, vice-admiral.'

Pitchbert turned to me and grasped my wrist. 'The appendix, Loftus. Where is it? For God's sake, give it up. I'll do new pardons.'

'No marines, vice-admiral,' I said. 'Dammit, you've broken our agreement.'

'Swearing at an officer, Loftus,' said Gamble, pointing with his blade. 'I shall add that to the schedule of charges on your head. And since it occurred aboard a Navy commissioned vessel,' he smirked, 'for the *Diamond* is again such, so I shall deliver verdict and punishment the moment we have got back aboard the *Bounteous*, without waiting for any Admiralty Court.'

'Loftus, what about your side of the bargain?' protested Pitchbert.

Gamble snorted. 'If I may interject, sir, there's no more bargaining.' He bent towards me, so close that every livid scar, all the hills and dales of the damage Eli had inflicted with his forehead, showed up in tumescent relief. 'And you, Loftus, are going on the winding rack before you hang.'

I looked at Pitchbert, but he remained silent, deflated.

Gamble waved his arm in a triumphant sweep along the shoreline. 'The near terrain looks adequate for a plantation and I intend to disembark a marine force to lay claim in Her Glorious Majesty's name. I shall declare this land for the Queen of England and fly the flag over it preparatory to bringing in good church-going settlers. It'll read rather well in my reports, do you not agree?' He straightened and gazed over the rail. 'Vice-admiral, I have ordered the *Bounteous* to close so we can proceed without delay.'

The vice-admiral and I looked round together. There was the great warship, reaching steadily along with topsails set and drawing, progressing on her stately way. Just then the breeze faltered and the canvas flapped limply as though she were borne along more by current than wind. In these pools and shallows, if Spatchears had been right, the spring tides would be running stronger than they had for a century, or perhaps ten centuries.

'Gamble,' said the vice-admiral, eyeing the warship's course, 'the way in is narrow.'

The captain gave a confident laugh. 'You have been sorely misled, sir. Why, I saw for myself when we brought the *Charity* in, a fifty gunner could pass through that channel.'

Caring nothing for the Navy's arguments and sick to my guts, I turned away and gazed over the rail to where the sea shone with bright hues and sunlight danced mockingly on the ripples. Almost in sympathy with the foreboding in my heart, the sun faded behind a passing cloud and a breath of wind fluked across the anchorage, rocking the schooner, shifting her gently in the dying breeze. Despairing, I dropped my forehead on to the rail. By now, it was clear my plan was in ruins. Perhaps it never could have succeeded, for Spatchears must be insane after all, the tables a nonsense, his heralded prediction nothing but a fantasy.

Gamble bore on. 'Loftus, I have ordered the bosun reeve a good new manila rope on the rack's winding drum,' he said, 'to reduce the influence of stretch, do you see, and impart the best mechanical advantage.'

Staring into the captain's bland, complacent features, I saw a man animated more than anything by the cruelties his Naval authority allowed him to exercise. Contempt and hatred welled inside me. He stood not a yard off, his cocky head framed against the purple of the sky in the distance beyond the *Diamond*'s quarter, the livid injuries and blood-dried weals across his nose and mouth highlighted by the cloud-obscured sun's slanting shades. The mauve light glowed so that each ridge and furrow of the scars, even the very pimples of his nose, cast a minute shadow and stood out in prominence. Still his voice droned on, lifeless and dull, mocking all my hopes. Struggling against the beefy marines holding me, I sought to move towards him, with only murder in mind.

But wait. Slanting light? A purple hue on the far horizon? I looked again. The rays striking Gamble's crooked face seem angled and diffuse. The glare of day was diminishing. The bright green coco palms along the shore, the white strand, the opalescent blues of the clear pool we were anchored in – all the colours of land and sea alike were fading. The sunlight shaded darker by the minute. Surely this shadow was caused by no passing cloud? I lifted my gaze. In the deepening blue above, there was not a single billow to be seen.

The time, I thought, my heart pumping – what time is it now? Well past the predicted hour, nearly half a glass after local noon, long beyond Spatchears' prediction.

Gamble continued to observe the *Bounteous*'s approach, prating on about the new lands he would name for the Sovereign Queen. But Pitchbert's gaze was directed skyward, mouth open, lips parted in surprise. In the waist, the other marines began to speak in puzzled murmurs, whispering to each other. One of them cast his eyes heavenwards, another clasped his hands in prayer. A third dropped his musket with a clatter. At the sound of the fallen weapon, Gamble whirled on the soldier.

'Retrieve your weapon, that man,' he snapped.

The marine ignored him, head tilted, mouth agape.

As always in these latitudes, near the top of its daily arc, the sun stood in the noon sky directly above an observer. Craning my neck in fascination, I saw the oddest thing, a spectacle to remain fixed in my mind for ever. Until my last breath, I shall not forget the vision that presented itself that noonday by the coast of Cuba.

Although still too bright to view directly, the great fiery sun was being vanquished, overcome by degrees. A growing black hemisphere had taken a giant's bite from it. All around, the canopy dimmed, losing its brilliance just as though the Tropick dusk had fallen suddenly upon the Earth. But this was different. The colours were not those of manjoes and blood, as at many a sunset hereabouts, nor did the clouds display their common pink and silver twilight pattern of a mackerel's back. The shapes and

284

hues were far from those of evening, let alone of noontime. Instead, the sky was darkly tinged like the guava juice we had drunk with the natives at Tranquil Inlet. No clouds were anywhere to be seen, for even the tradewind cotton-balls had disappeared. All the time, the sun – despite being so near its zenith height – was fading as the black half-circle advanced across its face.

It dimmed further. As one man the marines fell on their knees, some chanting prayers and working rosaries with fevered fingers, others jabbering incoherently. Gamble strode forward shouting for them pick up their muskets and stand to attention. They utterly disregarded him.

By now the sun had shrunk to a quarter circle, a mere crescent. The air chilled and I shivered. A breeze sprang up, ruffling my hair as if it had come vertically, raining a wind down from above. From the darkening sky, sudden vicious gusts swept the decks, trembling the belay pins in their rack and rattling loose blocks. The *Diamond*, unsettled like a nervous mare, swung on her anchor this way and that. All at once the gusts strengthened and torments of wind punched in from every direction. The schooner's bows sheered, snatching viciously at her cable.

Shouts went up from over the water, reaching us above the buffeting wind.

'She's dragging!' came a cry of alarm.

Across the reef-encircled pool, the *Charity*'s shadowy form was still visible in the weakening light. She had twisted out the flukes and sprung her anchor. In the grip of an astronomickally-strengthened current, she dragged helplessly across the pool towards the reefs. Her windlass clanked as more cable was run out but it failed to halt her progress.

The light began to wax and wane as if screens were being passed in front of the source. The sun shrank to nothing more than a jewel of light, flashing its single facet, reduced by the second. Now the sky was black all over. Absurdly, like a cowering God-fearer, I imagined the Devil himself riding above,

285

his huge cape enveloping the source of light and plunging the earth into a perpetual, frigid darkness.

A terrible, inhuman moan rose up right behind. The two marines still pinning my arms were struck rigid. From the hatchway there emerged into the gloom an emaciated figure, bony hands waving, the skull-like face illuminated in the last ghostly glows of the wounded, dying sun. The apparition paused, its enraptured countenance lifted to the sky. Then the spectre began its chant.

'O *Deus ex machina*! O declinations and conjunctions! Eight and seven and six and three!'

The warbling voice, rising in pitch to reach an inhuman wail, trembling and rattling in his mucous-ridden throat, gripped the entire complement of soldiers in spellbinding fear.

'My integers, O my logarithms! Fours and sixes and nines and ones!'

The marines capitulated. They cast themselves down on the deck-boards, begging for absolution and deliverance from Hell, until the babble of their prayers and religious incantations became a cacophony of clashing cries and shouts for mercy. Releasing their grip, my captors too prostrated themselves.

The Observator's rantings fell to a hoarse, painfully drawn whisper.

'Signs and symbols, equations and vectors, *Deo gratias*,' he breathed, his head waving from side to side. 'Plus twenty four, minus twenty four – forty eight's the difference.'

Though free, I stood immobile, unable to act. Never had I dreamt the event would be like this. I had foreseen, coldly and clearly from the dry tabulations and calculations and columns of figures, that there came simply a period of darkness followed by a re-illumination of the day. And the unexpected night had been my plan, our chance to dash off in the *Diamond*, leaving the *Charity* blind and trapped amongst the reefs while we outpointed the lumbering warships and got away. I had foreseen nothing of the transfixing nature of the event itself. Now, gripped by its grandeur and its terror alike, my mind defied the common sense that urged me to take advantage and press on. Instead, I reeled with the others, in thrall to the forces of Deity and Nature altering the Universe, upsetting the balance of everything. The stage on which we stood was tilting. We are angling towards the abyss, I thought, and reaching the end of the world.

Gamble's strangulated voice brought me back to my senses. He was yelling at the marines.

'Get up, you fools! It's only an eclipse of the sun.'

Far from rising at their captain's command, they threw themselves flatter before the mighty unknowable forces of their God, kissing the decks and calling for a priest, or an absolution, or their mothers.

Suddenly a pitch black shade raced in from the sea, so fast that in an instant its shroud was upon us and past. The edge of the Moon's sphere had covered the last golden shard of the sun, extinguishing it altogether. In that second, we were plunged into total night, cast completely under the shadow of the Moon.

The winds fell quiet. The marines quitted their wailing. Even Spatchears stopped babbling. In the stillness, utter silence reigned. I could not see six inches in front of my face, so total was the blackness.

Now the sun was quite gone from the sky, save for a smoky haze around where it once had beamed unchallenged. Overhead, the jet black canopy was littered with brilliant, twinkling stars. The planets shone out clear – Venus and Jupiter, masters of the night sky, suspended insouciant as ever, as though nothing was untoward.

But this was no ordinary time. A shrill, bubbling sound arose, like a busy little burn high on the moors. Ashore, though the animals and birds had gone to sleep or rest believing it to be night, in the darkness, insects awoke. The cucarachas began to sing and the moskeets to whine. The tree-frogs too, those tiny creatures that chirrup loud enough to wake the dead, added their voices. Millions of crawling, nocturnal creatures, tens upon tens of millions, trilling in unison – the sound enlarging suddenly like a wick turned up on a lamp – had embarked on their night-time chorus.

The eclipse has come late, I found myself thinking. At once, the absurdity of such a notion struck home, for the event could not be late, only the prediction wrong. Twenty four minutes before noon, Spatchears had promised, yet it had come after the sun passed its noon meridian. Exactly twenty four minutes after. Then I remembered the eclipse's duration. It would last, so the Observator had insisted, six and one half minutes. If he was right, then I had only this brief time in which to act before the light returned. I stamped my feet on the deck-boards. The wood felt solid. I reached out and touched the rail. It was smooth, still warm from the day's heat. Six and one half minutes. In the pitch darkness, surrounded by the eerie sounds of night, I had to act.

Without a sound, I fell on the startled Pitchbert, took hold of his weskit and flung him bodily against Captain Gamble. Both men lashed out in the dark, cursing, neither realising in the gloom who the other was. Snatching up the soldiers' fallen muskets, I herded the two big marines forward into the waist. They stumbled blindly, yet I knew every inch of these boards – every belay, every stow and step and rail. I moved surefootedly in their wake, issuing terse commands to their companions.

'Kick your muskets towards my voice,' I ordered. In the grip of superstition and fear, they complied at once and I cleared the weapons safely to one side.

'Up, fellows,' I said, encouraging them to the rail with a musket stock. 'Over the side and into your launch.'

If their faces had been visible in that pitch of night, they must have been pale with fear. Groping for the boarding rope, they hauled themselves up on to the rail, still praying and calling for salvation, and fell down unsighted into their boat. Moments later, I saw the glowing phosphorescent splash of the blades as the launch thrashed away, circling, trying to make towards the sounds

288

of confused hue and cry issuing from the troubled *Charity*.

'Eli, make sail! Boys, get the anchor!' I shouted.

Like me they had been overtaken by the magnitude and strangeness of the spectacle, quite forgetting my warnings that when a great darkness came, then was the time to act. Now at the sound of my voice they responded, moving quickly and noiselessly about the decks. On the quarter Captain Gamble barked nervously at his men, but they were gone. Keep talking, Percy, I breathed, padding silently back bearing a long-musket. Pointless orders and futile curses came in a stream from his deformed lips, allowing me to home in on him. The gun was a mere barrel's length from his chest when I sprang back the lock with a loud click.

'Cast down all your weapons, captain,' I told him, prodding with the muzzle. When his pistol and cutlass clattered to the deck-boards, I said, 'Now jump overboard.'

I heard his foot mount the rail. Then he hesitated. Beneath my finger, the trigger moved infinitesimally. Did he know he was within the twitch of a muscle of losing his life? I checked myself. The spring was strong and it held.

'Go,' I ordered. 'Over the side with you.'

There was a grunt as he climbed over. Was it my imagination or did he truly pinch his scab-encrusted nostrils fussily between two fingers before descending feet first into the black water below? There was a splash and a greenish glow of foam, the only source of light in the whole world under the eclipse's shadow. Then he stroked away in the direction of the commotion from the *Charity*.

Right forward, the *Diamond*'s windlass clanked busily as the anchor came up, fathom by fathom. I started for the waist, intent on making sail, and ran into something soft and pulpy. It was Pitchbert's sweating form. He was down on his knees, in a trance, hands clasped together as if in prayer.

'You too, vice admiral   time to go,' I told him, with the musket's muzzle at his arse.

'It's beautiful – gorgeous,' he murmured, rising and groping for the rail. 'What a wonderful work.'

'Just the Moon covering the sun,' I said, prodding him with the long-musket.

'How did you do it, Loftus?' he said. 'Get under the path so exactly?'

'The tables. The appendix, as you call it. Now, over the side.'

'O, glorious works!' His voice was close and breathy. 'Don't you see, man? We can return in triumph to London. You'll get a free pardon, I'll be made earl or duke. We can bargain still.'

'I shan't bargain with you again, not for all the riches on God's Earth.'

'But it was Gamble's fault. The marines were his idea.'

'Do you think it matters to me? Into the sea you go.'

'I can't swim!'

'Dogs can. Think of them and you'll work out the method.' Dropping the musket, I grabbed his ankles and swung his legs up. With a shriek, he pivoted, clawing at the rail, arms waving. When I shoved, he lost balance and disappeared. Half a second later, there came a satisfying splash followed by a pitiful cry and a gurgle. But he found the way to swim.

It was still inky black. I made my way into the waist and joined Eli to help hoist up sail. The windlass clanked and groaned with the boys' efforts until Gaspar's voice came through the thickness of the gloom, 'Anchor cable up and down, captain.'

The breath of a breeze brushed my face and the *Diamond*'s bows swung through a great arc. The sails flapped and bellied, then filled. Grabbing the tiller-bar, I sensed the waters passing over the rudder blade. The helm answered and she pointed her head downwind. The current was strong, but running which way? Then I realised the compass lamp was unlit. Dammit, in the darkness, how could I get my bearings?

I faltered. Of a sudden, a field of light appeared in the far distance. The six and a half minutes had passed. Where earlier, the near edge of the Moon's shadow had raced across the sea and plunged us into that final, extinguishing blackness, now the cast of its far limb came flying across the leagues as if they were mere fathoms. It flashed overhead at an unimaginable rate and at once the darkness lifted. The sun showed a thin circle of fire with – at the top limb – a sparkling blaze of flame for all the world like the diamond ring on a queen's finger.

The half-light gave enough to get a bearing on the land. With renewed force, the wind returned, gusting this way and that, boxing about and sending the compass card swinging wildly. Uncertainly, the *Diamond* gathered way. But where was the escape channel? A touch came at my arm and there was Spatchears, his face shining like a schoolboy's.

'Four six eight and ten! O, my predictions were right,' he trilled.

'Your predictions were only half right, Observator Spatchears,' I said, brushing him aside to get a clear view. The event had surely tipped him over the edge and back into lunacy.

He held out a paper, his eyes bright and alert. 'No more numbers, not even eleven fifteen twenty two or forty nine – just lines. Your *vade mecum.*'

It was my pilot's sketch. Lord, I thought, gratefully snatching it up, some vestige of sanity must remain in the old man's mind.

A chorus of shouts and alarms rose up on our larboard side. In the growing light, we saw the *Charity*, borne along in the grip of current and wind, falling back with her anchor bouncing uselessly along the bottom. She stopped dead and canted over a few degrees. Men ran to the side rails, pointing down in alarm.

'She's hard aground!' came the cry.

The *Charity* heeled further, settling on the reef's edge, her fate fixed. There came a hollow booming sound as she loosed off a piece. It was a wild shot from a figure bent over the forward swivels, fury getting the better of his aim. With his men beyond orders, Captain Gamble had acted alone, and futilely.

Across to our steerboard side, with the sun strengthening by the minute, a morning twilight illuminated the greenish waters of the coral reefs. Beyond I saw a band of blue. Glancing from the plan to the compass and back, I reckoned it must be the deep water channel.

'Harden sheets,' I called, pushing the tiller-bar to larboard. Our bows swung over.

I ordered Jan up the ratlines to spy out the way from the vantage of height and give the course to steer. Full daylight was almost restored and the blue-black smear of the channel became clearer by the minute.

'Look, look – the *Bounteous*!' called Jan, pointing.

There was the warship, revealed once more in the daylight, nearly a league away at the edge of the reef field. I needed no magnifying tube to tell me the story. She was stopped in the water, her topsails aback.

'By all the sinners,' cried Eli Savary, 'she's stuck faster than a whore on a jack-tar!'

Distantly astern of her was the *Forbearance*, keeping well off the shoals, unlike her sister warship, but in the wind and current she had sagged far to leeward and would need half a day's sail just to draw level. The *Diamond* would be over the horizon in an hour.

From the *Charity*, I heard Gamble bawl at his men to engage in their gunnery work, but the Navy schooner had settled on the edge of a steep coral bank, her guns one side pointing high in the air and, on the other, into the water. As we swiftly approached to pass her by and run through the channel, there were voices raised in argument.

'You disobeyed my orders.' It was the vice-admiral. 'You endangered Her Majesty's ships for no good purpose.'

'On the contrary,' came Gamble's petulant reply, 'it is you who acted without good reason – for no prize, no land claim, no war purpose, merely this diverting appendix.'

'The appendix is worth more than any dam' prize, you oaf!'

'You'll have little chance of convincing the Court-martial of that. Not when they see my evidence of your bargaining with a common pirate and wanted criminal.'

'You're on a charge, Gamble,' spluttered Pitchbert. 'Good God, you've put two Navy vessels hard aground in as many minutes.'

'As is my right, I shall be bringing counter charges, vice-admiral,' was the rejoinder, 'based on my detailed reports covering all the mishaps.'

Their argument raged on. We swept past all but unnoticed as the Navy – disabled, reef-bound, incapable of fighting – disputed and contested amongst themselves. Meanwhile, skimming the corals, consulting my sketch of the reef field, I short-tacked the *Diamond* back and forth along the narrow channel until at last it broadened. Beyond lay the open sea.

'We're bearing off,' I called, pushing the tiller over. 'Ease sheets.'

The compass needle swung. With every passing second, the tradewind breeze reasserted itself, strengthening and carrying the schooner clear. The sun shone so strong and clear it was nigh impossible to believe that a quarter of an hour before we had been benighted by the totality of an eclipse. The day was as bright as an ordinary Tropick noon.

Or even, I smiled, twenty four minutes either side of it.

'All is lost – lost,' muttered Noah Spatchears, huffing and gasping after a prolonged coughing bout. 'I cannot go to England.'

I glanced around at my fellows' glum faces. The *Diamond* was anchored in a river mouth along the deserted Florida shore, a swampy disease-ridden land of no imaginable colonial or commercial value whatsoever, giving it the advantage of being free of Spanish and English patrols. With Pitchbert's pardons lost to us, my plan had been to meet the Charlestown packet off the Carolina shore, put the Observator aboard and send him safe to London with the volume and the code. We had completed

293

more than half the long voyage when the astronomer unexpectedly confessed he had discovered a 'terrible flaw'. So we had all – Eli, Gaspar, Jan, the one-armed Hap and myself – packed into the cramped day-cabin to hear him out.

'But you must have remembered the code right,' I insisted, waving the sheaf of parchments under his nose. 'Or almost right. Your prediction was out only by forty eight minutes – twenty four the wrong side of the zenith.'

'Yes indeed,' he said quietly, 'all but good enough for the transit.'

'And not for the Navigation?' I said, remembering our discussion.

Old Noah's sunken countenance crumpled into a parody of dementia. 'O the code's inversed, the Universe reversed! O dear, O dear, *festina lente*. Too much haste and discombobulation.'

'Perhaps just a figure or two missing from the code was enough to reverse the timing?' I suggested hopefully. Earlier, I had wondered if the two pages torn from the volume itself during our Martinique encounter could be to blame, but he had assured me they were not.

'O nooo-ooooo, *mea culpa*,' he puffed, 'it's wrong, wrong, wrong!'

I laid a hand on his wrist. 'What? What is wrong with the code?'

'Confused, O so confused, my poor head. The code's not wrong.' Again, he wore the fearful, haunted look of insanity. 'The drawers – stealing the book,' he breathed, shaking his head. 'In my haste, when I broke into Sir Thomas's cabin, I must have laid hands on the wrong set of tables.'

'What the Devil do you mean, the wrong set of tables!' I shouted, falling back in despair. Every time the old lunatick spoke, it seemed, there dropped from his lips some new and destructive revelation. Trying to calm myself, I said carefully, 'The tables are the same. What difference does it make which set you stole? You had two copies of the tables made by the scribe

294

at Greenwich and they were both flawed by similar means, you said.'

'They were not exact copies.' He hesitated. 'They were flawed by similar means, but by different measures. O dear, yes, indeed, each copy of the tables had its own set of errors. Thus, there is not one version of the tables, but two, and likewise of the codes.'

'Two codes for two tables?' I said, not wanting to believe it.

'Yes, but only one for each.'

My head spun. 'You mean, they must match?'

Spatchears nodded vigorously.

'Two codes, two tables, and they must match or the tables cannot work,' I repeated dumbly. 'And at this late stage, you discover that we possess the wrong tables for your remembered code?'

Noah Spatchears groaned and put his head in his hands. 'Forgot my own symbols – misread the signs.'

'You put signs or symbols in the tables to distinguish the one from the other?'

'Indeed, but I fear they were too simple, so I forgot which was which. O, if only I had devised something more complicated and systematick.'

'So you committed to memory an enormously arcane code,' I said with growing incredulity, 'and then could not keep hold of a few simple symbols?'

'My mind whirls like the heavens. All at sea, the stars mixed up. The heavens plagued with stars! The Demons of the sky! The Protestants, the bankers –'

'Hush, sir, calm yourself.' His rambling interfered with my ability to think. A new notion had struck me. I was thinking of Commodore Filligrew, imagining him detailing a Navigator to work out sights using his tables and code, then encountering the same persistent, frustrating flaws I had found.

'So this explains the great mystery,' I said at last, 'why Filligrew's been chasing us. Not to stop our tables getting to

London first, but because like us he's realised his tables and code don't pair up.'

'Well, if you say so,' said Eli, shaking his head and reaching for his baccy pouch. 'It's harder to make sense of than using a jellyfish to caulk a seam.'

The Dutch boy got the point. 'So he's got to get your tables, sir, to make the match?'

'Exactly so, Gaspar. It's nothing to do with any damm'd so-called appendix – that's some game of his own making. What he wants is our tables. Or indeed, our code.'

Eli paused in stuffing the bowl of his clay. 'Aye, well that's simple enough,' he said, 'even for my poor old head.'

I barely heard him. 'And by the same token, my good fellows, we want to barter his tables for ours. Or his code for ours – either way.'

I stood up and paced awkwardly round the cramped cabin. It seemed so easy to say – exchange the tables or code – and so inconceivable to do. Yet something must be done, for it was no longer my pardon alone at stake. The Navy's ire would be sorely inflamed by the eclipse fiasco and every man aboard the *Diamond* held liable. Now we all faced being hunted down like animals for the rest of our lives, every one of us. There had to be a way of saving these loyal fellows from that fate.

Noah Spatchears, dabbing at his mouth with a disgusting cloth, leant forward conspiratorially.

'O yes, captain, you must seize the chance. And when you retrieve the other tables,' he said, pointing a knuckly old finger at me and smiling as if addressing a schoolboy, 'you shall know them by the secret symbols marked on every page. And I have now remembered them all, every one!'

I shot him a fierce look. 'Retrieve Filligrew's tables? You make it sound an easy matter, Observator. What do you imagine, that our little schooner should go chasing after that mighty flota and ask for them back?'

Eli held a match poised above the striker. 'That's about as

much sense,' he said, 'as a jack-tar swimming after the sharks who've taken his tunny fish.'

He struck the match and the flame hissed, lighting his weather-beaten face. But in its flaring glow, his canny old eye gleamed.

23

DRAGON'S MOUTH

Dipping the muffled oars into the black, oleaginous waters by Port-of-Spain, I sent the launch a few pulls closer through the night's enveloping cloak of heat and stillness. Streaks of yellow danced on the wavelets and above soared the high stern quarters of a grand ocean-going bark, its mullions glowing with lamplight. I stroked right under the towering bulk of the great ship. My visit was timed for the deepest watch of the night, the hour before dawn, when a ship's company is most off its guard.

No breeze rustled the surface, yet the bark rocked on a lazy swell undulating the smooth waters of the Golfo Paria. Each time the stern rose and she canted over with the silent swells passing under her keel, her underparts sucked clear of the surface with a watery sigh. Trails of weed hung down, dripping and slimy, before she tilted back again and sent bubbles of trapped air gurgling upwards like the gasps of drowning men. Perhaps, behind the high gallery, her commander grumbled in his bunk at these uneasy shifts or, if he were still at his papers, spilled his ink or lost his reading place.

The launch's gunnels bumped gently alongside. I coiled the painter over my shoulder and, when for an instant the ship settled on an even keel, lunged forward aiming a boarding axe into the timbers above her waterline and to one side of the massive rudder jutting from her transom. Hoping any idler below would dismiss the thud of the axe as a mere rumble of movement somewhere deep inside the booming hull, I swung out of the launch and caught hold of the rudder fixings. Reaching up to grasp the chains emerging from the steering gear, I made off the painter and let the launch fall clear. I would be back for it within the half-glass.

Ducking between the chains and the iron-banded boards of the rudder blade, I continued up the transom panting with effort, for the wooden wall here was tilted back. My feet scrabbled for grip on the gilded decorations but the carvings offered toeholds and the timbers were dry, so I soon gained height to come under the gallery itself. Here I paused, breathing hard, listening for a step on the walkway. I leaned outwards to get a view beneath the gallery rail. Seeing nothing, I slipped noiselessly over the bar and stood outside the stern windows.

They were propped open on their deadlights to catch any cooling waft of air. Across the Great Cabin, lit by a flickering oil-lamp, stood a chart table, a chaos of books and papers strewn over its polished surface. From an ink-stand, quills stood up sharpened and ready. In the midst of all this, his back towards me, was the bulky figure of a grey-headed gentleman, slumped as though in the throes of his work when sleep overcame him. Irregular snores rose into the still fug of the cabin.

Taking a pistol from my belt, I slipped under the deadlight and padded into the room. The gentleman stirred.

'Sir Thomas,' I said.

Startled, the commodore lifted his head and, catching sight of me, scrabbled on the table as if seeking a weapon.

'Don't move or call out,' I breathed, lifting my pistol higher.

He rubbed his eyes, taking in the new circumstance. Recognition came quickly.

'Well, well, it's Matthew Loftus,' he said. 'I chase you about the Caribbee Sea for months and now you do me the service of appearing in my Great Cabin.' The slight dip of his head was accompanied by the stifling of a yawn. 'How did you know I was in Trinidad?'

'The Filligrew flota's not hard to find. The whole island chain knows your whereabouts.'

He stretched languidly. 'Well, my dear fellow, now you've found her, you shan't get off the *Prometheus* again.'

'O, I think I shall. I have come to treat with you, Sir Thomas.'

'To treat?' He laughed, then said, 'On what possible grounds?'

'Your advancement to the Admiralty Court. No tables, no appointment.'

His eyes widened, and he thought for a moment. 'Ah, George Pitchbert and his babblemouth habits, of course.'

'Indeed so. The vice-admiral and Percy Gamble forgot themselves enough to discuss you in my presence.'

Filligrew stretched again, and yawned. 'Aye, the Admiralty believes I saved the tables for the Navy. A magnificent achievement, they concede, and one they are obliged to reward.' He studied the muzzle of the gun, pointing directly at his head. 'Loftus, do you have any comprehension of what a position at the Admiralty Court means?'

'That you'll hang a lot of innocent seamen.'

'True, but the administration of justice is a small part of the post.' He leaned back comfortably, arms behind his head. 'Think of the commissions, man. Letters of marque. Divisions of prize money. Allocation of patrols. The patronage, the rewards, the spoils – Lord above, the opportunities are boundless. Far better to accumulate wealth and glory by issuing decrees from the comfort of a mansion in Jamaicka than by roaming about the seas on lurching ships, eating vile biscuit and salted fish, getting shot at.'

'And all that will be beyond your reach,' I said, 'as soon as your tables are found to be useless. You can bluff and bluster all you wish, Sir Thomas, but I know your tables do not work with the code you possess.'

'And your tables likewise cannot work, for you have no code at all.'

300

'O, but I do have a code.'

He sat up, startled for a moment, then smiled again. 'It seems you may have swallowed that old lunatick's damm'd lies and rants. The other code is lost – if there ever was one.'

'Indeed there is a second code, and with great difficulty I have retrieved it.' I gave an infinitesimal tilt. 'There are now two codes and two tables, and each of us has a mismatching set.'

He put his fingers together, working it out. 'Ah, perhaps I should have tested Spatchears a little harder.'

'You must come to terms, Sir Thomas. I propose a straight-forward exchange. To correct the error, as it were.'

'And do you imagine, Loftus, this exchange shall save your neck?'

'Aye. And your career.'

He smiled. 'I have only to put you upon the rack until you squeal out where your tables are hidden.'

'It can't help you, Sir Thomas. If I'm not back from the *Prometheus* in time, Observator Spatchears – who is safe and well a long way from here – shall release letters to the Admiralty in London revealing the truth, namely that your tables do not work and never can.'

For an instant he appeared unsettled, then regained his usual demeanour. 'Most impressive. You planned well. But I do not fear Spatchears and his letters.'

'I think you do. Your appointment rests on the tables proving effective.'

'Wrong. It rests on a belief that they work – the belief, mark you, not the reality. Specifically, on Pitchbert's belief.' Filligrew leaned forward, elbows on the table, hands clasped beneath his chin. 'The vice-admiral shall sign my advancement the minute I reach Port Royal and formally hand over the tables. Once his seal is upon it, my appointment can be rescinded only by direct prerogative of the Monarch. Loftus, you have miscalculated once again.'

Six bells clanged distantly overhead. I listened hard, straining

301

to hear the faint stirrings deep in the bowels of the great bark that would mean she was rousing herself to life.

Filligrew was still speaking of his future. 'The great Sovereign Queen Anne herself, Loftus – imagine that! By the time any flaws are revealed, I shall be well entrenched, very much richer and highly influential. Even the Monarch herself may give pause before attempting to unhinge me, for patronage is a powerful instrument when judiciously wielded.'

I met his steady gaze. 'Pitchbert won't sign because he thinks you haven't got the so-called appendix.'

Sir Thomas continued to look pleased with himself.

'Not so. The vice-admiral believes the mythical "appendix" is not crucial but merely an extra bit of the work, a few more stars and observations – worth having, but not vital. You see, he has never been interested in the minutiae of the matter.'

'Then why was he so intent on getting it?'

In the ensuing silence, I heard the distant tread of sentries on the sleeping ship's quarter-deck high above. Dammit, I had planned to be away quicker than this. Filligrew used both hands to smooth his beard, straightening the bristles and bringing them to a point at his chin.

'Pitchbert saw an opportunity to dish me. We are rivals, Loftus – rivals in ambition. He went haring off intent on getting his hands on the appendix first, as I knew he would. I hoped of course that he would bring back your tables, thinking he had found the appendix and could therefore claim a little of the triumph and diminish mine. Yet in the end it went to my advantage.'

'Hardly. The mission failed entirely.'

'O, you got away without giving up your volume,' he said, with a shrug, 'but in doing so you proved to the credible Pitchbert just how well the tables work, did you not? Ever since that eclipse escapade of yours, he's been frothing about the marvellous event and the efficacy of the Method.' He gave a throaty chuckle. 'You, Loftus, by your own ruse, converted Vice-

Admiral George Pitchbert from my greatest rival into my sternest advocate. He is about to journey home to London to cover himself in the reflected glory of Commodore Filligrew's success, while I bask in the Admiralty Court's splendour and munificence in Jamaicka. You've altogether miscounted the politickal arithmetick of the thing. Pitchbert's going to sign, and there's nothing you can do or say to stop him.'

He seemed so damm'd confident. Had I truly, in emphatically demonstrating the tables' powers, destroyed my sole lever?

'Tripped up, I'd say, Loftus,' Sir Thomas continued, 'by your own marlinspike.'

The *Prometheus* shifted her vast bulk on the sluggish swells rolling into Port-of-Spain, and a hundred and fifty feet away at the beak her anchor chains rumbled. Somehow, I half guessed what was coming next.

'And once I am appointed to the Jamaicka Court,' he continued, with the air of one addressing a simpleton, 'you shall enjoy the privilege of becoming the very first convicted criminal in whose honour I don the black cap.'

There were sounds all along the great ship's length – launches bumping alongside, murmured commands, the faint sound of piping somewhere – as if she and her hundreds of seamen and idlers and officers were sleepily coming awake for the day.

'Before hanging you, I shall torture you for your tables then sail to London and reveal that the ones Pitchbert brought back are useless. Despite this vice-admiral's blunders, they'll say, Filligrew has saved for the English Navy the greatest advance in the Longitude of the last hundred years, and perhaps the next. I shall kneel before a grateful Queen to be covered in further glory, and all at George Pitchbert's expense. You might as well give up the tables now, Loftus, and save yourself a racking. You've really no other choice.'

I raised up the pistol, the muzzle bearing directly on to the commodore's face from six inches distant. Half of me was thinking, if all is truly lost, why should he live?

'You had choices, Sir Thomas, in the past,' I said, my jaw clenched.

He narrowed one eye along the line of the barrel. 'Meaning?'

'You sent a ruthless authoritarian fool after me, who executed an innocent man.'

He sucked his teeth. 'Gamble? He was only following Navy practice. Deserters must be hanged.'

'Adam Pyne was no deserter, dam' your eyes.' Keep hold of your temper, I warned myself.

'You forget, at the Witness Isles, the boy ran away from the *Prometheus*.'

My palm was sweaty around the pistol's handle, the trigger growing slippery. 'The Navy cannot hang a man,' I said, my voice rising, 'for leaving a private ship.'

'But my flagship had Navy commissions at the time. Either way, Pyne was a common no-good jump-ship.'

My temper broke. 'He was worth ten – a hundred – of you!' I shouted. 'Or a thousand of your blasted Gambles or any damm'd admirals!' The commodore sat back in alarm as I waved the muzzle under his nose. 'That boy was as loyal as they come, ready to give his life for the English Navy. He was choked to death swinging from the cross-jack of one of Her Majesty's ships, killed by a cruel, self-serving imbecile. And it was you, Filligrew, who sent the man who did it.'

The blood pounded in my temples and the sweat stung my eyes. I all but discharged the pistol into his face there and then. There was a brief silence before I slowly lowered the weapon.

'What's done is past altering,' I muttered. The pistol drooped.

Filligrew breathed again. 'By Satan's bollacks, Loftus,' he whistled, 'the rats must be in your briches. You were a more reasoning man when I first met you. Perhaps the company of that most charming girl softened you.'

Instantly, my fingers tightened again on the smooth handle of the pistol, damp under my sweating grip.

'How dare you even speak of her,' I breathed.

He put up his arms, spreading his fingers in an open-handed gesture. 'I was only about to remark on how courteous a letter she writes, and in such a flowing, delicate hand.'

'What letter?' I snapped.

'Why, she has courteously sent me a note of gratitude.'

I gaped. 'When did you receive it?'

'Some days since. It was written before she – well, let us say, before she departed.'

'What in Hell do you mean?' I aimed the muzzle again at his face. 'Give it to me.'

Hastily scrabbling about on the table, scattering documents and chartings, he found a sheet of parchment. I snatched it from him. The writing leapt from the page, her hand familiar from so many cargo manifests and crew lists. She explained to Filligrew – *'dearest, most generous Commodore'* – that through starvation and disease exacting their toll, the plantation had become untenable. She thanked him for supporting the venture, but her father had ordered her on to the last trading vessel to call in, which was making for Port Royal, whence she would shortly embark a packet ship. Mister Jeffreys – *'the kindest and most loyal of fathers'* – would stay to see affairs brought fully to a close before handing ownership of the plantation to the overseer and his wife, whereupon Mister Jeffreys would himself depart likewise from Cala Arena for ever. In a last kindness, she begged that the commodore might assist her father's passage, for he had fondly given his daughter the very end of his money and they were now quite ruined.

And one more paragraph. If ever the destiny of Matthew Loftus rested in the commodore's palm, would Sir Thomas accept from her – as a simple, honest and most respectful woman, and taking into account his innocence of the crimes of which he stood accused – a plea for leniency and fairness. Then below her name, a crushing postscript: she beseeched Sir Thomas be so kind as to keep from him her whereabouts or intended destination.

I lowered the paper. 'When was this? How long ago was it written?'

'The letter's undated, Loftus.' He sounded amused. 'Why so keen an interest? After all, it seems she no longer loves you.'

'Hold your noise, blast you!'

Again came a clanging from far above on the quarter-deck. Seven bells, and soon the ship would be fully awake. Already there were shouts and the movement of men about the decks as the watch above prepared to rouse up the watch below. In five minutes, the bark would be alive with men going about the tasks of the day.

Filligrew sat stroking his beard. 'A touching plea, was it not? I sent off some passage money for the uncommercial Mister Jeffreys.'

I tried to gather my thoughts. 'When did she leave Cala Arena? Do you know what happened there?'

'No idea at all. What does it matter? Ghastly Hellish place, to my mind, not worth the candle. Pity I wasted good roundshot and powder in securing it. It'll be another two weeks before any fresh despatches reach us from Port Royal. It's a beat against the trades to gain the Lesser Antilles from Jamaicka, and, my dear man, there's war.'

Dizzily, I gripped Abigail's letter with both hands and searched again for a date, or any clue. I thought back to the day we had arrived at Cala Arena. Had I looked at her face, or even that of Mister Jeffreys? No, I had turned away. What if – or was this a wild, insane hope – but what if the overseer and his wife had worn the Jeffreys' cast-off clothing? Perhaps it was their corpses we had buried, not Abigail's and her father's. I remembered the Negroes said the overseer, not the merchant, had fired the shot that set off the slaughter. If Eli and Gaspar, hiding in the forest, had not been to the settlement for weeks before the attack, they could not have known if Abigail had been gone before the onslaught. But had she?

There was noise in the passage outside and I glanced up in

306

alarm. Intent on the letter, I had let the pistol carelessly dangle. Suddenly Filligrew moved. His hand was on it in a flash and the muzzle pointed at my belly. Next moment the door burst open and a portly figure entered wearing the full Navy uniform of a high ranking officer. Stepping briskly into the cabin, waving a paper, he approached the commodore.

'Good morning, Sir Thomas,' said this gentleman. 'I make no excuse about coming aboard so early. It's a singularly important matter – my despatch to the Admiralty describing Gamble's failure to retrieve the appendix. You must countersign –'

Suddenly he caught sight of me. The paper fell from his hand and fluttered to the cabin sole.

'By the Sovereign's bedchamber, can it be Loftus?' exclaimed Vice-Admiral George Pitchbert. His expression was one of pure confusion. Then he caught sight of the pistol in the commodore's hand. 'Why, Filligrew, you've captured him. How – ah, how splendid. What a clever cove you are. Good Lord, but the fellow isn't tied or shackled. Guards!'

Before either of us could move, he was at the door calling for marines. I stared at Filligrew, amazed. What in Hell's name was going on? Without thinking, I had assumed the vice-admiral to be at the Navy station in Port Royal.

The commodore shook his head angrily, hissing, 'Loftus, reveal nothing, or you're shark-meat. I'll bargain with you.'

Two marines entered. Again, my feet were locked in chains. Pitchbert's gaze flicked from me to Sir Thomas and back, and it was clear as lagoon water what he was thinking. He was convinced that we had spliced up a plot at his expense.

'Caught unawares, eh?' said the vice-admiral, suspicious eyes darting this way and that. 'Badly caught out, I think, Loftus.'

Sir Thomas sprang the pistol's lock back to rest, then got up and paced about the sole, stopping before the sternlights, where the grey of dawn glimmered. The vice-admiral arranged himself in a chair opposite me.

'So, how did you find the fellow, Filligrew?' he said, rubbing

307

his hands and beaming uncertainly at us both. 'Doubtless fell upon him carousing in Port-of-Spain, eh? No matter, we have him. Lucky I was here for the negotiations. Damm'd tricky at the bargaining table, these Dago ambassadors.' He seemed to enjoy my look of surprise. 'Under the impression that Spain was allied with France in this war, were you, Loftus? They may think so in Paris but the Spanish colonies are too keen on their lucrative trading arrangements. With the enemy. In secret. That's why I've come with the commodore's flota. I could hardly haul into enemy territory in the *Forbearance*, flying the English standard, could I?'

Sir Thomas turned. With a sardonic glance my way, he said, 'I trust, vice-admiral, you are comfortable aboard the *Saskia*?'

'Very amenable billet, most pleasing bark,' said Pitchbert. 'Now, Loftus, I've related to the commodore the entire tale – the loss of the *Bounteous*, the *Charity* out of commission and all that. Gamble's going up for Court-martial. Of necessity, there are further charges on your head too.'

A brief silence ensued, disturbed only by the drumming of Pitchbert's fingers. He was trying to work things out, and so was I. Both these gentlemen, it now transpired, might desire to treat with me – Filligrew to prevent the revelation to Pitchbert that his code and tables mismatched, the vice-admiral seeing a new chance to get hold of the 'appendix' and garner a portion of the glory.

Pitchbert took a deep breath. 'Sir Thomas, as the senior commander – unofficial but *de facto* – within a flota engaged in Her Majesty's cause though not flying her standard at present, I request that you discontinue your presence in this Great Cabin.'

The commodore spun round. 'Are you asking me to leave my own quarters?'

'Forthwith,' said Pitchbert, glaring. 'And not requesting – commanding.'

Filligrew still held my pistol. The vice-admiral wore a cutlass at his waist. For an instant, I imagined them fighting over me, a confrontation that would be hard to explain to Her Majesty even in such cravenly couched despatches as those Gamble excelled at. In an instant, though, Sir Thomas knew he must back down to the senior man.

'Very well,' he said, reaching the cabin door. 'But I shall make the most severe protest in the highest quarters.'

When he had gone, Pitchbert shifted his hindquarters uncomfortably.

'An irascible fellow,' he remarked with a shake of his head. Then, leaning closer, he said, 'Filligrew is going to hang you like a common pirate as soon as his flota touches at Port Royal. Do you understand?'

'Aye sir, I do.'

'That escapade with the eclipse – very clever! Less so to let yourself run into the commodore's hands, but let that pass. The point is, Loftus, what about these works?'

I sighed. 'You want the appendix, I assume.'

He appeared shocked. 'Good Lord, no! Things have moved on since then.'

My bewilderment must have been plain.

'Don't you see, Loftus? The appendix is irrelevant and I no longer care if you have it or not. The point is, Filligrew has the tables and time has run out. I must sign his appointment before I return to London, after which all I can do is promote my own meagre part in saving the thing for the nation.'

I was nonplussed. 'Then why do you want to talk to me alone?'

'I can put in a plea for leniency, Loftus. Filligrew shall have to take note of it, coming from a vice-admiral. That's all I can offer. What I want in return is that you resolve the flaws – this difficulty of the flaws.'

What flaws could he be talking about? He had never understood the Astronomy, never even got the Method's name right, and remained confused over the appendix. How much did he know of the codes? Did he understand about the mismatching sets?

The vice-admiral smiled sadly. 'You see, Captain Gamble – no doubt in an attempt to dissuade me from putting him to the Court-martial, though it's too late – has been explaining this Lunar Longitude complexity to me.'

'Gamble has been explaining this?' I spluttered, unable to disguise my incredulity.

'He maintains that this Lunar Distinction business is a delusion, and the eclipse prediction nothing more than a lucky stroke. The tables might advance certain aspects of astronomy but no one could Navigate by this method.'

I sat back in amazement. Had the vice-admiral taken his lessons from, of all people, the Navigationally illiterate Gamble?

'He is quite wrong, of course, Loftus, but he is not alone. How many doubters there are, so many conflicting claims! Yet I have seen with my own eyes how effectively the Method works. The pity is that there were no properly witnessed reports of the eclipse. Rather, to your prediction of it. What I want is for you to write out exactly how it was achieved, how you used the Lunar Longitudinal Distance. Get it all down, make the most convincing story of it – a story with which I can enthrall the halls of the Admiralty, amaze the Royal Society and astonish even the Royal Court. Write it all out, and in clear manuscript too. You shall have a scribe for the purpose. In return, you win a vice-admiral's formal plea for leniency.'

He was so pathetically eager to glean some shred of glory from the tables that I began to see a way to regain an advantage.

He tapped my arm. 'Can we not make such a bargain? A leniency plea for a little work of dictation?'

Shifting my limbs in the chair, awkwardly hauling at the shackles, I said at length, 'What value, sir, is there in a written statement of mine? I am a wanted man. What would my testimony be worth? Or indeed that of the lunatick Spatchears?'

'Well – perhaps. I think –' He became irritated. 'Loftus, what the Devil are you angling at?'

I bent close across the table, the foot-chains clanking again.

310

'As you rightly say, sir, what's really needed is for a personage of stature to take up the cause, to sway the disbelievers, bring the tables to the attention of the highest. A gentleman of standing, who could influence the Natural Philosophers of the Royal Society. One whom the Monarch Herself and indeed Her Parliament would heed. One such as yourself, sir.'

'O, indeed – that's what's wanted.' He cleared his throat. 'How could this be done? Via the testimony of these Philosophers, as you call them?'

'Not good enough, vice-admiral. They quarrel and dispute too much. I have something else in mind.'

He craned forward. 'What? What's your notion?'

'A demonstration, before unimpeachable witnesses.'

He leaned back again, frowning.

I bore on rapidly. 'An incontestable demonstration that the Lunar Distance Method works beyond all doubt. A proof set up in the most dramatic way, which you would then bring to the attention of the wider world.'

'Dramatic proof?' said Pitchbert in growing excitement. 'Go on.'

'The exercise is this – to visibly and publickly show that a sea-going war flota can Navigate a long passage using nothing but the tables.'

He sucked air. 'Good Lord!'

'Furthermore, the entire procedure would be witnessed by the most reliable and independent observers – that is, serving officers aboard the barks of Her Majesty's Navy.'

'Why, Loftus, I congratulate you,' he cried, his face lighting up. 'Incontestable proof from the most virtuous and credible of witnesses! What a most splendid notion.'

I smiled. 'Show the faithless how wrong they are, convert a sceptickal world. Get the proof you need. Think of the glory.'

'By God's lights, I certainly shall. Get the proof, I mean.' All at once, he spoke without pausing for breath. 'I'm beginning to see how it shall be arranged, Loftus. All the officers of the flota,

311

even those irritating midshipmen, should observe the exercise minutely, be obliged to scribble up in their logs every detail of the voyage like the trained mongrels they are. Meanwhile, the Navigator directs the course by the Lunar business alone. Is that possible? Aye? Then, when the destination is gained with undreamt-of accuracy, there shall stand the proof. The Lunar Distinction Measure trounces the old ways for all to see!'

I nodded vigorously. 'And you, vice-admiral, return to London and present our Monarch with the crowning evidence.'

He closed his eyes, his features suffused with a beatific smile.

Lord, I thought, he's taken it like a barracuda swallowing a red snapper. I leaned back and considered Filligrew's dilemma. If he prevented the demonstration, he gave the game away about the tables. If he did not, Pitchbert stole his glory.

Suddenly, a dry hand grasped my wrist. The vice-admiral's face was close, smiling, almost pleading.

'What do you say, Captain Loftus? Can you do it?'

I pretended to mull it over, then said with a wan smile, 'As a man about to be hanged, sir, I have nothing left to lose. But by the same token, neither have I any incentive to help you.'

His smile disappeared. 'Then – what about your pardon? I shall reinstate it. Despite all your crimes.'

'Sir Thomas intends to hang me.'

'O, I still have sway. Don't forget, his appointment to the Court lies in my hands. I haven't signed yet.'

'He says you've no choice but to sign. The Admiralty would not countenance your refusal.'

'But suppose the tables are shown not to work – just speculating, Loftus – then I am justified in withholding my seal. I lose nothing by demanding this proof. On the other hand, if the tables do work, then I share in the recognition.'

We were together in the Great Cabin, the renegade and the vice-admiral, working out our prospects like post-captains reckoning up their prize monies.

'Well, Loftus? Have we a deal?'

312

'Let me make sure I understand. If you order the demonstration, you want me to Navigate using the Lunar Distance Method based on the tables and appendix?'

'Aye, that's the idea.' His head bobbed up and down, the pigtail bouncing lightly on his neck.

'And I shall have the freedom to Navigate according to my knowledge of the Method?'

He nodded. 'Indeed you shall.'

'With all the tables and instruments and almanacks I require to hand?'

'All the necessaries.'

'And a boy scribe or two?'

'Of course.'

'In return, I shall win a free pardon, given in writing with your seal?'

He sighed. 'Aye, a written, sealed pardon.'

'And pardons for each of my men aboard the *Diamond*?'

A minuscule pause, then he shrugged and said, 'Aye.'

'Witnessed by an officer, and with your seal fixed upon them?'

'As you wish.'

'Unconditionally?'

'Aye.'

I sat back and breathed deeply. 'Very well, it's agreed. To where shall I Navigate, vice-admiral?'

He beamed, the grey eyes wrinkling at the corners. 'Why, to Port Royal, of course. That is where Filligrew and I are journeying on the completion of our affairs here. It is also where I embark a returning Navy vessel bound for Portsmouth. Moreover, it makes the perfect test – a voyage across a hundred and fifty leagues of open sea with no landmarks from our departure point at the Boca de Dragones outside the Golfo Paria till we spy Jamaicka. Loftus, you shall deliver us to the shore within sight of Plumb Point and the Palisadoes, by the approach to Kingstown Bay. What a triumph!'

I felt lightheaded. The dim cabin whirled. I thought of that

313

bright morning – it seemed an age ago – when I had brought the old *Cornelius* into Kingstown Bay past that very same Plumb Point and the Palisadoes, with Adam piloting us past the dangers, dear Abigail drawing up her manifests, the flyer's holds laden with a cargo for honest trade with the sly merchants of Sally Cox's Tavern and my heart so full of hopes.

'Loftus, such a feat of pure Navigation has never been done,' said Pitchbert. 'Never even been attempted. Are you absolutely certain you can do it?'

I smiled. 'The eclipse, sir. Think how well the eclipse worked.'

Vice-Admiral George Pitchbert looked me in the eye.

'Very well, Loftus, it's agreed,' he said sternly. 'You shall Navigate the Navy's flota.'

24

STAND OFF

From the high quarter-deck of the *Prometheus*, I watched the purposeful flota creaming along in the grandest style. All told, we counted five barks, a magnificent parade of sail running in ragged line astern on a northwesterly course, yards braced for a broad reach, surging and yawing down the Caribbee swells. Perhaps I should contrive to join the Navy, I grimaced, if only to enjoy more often such uplifting sights.

In the van were Filligrew's private ships, the mighty flagship the *Prometheus* and her smaller sister the *Willingminde*. Between these was an all-too-familiar sight, the lovely three-masted flyer, the *Saskia* – my once-beloved *Cornelius*. I sighed, thinking how splendid and graceful she looked.

Next came the heavily armoured, lumbering three-decker the *Forbearance*, the vice-admiral's flagship, with which we had rendezvoused outside the Boca de Dragones. She was Pitchbert's only remnant. The *Charity* – not before an enduring struggle – had been repaired and refloated off the reefs but, leaking like a muslin cloth and with too many frames gone, she had been ignominiously broken upon the spit at Port Royal for her remaining good timbers. The thirty-gun *Bounteous*, her men safe home but the valuable armaments unsalvageable, rotted still on that reef far away on the unknown Cuban shore, her planks gripped forever by unyielding coral heads. Her erstwhile captain,

315

Percy Gamble, never again would strut about her quarter-deck issuing condemnations and punishments to the innocent and deserving alike. Instead, he languished in a prison box deep within the *Forbearance*'s wooden walls, in transport to face the stern judgement of an angered and affronted Navy.

Ploughing along gamely in the wake of these magnificent barks, with all her canvas set in hopes of keeping up, came the fifth and puniest vessel of the fleet. Through the spy-glass, I saw Eli's figure bent at the tiller-bar and with something of a smile remembered how, early that morning in the hidden anchorage of the Bahia Escotia, my crew had all but opened fire as the launch approached. Then they had heard the cry, 'Ahoy, the *Diamond*!' and recognised their captain.

Breathing deeply, I savoured the freshness of the tradewind breeze and the afternoon sunshine. All day, I had been incarcerated below, not imprisoned for once but rather ensconced in the splendour of the Great Cabin with all the means of Navigation to hand. Under the gaze of the vice-admiral and the commodore, I had pored over the Spatchears tables – Filligrew's own copy, of course – running my finger up and down the columns of the code, consulting the *ephemerae* and busying myself with calculating the sights as we sped onwards.

Before putting to sea, Pitchbert had called together his officers and explained their task. It was to be the great proving trial, he informed them sonorously, of the Lunar Distinction Method. The flota would set its course solely by the new Method, under the direction of Captain Matthew Loftus. Meanwhile, all officers were to maintain their sailing logs in the utmost detail and sail their barks by the well-practised and familiar method of dead reckoning.

They were to record meticulously every swing of the compass needle, every cast of the log-chip, every quarter knot of change in speed, each wavering breath of the tradewind's strength. The sailing-masters were to note the minutest shift of the breeze's direction, the set of the sails, the speed of their barks through the water, the angle of their wakes and the line of the wave-train. They were to record their notion of how strong the current might run, their guess at its constancy and their estimate of its set. And too, the Navy's best practices of the Mathematickal Navigation were to be pursued in careful and recorded detail. At each noon of this five or six day voyage, instructed the vice-admiral, every officer with a grasp of latitude sailing was to sight the sun's zenith and make his own calculation of the degree. At sunrise and sunset they were to swing their cross-staffs along the horizon to catch the azimuth and check the deviation of their compasses, and further, they were commanded to consult the Navy's almanack – if they had such aboard – to allow for magnetick variation as we progressed west and north.

Not the least matter of Navigation nor of seamanship was to be forgotten, no manner of our sailing ignored, no deducement nor reckoning missed out, no rule of thumb nor line of eye discarded. Every deck officer and midshipman, every master and bosun and all the longest serving tars and time-worn sea-daddies were to bear witness to the finest degree and to the smallest of details, day and night, of every passing minute of the voyage.

One man alone was to be denied all of this. I was to stay below and work from celestial sightings of the sun and the Moon, consulting the books and almanacks and tables, entering the columns and the logarithms and, from all these, calculating the course to steer. Only briefly was I allowed on deck, for the sole purpose of overseeing the taking of the latitude angles and identifying stars or planets for Moonshots. While I stood on the quarter, the compass card was to be covered and the log-line packed away in its cuddy-box. No orders might be given the helmsman, no talk of course or distance run allowed to reach my ears.

Thus there were to be two quite separate means of directing the barks towards Jamaicka. On the one hand, recorded in the logs, was the Navy's common practice, employing all traditional seamanship combined with the simple Navigational calculation of a latitude, as had been done for centuries. On the other, there was Matthew Loftus shooting the Moon against the sun by day, sighting the Moon against the stars at night, and using nothing but the tables and almanacks and predictions and arithmeticks and logarithms of the new, untested Lunar Distance Method.

I marvelled at Vice-Admiral George Pitchbert's faith. And his utter delusion.

Three young Navy midshipmen stood on the quarter-deck nearby, busy taking sights under my close direction. They swung their unwieldy back-staffs across the horizon, then traversed it again to the opposite quarter to where, in the middle sky against the endless blue roof behind cotton-ball clouds, appeared the crescent Moon in her most ghostly shades. All but effaced by the sun's brilliance, she arced gracefully downwards to meet the sea-horizon. In a few hours, she would be invisible once more. Through the coming night, the flota would plunge blindly on, its safe passage resting on my calculations alone.

There was a touch at my elbow.

'Fine sailing here on the *Prometheus*, I must say, Loftus,' said the vice-admiral. 'More comfortable than the *Forbearance*. By God, Filligrew does himself well with his barks. Now, are you finished?' He smiled conspiratorially, rubbing his palms together. 'Don't want you seeing too much up here, do we?'

'Indeed not, sir,' I agreed. 'I shall next report back on deck at twilight to get a sight before Moonset.' Then I briskly addressed the midshipmen. 'Now you fellows, take yourselves below, if you will.'

The boys packed away their instruments and scrambled past me to the companionway. Giving the vice-admiral an encouraging nod, and with a last lingering glance around, I stepped below. In those brief minutes on deck, unbeknown to Pitchbert, I had taken the most careful note of the course and sneaked a glimpse of the sailing log. I had studied all the sailor's signs too – the set of our sails, the line of our wake, the direction and strength of the breeze, and my guess at the current. I had taken note of a dozen other aspects that a Navigator finds so essential, not for astronomickal calculations but for deduced reckoning. Pitchbert had no idea his Navigator was in truth going by the oldest ways of all.

In the Great Cabin, Sir Thomas Filligrew scowled out through the sternlights, hands clasping and unclasping behind his back. Already seated round the table were the midshipmen, boys of twelve or thirteen, my scribes and helpmeets, each one poring over his papers and quills, sucking the points thoughtfully, scratching his head over rows of numbers. They looked quite defeated.

The commodore gave an irritable wave of his hand. 'Can we not clear these minions away, Loftus?'

'Midshipmen, dismissed to the galley,' I said, and they jumped up, scrabbling at the papers in their haste to get off. As soon as the door had closed, Filligrew marched over and pointed a finger in my face.

'Loftus, you may trick Pitchbert but you can't fool me. I'm calling my captains and officers together this night to plan our sailing to the utmost so that we fetch Port Royal by dead reckoning. Then the vice-admiral shall be convinced the tables have worked. But, by God's bollacks, once he's safe away to England I'll wreak my revenge.'

I shrugged. 'He's written the pardons and I'll be gone long before you get the chance.'

'Dammit, I shall chase you down,' he snapped.

I leaned back in my chair, tapping the chart with a quill. 'First, you've got to get this flota safely to Port Royal.'

'I know that, man.' He strode to the window and stared out.

'And you know that no bark has ever made such a passage on dead reckoning alone. From the Bocas to Kingstown Bay is one hundred and forty six leagues by the rhumb line, as the Navy's chartmakers reckon it, or four hundred and thirty eight land miles by the mapmaker's measure. The current varies from nothing to a knot and a half. The wind may shift daily from north by east to south by east. From Cabo Paria at the eastern-most tip of the Spanish Main at Venezuela where we took our departure point from the land, we'll be at sea for five days, six, perhaps. By then the dead reckoning might be out by fifteen or twenty leagues. Along the way, we shall have to scrape past many dangers. There's the island of Blanquilla, high but dark and unlit, then the low lying Morant Cays, then –'

'Enough, Loftus. My captains shall take care of all that.'

'If they know their latitudes,' I said with a shrug, 'which I doubt. And we're bowling down the rhumb line as if we had a way of telling our Longitude too. A Lunar Distance Method, for example.'

From the commodore's tetchy back, it was easy to imagine the glowering look on his features. Good, I thought, the doubts are starting to bite. Filligrew has to crack sooner or later.

'If the English Navy, Sir Thomas, were the first to work out how to sail a course direct to Jamaicka, what a boon to war and commerce.' I relished reminding him of this – any means of adding to his discomfort. 'It would be a defining advantage in Her Majesty's present conflict. We'd likely win the war in a month.'

'Dammit!' His temper was fraying. 'Just because a voyage of this length has never been done before by dead reckoning doesn't mean it can't be done now.'

'It's never been done precisely because it cannot. The grand experiment is set to become the Navy's most dramatic proof that lack of a Longitude drives barks on to reefs and rocks. In which case, if we don't drown, then not only shall I swing from the gibbet but so, commodore, shall you.'

He stared out of the rocking mullions at the broken, swirling wake the *Prometheus* left astern as she careened down the Caribbee swells.

'My captains may not be the best of Navigators, Loftus, but they are damm'd fine seamen. If anyone can do it, they can.'

'Aye, but let's see what tale your brave officers tell when night falls.'

He spoke exasperatedly. 'They can reckon their barks through the night as well as the day.'

'No doubt they can. Nevertheless may I invite you, Sir Thomas, to take a closer look at the rhumb line?'

Gesturing at the chart, I laid the rule carefully across the line of our course. With a frown, he stepped over and studied it for barely a second.

'Blast you,' he muttered.

Without another word, he stormed out, leaving me to ponder the subtleties of Navigation, and to work even more diligently on my own dead reckoning.

At six and a quarter of the clock by the ship's time, I was again on deck savouring the evening air. It was middle twilight and already the canopy was crowding with bright stars. Centre stage blazed the brilliant lamp of Jupiter himself, while some thirty degrees of arc to the east and suspended low over the horizon shone the last of the Moon.

At the rail my midshipmen, with the *Prometheus* swaying beneath their feet, swung their instruments now towards the Moon, now back to Jupiter, pausing to squint in the darkness at the miniature scales and read off the angles.

'Not like that, Gudgeon,' I said, loud enough for the vice-admiral to hear, and took the piece from the hapless midshipman's hand. 'Look man, have you never been properly taught?'

Planting a foot in the scuppers, I leaned forward with my elbow on the rail and raised up the staff.

'Like this, midshipman. Try again, will you?' I said, handing back the instrument and turning to the vice-admiral with a helpless shrug. 'For the Lord's sake, how can a Navigator rely on sights from ones so unpractised?'

'I'm impressed, Loftus,' he said, perhaps recalling that Gudgeon had served his time and supposedly learnt his arts under Percy Gamble aboard the *Bounteous*. 'Can't think why we haven't got you signed up to Her Majesty the Queen's Naval service.'

A knot of figures had gathered across the quarter-deck by the leeward rail, huddled in consort. It was the meeting of Filligrew's officers. At his signals they had come aboard by launch while the flota was underway, a tricky enough procedure at anchor, let alone in a seaway. It left their uniforms soaked in the salt Tropick waters and the thin cotton hose clinging stickily to their legs, their knees bruised from clambering up the rollicking topsides and no doubt their tempers more rattled than ever. They have good reason to be on edge, I thought with grim satisfaction, for if they are now bent on persuading Sir Thomas to abandon this proving trial as insanely perilous – thereby exposing the tables' flaws – I wish them all the luck of a convicted pirate on the Port Royal scaffold.

Taking up the parchment scraps on which the midshipmen had scrawled their mysterious angles, I headed for the companionway. Sir Thomas stepped across to intercept me.

'My officers insist we come off two points at once, Loftus,' he rasped in a low voice. 'You know why.'

'Steer off, Sir Thomas?' I spoke loud enough to cause Pitchbert to whirl round. 'The Navigation is true, isn't it, by our tables?'

The vice-admiral was at our side in an instant, shooting wild glances from one to the other.

'What the Devil's going on?' he said. 'What's this about steering off?'

I smiled. 'There's no cause for alarm, sir. The commodore's officers are unused to the notion of going by astronomy and calculations, that's all.'

Pitchbert gestured impatiently. 'What precisely is this gathering about, Filligrew?'

The commodore gave a barely perceptible bow. 'Routine discussion, vice-admiral, nothing more. There are some dangers between here and Port Royal.'

'What dangers?' snapped Pitchbert.

'A group of islands, vice-admiral,' said the commodore.

'Where?'

'Ahead on the rhumb line.'

'Well, I'm sure Loftus knows all about them.'

I spread my palms. 'We'll clear them by a league or more, according to the tables and my Navigation.'

'Well, Sir Thomas?' demanded Pitchbert. 'You're absolutely confident in these tables, I take it?'

'Vice-admiral, these islets are very small, dark and low, quite unmarked in any way.' Sir Thomas's tone was tense. 'As is the way with insignificant lands, no one knows their true and exact latitude. Our present course may take us a touch close, so my advice is merely to come two points off the wind.'

'Sir, we shall fall of our track for Port Royal,' I cut in. 'It would ruin the proof.'

'It's merely a small adjustment,' said Filligrew testily, 'for prudence's sake.'

'Adjustment? Prudence?' fumed Pitchbert. 'You might as well suggest we heave to for the night, dammit.'

The commodore spoke irritably. 'That's exactly what I would do in such a circumstance as this.'

'Not this time, Filligrew, not this time.' Pitchbert wagged a finger under his nose. 'It would show lack of faith in the tables. Think of the logs being examined by the academicians at the Admiralty in Greenwich. No, sailing boldly on through the night and safely passing all dangers ahead is precisely the point. No other fleet would dare. Altering is out of the question.'

The commodore gazed out over the length of the *Prometheus* as if he could see into the chasm of the night beyond her plunging bowsprit. The sun had set, leaving nothing more than a pinkish smear under clouds low on the western horizon. The Moon too was gone and a heavy darkness had descended. Now the seascape spread around us black and empty save for the twinkling lights of the company of barks, all plain sail spread, forging across the swells. I glanced down over the rail. Eighteen feet below the quarter-deck at the waterline swirled a wash of white foam spinning out astern in a hissing wake as the ship pressed her four hundred tuns swiftly onward. Seven knots, I reckoned. We were covering better than a whole league with every turn of the half-hour sand-glass. Good God, I thought, I've got to get this right.

Pitchbert addressed Filligrew again.

'Tell me, what are they called, these islets you spoke of?' He cleared his throat. 'It's been a while since I was obliged to study any charts myself.'

Sir Thomas paused, weighing his words. At length, he said, 'They go by a Spanish name, vice-admiral, Los Testigos.'

'Testigos?' said Pitchbert, turning to me, half amused. 'Most odd, these Dago names.'

'In English,' I explained, 'we'd call them the Witness Isles.'

Not many minutes later, I sat alone in the Great Cabin, fretting. How much longer could Filligrew hold out?

Above the splashing surge of water past the flagship's speeding hull came the sound of launches bumping alongside as Filligrew's officers scrambled down into the leaping boats, to be stroked quickly away to their ships. The flota foamed along at six and seven knots, the current driving us faster by a half knot again, a mad, headlong dash into the night.

Few sea-charts even attempted to mark the hidden rocks of the Witness Isles, for they were considered of little military or politickal use. Further, no chartmaker could confidently place them on the grid with more than the vaguest estimation of their latitude for, being off the usual sea routes, they were infrequently sighted. As for their Longitude – or indeed the flota's – who had the merest guess? Yet every captain and Navigator in the Caribbee Sea knew full well the isles lay somewhere southwest of Grenady, perhaps thirty leagues or so from Trinidad, and their lurking presence was one good reason why warships, cruzers and frigates never sailed this course. The native fishermen might have their ways of finding the islets, but not the Sovereign's Navy.

Still we bore on regardless, careering down the rollers at top speed. This Moonless night the lookouts would never spy surf glowing at the reef's edges. I imagined the grinding and tearing as all five vessels dashed themselves on the rocks, timbers rent apart on those jagged teeth, hull bottoms torn out. Vivid memories flooded into my mind of the poor *Hannah Rebacka*, reef-stricken, ripped open and heeling in her final agony. I swear I heard again the cries of drowning men as her decks came awash and she slid below the surface.

I thought too of the *Diamond*, faithfully following the flota, her crew trusting unquestioningly as I led them into danger. How I wished now for a quiet confident word from Will Wrack, or a gruffly spoken gem of sea-lore from Eli.

Concentrating on the sea-chart, yet again I checked our position. Doubts began to eat away at my resolve, like maggots on a rotting flesh wound. How certain was my dead reckoning? How good were the latitude sights? Supposing Filligrew's officers were right about the proximity of the flota to the land? After all, in truth my own estimation might be many leagues awry. What if innocent men drowned? Their curses would follow echoing in my ears even as I sank to my own salty grave. Surely Filligrew must call the game off soon. Or would I crumble first?

'Lord, I can't let it happen,' I said out loud, half rising.

With a crash, the door flew back on its hinge and in marched the commodore.

'Blast you, Loftus – blast you to Hell and back,' he rasped. The door slammed shut behind him. He strode over and with one movement swept all the books and papers and charts and instruments off the table. They fell with clatters and thuds. He lowered his face right next to mine, his breathing uneven, his eyes betraying the strain.

'Don't try me any more,' he said hoarsely.

The ship rumbled onwards. What depth was there now beneath her keel?

'Speak, Loftus – are your terms the same?' he said, trembling with anger. 'Quickly, man, there's too much at stake.'

I swallowed hard and said, 'Aye, my terms are the same – the exchange in return for freedom and Pitchbert's pardons.'

'There's more, dammit,' he said. 'Get me out of this fix. Call it off without letting him know.'

'Say –' I began, then halted. 'Tell Pitchbert it's my error. Let him think the mistake is mine.'

'Aye, indeed he shall!' he said, and turned to go.

I was up out of my seat, grasping him by the arm.

'Commodore, there's one thing more.'

He surveyed me with scorn. 'What else can you possibly demand?'

'The exchange must be done under the guarantee of your life.'

'What the Devil do you mean?' he rasped.

'We must go together to the *Diamond*,' I said, holding his eye, 'or the deal is off.'

He knew his bargaining power had run out. His voice sank to barely more than a whisper.

'What choice have I?' he breathed.

'None. For pity's sake,' I pleaded, 'give the order.'

He turned and ran up the steps, with me following half a pace behind. Gaining the quarter in a dozen strides, he barked out a rapid stream of orders.

'Helmsman, haul over six points to larboard. Sailing-master – come on a reach. Hurry, blast it – get moving!'

The helmsman blinked in astonishment. Without waiting, I fell on the spokes and sent the wheel spinning.

'Signalsman – all ships steer off hard to larboard,' ordered the commodore.

The signalsman called for his assistant and, with fumbling hands, snatched at the coloured lamps to run them up the haul-yards. Filligrew shouted again at his sailing-master and seamen appeared from everywhere, running for the sheets and braces. The noise from aloft told its own tale, for the *Prometheus*, braced for broad reaching, protested mightily. Her great yards groaned and a hundred blocks creaked under the strain. Fighting the wheel, I felt the juddering rush of water over the plane of the huge rudder twenty feet below as it strained against the flow. The great bark took an age to respond.

The dim outlines of her enormous white sails swung dizzily across the night sky. They flapped and luffed, and the bark's speed fell away. A dozen jack-tars ran about the weather-deck shouting for slack or belay, while yet more sweated at the capstan to bring round the overstrained yards. The ship tilted as a high swell passed underneath, catching her on the broach. She swayed down its back then lurched heavily upright, wallowing in the trough. The compass card whirled in its bath of oil and settled. She had come round.

All the ships of the flota at once responded to the flagship's lead. In the glimmering starlight, I picked out the *Diamond*'s tiny lamps well astern and, thank God, already swinging to leeward. She was altering to run parallel with the *Prometheus*.

Silently cursing Filligrew to Hell and back for holding on so long, I became aware of someone beating on my shoulder.

'Loftus, Loftus!' It was the vice-admiral. 'What have you done?'

I faltered. 'Sir – I – moments ago, I discovered an error. A flaw – in the Navigation.'

'Flaw? What flaw?'

Filligrew came up, breathing hard. 'By the blood of Mary, you cut things fine, Loftus.'

The vice-admiral clutched at my shirt. 'For God's sake, man, is the fault with your Navigation or with the Method?'

I stared at the commodore. He made an infinitesimal movement of his head.

'With me – with my reading of the tables, sir,' I stuttered. 'A grave error in my interpretation. The fault lies with me, not the Method.'

Pitchbert relinquished his grip on my shirtfront and let out a moan.

'Thank God, thank God, and blessed be our Queen,' he breathed. 'Loftus, you must write a full explanation. The officers shall make it clear in their logs. There must be no questioning of the demonstration.'

'Aye aye, vice-admiral,' I said, sounding contrite.

Pitchbert passed a large white cloth across his brow. 'How far off our intended course must we sail?'

'Not far,' I said, 'a league or two at most.'

'Praise be. Can we then sail onwards to Port Royal without further tribulations?'

'Aye, I trust so, sir, when we're clear of the isles. But we should heave to while I calculate a new course.'

'What do you say, Filligrew?'

The commodore glared. 'I'll do as our Navigator recommends.'

'Then heave to,' said Pitchbert, trembling. 'Good God – my proof! What a trial this is!' The vice-admiral draped himself over the rail, mopping his brow. 'Filligrew, have you good brandy?'

'The cabinet in my private quarters,' said Sir Thomas through gritted teeth.

'Then I shall repair below for relief from this tension.'

As the vice-admiral tottered off towards the companionway, I stepped close to Filligrew and said, 'It's time, commodore, to put our agreement into effect.'

Some minutes later, the *Prometheus*'s launch hauled off across a lumpy sea, twelve blades splashing patches of glowing phosphorescence on the water's black surface. Sir Thomas and I sat silently in the sternsheets facing the oarsmen. Hidden at my belt nestled a brace of loaded pistols, while tucked under the commodore's arm was a commodious leathern satchel.

All around, the lights of the flota flickered as the stopped barks rolled sickeningly on the Caribbee surges. The distance opened and the flagship's signal lamps, arcing back and forth, disappeared from sight only to reappear riding high on the following swell. Rowing upwind, hard won work against the wind and waves, we slowly approached the dipping lamplights of the *Diamond*.

'Fellows,' I called when we came in hailing distance. There were whistles and grunts of surprise as we drew under the schooner's lee and bumped alongside.

'What's happened?' they said.

'Are you all right, Captain Matthew?'

'By Saint Mary's tears, where in Hell are we?'

A passing swell heaved the launch to the height of her rail, and my seamen reached down eagerly to help me aboard.

'Let the commodore come up first,' I said, standing aside.

In the feeble lampglow, I registered their astonished faces as Sir Thomas Filligrew stepped over the *Diamond*'s rail. Then I scrambled quickly up after and said, 'Dismiss the launch, Sir Thomas.'

'What?' he hissed. 'You said I'd go free after the exchange.'

I had a pistol levelled at his stomach. 'You'd set the flota after us in minutes. Tell off the launch.'

'Dammit, why did I trust a blackguard like you,' he muttered, and called down to the oarsmen. After confirming they had heard the order correctly, they rowed slowly off shaking their heads and wondering why the commodore had transferred in the middle of the night to such a vessel.

'Put her head to the wind, Eli,' I ordered. 'We shall be tacking on a long, hard beat a point east of north.'

'Aye aye, Captain Matthew,' he said, and went smartly off to get the schooner under way.

'A long beat north, Loftus?' said Sir Thomas. 'What by the merry bells of the dogwatch have you cooked up?'

'The vice-admiral shall find my instructions in the Great Cabin when he wakes,' I reminded him, 'so you'll be picked up in due course.'

'From where?'

'From the Witness Isles.'

'But I thought – I mean, we're right by the blasted place. Only

329

a sea-mile or two off, that's why we hauled to a stop.' He whirled around, looking out into the darkness as if he might spy out the nearby land.

I swept my arm around the pitch dark sea-scape. 'According to my reckoning, Sir Thomas, for a good seven or eight leagues in all directions there's no land anywhere.'

He started to say something, then thought better of it. Instead, he slumped to the rail and leant on it, his head hanging in defeat.

As the schooner got slowly under way, I reached up and extinguished our signal lamp. Eli came aft and took up the tiller-bar, sweeping it across the width of the deck. I moved over to the weather rail on the high side, next to the silent, fuming Filligrew. The boys sheeted home the big staysail and she paid off with the old salt steering to come hard on the wind, whereupon the *Diamond* heeled to the breeze and gathered way, a wake fanning from her stern as she climbed and dived over the steep swells. Soon the lamps of the combined Navy and privateering flota, carrying all the officers and men and boys engaged in Pitchbert's great demonstration, began to recede, flickering and faltering behind the high-running swells. Then the lights vanished altogether.

There was a long pause before the commodore spoke.

'Dam' you,' he said finally. 'Loftus, how the Devil did you work that?'

'You were kind enough, Sir Thomas,' I reminded him, 'to leave me a cross-staff at my marooning and I got the isles' latitude pretty well. Even so, until you ordered the flota hauled over, I was on tenterhooks at the thought of striking. After all, my own reckoning might have been out by leagues.'

'But it was not, was it, Loftus?'

I smiled. 'I think not, commodore.'

He sighed. 'Pity you never agreed to become my Navigator. Just imagine all the spoils and prizes we'd have taken.'

For a full minute, we studied the *Diamond*'s progress as she smashed her way northwards, heeling hard, her canvas hauled flat, every sheet straining. I marvelled once more at the speed and weatherliness of our little craft, and wondered if the commodore too might admire her in the slightest degree.

'How's she going, old salt?' I sang out to my steersman.

'She's a tiger on the wind, captain,' Eli called cheerily.

I turned and faced the commodore on equal terms. 'When we get there, Sir Thomas, with due formality and circumstance as befitting your position, I shall maroon you.'

In the shadowy gloom, I searched his face for the hint of a smile, the thinnest recognition of our altered circumstances, but there was none.

Then I bowed. This time, he had the grace to return the compliment.

25

Tables Turned

Early next day not half a glass after the dawn lifted, from high at the maintop came Gaspar's excited babble.

'Fine on the larboard bow!' he cried, and the boys took turns scrambling up the ratlines to report seeing hazy blue-grey shapes low on the sea-horizon. Soon we came near enough to distinguish the terrain. If he recognised the archipelago – which the Spanish had named in honour of the highest of Catholick Saints, the Apostles of Christ, or the Witnesses – Filligrew revealed not a sign of it.

We made our tacks shorter until we fetched Isla Grande on the beam. At once the schooner bore away on to a reach and entered the gap named Crab Strait. Steering into the little cove, I spied the narrow strand where our shelter had stood. A pang shot through me at the memory of finding Adam half alive on the shore, and the hard days of sickness when we had striven for sustenance and fought for deliverance. Briefly, I wondered if we might find a pair of emaciated, half-dead Spanish pirates there, but the place was as deserted and abandoned as the day I had first set foot upon it.

Two boat lengths off the beach, we let fly sheets and with a rattle the anchor went down in six fathoms. She fell back on her cable, the bows snatched straight, and the *Diamond* lay swinging to an erratic breeze, the tradewind baffled under the hillside's lee.

'A temporary home, Sir Thomas,' I said. 'Until the flota reaches here in a few days.'

He grimaced, perhaps wondering whether an upstart amongst his ambitious captains might seize the chance, tear up the sealed orders left in the Great Cabin and launch his bid for the commodore's command. Yet there was one man who would, I knew for sure, make the Navy barks haul up to Los Testigos – a man ready to crawl into the bilges of a slaving bark to find a piece of gold braid or slop out the piss-dale of a warship in the name of his own advancement. If he had to run his barks halfway around the Caribbee Sea and back again, Vice-Admiral George Pitchbert would fetch the isles come what may, for my note told him where to find the precious tables. Commodore Filligrew, it explained, had not only gone to Los Testigos but taken the volume with him.

The boys sent down the *Diamond*'s launch and off-loaded stores enough for a man for a whole month, let alone half a week. The marooned commodore could gorge himself on ship's bread and saltfish with a sun-warmed keg of small beer to wash it down, while the flota laboriously beat and tacked and hauled its way up to weather.

'Two pistols, Sir Thomas, cleaned and empty,' I said, handing over a brace of the commodore's own from the box in his Great Cabin, 'along with wadding and a horn of dry powder. When our anchor's up, I'll toss you a bag of ball.'

He patted his leathern satchel. 'And our bargain?'

'Indeed,' I said, and went towards the companionway. At once, I heard a snuffling and coughing from the steps below. To my consternation a grizzled head popped from the hatch, followed by the stooping shoulders of one who has spent his life pursuing academic endeavours in enclosed cells of learning. In his hand, the old fellow clutched a roll of parchments, thirty or forty sheets, tied with a ribbon. He blinked in the noonday brightness.

Grasping the parchments, I hissed, 'Observator Spatchears, I ordered you to remain out of sight.'

Filligrew's composure departed him. 'Spatchears? Good God, I never thought to see you again.'

The astronomer must have recognised the man who had put him ashore at the hell-hole that was Cala Arena and left him for dead, for he instantly lapsed into a familiar derangement.

'O the shadow of my cell, the Moon's in shadow!' he cried, eyes starting. 'O *tempora*, the tables cannot predict. The experiments are unfinished, the numbers incomplete!'

'Quiet, sir,' I hissed, putting my hand on his pate and pressing down hard. 'Below with you, for the Lord's sake.' To my relief, he dipped back down the steps and returned to his quarters, still reciting numbers. Turning to the commodore, I managed a smile. 'Your copy of the code, Sir Thomas. To match your tables.'

I held out the parchment rolls.

'The code?' he said, eyes narrowing. 'Why not the tables?'

'Commodore, my tables are safely hidden away.' The volume nestled at the base of the *Diamond*'s sixty-foot hollow mainmast, with its line attached, ready to be drawn from the truck at the top. 'Here is the second code. Take it and you have your matching set.'

His face darkened. 'There's some trickery here. I heard the old lunatick say the numbers are incomplete.'

Spatchears had been thinking of his not-quite-remembered code. I moved quickly to cover the commodore's suspicion.

'The man is a perfectionist, is he not?' I grimaced. 'And all the more awkward for that. He meant, of course, that the Royal Observatory's work is incomplete.'

'Incomplete?' repeated Filligrew idiotically. 'The Observatory?'

'Sir Thomas, as you yourself reminded me at Flawless Cove, despite the magnificent advances made by our mutual friend Noah Spatchears, the full set of almanacks for the Lunar Distance Method remains some years from completion, let alone publication. Particularly if John Flamsteed has his way.'

His brows furrowed and he muttered, 'Indeed so, the Astronomer Royal's endeavour is incomplete, I grant. Aye, until

334

then the Lunar Method's a partial solution.' Then a flush of temper suffused his face. 'Dammit, Loftus, it's an excellent Method in theory, our best prospect by far for the Longitude. I'll oblige you not to diminish its significance.' He patted the satchel, cradling it like a prize. 'Think of the advantages to the Navigation when the work's all done. Why, the whole undertaking is worthwhile if just one single bark is saved.'

I smiled sadly. 'Like the *Hannah Rebacka*?'

It caught him, and he looked momentarily stunned. 'Well, perhaps so,' he muttered, 'perhaps so.'

I held out my parchments. Hesitantly, he reached inside his satchel and then, as if resolving a doubt, quickly pulled out a similar scroll. We handed the documents over in such a manner that for the briefest instant, each held both sets of code in his grasp.

Taking Filligrew's parchments, I unrolled them, glanced again at the pages and saw Spatchears' secret symbols. Inside the roll, I found several further papers, and checked the names of the men concerned, the witnesses' names, and all the signatures and seals. Sure enough, they were the vice-admiral's true pardons, not bought, but fairly obtained.

The commodore examined his own document. It was the memorised version of the code, written in poor Adam's hand – though Filligrew knew nothing of all that difficult retrieval. Each leaf was also enscribed with Spatchears' own signature. Satisfied, Sir Thomas opened the satchel ready to tuck in the rolls alongside his own tables. As the flap opened, fleetingly I glimpsed the other leather-backed volume. An inner voice urged me simply to seize it and keep all the tables and codes for myself. Perhaps Filligrew caught my glance, for he hastily closed the satchel.

'I take this on trust, Loftus,' he said, holding up the parchments. 'We have an agreement between us.'

I acknowledged that we had.

'And this is the proper code?' he asked, still seeking confirmation.

'As the truth is my witness,' I told him, 'the code you have is the one constructed to match your tables.'

'Good. Then, Captain Loftus, may the Lord overlook all your ambitions and hopes.'

'Aye, and may the Fates overlook yours, Sir Thomas,' I replied. 'Into the launch, if you will.'

With that, we clambered down together. Gaspar and Jan rowed until the boat's stern grazed the warm sand where wavelets lapped rhythmically. A breeze swayed through the coco palms, swishing the giant green fronds high above. Below them, the remnants of our shelter were still just visible. For me, it was all too familiar.

When the commodore had splashed disconsolately through the shallows and onto the strand, we backed the boat off and, some fathoms clear, I heaved to the foreshore a shot-bag for his pistols. As we stroked away, Filligrew stood alone on the beach, surrounded by a sorry little collection of boxes and stores, his shoulders drooping and his gaze resting somewhere in the half distance.

And all the time, he clutched that leathern case, hugging it close.

With Carolina falling astern and the Observator Spatchears safe on the packet for London, I sat quietly on the *Diamond*'s quarter scanning the sea-horizon and the curve of the ocean ahead. Eli, whose fanciful sea tales and salty memoirs kept us entertained through the night watches, steered our course, smacking and chewing on an enormous baccy plug bequeathed to him from poor Will Wrack's supplies. In the waist, Gaspar and Jan rested under the rail, talking animatedly together in Dutch. Hap, bless his strong heart, had hauled himself one-handedly up the ratlines and was perched at the maintop, keeping lookout.

Scratching the bristles on his chin, Eli Savary said, 'Back there on those Tosteegey Islands, captain, I thought old Noah had blown you apart. Incomplete, he pops up and says. And

336

Filligrew's face! Should be embroidered on a flag-cloth. Enough to frighten the savages, let alone the Navy.'

I smiled. 'And what about when the Admiralty in London discovers Filligrew's version of the code is not quite what it should be? Ours, on the other hand, is perfectly whole and original, as the Royal Society's Natural Philosophers shall discover when the Observator calls with his satchel.'

'What a palaver that was, Noah remembering those log-and-rhythms,' said the old salt, jaws champing.

'And forgetting,' I pointed out, 'that he had got the wrong tables.'

Eli chewed pensively for a minute or two. 'Captain, do you reckon the old boy can stay out of a spin?'

'O, he's lucid enough about his purpose. He'll go straight to Robert Hooke Esquire, Curator of Experiments, and the works shall be published at once.' I chuckled. 'Before you can say Lunar Distinction Measure.'

With unfailing accuracy, Eli Savary aimed a stream of rancid baccy spittle over the rail.

'Aye captain,' he said, 'whatever that may be.'